THE
CHALICE

Also by Nancy Bilyeau

The Crown

THE
CHALICE

NANCY BILYEAU

First published in Great Britain in 2013 by Orion Books,
an imprint of The Orion Publishing Group Ltd
Orion House, 5 Upper Saint Martin's Lane
London WC2H 9EA

An Hachette UK Company

1 3 5 7 9 10 8 6 4 2

A CIP catalogue record for this book is
available from the British Library.

ISBN (Hardback) 978 1 4091 3309 4
ISBN (Trade Paperback) 978 1 4091 3310 0
ISBN (ebook) 978 1 4091 3311 7

Typeset by Input Data Services Ltd,
Bridgwater, Somerset

Printed and bound in the UK by CPI Group (UK) Ltd,
Croydon, CR0 4YY

The Orion Publishing Group's policy is to use papers
that are natural, renewable and recyclable products and
made from wood grown in sustainable forests. The logging
and manufacturing processes are expected to conform to
the environmental regulations of the country of origin.

www.orionbooks.co.uk

To Kate McLennan, for her encouragement, just when I needed it

And Jesus said, 'Father, if you be willing, take this cup from me.'
—Luke 22:42

PROLOGUE

When preparing for martyrdom on the night of 28 December 1538, I did not think of those I love. Hiding in a narrow cemetery with seven men, all of us poised to commit violence at Canterbury Cathedral, I instead stared at the words carved into the tombstone I huddled behind: 'Here lieth interred the body of Brother Bartholomeus Giles, of Christ-Church Priory, Canterbury, who departed this life on the sixteenth of June, 1525.'

How fortunate was Brother Bartholomeus. He prayed, sang, laboured, and studied, and after his body weakened, was moved to the infirmary, to die there, blessedly ignorant that his was the last generation to serve God in an English monastery. This humble monk had known nothing of the Dissolution.

A gibbous moon hung above me tonight, swollen and bright in the sable sky, illuminating all the gravestones and memorials. But somehow it was a soft moon, not the sharply detailed orb I'd seen on other winter nights. It must be because we were near the sea. I'd been to Canterbury one other time – the same journey during which I learned of my destiny. Against my will, I was told of a prophecy. It was one I feared above all else. Yet here, tonight, I stood ready to fulfil it.

We had each of us picked a stone of concealment in this graveyard, a paean to a departed brother. These seven were like brothers to me now, and one most particularly so. Brother Edmund Sommerville, standing but a few feet away, looked over, and I nodded my readiness. We both knew the time approached. He blew on his frozen fingers, and I did the same. Our hands must be supple enough to grip the weapons we'd brought. I carried a rock with a sharp edge; Brother Edmund held a cudgel. We had no training in combat. Our faith would supply the needed strength.

After King Henry VIII ordered the suppression of our home, Dartford Priory, we had become, to the world, simply Edmund

Sommerville and Joanna Stafford. I'd struggled to prevent that. In the last months of Dartford Priory's existence, under duress, I'd searched the convent for the Athelstan crown, an object that Bishop Stephen Gardiner swore to me would stop the destruction. But the search took unexpected – and deadly – turns, and when it was over, our priory, 180 years old, closed its doors forever, as did the other monasteries. So ended the chaste splendours and humble glories of the only house for Dominican sisters in England. We had no choice but to relinquish our habits and veils and depart. I moved into the town close by and, with a handful of other priory refugees, tried very hard to make a new life for myself. Now that was over, too. The cruelty of the royal court had swung close to me once more. I'd seen fear and treachery and loss – and courage too – and innocent blood spilled on Tower Hill.

The figure of a man darted through the cemetery. In the moonlight, the face of Brother Oswald, a one-time Cistercian monk, was a sliver of ivory within his hooded cloak. His wounds of face and body, inflicted by those who hate us and call us Papists, were hidden.

'We will move on the cathedral soon,' Brother Oswald said in a ragged whisper.

My hand tightened on the side of the gravestone. Within moments, men sent by King Henry would emerge from this dark cathedral carrying a sacred wooden box. And we would be waiting.

Thomas Becket, archbishop of Canterbury, was murdered inside that cathedral 368 years ago because he would not submit to the will of an earthly king. After his death, Rome proclaimed Becket a saint. His grave became a shrine – the holiest destination in all of England. But Henry VIII had declared our revered saint a criminal, stripping his shrine. Tomorrow was the anniversary of Becket's assassination. Before the first valiant pilgrims arrived, the desecration would have taken place. King's men were at this moment stealing the feretrum, the adorned box containing the bones of the archbishop. The remains of Becket would be burned, his ashes scattered to the wind.

It was the final cruelty from the king who had already taken everything from me and from all of us who had lived enclosed and spiritual lives.

'I heard the prior's prayers from the side door,' said Brother Oswald. 'He begged the king's men to be allowed to pray before they took away the feretrum, and they relented. We shall go to the street in a few minutes.'

The monk crossed himself. 'God will be with us,' he said, a little louder. 'We do His work tonight. Do not forget – the Holy Father will bless us. He has no knowledge of our business here, but once it is done, all Christendom will give profound thanks.'

Not much time remained. Brother Oswald, our leader, dropped to his knees and prayed, his hands trembling with fervour. Thirteen months ago, when Brother Edmund and I met him, he was a monk who smiled, suffused with hope. Brother Oswald had been turned out of his monastery but was confident he'd learn God's purpose by roaming the land with a dozen other displaced monks. Weeks ago, I found him again, this time fending off blows. There were no more smiles from Brother Oswald. But when was the last time I had smiled, or, for that matter, eaten a meal or slept a night through? I wasn't sure.

A dog barked on the cobbled street between the cemetery and the cathedral. Its mad cries echoed off the towering cathedral. I hunched over, covering my mouth with my hand so my warm breath wouldn't form a white cloud above the tombstone.

Another dog answered, farther down the street. The first beast ran toward it, barking ever more frantically. Then they ran together, through Canterbury, seeking mischief. Their sounds died away.

'Sister Joanna?'

It was Brother Edmund. Even lit by moonlight, the change in him startled me. His determination to take this course of action several days ago had blessed my friend with a serenity of purpose. But now his brown eyes flickered with pain.

'Are you no longer of a mind to do this?' I whispered.

He opened his mouth and then shut it. 'Is it Sister Winifred?' I asked. I knew how much he loved his younger sister. As did I – she was my closest friend.

He still didn't answer. The others were finishing the Rosary; the sounds of murmured prayers and clicking beads drifted across the graves.

'And you – what of Arthur?' Brother Edmund finally said.

I looked down at Brother Bartholomeus's tombstone. I didn't want Brother Edmund to see my eyes, fearing he would read my thoughts.

For it wasn't Arthur, the orphaned boy who depended on me, who had leaped into my mind but a grown man. I could see the angry face of Geoffrey Scovill and hear his words once more: 'You're a fool, Joanna. What you're doing is madness – and it will change *nothing*.'

If I were killed here, tonight, on the streets of Canterbury, it would free Geoffrey, the constable who had helped me time and again. Our bond, so fraught for so long, would be severed and he could begin a new life. He was twenty-nine years old, two years older than I. Not quite young, but not old either. This was a selfless goal. I should have taken strength from it, and yet I felt quite the opposite. My belly leaped and tumbled; I was so dizzy I had to rest my forehead against the gravestone.

'It is time, brothers – and sister,' said Brother Oswald. The others stepped out from behind monuments. Brother Edmund moved forward with determination. I pushed off from the grave marker with one hand – clutching my sharp stone with the other – and took my place in the line moving slowly toward the street.

The gate creaked as our leader pushed it open and slipped through.

One of the monks cried, 'They're coming out!' Lights moved deep inside the cathedral.

There was a loud clattering of hooves on the narrow cobbled street, and a single man on horseback appeared. I recognised his green-and-white livery as Tudor colours. He was a king's soldier – he must have been stationed outside while the others charged into the cathedral. He pulled up on his horse and stared at us, arrayed before him in an uneven line.

One of the monks next to me hissed. It was taken up by another. Then another.

The soldier flinched in his saddle; his mouth dropped open. He was young, I could see that now. Eighteen at the most. In our long tattered cloaks and robes, hissing at him, we must have seemed terrifying wraiths.

He shook the reins and kicked the side of his horse, to return to the front of the cathedral and doubtless warn the other soldiers. Brother Oswald scrambled after him, and his followers went with him.

Brother Edmund looked at them and then at me, torn.

'Go, go, go,' I choked. 'Don't tarry.'

I pushed Brother Edmund away from me with all my strength. To my relief, he went. But I couldn't follow. My legs were frozen. The moon spun slowly in the sky.

A distant door opened with a thud and men cried out. I could hear it all, the noises boomed from the front of the cathedral, but I couldn't see anything. A noise pulsed in my ears. It was like the roaring sea. Snow came down faster, in stinging gusts. I stuck out my tongue to taste the flakes – I'd do anything to stave off fainting.

I staggered to the wall of Canterbury Cathedral. How could I be struck down by such weakness? This was what was supposed to happen – and my place in it was critical.

'*What you're doing is madness – and it will change nothing.*'

I kept hearing the words, scornful yet pleading, of Geoffrey Scovill. It was as if he sapped my strength from miles away. Frustrated, I grabbed the bricks to pull myself along the wall. I had to fight alongside Brother Edmund and the others. No matter the consequences, I'd finally determined to do this, to stop hiding from the future.

I dragged myself to the end of the wall.

Two fresh torches blazed on either side of the entranceway. Cowering in the doorway was the plump prior, his hands cupping his shiny face. He had no idea of our plans tonight, any more than he had of the royal mission to defile Becket's shrine. It had been easy for the soldiers to despoil the cathedral. That was one thing that always worked in King Henry's favour: the paralysis of the faithful, our inability to resist the destruction of our faith because we couldn't believe this could actually be happening to us. Until tonight. Each of us had sworn to take control of our destiny by trusting in God and believing that this was what He wanted us to do. It did not matter whether we survived. Only whether we succeeded.

In front of the prior stood four of the king's soldiers. I had expected more than this. One man carried a long box – the freretum. The others charged forward, to confront the monks, who formed a semi-circle on the street.

Brother Oswald thundered: 'In the name of the Holy Father, I command you to cease your desecration.' His hood fell back. In the torchlight his albino skin glowed like an advent candle of purest white wax.

I was accustomed to Brother Oswald's pallor, but the sight of him had a terrifying effect on the soldiers. One of them cried, 'God's blood, what *is* he?'

My attention was drawn to the aged box, gripped by a king's soldier. Within seconds, my dizziness evaporated. A fiery rage surged through me, singeing every inch of my body. Everything I'd been told in London was true – the night before the anniversary, the king's men were secretly removing the holy remains.

I could not let them defile the bones of Saint Thomas.

This is the city where it began, I thought as I raced towards the door gripping my rock. *And this is the city where it will end.*

PART ONE

Ten Years Earlier

1

B efore the lash of the wind drew blood, before I felt it first move through the air, our horses knew that something was coming.

I was seventeen, and I had made the long journey down to Canterbury from my home, Stafford Castle. At the beginning of each autumn my father travelled to London to attend to family business, but he had not wanted me or my mother to accompany him. A bout of sweating sickness struck the South that summer and he feared we'd lose our lives to the lingering reach of that disease. My mother would not be dissuaded. She told him she feared for *my* life if I did not take the healing waters at a bath she knew of in Canterbury, to cure me of melancholia.

Once in London, my father remained in our house on the Strand, seeing to business, while we rode on with two servants to Canterbury. The day after we arrived, my mother, greatly excited, took me to the shore overlooking the sea. But when we reached it, and I gazed for the first time at those churning grey waves, my mother's temper changed. She had not seen the sea herself since coming to England from Spain at fourteen as a maid of honour to Katherine of Aragon. After a few moments of silence, she began to weep. Her tears deepened into wrenching sobs. I did not know what to say, so I said nothing. I touched her shoulder and a moment later she stopped.

The third day in Canterbury I was taken to be healed. Below a tall house on a fashionable street stretched an ancient grotto. We walked down a set of stairs, and then two stout young women lowered me into the stone bath. It brimmed with pungent water bubbling up from a spring. I sat in it, motionless. Every so often, I could make out strange colours beneath the surging water: bright reddish brown and a deep blue-grey. Mosaics, we were told.

'A Roman built this bath,' explained the woman who administered the treatment. 'There was a forum in the city, temples, even theatres. Everything was levelled by the Saxons. But below ground it's still here. A city below the city.'

The bath mistress turned my head, this way and that. 'How do you feel, mistress? Stronger?' She so wanted to please us. Outside London and the ranks of the nobility, it was not known how much our family lost in the fall of the Duke of Buckingham, my father's eldest brother. He was executed after being falsely accused of high treason, and nearly all Stafford land was seized by the Crown. Here, in a Canterbury bath, we were mistaken for people of importance.

'I feel better,' I murmured. The woman smiled with pride. I glanced over at my mother. She refolded her hands in her lap. I had not fooled her.

The next morning, I expected to begin the journey back to London. But while I was in bed, my mother lay next to me. She turned on her side and ran her fingers through my hair, as she used to when I was a child. We had the same black tresses. Her hair thinned later on – in truth, it fell out in patches – but she never greyed. 'Juana, I've made arrangements to see a young nun,' she said.

There was nothing surprising about her making such a plan. In Spain, my mother's family spent as much time as possible with nuns and monks and friars. They visited the abbeys that dotted the hills of Castile, to pray in the churches, bow to the holy relics, or meditate through the night in austere cells. The religious houses near Stafford Castle could not compare. 'Not a single mystic within a day's ride of here,' she'd moan.

As we readied ourselves, my mother told me about Sister Elizabeth Barton. The Benedictine nun had an unusual story. Just two years earlier she'd worked as a servant for the steward of the Archbishop of Canterbury. She fell ill and for weeks lay senseless. She woke up healed – and her first question was about a child who lived nearby who had also sickened, but only after Elizabeth Barton lost consciousness. There was no way she could have known of it. From that day on, she was aware of things happening in other rooms, in other houses, even miles away. Archbishop Warham sent men to examine her and they concluded that her gifts were genuine. It was decided that this young servant should take holy vows and so be protected from the world.

The Holy Maid of Kent now resided in the priory of Saint Sepulchre, but she sometimes granted audiences to those with pressing questions.

'Her prayers could be meaningful,' my mother said, pushing my hair behind my ears. There was a time when meeting such a person would have intrigued me. But I felt no such anticipation. With our maid's help, I silently dressed.

When I first left the household of Queen Katherine over a year ago, I would not speak to anyone. I wept or I lay in bed, my arms wrapped around my body. My mother had to force food into me. Everyone attributed it to the shock of the king's request for an annulment – the queen, devastated, wailed loudly; the tall, furious monarch stormed from the room. This happened on the first day I entered service, to be a maid of honour to the blessed queen, as my mother had before me. The annulment was without question a frightening scandal. But, from the beginning, my mother had suspected something else. She must have pressed me for answers a hundred times. I never, ever considered telling her or my father the truth. It was not just my intense shame. George Boleyn bragged that he was a favoured courtier. His sister Anne was the beloved of the king. If my father, a Stafford, knew the truth – that Boleyn had violently touched me, his hand clapped over my mouth, and would have raped me had he more time – there is no force on earth that could have prevented him from trying to kill George Boleyn. As for my mother, the blood of ancient Spanish nobility, she would be even more ferocious in her revenge. To protect my parents, I said nothing. I blamed myself for what happened. I would not ruin my parents' lives – and those of the rest of the Stafford family – because of that stupidity.

By the time summer ended in 1527, a certain dullness overtook me. I welcomed this reprieve from tumultuous emotion, but it worried my mother. She could not believe I'd lost interest in books and music, once my principal joys. I spent the following months – the longest winter of my life – drifting in a grey expanse of nothing. The apothecary summoned to Stafford Castle diagnosed melancholia, but the barber-surgeon said no, my humours were not aligned and I was too phlegmatic. Each diagnosis called for conflicting remedy. My mother argued with them both. When spring came, she decided to trust her own instincts in nursing me. I did regain my health but never all of my spirits. My Stafford relatives approved of the quieter, docile Joanna

– I'd always been a headstrong girl – but my mother fretted.

That morning in Canterbury, when we'd finished dressing, my mother declared we had no need of servants. The priory of Saint Sepulchre was not far outside the city walls.

Our maid was plainly glad to be free of us for a few hours. The manservant was a different matter. 'Sir Richard said I was to stay by your side at all times,' he said.

'And I am telling you to occupy yourself in some other way,' my mother snapped. 'Canterbury is an honest city, and I know the way.'

The manservant aimed a look of hatred at her back. As much as they loved my father, the castle staff loathed my mother. She was difficult – and she was foreign. The English distrusted all foreigners, and in particular imperious females.

It was a fair day, warmer than expected for the season. We took the main road leading out of the city. Majestic oaks lined each side. A low brick wall surrounded Canterbury, most likely built by the Romans all those centuries ago.

As we neared the wall, my horse stopped dead. I shook the reins. But instead of starting up again, he shimmied sideways, edging off the road. I had never known my horse – or any horse – to move in this way.

My mother turned around, her face a question. But just at that moment, her horse gave her trouble as well. She brandished the small whip she always carried.

The winds came then. I managed to get my horse back onto the road, but he was still skittish. The wind blew his mane back so violently, it was like a hard fringe snapping at my face. By this time, we had managed to reach the gap in the wall where the road spilled out of Canterbury. All the trees swayed and bent, even the oaks, as if paying homage to a harsh master.

'*Madre*, we should go back.' I had to shout to be heard over the roar.

'No, we go on, Juana,' she shouted. Her black Spanish hood rose and flapped around her head, like a horned halo. 'We must go on.'

I followed my mother to the priory of Saint Sepulchre. Dead brush hurtled over the ground. A brace of rabbits streaked across the road, and my horse backed up, whinnying. It took all my strength on the reins to prevent him from bolting. Ahead of me, my mother turned and pointed at a building to the left.

I never knew what struck me. My mother later said it was a branch, careening wildly through the air. All I knew was the pain that clawed my cheek, followed by a thick spreading wetness.

I would have been thrown but for a bearded man who emerged from the windstorm and grabbed the reins. The man helped me down and into a small stone gatehouse. My mother was already inside. She called out her gratitude in Spanish. The man dampened a cloth, and she cleaned the blood off my face.

'It's not a deep cut, thank the Virgin,' my mother said, and instructed me to press the cloth hard on my skin.

'How much farther to the priory?' I asked.

'We are at Saint Sepulchre now, this man is the porter,' she said. 'It's just a few steps to the main doors.'

The porter escorted us to the long stone building. The wind blew so strong that I feared I'd be sent flying through the air, like the broken branch. The porter shoved open tall wooden doors. He did not stay – he said he must see to the safety of our horses. Seconds later, I heard the click of a bolt on the other side of the door.

We were locked inside Saint Sepulchre.

I knew little of the life of a nun. Friars, who had freedom of movement, sometimes visited Stafford Castle. I had not given thought to the meaning of enclosure. Nuns, like monks, were intended to live apart from the world, for prayer and study. That much I knew. But now I also began to grasp that enclosure might require enforcement.

There was one high window in the square room. The wind beat against the glass with untamed ferocity. No candles brightened the dimness. There was no furniture nor any tapestries.

A framed portrait of a man did hang on the wall. The man wore plain robes; his long white beard rested on his cowl. He carried a wooden staff. Each corner of the frame was embellished with a carving of a leafed branch.

My mother gasped and clutched my arm. With her other, she pointed at a dark form floating toward us from the far end of the room. A few seconds later we realised it was a woman. She wore a long black habit and a black veil, and so had melted into the darkness. As she drew nearer, I could see she was quite old, with large, pale blue eyes.

'I am Sister Anne, I welcome you to the priory of Saint Sepulchre,' she said.

My mother, in contrast to the nun's gentle manner, spoke in a loud, nervous tumble, her hands in motion. We were expected, she said. A visitation had been granted with Sister Elizabeth Barton, the storm roughened our journey, and I'd been slightly injured, but we expected to go forward. Sister Anne took it all in with perfect calm.

'The prioress will want to speak with you,' she said, and turned back the way she came, to lead us. We followed her down a passageway even darker than the room we'd waited in. The nun must have been at least sixty years of age, yet she walked with youthful ease.

There were three doors along the hall. Sister Anne opened the last one on the left and ushered us into another dim, empty room.

'But where is the prioress?' demanded my mother. 'As I've told you, Sister, we are expected.'

Sister Anne bowed and left. I could tell from the way my mother pursed her lips she was unhappy with how we'd been treated thus far.

In this room stood two wooden tables. One was large, with a stool behind it. The other was narrow, pushed against a wall. I noticed the floor was freshly swept and the walls showed no stains of age. The priory might have been modest, but it was scrupulously maintained.

'How is your cut?' my mother asked. She lifted the cloth and peered at my cheek. 'The bleeding has stopped. Does it still hurt?'

'No,' I lied.

I spotted a book mounted on the narrow table and decided to inspect it more closely. The leather cover was dominated by a gleaming picture of a robed man with a white beard, holding a staff – similar to the portrait in the front chamber but more detailed. The beatific pride of his expression, the folds of his brown robe, the clouds soaring above his head – all were rendered in rich, dazzling colours. Running along the square border of the man's picture was an intertwined branch: thin with slender green leaves. With great care, I opened the book. It was written in Latin, a language I had dedicated myself to since I was eight years old. *The Life of Saint Benedict of Nursia*, read the title. Underneath was his span of life: AD 480 to 543. There was a black bird below the dates, holding a loaf of bread in its beak. I turned another page and began to absorb the story. Underneath a picture of a teenage boy in the tunic of a Roman, it said that Saint Benedict forsook his family's wealth, choosing to leave the city where he was raised. Another turn showed him alone, surrounded by mountains.

I'd been concentrating so closely that I didn't hear my mother until she stood right next to me. 'Ah, the founder of the Benedictines,' she said. She pointed at the branches that stretched across the border of each page. 'The olive branch is so lovely; it's the symbol of their order.'

My finger froze on the page. I realised that for the first time since last May, when I submitted myself to the profligate court of Henry VIII, I felt true curiosity. Was it the violent force of the wind – had it ripped the lassitude from me? Or had I been awakened by this spare, humble priory and the dazzling beauty of this, its precious object?

The door opened. A woman strode into the room. She was younger than the first nun – close in age to my mother. Her face was sharply sculpted, with high cheekbones.

'I am the prioress, Sister Philippa Jonys.'

My mother leaped forward and seized the prioress's hand to kiss it and go down on one knee. It was not only theatricality: I knew that in Spain, deep obeisance was paid to the heads of holy houses. But the prioress's eyes widened at the sight of my prostrate mother.

Pulling her hand free, the prioress said, 'I regret to hear of your mishap. We are a Benedictine house, sworn to hospitality, and will offer you a place of rest until you are ready to resume your journey.'

My mother sputtered, 'But we are here to see Sister Elizabeth Barton. It was arranged. I corresponded with Doctor Bocking while still at Stafford Castle.'

I stared at my mother in surprise. My impression had been that the trip to Saint Sepulchre was spontaneous, arranged in Canterbury or London at the earliest. I began to comprehend that the healing waters served as an excuse to get us here. Coming to Saint Sepulchre, without servants to observe us, was her purpose.

'I have not been informed of this visitation, and nothing occurs here without my approval,' the prioress said.

Most would be intimidated by such a rebuff. Not Lady Isabella Stafford.

'Doctor Bocking, the monk who I understand is the spiritual advisor of Sister Elizabeth, wrote to me granting permission,' my mother said. 'I would have brought his letter as proof, but I did not expect that the wife of Sir Richard Stafford – and a lady-in-waiting to the queen of England – could be disbelieved.'

The prioress clutched the leather belt that clinched her habit. 'This is a priory, not the court of the king. Sister Elizabeth is a member of our community. We have six nuns at Saint Sepulchre. *Six*. There is much work to be done, earthly responsibilities as well as spiritual. These visits rob Sister Elizabeth of her health. "Will this harvest be better?" "Will I marry again?" She cannot spend all of her time with such pleadings.'

'I am not here to inquire about harvests,' snapped my mother.

'Then why are you here?'

With a glance at me, my mother said, 'My daughter has not been well for some time. If I knew what course to take – what her future might hold—'

'Mama, no,' I interrupted, horrified. 'We were ordered by Cousin Henry never to solicit prophecy, after the Duke of Buckingham's—'

'Be silent,' scolded my mother. 'This is not of the same import.'

There was a tap on the door, and Sister Anne reappeared.

'Sister Elizabeth said she will see the girl named Joanna now,' the elderly nun murmured.

'Did you tell her of these guests?' demanded the prioress.

Sister Anne shook her head. The prioress and nun stared at each other. A peculiar emotion throbbed in the air.

My mother did not notice it. 'Please, without further delay, show us the way to Sister Elizabeth,' she said, triumphant.

Sister Anne bowed her head. 'Forgive me, Lady Stafford, but Sister Elizabeth said she will see the girl Joanna alone. And that she must come of her own free will and unconstrained.'

'But I don't want to see her at all,' I protested.

My mother took me by the shoulders. Her face was flushed; I feared she was close to tears. 'Oh, you must, Juana,' she said. '*Por favor*. Ask her what is to be done. Sister Elizabeth has a gift, a vision. Only she can guide us. I can't cope with this any more all alone. *I can't*.'

I had not realised how much my spiritual affliction troubled my mother. Her suffering filled me with remorse. I would go to this strange young nun. The visit should be brief; I intended to ask few questions.

The prioress and Sister Anne spoke together, in hushed tones, for another minute. Then the prioress beckoned for me alone to follow.

She led me down the passageway, through the front entranceway, and down another dim corridor. Following her, I thought of how the elegance of her movements contrasted with the ladies I'd grown up with. Hers was certainly not movement calculated to draw admiration.

It was grace that derived from simplicity and economy of movement.

I also tried to plan how I could speak to Sister Elizabeth Barton without disobeying the command of Lord Henry Stafford, my cousin and head of the family. It had been the prophecy of a friar, much distorted, that was the basis for arresting my uncle, the Duke of Buckingham. During the trial, he was charged with seeking to learn the future – how long would Henry VIII live and would he produce sons – so that the duke could plot to seize the throne. Afterward, my cautious cousin, his son, said repeatedly that none of the family could ever have anything to do with prophecy. My father agreed – he harboured a personal distaste for seers, witches, and necromancers. It was one of the many ways in which he differed from my mother.

The prioress rapped on a door, gently. She hesitated, her eyebrows furrowing, and then she opened it and we stepped inside.

This room was tiny, as small as a servant's. A lone figure sat in the middle of the floor, slumped over, her back to us. There was no window. Two candles that burned on either side of the door provided the only light.

'Sister Elizabeth, will you attend Vespers later?' asked the prioress.

The figure nodded but did not turn around. The prioress said to me, 'I shall be back shortly,' and gestured for me to step forward.

I edged inside. The prioress closed the door.

Sister Elizabeth Barton wore the same black habit as the others. She didn't turn around. I felt awkward. Unwanted. The minutes crept by.

'It's a wind that brings no rain,' said a young voice.

'Indeed, Sister,' I said, relieved that she spoke. 'There wasn't any rain.' But a second later I wondered how she knew anything about the elements without a window in the room. Another nun must have told her, I concluded. Just as someone told her my name – the monk Doctor Bocking, perhaps. I did not believe that she possessed the powers my mother spoke of. Although devout, I held closer to the spirit of my pragmatic father in such matters.

White hands reached out and Sister Elizabeth turned herself around, slowly, sitting on the floor. This nun was but a girl, and so frail-looking. She had a long face, with a sloping chin.

As she gazed up at me, sadness filled her eyes.

'I did not know you would be so young,' she whispered.

'I am seventeen,' I said. 'You look to be the same age.'

'I am twenty-two,' she said, and continued: 'You have intelligence, piety, strength, and beauty. And noble blood. All the things I lack.' There was no envy. It was as if she mulled a list of goods to be purchased at market.

Ignoring her assessment of me, which I found embarrassing, I asked, 'How can you say you lack piety when you are a sister of Christ?'

'God chose me,' she said. 'I was a servant, of no importance in the world. He chose me to speak the truth. I have no choice. I must submit to His will. For you it is different. You have a true spiritual calling.'

Sister Elizabeth Barton was confused. 'I am not a nun,' I said.

She suddenly frowned, as if she were responding to someone else's voice. She slowly rose to her feet. She was spare and small, at least three inches shorter than me.

'Yes, the two cardinals are coming,' she said. 'It will be within the month. They will pass through on the way to London. I will have to try to speak to them. I must find the courage to go before all the highest and most powerful men in the land.'

My mother had said nothing of Sister Elizabeth leaving Saint Sepulchre to go before the powerful. 'Why would you do that?' I asked.

'To stop them,' she said.

I was torn. A part of me was curious, but another, larger, part was growing uneasy. There was nothing malevolent about this fragile nun, yet her words made me uncomfortable.

At last the curious part won. 'Whom must you stop, Sister?' I asked. 'The cardinals?'

She shook her head and took two steps toward me. 'You know, Joanna.'

'No, Sister Elizabeth, I don't.'

'Your mother wants to know your future – should she marry you off in the country to someone who will take you with meagre dowry, or try to return you to the court of the king? Your true vocation leaps in her face but she cannot see. Poor woman. She has no notion of what she has set in motion by bringing you to me.'

How could the Holy Maid of Kent know so much of my family? Yet I said, nervously, 'Sister, I don't know what you are talking about.'

Her lower lip trembled. 'When the cow doth ride the bull, then priest beware thy skull,' she said.

My stomach clenched. At last, I had heard a prophecy.

'Those are not my words,' Sister Elizabeth continued. 'They come from the lips of Mother Shipton. Do you know of her?'

I shook my head.

'Born in a cave in Yorkshire,' she said, her words coming fast. 'A girl without a father – a bastard of the north. Hated and scorned by all. Not just for deformity of face but for the power of her words. Crone, they call her. Witch. It is so wretched to know the truth, Joanna. To see things no one else can see. To have to try to stop evil before it is too late.'

'What sort of evil?' The instant I asked the question, I regretted it.

Again the nun's lower lip trembled. Her eyes gleamed with tears.

'The Boleyns,' she said.

I stumbled back and hit the stone wall, hard. I felt behind me for the door. I hadn't heard the prioress lock it. I would find a way out of this room. I must.

'Oh, you're so frightened, forgive me,' she wailed, tears spattering her face. 'I don't want this fate for you. I know that you've already been touched by the evil. I will try my hardest, Joanna. I don't want you to be the one.'

'The one?' I repeated, still feeling for the door.

Sister Elizabeth stretched her arms wide, her palms facing the ceiling. 'You are the one who will come after,' she said.

The gravity of her words, coupled with the way she spread her hands, chilled me to the marrow.

Sister Elizabeth opened her mouth, as if to say something else, and then shut it. Her face turned bright red. But in a flash, the red drained away, leaving her skin ashen. I looked at the candles. How could a person change colour in such a manner? But the candles burned steadily.

'Are you unwell, Sister?' I said. 'Shall I seek help?'

She shook her head, violently, but not to say no to me. Her head, her arms, her legs – every part of her shook. Her tongue bobbed in and out of her mouth. After less than a minute of this, her knees gave way and she collapsed.

'It hurts,' she moaned, writhing on her back. 'It hurts.'

'I will get you help,' I said.

'No, no, no,' she said, her voice a hoarse stammer. 'Joanna Stafford … hear me. I … beg … you.'

Fighting down my terror, I knelt on the floor beside her. A trail of white foam eased out of her gaping mouth. She thrashed and coughed; I thought she would lose consciousness. But she didn't.

'I see abbeys crumbling to dust,' she said. The choking and thrashing ended. Incredibly, the voice of Sister Elizabeth Barton boomed strong and clear. 'I see the blood of monks spilled across the land. Books are destroyed. Statues toppled. Relics defiled. I see the greatest men of the kingdom with heads struck off. The common folk will hang, even the children. Friars will starve. Queens will die.'

Rocking back and forth, I moaned, 'No, no, no. This can't be.'

'You are the one who will come after,' she said, her voice stronger still. 'I am the first of three seers. If I fail, you must go before the second and then the third, to receive the full prophecy and learn what you must do. But only of your own free will. After the third has prophesied, nothing can stop it, Joanna Stafford. *Nothing.*'

'But I can't,' I cried. 'I can't do anything. I'm no one – and I'm too afraid.'

In a voice so loud it echoed in her cell, Sister Elizabeth said, 'When the raven climbs the rope, the dog must soar like the hawk. When the raven climbs the rope, the dog must soar like the hawk.'

The door flew open. The prioress and Sister Anne hurried to the fallen nun, kneeling beside her. Sister Elizabeth Barton said just two words more, before the prioress pried open her jaw and Sister Anne pushed in a rag. She turned her head, to find me with her fierce eyes, and then she spoke.

'The chalice …'

2

On a dismal Tuesday night, ten years after that visit to the seer and two months before the desperate mission to Canterbury, I lay sleepless in my bed. I mourned the past and worried for the future, but without any conception of what was to come. The events of the following day would set me once more on the path to prophecy that Sister Elizabeth Barton warned of long ago. But as I stared at the ceiling, there was only one thing predictable: the depth of the next day's mud.

The rain began hard on midnight, hours after I crept into bed. It was a fine bed: a mattress placed on a board, propped up on four short wooden legs. By any measure, it was more comfortable than my old bed at Dartford Priory, a straw-stuffed pallet laid on the stone floor of the novice dormitory. We slept in stretches there: after Vespers we rested for a few hours, then awoke to the bells calling us to Matins, at midnight. After that observance, we'd return to our dormitories, to sleep until the pealing of the bells announced Lauds.

Now there was nothing to disturb me between sunset and sunrise, yet sleep eluded me as it had so many nights before. I listened to the rain and to the light snoring of Arthur, on the other side of the small room.

'With you, Arthur will be safe,' my father said to me last winter. He'd come to plead with me to take care of Arthur, then four years old, the only son of my cousin Margaret. She was gone, and my father soon followed, his health broken by his imprisonment in the Tower and the other horrors of the past year.

To all of England, Margaret Bulmer – the bastard daughter of my uncle the Duke of Buckingham – was an infamous traitor, burned at the stake at Smithfield for her part in the Pilgrimage of Grace. But to me she was the trusted companion of my childhood. I would never regret going to Smithfield, breaking the rule of enclosure of my Dominican Order, to stand by Margaret. Of course I would protect and care for her son. And I would never reveal to a living soul the truth of his birth – that he was not the child of Margaret's husband.

I'd always found it a soothing sound, the drumming of rain on windows, both at Stafford Castle and at Dartford Priory. And why not? The elements never impeded me. Before Arthur, I spent most of the hours of the day inside.

But now I was at the mercy of the elements. Only vigorous play kept Arthur occupied: running and climbing and digging and tossing balls. As the rain grew stronger, a dread took hold of what the next day would bring. How could I cope with Arthur if a rainstorm trapped us inside? I'd need all my strength to manage him ... yet the sleepless minutes stretched into hours. My thoughts coiled round and round in my head.

'We must not submit to sorrow,' Brother Edmund often said. He was correct. But it wasn't quite sorrow that plagued me. It was my inability to understand why God allowed this to happen: the dissolution of the monasteries, the end of our way of life. I had been told over and over to submit to the will of Christ Our Lord. To my shame, I found that very difficult. More than anything else, I felt lost.

Finally, mercifully, a sodden exhaustion silenced the questions and I found sleep.

It was Arthur's firm shake of a shoulder that woke me, just after dawn.

'Joanna – hungry.'

As weary as I was, the sound of Arthur's halting voice – he did not speak as well as most five-year-olds – and the sight of his round, handsome face heartened me. I pulled myself from bed, dressed him in his child's gown, and led him downstairs, his warm little hand clutching mine.

I lit a fire in our kitchen and sliced the bread. I discovered most of the cheese had gone rancid but managed to find a decent slice for Arthur. My serving girl, Kitty, often forgot to store food properly in our tiny larder. I was her first employer. She lived with her parents nearby and came in most afternoons to sweep, wash our clothes and linen, churn and cook. None of it was done well. But she was kind and needed money and I sought to help. Arthur was gobbling his second piece of bread when a knock sounded on the front door.

'Sister Bea!' he crowed.

Into my home slid Sister Beatrice, shaking the rain off her cloak. Droplets clung to her long blonde eyelashes. She'd been a novice before me and left the priory for more than a year, but returned as a lay sister a few months before its closing. Now, like myself, she was in limbo: a woman forced from a religious life but not of a mind and spirit to embrace the secular world.

As Arthur reached up to hug her waist, Sister Beatrice gave her usual smile, a curve of her lips without the showing of teeth. She was a woman sparing of words. I'd not seen a blush on her white skin nor anger in those slanted green eyes.

As I handed her a hunk of bread, she took a long look at me. I suspect my near-sleepless night had left my face a misery. But she didn't make inquiry. Neither of us meddled in the other's troubles or secrets.

'I'll be dressed in a moment,' I said, for I was still in my nightclothes.

'After you return from Mass, shall we all go to the Building Office?' she asked. Sister Beatrice looked after Arthur while I attended Mass, for he simply could not keep silent in church.

In an instant my torpor fell away. 'Oh, yes, I'd forgotten. It's the first Wednesday of the month. Hurrah!' I danced with Arthur through the kitchen. He laughed so hard that bits of half-chewed bread flew through the air.

Today was the day to secure my tapestry loom.

At the priory, we'd woven tapestries, exquisite silk ones. They were sold to hang on castle walls. Each one told a story based on ancient myths or parables in Scripture. Novices had been expected to weave for at least three hours a day, when the light was strongest. My mother personally trained me in needlework and, although tapestry work was very different – we sat at a large wooden loom, sometimes pressing foot pedals – I took to it at once.

Four months ago, I'd had the idea to continue the tradition of Dartford tapestry-making as a private enterprise. The challenge was securing a loom, since of course the priory's was carted away at our dissolution, as was every other object we possessed. Such looms were not even constructed in England, so I ordered one from Brussels, the centre of tapestry production for all of Christendom, and arranged to have it shipped from the Low Countries to Dartford. It was no simple matter, because of all the trade difficulties, but I managed it. The first Wednesday of the month was the day when new imported goods were distributed to waiting customers, at the Building Office.

I raced up the stairs to dress, wriggling into my kirtle and pinning up my thick black hair. I pulled my cleanest white hood over my hair.

I kissed Arthur on his cheek and scrambled out the door, calling over my shoulder, 'Be ready by the time I return. I shall bring reinforcements!'

3

When I stepped out the door, I plunged into the heart of town. I lived on the High Street, in one of the two-storey timber-framed buildings that faced the church.

From behind our priory walls, Dartford had seemed a good neighbour – a friendly, well-ordered place. Three hours on horseback from London, the town was known for its safe travellers' inns, its proud shops, and, of course, its five-hundred-year-old church. There was another Dartford, though. One that was not so well ordered. The shambles was closer to the church than usually thought desirable in a town this size. The stench of it, the butchered animals and dead fish, was a constant unpleasantness. I wondered why the town fathers did not have such a malodorous site moved.

The shambles was a reminder that beneath the pleasing surface of Dartford lurked ugliness. It was a reminder that I too often ignored.

That very morning, heedless, I leaped across the puddles in the street to reach the pride of the town: Holy Trinity Church. Its square Norman tower, with five-foot-thick walls, could be seen for miles.

I'd made it across the street when I heard my friends' voices behind me.

'Sister Joanna, a good morning to you.'

Brother Edmund and Sister Winifred bore such a strong resemblance to each other: slender, with ash-blond hair and large brown eyes. As I waited for them to reach me in the doorway, I scrutinised Brother Edmund's sensitive features, more out of habit than necessity. For years he had struggled with a secret dependence on a certain tincture, made from an exotic red flower of India. At the priory he'd confessed it to me and vowed never to weaken again. Ever since, I'd studied his eyes for the tell-tale sign of the potion: a preternatural calm, a blank drowsiness. When the priory was dissolved, Brother Edmund continued his work as an apothecary and healer. The priory had had two infirmaries, one inside its walls and the other, for the benefit of the town, outside it. Brother Edmund kept the town's open, supplying it himself, and practised his skills on any who desired it. I worried that his proximity to the tinctures of his trade would weaken his resolve. But today, as every day for almost a year, his eyes were clear.

When they reached me, I realised it was Sister Winifred who deserved my concern more than her older brother. Her skin was ashen; her cheekbones stood out in her face. I knew the marshy air of Dartford wreaked havoc on her, especially after a sopping night.

'Are you well, Sister?' I asked as the three of us entered the church.

'Oh, yes,' she said quickly.

Our footsteps echoed as we walked across the church, which was alive with light. Brilliant candles flickered everywhere: at the grand high altar, at the chapel of Saint Thomas Becket, and on the floor clustered around the brass memorials, honouring the dead gentry of Dartford.

We were the only people visible on the floor of the church. Yet we were not alone. High above the vestry, through three vertical slits, a candle gleamed. And a malevolent dark form moved between those carved slits.

Father William Mote, the vicar of Holy Trinity Church, was watching us from his private room.

Brother Edmund glanced up; he, too, took note of the priest's surveillance. He put his arm around Sister Winifred, patting her on the shoulder as he guided her to our destination at the southeastern corner of the church: the altar of Saint Mary the Virgin.

I do not know exactly how it happened, that we, the refugees of Dartford Priory, were shunted off this way. No one ever said we were unwelcome at Holy Trinity. It was all done as if it was for *our* benefit: 'Your Dominican Order reveres the Virgin – wouldn't you be more comfortable in a chapel devoted to Her?' And we would hear Mass exclusively from doddering Father Anthony rather than Father William. The final insult was the timing: to prevent any 'confusion', we attended separate Mass.

I made a tally of all the good that our priory had done for generations – not just as landlord and employer but also as sponsor of the almshouse and the infirmary. And what of our role as teachers? The priory was the only place where girls of good local families could learn reading and writing. Nothing took its place. And yet now we were treated like inferior animals to be culled from the herd. I dipped my fingers in the stoup of holy water at the side of the chapel entrance. But before I followed Sister Winifred inside, I whirled around to glare at Father William's high spying place. *You should be ashamed*, I thought.

Brother Edmund shook his head. Just as I stood watch over him for signs of his weakness, he did his best to help me master mine – my temper.

I took my place before the statue of the serene Virgin. It was of some comfort that we took Mass in such a chapel. A colourful wall mural of Saint George slaying the dragon dominated the room.

There was a stirring behind me. The others were arriving, the six nuns of Dartford who still lived in community. They were the vestiges of the priory, attempting to live out the ideals of our order. When King Henry and Lord Privy Seal Thomas Cromwell dissolved the priory, most of the sisters returned to their families. Our prioress departed for the home of a brother, and none of us heard from her again. But Sister Rachel, one of the senior nuns, had years earlier been bequeathed a large house a mile from the centre of town, and five others joined her there, pooling their pensions. Arthur's rambunctiousness made my joining the sisters in their community impossible, and so I, like Brother Edmund and Sister Winifred, leased lodgings from Holy Trinity Church.

Morning Mass was when we could all be together again. At the priory, we had chanted the Psalms at least four hours a day – the liturgy was the core of our commitment to God. To be reduced to a single observance was difficult, but without daily Mass we'd be plunged into confusion.

Sister Eleanor strode forward, water dripping from her clothes. Yes, the hem of her kirtle was drenched from the mile's walk in the rain, but she'd never complain. She'd been appointed *circatrix* of Dartford by the prioress – the enforcer of rules. From what I could tell, she considered herself the leader now, though Sister Rachel – ten years older and the actual owner of the house – also had firm ideas of how they should conduct themselves.

We all stood in the same exact place every day, re-creating the hierarchy of our lost world. Sister Winifred and I, the two ex-novices of Dartford, were in front. The tense Sister Eleanor stood behind us. Next were the two nuns who also held office while at Dartford: Sister Rachel, the reliquarian, and Sister Agatha, the novice mistress. Then came the final three. Brother Edmund stood across the aisle, alone, continuing the strict division of man and woman.

I struggled to hide my impatience as we waited for our assigned priest. The only sounds were the sizzle of an altar candle or one of Sister Agatha's loud sighs. I turned around; her eyes met mine with a little nod. Of all the sisters, I missed her the most, my warm-natured, gossipy novice mistress.

Finally we heard the shuffling feet of Father Anthony.

'*Salve*,' he said in his creaky voice.

A moment after he'd begun Mass, I looked over at Brother Edmund. This was not correct. My friend, who was as proficient in Latin as I, cleared his throat.

'Father, forgive me, but it is not the beginning of Lent.'

The priest blinked rapidly, his mouth working. 'What day is it?'

'It is the second of October, Father.'

'What year?'

Brother Edmund said gently, 'The Year of Our Lord fifteen hundred and thirty-eight.'

Father Anthony thought a moment and then launched into an appropriate Mass.

How far we had fallen. I ached to remember: sitting in my novice stall, singing and chanting, the lavender incense so heady it made me swoon. Or plucking cherries from a tree in our orchard. Or leafing through the precious books of the library. This morning, I could feel the same longing from the others, pulsing in the very air. Yet what was to be done? The monastic life was extinguished in England.

After taking communion, we walked together through the larger church. Because Father Anthony had made such a late start, the towns-folk were already trickling in for their regular Mass. One woman knelt at the altar, tenderly replacing the candlesticks with new ones she'd just polished.

I heard a strange noise as we passed the centre aisle: the sound of a man weeping.

'Ah, it's Oliver Gwinn,' said Brother Edmund. 'His wife died yesterday.'

I peered up the aisle. A large man stood alone, his shoulders shaking.

'That is so sad – they were devoted,' said Sister Winifred. Because of their work in the infirmary, they knew the townsfolk better than I did.

'We must try to help him,' said Brother Edmund.

Sister Winifred said, 'But what of the rules?'

I winced. Brother Edmund had been told that he could not perform the work of a friar inside this church. Dominican friars chose a life that involved not just studying God's wisdom but giving comfort to the people who needed it, the sick and poor and bereft.

Brother Edmund stepped forward as if he had not heard his sister. I went with him up the aisle, fiercely proud, as always, of my friend.

I heard the footsteps of someone hurrying to catch up – my heart pounding, I whirled around. Was a parishioner already trying to prevent us from providing counsel? But it was my erstwhile novice mistress Sister Agatha, her eyes bright with interest.

'Master Gwinn, can I be of service to you?' asked Brother Edmund. 'I grieve for your loss. Your wife was a wonderful woman, a good Christian.'

Master Gwinn turned slowly. He wore the clothes of a prosperous man and had a thick black beard salted with grey.

'Yes, she was, Brother,' he said, his voice rough and broken. 'It is very good of you to make inquiry. I confess, it's a bitter blow. I've spent every day with my Amy since I was twenty years old. Our children – our grandchildren – I don't know what to do.'

Brother Edmund laid a hand on the widower's broad shoulder.

'She is in a better place, be assured,' he said. Although I knew better than anyone that Brother Edmund was not always certain of his own strengths, when he helped others, he radiated a confidence that helped many through their struggles.

It was no different for Master Gwinn, who nodded in gratitude.

'Oh, you poor man – you poor, poor man.' It was Sister Agatha who spoke, as she stepped toward Oliver Gwinn, her own eyes filled with tears. 'You loved your wife so dearly.'

He looked at Sister Agatha and his exhausted, homely face was transformed. Instead of weakening him, her words of sympathy seemed to strengthen him. 'Thank you,' he said.

'Are these people bothering you, Master Gwinn?' said a high, nasal voice.

At last, the chastisement. But who would it come from, I wondered.

A woman of like age to Oliver Gwinn's pushed her way forward. She too was well dressed; her russet kirtle stretched over an enormous, sagging bosom. Her thick dark eyebrows nearly met in the middle, over ice-cold blue eyes.

'We are *helping* Master Gwinn,' I said to her.

She looked at me, and the rest of us, her face filled with distrust.

'Yes, Mistress Brooke, they are helping me,' said the widower.

'But that is not their duty – it is Father William's,' she said, pointing. 'And he comes now.'

I tensed as the vicar of Holy Trinity Church approached. He wasn't hurrying. Father William never rushed; he had an indolent stride. The customary smile stretched across the lower half of his face. Above, his eyes examined us with the distaste of a man facing a perpetual running sore.

I realised someone else surveyed me – Mistress Brooke had not moved.

'I know who you are,' she said to me.

'Do you?' I shrugged. It was the shrug of my mother, I fear, one of her more imperious Spanish gestures.

'Is there a difficulty here?' asked Father William. He rarely addressed us by name, to avoid having to use 'Brother' or 'Sister', honorifics we were, strictly speaking, no longer entitled to. The kinder townspeople still used those names, out of respect. Father William was not kind.

Brother Edmund, several inches taller than the vicar, inclined in a conciliatory half bow.

'None at all, Father,' he said.

'Then I must ask you to join me in the chapel of Saint Thomas Becket,' he said. 'I've already asked the others to await us. I have something to say to all of you.'

My spirits sank to the stone floor. I could feel Mistress Brooke's glare on my back as I trailed the others down the aisle, to the chapel.

Sister Rachel, Sister Eleanor and the rest of the nuns stood there, uneasy. We joined them, forming a defensive half-circle.

Father William folded his hands together to address the group.

'I feel it is only right and proper to prepare you for what is to come,' he said. 'Lord Privy Seal Thomas Cromwell, our Vice Regent of Spiritual Affairs, has devised certain articles to be read before all the people of England. The king approved such articles, and so Archbishop Thomas Cranmer drafted the letters that will soon reach every parish in the land.'

He paused to look at the nine of us in turn, saving me for last. His eyes glistened as he studied my face, which must have been filled with dread.

'There will be changes in the observance of religion,' he said. 'And you must conform, every one of you, to the will of our sovereign lord, the king.'

'We are obedient subjects of King Henry,' said Sister Eleanor. 'If you will only instruct us in what is expected.'

Father William shifted away so that he was addressing Brother Edmund directly. I had noticed before how uncomfortable he was with Sister Eleanor's role as our leader. He always endeavoured to speak to the lone man of our group.

'This church,' he said, 'is to be stripped.'

4

We left Holy Trinity in silence. The rain had stopped. A chalky white mist hung above the street, obscuring the buildings beyond the glazier's shop. It was as if a cloud had descended to earth. The stench of the shambles – the sour smell of rotting fish – encircled us.

Sister Rachel broke the silence. 'Heretical abominations,' she moaned.

'What are we to do?' whispered Sister Agatha.

Two men, curious, stood on the periphery of the mist. Whenever we – the diaspora of Dartford Priory – gathered together in town like this, we attracted attention.

'Sisters, hush,' ordered Sister Eleanor. 'We will not speak of this matter here, in the open. We will return to our house.'

They departed, walking two across, as if they were presiding down the cloister passageway and not a stinking, mud-riven street.

Brother Edmund, Sister Winifred and I remained, staring at one another as we struggled to take in what Father William just said. *Stripped*, what a terrible word. It meant that Mass would continue to be held at Holy Trinity Church. But the way we worshipped God – that would change. All of the candles were to be extinguished. Natural light would have to suffice from now on. The statues of the saints were to be removed as evidence of 'men's superstition and papist idolatry'. The brass plaques, loving tributes to the memory of Dartford's citizens, were to be torn from the floor. The mural of Saint George? Painted over. The chapel of Saint Thomas Becket would be dismantled, since the king regarded him as a rebel to royal authority, and all chapels and statues honouring him were to be destroyed.

Brother Edmund cleared his throat. 'I must go to the infirmary. The candlemaker has dropsy, I fear.' He turned to his sister. 'You don't need to assist me, if you'd rather go home for a time.'

Suddenly I remembered. 'My tapestry loom – this is the day I can take possession.' I tugged Sister Winifred's sleeve. 'Please come with me and Sister Beatrice to the Building Office.'

But Sister Winifred shook her head and coughed. Difficult moments often triggered one of her choking fits.

Brother Edmund signalled me to wait, and then hurried his sister across the street and into their home. When he returned he said, 'Perhaps tomorrow would be a better day for the loom?'

'But I've waited so long already, Brother.' I was much disappointed.

He frowned as he looked over my shoulder. 'She's watching us.'

'Who is?' I turned around. A woman's face peered out of the window of the church. I recognised that suspicious countenance. Mistress Brooke.

'Do you know her?' I asked.

'Master Brooke, her husband, built the largest house in the Overy.'

'That does not give her the right to order us about.'

Brother Edmund shook his head. 'Sister Joanna, please remember that we are without protection here in the town. We must, as Sister Eleanor said, conform.'

I gazed at the church window, at Mistress Brooke and the leaping candlelight that surrounded her face, light that would soon be snuffed. With all my heart, I did not wish to conform.

It was then that John staggered toward us on the High Street. Years ago John went mad and, when his parents died, the almshouse overseen by the priory took him in. He had cousins in town but they could not cope with him. When the priory fell, so did its almshouse for the poor and unwanted. John was transferred to the town almshouse. He hated his new surroundings, and his madness turned riotous, like soup boiling in a pot too long. He refused to trim his beard and claimed to be John the Baptist. By night he slept, unhappily, in the almshouse. By day he roamed the streets, shouting gibberish. The crueller young boys threw rubbish at him. We who had lived in the priory felt compassion for John. Yet, in his mind, the exiles from Dartford were to blame for his misfortunes. Brother Edmund was, unfathomably, his chief target.

'Behold the great river Euphrates,' John bellowed. 'The water dried up. I saw three unclean spirits like frogs come from the mouth of the dragon.' John turned this way and that, as if he were surrounded by rapt followers. 'Behold, here is that false prophet.'

Brother Edmund, who learned months ago that it did no good to reason with John, said to me in a low voice, 'Promise me to wait – do not go to the Building Office without me.'

'John never lays hands on any of us, I don't fear him,' I said.

'It's not John we should fear,' Brother Edmund said. 'Sister Joanna, I must get to the infirmary.'

He smiled at me a last time and hurried down the street, bound for the patients who needed him.

John staggered after him, pulling on his beard. He shouted: 'Brothers and Sisters, this man conjures up the spirits of the devils with his working of miracles. Do not follow him to the place the Hebrews call Armageddon!'

I turned away from John's madness and crossed the street, toward home. I regretted the lack of enthusiasm for my tapestry enterprise from Brother Edmund, Sister Winifred and the other nuns. It was no small venture, I knew that. Tapestry looms and silken threads were extremely costly. But there was no other way to begin – I must make an initial investment to create my first tapestry. The proceeds from its sale would buy the materials for the second one.

However, my pension and Sister Winifred's were very small: one hundred shillings a year. Novices received the least. And so I had purchased the wooden loom with my personal funds: the small inheritance from my father and the proceeds from the sale of his London house, along with part of my first year's pension.

'But that was all the money you had – what are you to live on if this should fail?' Sister Winifred had pleaded. 'And what do any of us know of running such an enterprise? Have you ever heard of a woman who sold tapestries by herself?'

I'd dismissed her concerns then, as I did now. My enterprise would *not* fail. Back home, while explaining to Sister Beatrice what happened at church, it hit me with savage force. From now on, I would not be able to worship God in the way that was most meaningful to me.

Sitting in the kitchen, my sadness flipped into fury. I had to do something.

'I'm going to the Building Office to secure my loom,' I announced.

'Did not Brother Edmund bid you wait for him?'

'Yes, that's true, but …' I floundered for justification, and then burst out with, 'He is not my *real* brother, not my father, and not my husband. He is a valued friend, but his concerns are unwarranted.'

My words of defiance drew a sidelong smile from Sister Beatrice. I realised how unprecedented this must be, my flouting of the wishes of Brother Edmund. We shared a bond that was impossible to explain to others, forged during our frantic struggle to save the priory. There had been one night, in a travellers' inn in the town of Amesbury, when we shared a room, that certain longings stirred. Brother Edmund left the room in the middle of the night rather than succumb to sin, while I dreamed a dream that disturbed me still. It was a night neither one of us ever spoke about, of course.

I said to Sister Beatrice, 'It's stopped raining, so we must take a walk in any case, for Arthur's sake.'

The Building Office was up the High Street that led to the wide road stretching from London to the coast of Kent. We stopped along the way to allow Arthur to jump in puddles. I needed to calm him before we reached the Building Office. I did my best to ignore the head shaking of the townsfolk. Many did not like such boisterousness.

When we reached the top of the street, I knocked on the new, shiny door. The Building Office sprang up but six months ago. Important purchases of all kinds were routed through here, but its chief purpose was to facilitate the largest endeavour seen in Dartford for at least a century: the construction of a manor house for King Henry VIII atop the rubble of the priory.

The door swung open and I thought of yet another reason why Sister Winifred would not have wanted to come with me. Gregory, once the trusted porter of Dartford Priory and now the clerk of the Building Office, ushered us inside.

'I wondered if we'd see ye today,' he said gruffly.

Unlike the other sisters, I did not blame Gregory for taking this position, for putting his knowledge of the priory in the service of destroyers. All of our former servants had to shift for themselves, without the benefit of pensions.

No, if there were work to be found in Dartford, it must revolve around the building of the new royal manor house. Although most dissolved monasteries were made gifts to men loyal to the Crown, King Henry was keeping this one for himself. But he had not preserved any part of it. Dozens of workmen had spent the entire summer swarming over the property, demolishing it.

I said, 'Yes, I've come to take possession of my loom.'

He gestured to an underclerk. 'Tell Jacquard to arrange for transport.'

I stiffened. No one was a less welcome sight to me than Jacquard Rolin, a man of the Low Countries hired to coordinate the ordering of materials. King Henry's taste ran toward French and Flemish décor, and Jacquard knew where to procure the latest designs in tile, furniture, windowpane, and, of course, tapestry. Jacquard had taken a persistent interest in my tapestry enterprise. Ordinarily I would have enjoyed such discussion. But we could never be friends, for Jacquard was a full Protestant, a follower of Luther, I'd been told.

Arthur stirred next to me. I tightened my grip on his hand and prayed he'd not disrupt business here.

The door swung open and I turned to see Mistress Brooke push her way inside.

'What business have you here?' I asked.

'What business have I?' she repeated, incredulous. 'My husband has been entrusted by the king to oversee the hiring of men to raise his manor house of Dartford.'

Gregory nodded his assent.

Her voice growing louder, she said, 'But I should ask why you are here, distracting the men from their business.'

'Joanna Stafford is here for her tapestry loom.' The voice was soft and cultured, with an accent. Jacquard Rolin came to stand next to Gregory. He was young and rather slight of build, and he always unsettled me. His red lips formed an insinuating smile. His eyes were large and liquid, brown with flecks of gold. I had seen his gaze dazzle others. For me, though, there was something … uneasy in those eyes.

'Tap-stree, tap-stree!' Arthur bellowed.

Mistress Brooke demanded, 'How is it that she, a girl of the priory, could have the means to buy a loom?'

'It is none of your affair,' I insisted.

Gregory winced. And Jacquard bit his lip, his face tensing. I wondered, fleetingly, why should Jacquard care if I quarrel?

'Tap-stree! Tap-stree!' Arthur jumped up and down.

'Silence this awful dim child,' Mistress Brooke said.

That tipped me into rage. 'He is neither dim nor awful, and his

name is Arthur Bulmer. He is the son of Margaret Stafford, the daughter of the third Duke of Buckingham, and he is due all respect.'

Jacquard shot over, to stand between us. He flourished a palm in
some sort of Low Country gesture.

With a smile, he said, 'Mistress Brooke, you have a letter in your
hand. Is it for your husband? Presently he is at the building site. Will
you permit me to facilitate?'

She nodded, her eyes still on me. 'A messenger from London
brought it to the house, for some reason. Sir Francis Haverham will be
here tomorrow, to check progress.'

'Tomorrow?' repeated Gregory. 'The king's master builder is
coming here tomorrow?'

Gregory called out an alert to the men in the back of the Building
Office.

'I shall claim my loom and then you can be about your business,' I
said to Gregory.

Jacquard cleared his throat.

'Joanna Stafford, there is something you should know,' he said.
'Brussels made a mistake.'

'What mistake?' I asked.

'Only half the loom was sent, although of course our record books
showed your payment was in the full amount. We will make inquiry
and ensure that the other half will arrive by the first Wednesday in
November.'

'I am to wait another month?' My voice rose even higher.

Mistress Brooke snorted. 'So what will be your course of action?'

'I will take the first half of it today,' I said.

A trio of men appeared to receive orders from Gregory. He told
them to prepare my loom for transport down the High Street.

But Mistress Brooke intervened.

'The men must make ready for Sir Francis,' she said. 'It is foolish
to waste effort on this girl's errand.'

Gregory peered at Mistress Brooke, the wife of his superior. 'I'm
sorry, Mistress Joanna, but I can spare no men today.'

'Then give me the loom and we will take it from here without the
help of men,' I said, Sister Beatrice at my side.

After a few seconds, laughter sounded from all corners. Arthur, not
understanding, joined in.

'Take us there – now,' I said to Gregory. 'You cannot deny me something that is rightfully mine.'

Gregory threw up his hands. 'Very well.'

It was Jacquard who led me to my loom. It was covered with a blanket in the corner of a warehouse heaped high with the king's possessions: bricks, stones, nails, rope, and tiles. He watched as Sister Beatrice and I lifted the wooden frame. Jacquard was a puzzle to me. I knew he'd come to England in a party of Germans invited to court by Archbishop Thomas Cranmer and had somehow ingratiated himself with the king and won this position. Why would a Reformer want to help furnish a king's manor house?

I focused on the loom. It was long and imposing, half of a square wooden frame. But surely we could carry it a short distance.

'I wish you luck today, Joanna Stafford,' said Jacquard.

Without looking at him, I picked up the loom with Sister Beatrice and we staggered forward.

On the street, we'd made it less than a dozen steps when my shoulders and arms began to burn and then tremble. Arthur skipped next to me. On the other side of him, I could see townspeople stopping to gawk.

The tremor in my arms turned to wild shaking. Sister Beatrice said, 'We can't do this, Sister Joanna.'

'We *will* do it.'

From behind us came Mistress Brooke's voice: 'Look at them. Disgraceful.'

Then came another voice I did not want to hear. 'The time for repentance is near,' howled John.

We had to keep going. I willed myself to keep going.

Sister Beatrice said to me, 'Rest, at least. Let's put it down for a moment and then continue.'

'No, Sister Beatrice. If we lower it, we'll never get it back up again.'

At that instant, Arthur jumped in a puddle and the rainwater spurted into my eyes. I flinched and, in the mud, I tottered. As I crashed headlong into the street, the loom fell on my right shoulder, pinning me down.

My body, my face, all were enveloped in cold mud. It smelled of firewood and rotten vegetables and horse dung. My eyes stung, I could see nothing.

But I could hear them.

'Look at you now, nun!'

'She's a foolish, foolish girl.'

Arthur wailed tears of confusion. I felt Sister Beatrice's hands on my back and then grappling with the loom, trying to lift it off me – but failing. After much struggle, I was able to lift my head. I could see the skirts and legs of at least a dozen people surrounding me.

'Behold the harlot of the false prophet,' thundered John. 'She does not dance today.'

'She should go in the stocks for this,' said Mistress Brooke. Someone else shouted eagerly, 'The stocks, the stocks!'

But then there was a new cry: 'Who are they?'

Sister Beatrice managed to pull the loom off me. With her help, I staggered to my feet, my shoulder throbbing. She wiped the mud from my face.

Now I could see what the others saw, what had drawn them away from me for the moment. A procession moved through Dartford. About twenty people, clad in the same livery of white and blue, rode fine horses. They surrounded, in protective formation, a couple. The blond man wore a blue doublet; it must be the family's chosen colour. But the woman was different. Perched in her saddle, she was clad in bodice, kirtle, and headdress of deepest red. It was as if a slash of scarlet glided down the street. Even from where I stood, I could see a ruby necklace glittering on her bosom. That single jewel cost more than what these townsfolk would earn over a lifetime.

When they'd come close, the woman spoke to the man accompanying her. They stared down at me. The man dismounted. He was handsome but rather stout, in his middle years.

Two men materialised with a bolt of fabric and hurled it in my direction. Only then was the lady helped from her horse. She stepped onto the fabric, which I realised was to serve as a path over the mud straight to me. Seizing the man's hand, she led him forward. She moved with a quick grace. Little diamonds woven into the tops of her deep red velvet slippers twinkled every time they emerged from her full skirts.

'It's you, isn't it?' the woman said in a melodic voice. Her face was crisscrossed with faint lines, like delicate parchment paper left too long on a table, unused. The hair visible beneath her Spanish-style gable hood was black with a few strands of grey. 'Joanna Stafford?' she asked.

'Yes,' I said. 'But I don't know you.'

'Oh, yes – you do,' she said. 'I'm Gertrude.'

The man moved forward and smiled. 'I'm your cousin, Joanna. I'm Henry Courtenay.'

5

Father William Mote never moved as quickly as he did that morning. The pastor of Holy Trinity Church flew down the High Street. When he'd reached us, his spindly knees shook from the effort.

'We are so honored by your presence in our town,' he said, bowing low before Henry and Gertrude Courtenay, who bore the titles marquess and marchioness of Exeter.

But the priest was ignored, for their eyes were on me alone.

'Don't you remember me?' asked Gertrude, her lip quivering. She was hurt that I, a bedraggled ex-novice flung into the mud, did not know her. It was all I could do not to laugh.

Henry had his arm around his wife's waist. Yes, his name and title were familiar to me. The Courtenays were kin to the Staffords – both families were in direct descent from Edward III and intertwined once more through marriages with the Woodvilles. The name *Courtenay* summoned up an aura of wealth and influence. But, to my knowledge, this couple had never visited Stafford Castle – where could I have seen them before?

Looking at his kind face, I found the memory.

'Your wedding,' I said. 'I was there. I was a child.'

'You were our flower maiden!' Gertrude's laugh bounced off the gawking faces of the townsfolk of Dartford who encircled us. Her elation was transforming. The wrinkles in her face receded, and her eyes, brown and wide-set, flashed brightly.

'Cousin Joanna, tell us – what happened to you here today?' Henry asked.

I began to explain, haltingly, about my plan for a tapestry business and how I'd tried to gain possession of the loom with the help of Sister Beatrice.

Henry Courtenay interrupted: 'But why did no one else assist you? Even if the men of the Building Office could not spare anyone, surely the occupants of the town would have stepped forward, to help? You are a sister of Christ.'

I looked past them, at the townsfolk gathered around. No one met my gaze.

'Do you have an explanation, Father?' Gertrude's voice was hard with anger.

'One will be found, my lady Marchioness,' Father William said, clutching his hands. 'I will personally discover why the people of Dartford showed no Christian charity to our Sister Joanna.'

It was then I heard Mistress Brooke's voice. 'But Father, you've always told us that the priory women—'

'Silence yourself,' the priest hissed.

At that moment I gave an involuntary cry. Arthur, confused, had pulled on my arm. Pain convulsed the shoulder on which the loom had rested.

'You were injured?' asked Henry. 'We must see to you at once. All guilt in this matter will be determined and addressed. Father, lead us into the church.' He beckoned toward Holy Trinity's high, square tower.

'No, not there.' It sounded more like pleading than I intended. 'I want to go home.'

Henry said gently, 'Then we will take you there.' He turned to a stern-looking man wearing the Courtenay livery. 'Charles, make further inquiries into this matter.'

Gertrude bent down to caress Arthur's smooth cheek. 'Is this he – is this Arthur Bulmer?'

'How do you know of Arthur?' I asked.

Gertrude Courtenay moved close to whisper in my ear. 'All who know the Lady know of you and Arthur Bulmer.'

The Lady?

Before I could question her further, they bore me to my house, handling me like a piece of Florentine sculpture. At the doorway, Henry paused, saying he would leave us for a short time, to see the church.

'Come, Edward, you will accompany,' he called out. A boy emerged from the small crowd of attendants, blond and handsome, about eleven years old.

'Do you seek a private Mass?' I asked, confused.

'My husband the historian has long wanted to see Holy Trinity Church,' Gertrude said, smiling. 'The body of Henry the Fifth was brought there. Isn't that right, my lord?'

'Yes, they stopped here when conveying the dead king up from Dover and held a special funeral Mass,' said my cousin Henry, bouncing on his heels with excitement. 'Perhaps young Arthur would like to come along.'

With regret, I told him that Arthur was not yet ready for church or any historical expeditions.

Henry said, 'Don't be so sure, cousin. Arthur, what say you? Care to come with me and your cousin Edward?'

Arthur stared at Edward Courtenay as if he were a young Apollo come down to earth. He nodded. Henry ruffled his hair. 'See? Arthur's a good boy.' He kissed his wife's hand. 'We won't be long, my love, I promise.'

Gertrude smiled her enchanting, childlike smile. Their eyes met, and a world of tender secrets swirled between them. Not accustomed to such intimacy, I looked away.

The man and two boys set off toward the church, followed by servants. Two of the family retainers remained outside my house, as if to stand guard.

The women led me inside. Upstairs, in my bedchamber, they removed my clothes and cleaned my face and throat and shoulders. Expert fingers worked healing ointment into my shoulder.

Gertrude herself did not touch my skin nor soothe my pain, nor sort through my garments. It was her lady in waiting, Constance, who performed all such tasks, with the help of a young maid. With a nod or a shrug, Gertrude directed the movements of Constance, a woman the same age as the marchioness, though fairer. Then Constance would order the young maid about. Freshly attired, I stood in the centre of the room while the maid pulled a comb through my thick hair. She had to yank hard, for I had more than a tangle or two. I did my best not to flinch.

Gertrude watched while sitting in the lone chair brought into my bedchamber for her comfort. Perhaps it was the dull light filtering in from the windows, but her sparkle had been extinguished. Her voluminous red skirts seemed to overwhelm her thin frame. Shadows pouched under her brown eyes.

As if she could read my thoughts, Gertrude said, a touch wistful, 'What is your age, Joanna?'

'Twenty-seven.'

She smiled. 'I would take you for twenty-one. You have such a fine figure, too. But of course you have not borne children. Women of Spanish blood are the handsomest, but we do not always age well.'

'You are Spanish?'

'Like your mother, mine came from Spain in the service of Katherine of Aragon. She married an Englishman, as did yours. My father was Lord Mountjoy. Surely you remember that?'

'I'm afraid I remember only the day of your wedding.'

Gertrude brightened. 'It was a spectacular wedding, wasn't it, Joanna? I wanted everything to be beautiful – and it was.'

My memory of that day deepened. I saw again the bridal couple, Henry and Gertrude, so young and splendid, meeting at the church door to take their vows before God. My cousin Margaret and I carried flowers in the procession, with all eyes on the exquisitely pretty Margaret rather than me. I never once minded that. I was so proud of her.

But now was not the time for reminiscences. I needed to hear the truth from the Marchioness of Exeter.

'How could you have recognised me today?' I asked. 'We haven't seen each other in many years, not since I was, as you say, a child. How do you know of Margaret's son? Who is the "Lady"?'

Gertrude fingered her ruby and took her measure of me, as if trying to decide how much to disclose. 'Yes,' she said at last. 'I came to Dartford today not only to see the town's church but to seek you out. I knew all about you and Arthur Bulmer from' – her voice dropped in reverence – 'the Lady Mary.'

Of course. Mary Tudor, the eldest daughter of the king.

Last winter, at Norfolk House, when Brother Edmund and I were in the greatest peril, I'd flung myself in the path of the Lady Mary, speaking Spanish to seize her attention. After she learned what I'd done for her mother – that after my own mother's death I'd nursed Queen Katherine in exile, during the last month of her life – the Lady Mary became an immediate champion. It was because of her intervention that my father was freed from the Tower of London. I'd received many letters from the Lady Mary, both before Dartford Priory was dissolved and afterward. An uneasy, solicitous tone entered the correspondence after I settled in town with Arthur instead of living with my relations at Stafford Castle.

'I know that the Lady Mary worries for me, but there was no need for her to send you to Dartford,' I said.

'No need? After what I saw here today?'

'It was my stubbornness, my pride, that caused the mishap on the High Street,' I said.

The marchioness sprang to her feet. 'You blame yourself?' she said. 'You have been cruelly wronged, to lose your place at the priory and now to endure insults at the hands of common folk. What happened to you, to all of the nuns and monks and friars, it is a great offence to God.'

It was rare to hear such open sentiment – and in front of servants. I tried to gauge the reactions of Constance and the serving girl to such criticism of the king. But they remained unmoved.

Gertrude herself took several breaths, as if struggling for control.

'What did the Lady Mary tell you about me?' I asked.

'I learned of you in letters, not in conversation,' Gertrude said. 'I haven't seen her since the spring. She can have no visitors. Cromwell sees to that.'

Again I was confused. 'The Lady Mary is fully reconciled with her father, the king.'

Gertrude said, 'Joanna, I know that you prefer a quiet life, but is it possible you do not know what's happening in our kingdom?'

'I know nothing,' I said simply. It was the truth. London gossip never interested me, not after my first foray into sordid court life. Years later, at Dartford Priory, I listened more carefully to news of the business of the kingdom, but that was because it directly affected the monasteries. Now I avoided all gossip – not that I heard much.

'These are most dangerous times for England,' Gertrude said. 'It's been four months since the signing of the Treaty of Nice—' She broke off. 'You *have* heard of the treaty?'

'I'm afraid not.'

'The king of France signed a treaty with the Holy Roman Emperor Charles. The pope himself brokered the peace. They have joined forces in war against the Turk.'

'Isn't peace between France and Spain a thing to be praised?' I asked, loathing my ignorance. 'How could this harm England?'

Gertrude made her way to my window. She peered outside, as if she feared someone stood just outside it, hanging onto the ledge, listening.

Turning to me, she said, 'The Turks may not be the only target of the Emperor Charles. He is by far the most powerful monarch in the world. The sun never sets on his dominions. Spain, the Netherlands, Austria, Burgundy, and parts of Italy, the colonies of the New World – all belong to one man. He has armies, navies. Not yet forty years old and the most powerful Catholic on Earth!' I saw a new side to Gertrude now, the courtier's wife who kept abreast of politics. 'And the emperor is bent on destruction of heresy,' she continued. 'There are rumours that the pope has charged him with cleansing England of Protestant taint. France was our ally for years. But now that King François has signed a treaty with Charles, not us, we are without a buffering force …' Her voice trailed off.

'Are you saying England could be invaded and attacked by both Spain and France?' I asked.

She nodded, fingering her ruby once more.

With a jolt, I understood all. 'The Lady Mary is cousin to Charles through her mother, and has always been devoted to him. If Spain declares war on England, then she is suspect.'

Gertrude nodded again.

How could the Lady Mary fret over me when *she* was in real danger? On her deathbed, Katherine of Aragon spoke of her fears for her daughter the princess, and had urged me to take vows at Dartford Priory because she believed the Athelstan crown was hidden within. She hoped I would protect Mary. But my charge did not end there. I had failed not only the vulnerable princess but also the dead queen whom I revered, because I was lost to sorrow over the destruction of my priory.

Aloud, I said, feebly, 'Lady Mary gave no hint of any of this in any of her letters.'

'She knows that all of her letters are opened and read by Cromwell,' said Gertrude.

Which meant that my letters to her were not private, either. I'd written nothing to the Lady Mary that could be construed as political, of that I was sure. But reports of Arthur's growth, dreams of a tapestry business, my missing my father – it was all so very personal.

'I can't bear to see you this distressed,' said Gertrude, her voice shaking.

I looked up, surprised. The marchioness barely knew me. But a greater surprise swiftly followed.

Gertrude Courtenay darted across the room to fling herself at my feet. Her large brown eyes glittered with tears. For the first time, I smelled her perfume: sage and chamomile and rosemary, laced with something strangely bitter.

'Finding you was an omen, it has to be,' she cried. 'I had planned to make inquiry at the church of your whereabouts, then send Constance with a message, to see if you'd receive me today. But to ride into town and see you thrown down before me at the moment of arrival? It can't be without significance. God has sent us both a sign.'

I stared down at her. 'What are you saying?'

'I am meant to save you – it is my purpose,' she said. 'Joanna, I have so much and you have so little. Let me help you. We will be as sisters. Leave this dreadful town and come away with me – now. Today.'

Gertrude Courtenay's offer of a home so startled me that I could not speak. 'But my friends ... my tapestries ... Arthur.'

'The son of Margaret Bulmer would be as welcome as you are,' she said, still kneeling at my feet. 'I would be honoured if you'd both share a roof with me.'

I could see that her proposal was sincere. As gently as I could, I said, 'Please, Gertrude, you must get up.' After she'd done so, I took her by the hand. 'To live in London and be part of the life of the court – that is not a choice for me.'

'I never go to court,' she said quickly. 'Henry must attend, of course, but since the death of Queen Jane, no functions require my presence. And we only spend four or five months of the year in London. In the spring, we return west. That's where many of Henry's properties are. It's beautiful in Cornwall; I would love to show it to you. The sea, the forests, the flowers—'

The sound of shouting downstairs interrupted her reverie. The marchioness beckoned for Constance, and the lady-in-waiting slipped out. I made for the door.

'Joanna, wait,' Gertrude said. Her elegant fingers closed around my wrist. 'Don't put yourself in harm's way again.'

I pulled free. 'This is my home,' I said. 'I must attend to it.'

I'd made it halfway down the stairs when I saw him. The two Courtenay retainers left to guard my house struggled with a single man. My front door hung open behind them. The young man, tall and strong, shoved his way forward, leading with his right shoulder, to the centre of my front parlour. Both of the Courtenay men tried – and failed – to stop him.

With a grunt, the taller Courtenay man fell back and drew his sword. 'Cease – or I will have cause to use this,' he said.

'Not until you tell me what has become of Joanna Stafford,' shouted the man.

'Geoffrey, I'm right here!' I shouted.

Geoffrey Scovill looked up at me. 'So you are,' he said.

6

A smile of relief split Geoffrey's face. With one hand, he pushed away the tip of the Courtenay sword that quivered in his face, saying, 'It seems this won't be necessary.' With the other he tugged on his doublet, half torn off in the struggle, to make himself presentable. 'Ah,' he said, 'I've lost a button.'

I burst out laughing, I could not help it. And Geoffrey laughed with me, a touch sheepish.

Here was the young underconstable of Rochester, who had come to my aid at Smithfield, the day of Margaret's burning. Since then our fates had intertwined, at times uncomfortably.

Today he looked different. His light brown hair was newly cut. He'd trimmed it into a straight fringe across his forehead, the same style I'd seen on men who followed London fashions. I'd never known Geoffrey to ape the styles of the day. His clothes, too, were freshly stitched, not the patched-together ensembles he commonly wore. But his deep blue eyes were familiar, crinkling with amusement in a face faintly ruddy from all the hours spent outdoors.

'What is so funny?' asked Gertrude, coming down the stairs. Her tone was light, though her step was determined.

It was with some difficulty that I managed to stop laughing. 'This man is my friend, Geoffrey Scovill,' I said, breathless. 'He is a constable in Rochester.'

I introduced the marchioness and Geoffrey bowed deep, but not before I saw surprise in his face.

'He told us he was the constable here – for Dartford – before he started acting like a madman,' said the smaller Courtenay man, suspicious.

'If you'd simply answered my inquiry at the door, there wouldn't have been a disturbance,' Geoffrey said.

'We don't answer strangers' inquiries unless my lord or lady orders us to,' the larger man retorted.

As I introduced Gertrude to Geoffrey, I noticed Sister Beatrice in the corner. She had not gone upstairs but she hadn't left my home, either. Now she clasped her hands with an excitement I'd never seen. 'Oh, Geoffrey, the appointment has been secured?' she asked.

'I don't understand,' I said. 'What appointment?'

'There is a need for a constable here in Dartford, and I've been approved for the position. I'm no longer charged with Rochester.' He spoke to me, yet his eyes darted in Sister Beatrice's direction. I was taken aback by this news. Geoffrey here, in Dartford, every day? It made me feel queer, uncertain. I had seen him just once in the last six months, in July. It was the afternoon he escorted Sister Beatrice and me to Saint Margaret's Fair. But it was an odd day. Geoffrey had been distracted; he did not seem to enjoy the music, the donkey races, the pole climbing, or even the archery contests. When daylight faded, he hurried us back to town and I saw him no more.

'What about Justice Campion?' I asked. The old justice of the peace had paid much of his wages, for he depended on Geoffrey's quick mind and vigour when a serious enough crime required it.

'Justice Campion has died,' Geoffrey said. 'But now I must know what happened today, and why you are under guard.'

I hadn't finished the tale when Geoffrey slapped his leg in anger.

'Couldn't Sommerville help you?' he demanded. 'Blast it, the man is of no use at all.'

'It's not Brother Edmund's fault,' I said.

'No, nothing ever is,' muttered Geoffrey.

I felt someone's gaze hot on me. It was Gertrude, standing by the wall. She had listened to the whole exchange. There was surprise in her eyes, and something else, too. That speculative look had returned, as if she were trying to decide which jewels to wear.

A knock sounded. Henry's steward, a serious-looking man named Charles, led in two people – Gregory from the Building Office and Mistress Brooke – and informed Gertrude who they were and what happened in the Building Office and on the High Street afterward.

Bubbles of sweat sliding down his brow, Gregory looked miserable. But Mistress Brooke exhibited only defiance. 'I've broken no law,' she declared. 'And I was brought here under protest. Although I know well enough why.' Mistress Brooke shot me a look of hatred.

Geoffrey, the representative of the law in the room, stirred to action. 'Not on the face of it, no. But your actions merit further inquiry, Mistress Brooke, which I shall busy myself to.'

'Constable, if I may?' said Gertrude, still standing near the wall. Without waiting for his reply, she took a step toward Mistress Brooke.

'Do you know who I am?' Her voice was a melodic caress.

'You are the Marchioness of Exeter,' answered Mistress Brooke.

'Yes, but do you know what that means?' Gertrude took another step. A diamond twinkled on her velvet shoe.

Mistress Brooke looked sullen.

'Permit me to explain it to you.' Gertrude folded her hands as if in prayer. 'My true and loving husband, Henry Courtenay, is the grandson of King Edward the Fourth. He was raised with our King Henry and his sisters. He is the most trusted of all of the king's relations. In fact, he is the only man who is allowed to enter the king's private chambers without being announced by the chamberlain. You have seen the servants who attend us. They are but a portion of our staff. The king allows us to give our men arms, to issue livery. Whatever we do, in the West, in London, or here, today, in Dartford, is sanctioned by the king.'

Mistress Brooke peered back at the door to the street. She did not like this.

'This young woman, Joanna Stafford, is my husband's cousin,' continued Gertrude. 'Therefore, she is also a relation of the King's Majesty. She is an intimate of the Lady Mary Tudor.' Geoffrey looked at me, startled. He had not been aware of my friendship with royalty. I wished Gertrude had not announced it.

'When you dishonour Joanna Stafford, you dishonour the nobility of this kingdom,' said Gertrude. Her voice was no longer melodic. 'For what you have done today, I could, with just a few words, crush you, Mistress Brooke. Is that something you can understand? You, your husband, your family. Today your husband oversees the hiring of workmen for building the king's manor house? Tomorrow he would be discharged. He'd be most fortunate to secure work lifting limestone from a quarry.'

Mistress Brooke's hands quivered at her sides as if she were struck with plague.

In truth, I felt ill too. A fever coursed through me, but not a weakening one. I, who had been powerless, witnessed power being wielded on my behalf. A dark gloating pulsed in my blood. *Yes, crush her*, I exulted. *Make her suffer.*

But hard on this excitement came another feeling: shame.

'No, please,' I said, reaching out to touch Gertrude's shoulder. 'I am not blameless. I provoked her.' Gertrude shook her head. As before, she was unwilling to see any fault in my actions. I searched through my mind, frantically, for prayers that could guide us. 'My lady, blessed are the merciful, for they shall have mercy shown to them. Blessed are the pure in heart, for they shall see God. And blessed are the peace-makers, for they shall be recognised as the children of God.'

The storm of rage that darkened Gertrude's cheeks receded. With a cry, she seized both of my hands in hers and gripped them so hard I winced.

'Joanna, thank you for showing me the Christian spirit I must cleave to,' she said. 'Through you I understand God's grace anew.'

She ordered that Mistress Brooke and Gregory be sent away. Geoffrey saw them to the door, speaking in a low voice to Mistress Brooke. A moment later, there was another stirring on the street. Henry Courtenay had returned, well pleased with Holy Trinity Church.

'Father William showed me a wonderful mural painting of Saint George in one of the chapels,' he said.

I wager he didn't tell you that the painting would be whitewashed by order of Cromwell, I thought. So Father William was nothing but unctuous to the marquess of Exeter. It must be that way wherever Henry Courtenay went. He was fawned over by men and women who were cruel to others.

'How did Arthur fare?' I asked. I half dreaded the reply.

'Look for yourself,' said Henry.

From the window, the High Street was like I had never seen it before – transformed into a place of play for Arthur. Courtenay men had cleared a long, empty space. Henry's son, Edward, tossed him a ball and Arthur leaped after it, laughing.

How Arthur glowed. It was as if he'd grown two inches in the last hour.

'Joanna, are you all right?' asked Henry. 'You're crying.'

I touched my damp cheeks. 'It's been difficult, just Arthur and me. I don't know if I am doing the right things. I worry for his future.'

I barely knew this cousin of mine, yet I was confiding in him fears I'd not shared with anyone, not even Brother Edmund.

'Ah. Well, for a beginning, he shouldn't be wearing a child's gown any longer,' said Henry. 'He's ready for the clothing of a boy, a boy of a good family.'

'Do you think so?'

'He's five years old. He's also ready for a tutor and for lessons in sport,' said Henry.

My face must have shown my disbelief.

'Arthur is strong and quick, Joanna. He may not be ready for a horn-book in his hand. But that is no impediment to living as a respected gentleman – or even to having a career at court. Norfolk's said often enough that it's book learning that ruined the nobility.' He laughed, not noticing how I stiffened to hear the name *Norfolk*. I'd never forget how the duke hounded me in the Tower of London, even striking me in the face when I didn't submit to his questioning.

'My husband is the finest father in all of England,' said Gertrude, joining us on the front steps. She stroked her husband's arm.

'Cousin Joanna, why not bring Arthur for a visit?' asked Henry. 'Stay with us for a time. We have a host of tutors. He needs to learn to ride and dance and handle himself. It would be good for Edward too, if a younger boy were about.'

'I've already invited Joanna to stay with us in London, but she said there was much for her to do here in Dartford,' said Gertrude lightly.

Henry spread his hands. 'Then come for a month. We could do much for Arthur in four weeks. In November you can return.'

As I looked at them, my heart pumped faster than at any other time that day, even when I was trapped beneath my loom in the street. Could I do this – stay with the Courtenays? It would mean living in London, the city I feared, the city where I'd watched Margaret burn. But Gertrude had already assured me that she'd not go near the king's court. They were both so eager to help. I would finally be privy to the wisdom of parents in raising a child.

'If you will pardon me for a moment,' said Geoffrey Scovill. Watching Arthur, I'd forgotten about Geoffrey, about Mistress Brooke – everything. But Geoffrey hadn't left, and now he had something to say to me.

Henry looked him up and down. 'And you are …?'

'This is a friend of Joanna's, his name is Geoffrey Scovill,' said Gertrude, with elaborate politeness. 'He is a constable.'

'I see.' Henry smiled at him, but his eyes showed confusion. He probably could not imagine why a Stafford would befriend a town constable.

'I would like to speak with Mistress Stafford for a moment in private,' said Geoffrey.

Henry's smile faded.

'Geoffrey knew my father.' At once, I regretted saying that. It sounded as if I were trying to elevate Geoffrey's status. But it served its purpose.

Curious eyes tracked us as I led Geoffrey out of the parlour. I closed the door once we were inside the kitchen. The wooden table still bore the crumbs of Arthur's bread and cheese from hours before. My young servant, Kitty, had never appeared. My stomach ached; I was quite hungry. And weary, too. I'd slept so little the night before.

Geoffrey grabbed me by both shoulders and pulled me toward him. We were so close I could smell the soap he'd scrubbed into his skin. It was ashy, bitter. The sort of soap that servants use because it costs next to nothing. Not the choice for a man who attempts a fashionable haircut. Alongside my shock at his grabbing me I felt a strange tenderness at Geoffrey's fumbling toward gentility.

'Joanna, listen to me,' Geoffrey said. 'You mustn't go with these people.'

'Why not?'

'It's not safe for you.'

I wriggled out of his grasp. I'd felt such relief at the prospect of the Courtenays helping me with Arthur. The grinding burden of raising him would be lifted. Now Geoffrey wanted to sour the plan.

I said, 'You do know that the Courtenays are one of the wealthiest families in the land? They have an army of servants. How could anyone hurt me while I am their guest?'

'That's not the sort of danger I am thinking of.'

'Then what?' I demanded.

He did not answer me. I could see he was weighing his words, trying to decide how to frame something. Much as Gertrude Courtenay had measured her words upstairs, when telling me of the Lady Mary.

'How does Sister Beatrice know you were planning to come to Dartford, to be the town constable?' I asked.

Geoffrey frowned in surprise. 'She wrote to me after the fair. I answered her letters.'

'I see.'

'I would have been only too happy to write to you, Joanna. But of course you sent me no letters.'

An awkward tension filled my kitchen. I couldn't correspond with him. Writing might have encouraged his hopes of more than friendship. I'd thought he no longer harboured such feelings for me, since I'd seen him only once since his declaration in the priory barn, last spring.

'At Saint Margaret's Fair,' I began, and then faltered.

'The fair? What of it?'

'You were not ... at ease. I don't know why.'

There was bewilderment in Geoffrey's face, but then it shifted to something else. He laughed. It was not the easy, boyish laugh of earlier.

'You have no notion, do you, Joanna? I've sometimes wondered if you were aware – I've thought, "No, she *has* to realise. She's certainly not stupid".'

'Realise what?'

'Your *effect* on men. How they respond to you, how they look at you. And then when you add Beatrice to it – God's blood! Two beautiful young women, novices no more but unmarried, fatherless, wandering about the countryside. One dark, one fair. I may have seemed ill at ease, Joanna, because I feared that in a crowd of men who'd downed ale, I might not be able to defend you. Fortunately, no one meddled with us. But I wager that was part of the reason the town wanted to put you in the stocks today. Your looks can be ... discomfiting.'

'This is *not* true,' I said, my voice rising. 'What you're saying is distasteful. And absurd.'

'Must I remind you under what circumstances we met?' he asked.

I winced at the memory of the ruffian who'd attacked me at Smithfield. I said, 'What does this have to do with the Courtenays?'

'Nothing. But their home is not a safe place for you. Not now. It's not anything that they've done – obviously they are noble people. But it is who they *are*.'

I heard Arthur laugh in the other room. He'd come inside. I wanted to return to him, and to my relations.

'I understand you have concerns for my welfare, Geoffrey,' I said. 'But I must tell you that rarely has a man struck me as sounder than Henry Courtenay. I know I can trust him.'

'As you knew you could trust Sister Christina?'

I took a step back from him, then another, as regret filled his eyes. The pain must have been written large on my face that he had said the name of the novice who had been my friend – and yet had murdered two people. He reached out, saying, 'I meant only that—'

I slapped his hand away and whirled round to the kitchen door. It was stuck. I had to get out of that room.

'Joanna, I'm very sorry.' His voice was low and thick.

'I want you to leave,' I said. Using the heels of both hands, I slammed against the door so hard that it burst open.

Everyone stopped talking. I struggled to present a calm face. Arthur scrambled over to me and I ran my fingers through his silky tangled hair, felt for the tops of his ears.

'Are you well, Joanna?' asked Gertrude, her eyes shifting to the left of me. Geoffrey must have appeared there, just behind.

'I am.' Thankfully, my voice had steadied. 'And I wish to accept your kind offer of a visit.'

The Courtenays rejoiced; Arthur jumped up and down. In moments, servants were dispatched, to pack our clothes. Gertrude wouldn't hear of waiting for a day.

Sister Beatrice was halfway out the door when I caught her. She must have been trying to follow Geoffrey. He'd left my home, as I'd asked.

'Would you help me upstairs, Sister Beatrice?' I asked. 'A matter requires your attention.'

In my room, she knelt next to me as I folded Arthur's clothes. I said, 'I understand now why you've remained in Dartford, so close to me – it was not for my friendship, I think. It has more to do with Geoffrey Scovill.'

'Yes,' she said, 'I have a certain feeling for him.'

At least there would be no more deception.

Sister Beatrice handed me a wool nightdress for Arthur. 'Geoffrey does not feel the same,' she said. 'I know that. But he may come to.'

Such brazen calm frightened me. 'What of our vows?' I asked. 'We're no longer inside priory walls, but the vows we swore to take as sisters still mean something.'

'Do you mean the vow of *chastity*?' she spat.

Sister Beatrice's face puckered like a cornered cat's. 'You know my life. I was mistress to an evil man. My body thickened with a child whom God took away, in His mercy. I was abandoned by all – by my own mother. She cursed me as a whore and drove me into the forest.'

I couldn't help but be moved by her sufferings. 'But you returned to the priory, as a lay sister,' I said. 'You were brought back into the community.'

'Because of Geoffrey.' She nodded, rapidly. 'He found me and I told him everything. Everything. Geoffrey did not criticise me or judge me. The only person who never has.'

And yet how Geoffrey criticised *me*. From the first, he'd argued with me, hectored me. Aloud, I said, 'I do not judge you.'

'You least of all among the women, Sister Joanna. But still you do. I don't hate you for it.' She squeezed my hand. 'You've been a friend. I did not cleave to you only because of Geoffrey. Beneath all your storm and fury is a kind heart.'

She opened her mouth and then closed it, as if unsure.

'Tell me,' I said.

Sister Beatrice took a breath. 'If we are being truthful today, then let us walk to the end of the path. I know that Geoffrey loves you. But it is *because* it is hopeless. That is the nature of his feeling for you. And you do not love him.'

There was the faintest echo of a question to what she'd last said. I thought, *She wants me to reassure her, to give her my blessing.* But suddenly I was awash in confusion. I truly did not know what I wanted from Geoffrey Scovill.

'Everything else is packed,' announced Gertrude's young maid from the doorway. 'My lady awaits you downstairs.'

The Courtenays swept me up then. Arthur was lifted onto the same horse as Edward, to his delight. But they gave me a horse, to be my own for the ride to London and during my stay as well. My mount was a chestnut mare with a bright eye. How was this possible – whose horse had she been until an hour ago? I wondered fleetingly.

I bade Sister Beatrice farewell and gave her money, asking her to pay my servant's wages for the month and make explanation. Her eyes cast down, she nodded. Her words were no more than polite. Perhaps it was because I had not eased her mind on that last question.

The Courtenay procession moved up the High Street, toward the juncture with the road to London. We passed the cross in the centre of the street, across from the market. I had never ridden a horse through town. It gave me a new, higher vantage, a slanting view into the windows of the homes and shops as we passed.

I should have been happy to leave Dartford, where hours before townsfolk sought to humiliate me. But I felt weak. *You're just hungry*, I told myself. *This is the right thing to do.* I clutched the saddle horn, to steady myself.

'Sister Joanna! Sister Joanna!'

I turned in the saddle. It was Sister Winifred, holding up her skirts with both hands so she could move faster. 'Stop! What are you doing?'

I motioned to the men to let her through.

'I'm visiting my relations,' I said. 'I'll be back in one month.'

'I don't understand.' She was crying. A yellow bubble trembled at her nose. 'When was this decided?'

'Today,' I said. *Brother Edmund won't understand either*, I thought, miserable. How could I have made such a decision without speaking to him? *And how will he feel that I left without saying good-bye?*

Two horses ahead of me, Gertrude Courtenay turned around. I half waved at her, struggling to convey that she shouldn't interfere.

'Please, Sister Winifred, please don't upset yourself,' I said, leaning down from my horse. 'I will write you – tomorrow. I will send word tomorrow. And I'll tell Brother Edmund everything.'

Sister Winifred stopped trotting alongside my horse. We kept moving and she stood there, in the street. It hurt my neck to keep twisting around, so I turned forward. A second later, I heard her cry out, her voice turned shrill: 'God preserve you, Sister Joanna.'

My horse, obediently following the others, turned onto the wider road to London. A thick grove of apple orchards stood on the left. A few thin wooden ladders remained propped against trunks of the highest trees. It was harvesting season. The light danced off the tree leaves. I blinked from the strength of that lowering autumn sun.

Suddenly there was shouting in the road. John charged out of the orchard, waving his staff. 'Behold the brood of vipers, which have taken into their bosom a daughter of Satan!'

Gertrude motioned for a servant. I kicked my horse to reach them, before John could be harmed. 'Do nothing,' I said. 'John is mad – a sorry creature of God.'

Henry Courtenay nodded, and bade the servants do something else. A shower of shillings flew through the air and landed at John's filthy feet.

He did not pick them up.

Rooted on the side of the road, John said, 'Prepare the way for destiny – ye must prepare, ye who have sinned before God. He sees all of your sins! He knows your repentance is false, false, and false.'

Gertrude covered her mouth with her hand. John's blather frightened her. Henry called out loudly, 'Ride on, everyone.'

We all shook our reins or kicked the sides of our mounts. I prayed that John would not follow us up the road. Courtenay patience might have its limits.

John did not follow. But he was not silent, and his cries rang in my ears long after we'd left the town of Dartford behind.

'The reckoning is coming, it is coming,' cried John. 'Armageddon is at hand. In the end it will devour you all!'

PART TWO

7

Only in the city of London could Suffolk Lane exist. All around it throbbed the roar and the stench, the callous crowds and hard, glittering brightness of the city. But Suffolk Lane itself was short, narrow, and quiet. A shadowed preserve. A tall brick manor house ran along the west side, imposing its will on the cobbled street. Almost two hundred years ago, the house was raised at tremendous expense by a Middlesex merchant made lord mayor of London five times over. The lord mayor gave his cherished house a name: the Red Rose. After his death, it passed into the covetous hands of the nobility. Two years after my cousin Henry married Gertrude, he took possession of the Red Rose. During my time with the Courtenays, I lived there and nowhere else.

My room was on the second floor, close to the southwest corner of the house and thus to Lower Thames Street, a thoroughfare following the curves of the river like a nervous suitor. On the Wednesday morning of the second week of my visit, I heard a man shouting from the direction of Lower Thames, though these were not the ravings of a madman. Peering out the window, I spotted him, standing erect on the corner, dressed in royal livery. The only words I could make out were 'the Emperor Charles'. I realised he was the town crier.

A lady should not lean out a window, but I pushed open mine to better hear his news. A puff of cool, dank air rushed in, eager to sully my perfumed bedchamber.

'The Turks defeat the Emperor Charles in the sea battle of Preveza,' shouted the young man. 'Thirteen imperial ships are lost. Three thousand Christian men taken prisoner by Barbarossa. The Muslim Turks of the Ottoman Empire gain strength and the emperor's forces are vanquished.'

He repeated his message a third time and then strode out of my view. I struggled to assess the significance of this news. I no longer shrank from the business of the world. I owed my allegiance to the Lady Mary, and she was affected by the battles of her cousin, the Emperor Charles. To be a true friend to her, I had decided to put aside my distaste of politics and make a study of the affairs of Christendom. What a morass to master, though. Was this naval defeat good or bad for the Lady Mary?

'I'll ask Gertrude,' I murmured as I closed the window to shut out the city.

On one side of my large bedchamber was a four-poster bed, hanging with gilt-edged curtains. On the other was a fireplace, its flames subsided to glowing red ash. Near the door, set in the oak panelling of the far wall, hung a tall looking-glass. As I passed it, I stopped short.

Who was this woman who peered back from the glass?

I wore a kirtle of dark gold, with full sleeves and low square neckline. My skirts were full; my Spanish hood was tightly fastened. I wore velvet shoes. A jewelled diamond pendant dangled from my throat.

I looked just like Gertrude Courtenay.

But how could it be otherwise? These were once her clothes. My first morning in London, Gertrude sent word and by noon they came running, the dressmakers of London. I was overwhelmed by the fuss, the eager eyes and toughened fingers of women jostling for commissions from the Marchioness of Exeter.

I wanted to say no. I tried to turn away the garments and jewels she pressed on me. It was not only that Gertrude's generosity exceeded what I felt was deserved. I had never been the least interested in fashion; indeed, how freeing it had been to wear a long, loose nun's habit at Dartford Priory. When I had to put away my white habit and purchase the clothing of an ordinary woman, I selected a few indifferent ensembles, in sombre colours. I had never sought to draw attention through finery.

'Joanna, I have nothing but respect for your humility, but there are other matters to consider,' Gertrude had responded. 'We are members of the families that have served their sovereigns for centuries. You and my husband have royal blood in your veins – a certain standard of appearance is called for. Do you think the Lady Mary dresses herself in rags? After mourning was over for Queen Jane, she returned to beautiful colours. She wears jewels. She listens to music – she even plays at cards. Everyone looks to her; every detail of her appearance is noted.

We who love the Lady Mary must also show pride befitting our rank.'

And so, with reluctance, I accepted the new wardrobe. I was two inches shorter than Gertrude and larger in the bosom. The first difference was easy to adjust for, the second less so. All of the bodices were tight. At first I felt imprisoned; I did not like to be so conscious of drawing breath. But the feeling of confinement passed after a few days.

When I opened the door to the upper corridor, I nearly collided with Alice, my maid.

'Do you need anything at all, Mistress Joanna?' Alice dipped a curtsy, her dark red hair gleaming beneath her cap.

'No, thank you. I am on my way to see the lady marchioness.'

'I believe she has moved to her receiving room,' said Alice and edged sideways, preparing to follow me.

My mind worked frantically. 'Alice, the fire in my room has gone out. I know that it is not your responsibility to bank it, but—'

'I will see to your rooms and wardrobe at once, Mistress Joanna.' Alice rushed into my bedchamber.

Relieved, I made my way down the corridor. Of all the things I had to accustom myself to, none was more difficult than a maid shadowing me throughout the house. Gertrude assigned Alice to me, and she was a willing young woman. But I'd had no personal attendants for years. Earlier in my life, my mother and I shared a maid at Stafford Castle, a surly countrywoman named Hadley. In truth, I preferred Hadley's heavy sighs of resentment over the smallest task to Alice's eagerness to please. Perhaps it was because my London maid continually asked me what I would be doing or where would I be going, so that she could best serve me. And I often had no answers. Arthur's days were kept busy and happy, alongside Edward Courtenay and his bevy of tutors. My place in the house was less defined.

True to her word, Gertrude stayed clear of the king's court. She'd not left the Red Rose since my arrival. Instead, people came to her. Everyone from dressmakers to apothecaries, jewellers to scholars, they sought to occupy as many minutes of Gertrude's time as possible. While doing business, she was always attended by her gentlemen ushers, maids and ladies, principally Constance.

It was mid-morning. The Red Rose whirred with busyness. The staff rose at five in the morning and worked steadily until sundown. It felt strange to be purposeless in the midst of it.

To reach the stairs leading to Gertrude's rooms, I had to pass by the one part of the house I did not care for: the great hall. It was a vast, empty room. Unused. On the first morning of my stay, before the dressmakers descended, Gertrude had pushed open its doors and walked with me down the length of the hall, as part of a house tour.

But something happened in that room. Something I had not been able to make sense of.

It was when I gazed at the fireplace. High enough for a man to stand inside without stooping, it was swept clean. No flames had licked its walls for months, perhaps years. Two carved limestone figures, jutting out from the overmantel, caught my attention. They were not what you'd usually see on a fireplace: winged lions, with mouths yawning open as if in mid-scream.

When I stepped closer, to examine the figures, a feeling of dread came over me. An instant later, I heard the fragments.

First the words: '*May Almighty God bless thee.*'

Next came a brief high scream, such as that of a child.

And then a ripple of men's laughter.

It all rushed through my head and was gone. I peered at Gertrude, and behind her, Constance. They didn't react.

'Did you hear it?' I asked Gertrude.

Gertrude, bewildered, shook her head. As did Constance, her face a blank.

I nearly confided in my cousin's wife. But the impulse dissolved. I followed Gertrude out the door moments later. After all, the departure from Dartford had not been without trials. I hadn't slept well my first night at the Red Rose. Perhaps these strains had done me ill. I certainly did not want Gertrude to think me unbalanced of mind.

Since that first afternoon, I'd had no cause to step inside the great hall. But each time I passed it, the memory of what I'd heard gnawed at me. Was it simply fancies, or something darker? Was it, in fact, a *vision*?

And with that I was propelled back to the terror of Saint Sepulchre and the words of Sister Elizabeth Barton.

My horrified mother bore me away from the priory that day in 1528. I told her only that the nun had experienced a fit, spouting gibberish about ravens and dogs; I omitted everything that came before.

I knew how susceptible my mother was to the visions of mystics. I had to prevent her from seeking further direction or, God forbid, from pushing me toward fulfilment of prophecy.

Although the experience at Saint Sepulchre was nearly as frightening as being attacked by George Boleyn, I did not descend again to melancholia. Instead, I made it clear to all that I would reside in Stafford Castle from that day forward. If danger existed for me outside the thick walls of my ancestral home, then I'd remain in the Midlands. It wasn't necessary, it turned out. It was not I who fell ill that winter, it was my mother. She sickened of an ailment and never recovered. I spent the next years caring for her. There was no more talk of finding another place for me at court or a husband. The importance of my future – the possibility I could advance the Stafford family through royal service or noble marriage – dimmed. My place was nurse to my mother, companion to my father, and helpmate to my cousin Henry's wife, Lady Ursula, who each year thickened with a new pregnancy. I heard of Sister Elizabeth Barton's activities during that time. Everyone did. Within months of my visit, she became famous. Two cardinals did indeed travel through Canterbury: Cardinal Wolsey, the king's chief minister, escorted Cardinal Campeggio to London. The Italian prelate was sent by His Holiness to hear the king's petition for divorce. Sister Elizabeth obtained an audience in Canterbury with Wolsey, and warned him of the dangers of a divorce. In the next several years, she met with many important people, always pleading with them to persuade the king to abandon his quest. She met with the king himself twice. The second time she informed him that if he married Anne Boleyn, he would be dead within three months. He wed her regardless, in 1533.

The king moved against Sister Elizabeth Barton after those three months had passed and her prophecy had been exposed as wrong. She was arrested for treason, along with her followers. In the Tower of London she was repeatedly questioned, until she signed a document recanting her predictions. In the spring of 1534, Sister Elizabeth Barton was executed at Tyburn, along with a handful of her supporters. Her low birth excluded her from the privilege of being killed at the Tower.

It had saddened me to hear of her death, but to my shame, I was relieved too. She had publicly recanted her visions, saying the men around her placed notions in her head. Some people thought Sister Elizabeth a tool of those who opposed the divorce; others said she was mad. Or driven by a tormenting illness. Whatever the cause, it meant that nothing Sister Elizabeth said to me was true. I was *not* singled out for some terrible task. When I went to the side of Katherine of Aragon in my dead mother's place, and later professed at Dartford Priory, I did not think I had any role to play in the future of the kingdom. When Bishop Gardiner forced me to take part in his plots, I did not make a connection back to Sister Elizabeth. What happened in my search for the Athelstan crown had nothing to do with the dead nun of Saint Sepulchre.

Still, I was careful to avoid astrologers, seers, mystics, and witches – anyone else who might spout prophecy. She had said that two would follow her. No matter how hard I tried, I couldn't free my mind of that.

When I was a little girl, I first heard the word *necromancy*. My father discovered that two Stafford servants had met a country sorcerer who carried a severed head in a bag and, if paid a shilling, would pose questions to it. After being placed in front of a magical mirror, the head would answer. My father said sternly, 'Men, this sorcerer is nothing but a charlatan. And even if he weren't, such practices stray very far from God. You risk damning your souls to hell if you traffic with someone who uses the flesh of the dead. That be nothing but necromancy.'

Whenever I was plagued by uncertainties, I often turned to the sensible words of my beloved father. Today I decided to banish my fears of strange visions by entering the great hall once more and seeing for myself that there was nothing amiss.

The room was brighter this time. Sunlight streamed through the long bay windows facing the inner courtyard of the Red Rose. It was but a vast, empty space – at least three times longer than it was wide. At the far end, up high, was a stone balcony. Doubtless for minstrels.

My velvet-clad feet padded soundlessly across the floor, to the spot where I'd heard the noises almost two weeks ago.

What a strange choice, to mount grotesque stone figures on a fireplace. What had possessed him, the house's builder? I remembered his name now, Henry Courtenay had told me it – Sir John de Poulteney. Why did he raise a manor house with a great hall, as if it were the country castle of a magnate? This room didn't belong on Suffolk Lane. His strivings saddened me. How impossible to explain the truth of the aristocracy, that beneath the arrogance – the shallow pride and invariable suspicion – there was ... emptiness. As empty as this room.

I drew even closer to the fireplace's two figures, the winged lions on opposite corners. Was it true the lion never closed its eyes, even in sleep? That it was the most vigilant of all God's creatures?

All at once, the dread consumed me, stronger this time. Like the feeling of helpless, galloping nausea just before vomiting.

I heard the fragments, but there was more. Now visions flashed before my eyes.

'*May Almighty God bless thee.*' It was a clerical blessing, but bestowed by a smiling boy, no older than eight, wearing bishop's robes that fitted him perfectly.

A high, young scream. Mocking adult laughter. But I also saw a second person, a man so tall he towered above a jostling line of other men. His shoulders were broad, his clothing ragged. But his face was that of a simple child: filmy eyes and a thick, wet lower lip that trembled. He looked straight into *my* eyes and shuddered, as if afraid.

I staggered back from the fireplace. My borrowed shoes slipped on the floor and I fell.

8

By the time I got up and scrambled to leave the hall, the visions and voices faded. I stood in the corridor, with my back pressed against the door, struggling to catch my breath – and to comprehend what I'd just seen and heard.

A young chestnut-haired man carrying a tray approached. He was one of the twins employed here. Outwardly identical, even to the length of their hair, they could be told apart by bearing. James was the capable one. Joseph was slower-witted. This day, it was definitely James who walked toward me. He did not look away, in the respectful manner of most of the manor's servants. Would I be the subject of gossip? 'That Stafford girl is a strange one,' he'd say in servant quarters tonight.

I straightened my shoulders and, with more determination than ever, continued on my way to Gertrude's rooms.

This had nothing to do with Sister Elizabeth Barton, I soon decided. It was possible malevolent spirits possessed the Red Rose. Perhaps Gertrude and the whole household would think me mad, but I had no choice but to tell her what had happened in the great hall.

My mother not only believed in spirits, she swore she'd made the acquaintance of a host of them, in the family's ancient castle of Castile. Of course my father scoffed at that, too. I once pointed out what others thought, that certain spirits were so restless they haunted the living. It could be because they'd died without Last Rites – or experienced such horrors in life that their souls roamed past burial. 'No, Joanna, when people die, they stay dead,' he said.

But I had experienced these sights and sounds myself, twice. And I was *not* mad.

When I crossed the threshold of her elegant receiving room, brushing by her gentleman usher, I saw that Gertrude was not alone. Constance was elsewhere, but two young girls, thirteen or so, who came from good families in the orbit of the Courtenays, perched on large pillows, embroidering. They served her as maids of honour would a queen, learning the fine points of conduct.

Gertrude herself reclined on her favourite cushioned chair, her head tilted back so far it rested on the chair's back. Her skirts were emerald green, gathered at her tiny waist. Her hands – younger and creamier than the skin of her face or throat – rested on the arms of her chair. Sitting next to her was a smooth-faced man somewhere between thirty and forty years old. He wore flowing black robes but was not a cleric. A round cap perched on his head, tied under his chin. A bag rested against his legs, stuffed with tall square objects that bulged against its burlap skin.

'I've never understood how you could know what she was capable of – such an insignificant person for so long,' the man was saying.

Staring up, Gertrude answered, 'Because I perceived her secret wish. What everyone has, even if they don't fully understand it themselves.'

The man leaned forward, eager. 'What was hers?'

'To escape from the dominion of her family. This was her way not only to escape from the brutish men of her clan but to rule over them.'

They couldn't have been speaking of me. But something about Gertrude's words – delivered with such canny detachment – gave me pause. I cleared my throat.

Gertrude's head snapped up and she swiftly assumed the expression I always saw when I entered her presence: a warm regard tinged with triumph.

The man jumped to his feet.

'Is this she?' he breathed. 'Could *this* be Mistress Joanna Stafford?'

His eyes swept up and down my figure. Inwardly, I raged at Geoffrey Scovill. I had never been aware of it before, but now each time a man looked at me, with that sly, prowling hunger, I heard Geoffrey's words: *'Your effect on men. How they respond to you, how they look at you ... your beauty can be discomfiting.'*

The man then kissed my hand. I felt his plump palm, his wet lips on my skin. For a wild instant, I was reminded of the slobbering mouth of the giant I'd seen in the great hall moments ago. It took all my self-control not to yank my hand away.

'What a very comely young woman you are,' Gertrude's guest said.

He let go of my hand and turned toward the marchioness. 'I detect a resemblance, my lady.'

'Mistress Joanna is my husband's relation, not mine,' she said. 'But we are both half Spanish. That would explain a likeness.'

He swept the room with both hands in a grand gesture. 'Then Mistress Joanna is the moon to your sun.'

I cringed, and wished myself elsewhere.

Gertrude tilted her head as she shifted in her chair. Just before making an observation, she would shift just so. 'Mistress Stafford does not invite compliments and, once made, she does not enjoy their presence.'

'Ah, yes, of course, the priory has left its mark,' said the man, his voice hushed in a show of respect.

Gertrude turned to me. 'This is Doctor Branch, one of the finest physicians in the land. He studied at Montpellier, for three years. I would never take consultation from one who had only attended our College of Physicians.' They chuckled together at some private joke.

'Are you or Henry unwell?' I asked.

She shrugged. 'Nothing new. My dear husband's digestion is always a concern. And I've never been the same since 1528. Doctor Branch's remedies are the only ones that help.' I knew well what struck England ten years ago – a vicious epidemic of sweating sickness, the same bout that killed so many just before my family and I travelled to Canterbury. The sweat left its mark on Gertrude. One night she confided she was unable to bear more children. Edward must be sole heir to the Courtenay line.

Gertrude frowned. 'You do not look quite yourself, Joanna.'

I did not want to tell Gertrude of my fear of spirits in the great hall, not in front of Doctor Branch, whose eyes still glistened as he continued to size me up.

'I heard a town crier tell news of the Emperor Charles and I wasn't sure of its import,' I said.

'The defeat at Preveza.' Gertrude slapped the arm of her chair with her palm. 'The Muslim Turk has laid low the Holy League.'

As always, I was struck by how well informed she was.

'Can this be true – the barbaric Muslim enslaves Christians?' exclaimed Doctor Branch.

'The emperor will prevail against them,' Gertrude said.

The doctor replied, 'For months I've heard rumours in London. Now that France is no longer our ally, we are isolated. Perhaps this defeat in the Mediterranean – the threat of the Muslim – will distract the Holy Roman Emperor from invasion of England.'

Invasion. The word chilled me, as it would anyone who lived on our island kingdom. As when I first learned of this looming threat, my next thoughts were for the Lady Mary.

Speaking carefully, I said, 'But the diplomatic alliances, and how they affect England – and the prominent persons who live here – they are unchanged?'

Gertrude and I locked eyes. 'Such persons are, from what I understand, still safe,' she said. Her chin lowered and rose. It was such a small gesture, not discernible, perhaps, to Doctor Branch. Yet I felt as if she had slipped into my mind, my innermost thoughts, and there reassured me. In our devotion to the king's daughter, we were in harmony.

'I am so glad you chose to join me, Joanna,' she said. 'It saved me having to send for you. Please sit across from the doctor.'

'But I am of sound health,' I said.

'Doctor Branch practises another art,' she said.

With growing dread, I watched Doctor Branch rifle through a bundle of papers. He pulled loose a single sheet, using great care. It was covered with globes, arrows, and diagonal lines.

'Doctor Branch is second to none in his mastery of astrology,' Gertrude said.

I gripped the back of the chair I was meant to sit in. 'I wish I had known of this idea ahead of time. Forgive me, but this is … impossible.'

The doctor, surprised, glanced up from his drawings.

'Impossible?' he asked.

'I cannot have my planets cast,' I said.

Gertrude's light laughter filled the room. 'What nonsense is this, Joanna? Surely you don't fear that astrology is the invention of the devil? Such an assumption was discredited centuries ago.'

'That is not why I am averse.'

'Then why?'

'My cousin, Lord Henry, made everyone in the family, all who lived at Stafford Castle, swear oaths that we would never have our planets cast. Not after what happened to my uncle, the Duke of Buckingham.'

'Ah, yes,' said Doctor Branch. 'The duke used a friar?'

'A monk,' I said. 'At his trial, the gravest charge laid against His Grace was that he dabbled in ... prophecy.' My voice, unfortunately, shook on the word *prophecy*. 'My uncle did *not* request the foretelling of the king's death nor ask whether there would ever be Tudor male heirs – such testimony was false. But he was found guilty, and we lost everything.'

A respectful silence filled the room. My breath, trapped between my tense shoulders during the story of my uncle's downfall, eased.

Gertrude said, 'We would never, ever, make inquiry into the king's future.'

She jumped up and encircled my waist with her arm, clutching me close. Her grasp was surprisingly strong.

'Doctor Branch is here to *help* you, Joanna. Once we know the date and precise time of your birth, we can determine the composition of your humours and best protect your health.' She pointed at Doctor Branch with her other hand. 'Please explain your art. You do it so well.'

The doctor patted the empty chair across from him. 'Will you sit, Mistress Joanna?'

'I do not wish to give offence, but I cannot take part in this.' I couldn't risk exposing myself to any sort of prophecy, no matter how benign. This was what I'd vowed on the cold stone floor of Saint Sepulchre.

Gertrude withdrew her arm. 'Doctor Branch is my guest – and my long-time friend,' she said, her tone cooling. 'I can't think why you wouldn't sit and listen. If afterward you still feel this way, then of course no one will force you, Joanna.'

I sat.

The doctor, now all seriousness, launched into his lecture. 'Our belief in the power of the stars and planets traces back to the earliest recorded history, Mistress Stafford. The Babylonians could see that their lives depended on the sun. Their health was governed by the fluctuations of the moon. Through diligent study of the skies over centuries, they learned that the four elements – earth, air, fire, and water – were controlled by the fluctuations of our heavenly bodies. Because of the work of Europe's great humanist scholars, we now know that Aristotle and Claudius Ptolemy gave great credence to astrology.' He paused. 'These names, perhaps, are not known to you.'

I answered, 'They are known to me, Doctor Branch. As is another man, Tacitus, historian of the Roman Empire, who called astrologers "a danger to princes".'

The physician's mouth hung open. Gertrude said: 'You must understand, Doctor Branch, our Spanish mothers followed the example of Queen Isabella. She believed females were worthy of classical education. Clearly, Joanna paid close attention to her studies.'

Plunging on, he said, 'All of the kings of Christendom employ astrologers, including King Henry. The marchioness believes you were born in mid-April, but I must know the exact date to—'

Interrupting him, I said, 'But I have already told you I am in perfect health.'

'Yes – today,' Doctor Branch said. 'But once I have cast your planets, I can determine the state of your humours, and what should be done to bring you into perfect balance in the future.'

And to think I had feared that the visions in the great hall might have some connection to Sister Elizabeth Barton. This was so much worse. Gertrude was pressing on me the thing I most feared – an audience seeking prophecy.

I took a deep breath and then said, 'The future is where I cannot go.'

'Joanna.' Gertrude's voice shot me like an arrow. 'This is foolish. Assurances have been given that once the doctor possesses the necessary date and time, no dangerous predictions will be made. And furthermore, I find it strange, this fear of yours. The Duke of Buckingham was executed seventeen years ago. You are not a humble adherent to the will of his son. If you were, you would now reside at Stafford Castle, with your cousin and his family. But you do not – you've shown nothing but perfunctory obedience to him thus far. And yet in this matter, you shiver before his distant command? I don't believe it.'

A tense silence thickened the receiving room. The maids on their pillows had stopped stitching. The doctor looked away.

'There is no other choice,' I said miserably.

Doctor Branch picked up his bag. 'Ah, well. I have other patients, my lady. Before I go, could I examine your husband's water? You did have it kept for me?'

A servant led the doctor out, to perform his water casting. I sat in my plush embroidered chair, under the baffled glare of Gertrude Courtenay.

'Doctor Branch is expensive, Joanna,' she said. 'I am not pleased with what occurred here today.'

I rose to my feet. 'If you will inform me of the doctor's fee, I will make arrangements to compensate you.' I curtsied low. On my way up, I saw the red patches flare in Gertrude's cheeks. Her chest rose and fell rapidly. She was as angry with me as she'd been at Mistress Brooke in Dartford.

'Leave me now,' she said. Her voice shook, as if with the effort needed to control it.

9

The rest of the day I endeavoured to find peace of mind, without success. I paced the large bedchamber, from the window on Suffolk Lane, autumn chill pressing through the glass, to the fire that Alice sent crackling again. The Courtenays had shown Arthur and me every kindness. If there had been a way for me to give Gertrude what she asked for, I would have done it most willingly.

Gertrude was astute enough to doubt my claiming a Stafford family edict. My cousin had commanded us to shun prophecy, but no, I did not live by his distant commands. However, to reveal the reason for my aversion – to describe my visit to the nun and condemned traitor all those years ago – would be dangerous, not only for me but also for her and Henry.

Desperate for distraction, I picked up the book I'd begun, an English translation of *The Life of Edward the Confessor*, by the Abbot of Rievaulx. But the struggles of the pious Saxon king failed to engage. I read a long paragraph, only to realise at the end that I hadn't absorbed a single word. I closed the book – it possessed a red engraved cover. All of the books in my bedchamber were of the highest quality. I knew that Gertrude had in the last two years quietly purchased books from the large monasteries dissolved at the king's command. She rescued the martyrologies and Rules of Saint Benedict and Pater Nosters from the brutish courtiers who'd taken possession of religious houses. On my first day here, she'd pressed into my hand an exquisite *Mirror of the Blessed Life of Christ*. And now she must see me as recalcitrant and ungrateful.

I was seized with longing for the friends I'd left behind in Dartford. It was difficult for me to cope with these tensions. Two more weeks remained of my visit, but if there were a way to leave today without giving offence, I would have done so. If only I could talk everything over with Sister Winifred – and with Brother Edmund.

I'd had three letters from her and one short one from him. I ached to hear his temperate voice and look into his brown eyes, full of probity and wit.

I sat on the edge of the bed – this plush, curtained bed that had been afforded me – and wailed like a muddled child. After a time, I felt spent and rather embarrassed. I rarely carried on like this.

Just after dusk fell, I heard the stirring of horses. Torchlight danced outside my window, as it always did around nightfall. Henry Courtenay, Marquess of Exeter, was returning home.

Unquestionably Henry could have occupied his own rooms at court. The king currently resided at Whitehall. But my cousin had received permission to live at home, with his wife and son. Every morning he heard Mass in the family chapel and then went directly to the river, to be rowed to the palace. As a close kinsman and noble, he must serve the king. Instead of taking our main meal at dinner, in the early afternoon, we ate lightly then and enjoyed a large supper after nightfall, with Henry at the head of the table.

It always moved me, the excitement over Henry's return. I had never observed such devotion to the master of a house. Doors slammed, the sound of running feet, calls flung from one floor to another. Every person, from the lowest scullery lad to the highest-ranking officer, hastened to present him or herself in the main antechamber, for evensong.

By the time I'd reached the top of the stairs, Henry stood just inside the doorway. Fresh candles soared everywhere. His household, more than sixty people, bowed or curtsied in waves. Gertrude, who always stood on the first step, curtsied as well.

I've been asked, by more than one person, what it was that made Henry Courtenay so compelling. His fate haunts the more sensitive souls.

Part of it was looks. He and the king, both the grandsons of Edward IV, inherited the Yorkist monarch's height, fair skin, and blue eyes. But Henry Courtenay had a simplicity to his manner, a calm and friendly directness. He never insisted on obeisance from anyone. Perhaps that was why it was given so willingly.

Gathered with the others on the stairs, I felt a familiar hand slip into mine.

'Joanna!' Arthur cried, with a radiant smile. 'I shot arrows today.'

How it brightened my spirits, to see Arthur so joyful. In just two weeks, his manner of speech had improved greatly. It was near miraculous.

We sang Henry's favourite hymn, what I'd soon learned was a household tradition.

To thee before the close of day
Creator of the world, we pray
That, with thy wonted favour, thou
Wouldst be our guard and keeper now.

My eyes landed on the twins, Joseph and James. The one I had seen earlier in the day sang with great fervour, but his brother's lips barely moved. I had heard that an accident befell Joseph as a child, leaving him diminished in mind. His twin protected him. Even now, he nudged him, to stimulate memory of the song.

When we'd all finished, Henry made his way to his wife. Along the way there was a smile for this servant, a reassuring nod for another.

'My lady,' he said, kissing Gertrude's hand.

'My lord,' she murmured.

In one way, at least, Henry was *not* like Edward IV, the infamous adulterer. Love of Gertrude was what guided him.

It was always a small group in the dining parlour: First the immediate family, and their relations, Arthur and myself. Constance and Charles, the respective heads of Gertrude's and Henry's households, dined with us, as did the family chaplain and a young tutor from Oxford University who led Edward's lessons. I sat on the same side of the long table as Gertrude, with Constance between us, and so could not see her face.

For the boys, archery was the focus of their days. As pheasant was served, Edward and his father talked over length of bow and accuracy of shot. Arthur listened, doing his best to follow the conversation.

I ached for a better future for Arthur than the one that seemed on offer in Dartford. Arthur was a *Stafford*. He should be trained in all the arts and sports of a nobleman. Both the Staffords and the Bulmers were houses in eclipse. Henry Courtenay was in the position – perhaps a unique one – of being both of the old nobility and in high favour with the Tudor king. No one could help Arthur more.

'Now Edward, what of Arthur – how did *his* lessons go?' Gertrude said. She leaned forward in her seat and twisted toward me. Her conspiratorial way of looking at someone – as if tossing a half wink your way – never failed to charm. In her uncanny way, she'd leaped into my thoughts and knew of my hopes for Arthur.

I smiled back at her, tentatively, and as I listened to Arthur's excited talk of his afternoon, I was able to taste my pheasant at last. The afternoon's episode had been put away, I hoped forever.

The conversation moved toward families the Courtenays knew in the west. Charles relayed some news gleaned from correspondence. This one's father had died. That one struggled with debt because of a bad grain harvest. It was very much like the conversations around the table at Stafford Castle. Detailed scrutiny of the lives of country families whom, when in our presence, no one actually cared about all that much. It infuriated my mother. She wanted to talk of the great events of the kingdom. But that was not the Stafford way. I realised that the Courtenays, too, never, ever talked of the king or his councillors or foreign affairs at table.

'Remember, the day after tomorrow is my party,' Gertrude said. 'Just a few friends. Only ladies. Cakes and sweet wines. Joanna will enjoy the company so much.'

She said it as if I already knew about the party, but I'd heard not a word. Henry beamed as I tried to hide my surprise. Had Gertrude forgotten to mention it? But she never forgot anything. And I was not at all sure I'd enjoy it: this had been one of my conditions of the visit to London – no contact with the court *or* its courtiers.

Had Gertrude waited to 'invite' me until we were in Henry's presence, so that I would be less likely to baulk?

Immediately I felt guilty for thinking this of her. Hadn't she put our quarrel over astrology behind her – and shown every interest in Arthur? This was on top of generosity and solicitude displayed each day of my visit.

Henry Courtenay laid down his fork and said, 'I do believe this is the moment to speak of another engagement, cousin Joanna. Every year in the autumn, I make a point to dine with my closest friend, Henry Pole, Baron Montague. It's set for November fourth, here at the Red Rose. I very much want you to join us. You know Montague, I believe.'

'Yes, I'm acquainted with the Poles,' I answered. My cousin Henry Stafford was married to Ursula Pole, and her siblings made regular visits to Stafford Castle. There were three brothers: Henry, the oldest, who always seemed to me very arrogant; Reginald, the middle son, a quiet scholar; and Godfrey, the youngest, a ruffian and my least favourite. Of more concern to me than the guests expected was the date: the first week of November. Later than I would have preferred.

'So it is settled – you will attend the dinner,' Henry said, smiling.

Haltingly, I said, 'Yes, but the other half of my tapestry loom will be delivered that week, and so, after the party, I shall need to return to Dartford.'

It seemed that everyone sitting at the table had a reaction to that – and not one of them favourable. Both Arthur and Edward cried out in disappointment. Gertrude looked aghast. But it was Henry whose expression pained me the most.

'Have you not had a happy time with us, Joanna?' he asked sadly.

How this pained me. It was my talks with Henry Courtenay that brought me the most happiness at the Red Rose. On a handful of evenings I joined my cousin in his study. He would speak with great enthusiasm about his favourite subject – the lives of past kings of England – as he patted the two dogs that begged for his attention. It was, I admit, a scenario that I'd envisioned for myself and my father at one time. I'd assumed I'd never have that family feeling again after he died last winter. Henry had given me back a taste of it.

Arthur was becoming more and more upset. 'No, no, I don't want to leave!'

'Don't be troubled, Arthur,' I pleaded, patting his hand. 'We shall see.' I shouldn't have brought up leaving the Red Rose in front of him this way, without preparation.

The conversation at the table returned to Gertrude's dinner. The Duchess of Suffolk would not be able to attend. I knew the Duke of Suffolk was considered the king's closest friend, and so her absence seemed no matter of regret to me.

Yet Gertrude said, 'The duchess wrote in her note to me that she wanted to make your acquaintance and regretted not being able do so.'

'Why would she want to do that?' I asked, apprehensive.

Gertrude said, 'I believe it is because of her mother, Maria de Salinas.'

My hand tightened around the knife I'd used to cut my pheasant. I was no longer present, in this comfortable dining parlour, but back in cold and shabby Kimbolton Castle, at the bedside of the dying Queen Katherine of Aragon. I'd nursed the exiled queen alongside Maria de Salinas, the queen's most devoted lady. She'd come from Spain as a young girl, as had my mother. And, like my mother and Gertrude's mother, she married an English nobleman, in her case, Lord Willoughby. I remember in the moments after the queen died at dawn, how Maria and I clutched each other, in blind grief.

'Lady Willoughby is dead,' I said softly. I knew that she followed the queen to the grave not more than a year later. 'Of all the ladies you've mentioned, because of her mother, the duchess is someone I would wish to meet.'

Gertrude looked at her husband as if seeking permission for something. He nodded. 'Duchess Catherine is very young, not yet twenty years old. She is Suffolk's fourth wife. But I regret to tell you she is an avid reformer in the matter of religion.'

As everyone else finished supper, I struggled to fathom Catherine Brandon, Duchess of Suffolk. How could she practise a faith that constituted painful heresy to the blessed queen, whom her mother revered?

After supper, as was my custom, I went to Arthur's room to spend more time with him. He'd recovered his high spirits from the scene at dinner this evening; I tried to play with him but was sore distracted.

I'd lost my balance at the Red Rose. The first two weeks had gone well enough, but beginning in the great hall this morning, things had become strained and confusing. Henry had gone direct from the table to discuss pressing matters with Charles. Such talks went on for hours. Perhaps if I confided in Gertrude – not about my terror of prophecy but about what I heard and saw before the fireplace in her house – it would begin to restore good faith.

After putting Arthur to bed, I made my way to Gertrude's rooms once again.

I could hear the sound of women's voices in the bathing room.

She was the only person I knew who'd had a room built just for bathing. Her maids cleaned her bedchamber and heated water in a huge pot hanging over the fire. I knocked on the door. Gertrude called out, 'Come in!'

The bathing room was small, dominated by a large wooden tub that, I knew, had been built to her specifications. Gertrude lay in it, her thick black hair piled on top of her head, the water up to her breasts. Herbs and potions swayed in the water. And peels of orange, a fruit grown in the Mediterranean. The steamy room pulsed with its sharp smell.

She sat up in the water, startled. 'I thought you were the maid, bringing water,' she said. Seeing her naked, I realised how thin she was. Gertrude's height and carriage were set off so well in clothes. But now I glimpsed the sharp triangles of her shoulders.

Constance sat in a chair pulled up close to the bath, a small box open in her lap, filled with bundles of letters. Gertrude held a letter in both hands. Without looking at it, she thrust it toward Constance.

The lady-in-waiting leaned over, but the letter slipped through her fingers and fell to the floor. It drifted to my feet, propelled by the curl of a draught. I picked it up. It was not written in English but in Latin.

'Joanna, I would of course enjoy speaking with you, but I need to finish my correspondence first,' Gertrude said. 'Would that be acceptable?'

The words were reasonable, but a brittleness underlined them. She wasn't angry, more afflicted with nerves. Her eyes were not even on my face but fixed on the letter I'd retrieved.

'Of course,' I said, and handed the letter to Constance, who pushed it into the box on her lap. 'Tomorrow, then?'

On the long walk to my bedchamber, the passageway lit by candles affixed to the walls, I wondered what had made Gertrude nervous in her bathing room. It couldn't be the letter. I'd only read one phrase: *de libero arbitrio*. Which, translated to English, meant 'of free will'.

Something about the phrase 'of free will' tugged at me, though. I searched the many conversations I'd had today. No one had said it, nor in the previous days either.

It wasn't until the middle of the night, as one restless dream shifted to the next, that I remembered. I bolted up in my bed, gasping for breath.

I'd heard those words in Saint Sepulchre ten years earlier, first from Sister Anne and then Sister Elizabeth Barton herself.

'*You must hear the prophecies of your own free will and unconstrained*,' the nun had told me. '*After you hear the third, nothing can stop it. Nothing.*'

10

'So, Mistress Wriothesley, how goes your husband's quest to find the king a new wife?'

The roomful of women who'd come to Gertrude's party dissolved into laughter. Mistress Wriothesley herself, plain-faced and heavily pregnant, shook her head, refusing to answer.

Cecily, the woman who posed it – younger and prettier than the wife of Master Thomas Wriothesley, king's ambassador – sipped spice wine from her glass and pretended to be sorry. 'We don't mean to pry into the secrets of the king's council, but really, what are we all to do?' she said. 'We've been a year without a queen. No positions to fill, no favour to fight over. It's intolerable. We all pray that His Grace takes a fourth wife – forthwith.' Everyone laughed again as Cecily giggled, rather helplessly, as if she had little to do with the words that came from her mouth.

I tried to concentrate on the song being played in this, the most beautiful room in the Red Rose. With Gertrude's exquisite taste – and Henry's money – every inch of the house was impressive. But the music room reigned supreme, which was all the more interesting since I'd heard it was installed before the Courtenays took possession. In this high, rectangular space, a frieze ran along three of the walls. The long stretch of sculpted decoration told a story, of a band of travelling musicians who arrive in a village and raise everyone's spirits. Whoever designed it had a feeling for the way music could transform lives. What a charming setting for the Courtenay musicians, who entertained Gertrude's guests on the lute and harp and with lovely madrigals.

Everything was in place for an enjoyable afternoon – but for the guests.

I had never been a person who was at ease in a party. But Gertrude assured me that her friends were pious and cultured and kind. 'I expect you to make lifelong friends today,' she said, squeezing my arm as we walked into the music room together. I had forced a smile in return. Common sense dictated that my seeing *de libero arbitrio* in one of her letters was a coincidence, nothing more. Nonetheless, I'd not confided in her about the visions in the great hall. For now, I would keep my own counsel on all matters that disturbed me.

'Ladies, I present my husband's cousin, Mistress Joanna Stafford,' announced Gertrude. Seven pairs of eyes studied me from head to toe, examining the borrowed brocades, headdress, and gems that covered my body.

The women ranged widely in age, from Cecily with her milk-and-honey girlishness to a woman everyone called Countess Elizabeth whose forehead puckered at the temples. Cecily sat with Lady Carew – or Lady C., as she was called – who made knowing remarks about her husband, Sir Nicholas Carew, evidently a courtier in high favour with the king. As I moved from guest to guest to shake hands, I was discomfited by their smiles, gracious but as cold as a frost-bitten pasture.

Gertrude's guests sat in pairs except for one woman who was alone, farthest from the music. She bore a fixed smile on her face that never left, even when she spoke. I guessed her to be the same age as Gertrude, who called her Lady R. with fondness. Her skin was alabaster white; gleaming, yes, but devoid of any depth or subtlety to its glow, like an egg kept overlong in a cupboard. She had grey eyes, set wide apart. In profile, she looked like any other woman. But when she faced me, with that toothy frozen smile and bulging eyes set far apart, she was something else.

Lady R. spoke now, seemingly to ease Mistress Wriothesley's discomfort. 'It is no fault of your husband's that negotiations proceed so slowly in Brussels for the hand of Christina of Milan,' said Lady R. 'She is the niece of the Emperor Charles.'

'And Duchess Christina has her own opinions of King Henry,' murmured Cecily.

Gertrude tapped the young woman on the shoulder, her diamond bracelet dancing up and down. She wore a dark gold velvet kirtle and skirts, a colour that enhanced her olive complexion. She'd stained her lips with a berry concoction. One could never forget that Gertrude had been a great beauty in her youth, and when the occasion warranted, could shrewdly assemble the wardrobe, jewellery, and cosmetics that set her off to best advantage. 'We must not repeat this particular piece of gossip,' she said.

'Not gossip,' said Lady C. 'It is established fact. Duchess Christina of Milan may be seventeen years old but she is no fool. She said to Master Wriothesley, loud enough for all to hear in the whole court of Brussels, "If I had two heads, one would be at the disposal of King Henry."'

Mistress Wriothesley put her hand on her round belly, even more distressed as the ladies screamed with laughter all around her.

Cecily said, breathless, 'We must all pray the king takes Christina for a queen, or one of the French princesses, and not look elsewhere in Europe.'

'Elsewhere?' echoed the countess's rotund daughter.

Someone groaned and said, 'Please don't mention the possibility of Cleves. I'm having too good a time for that.'

'Cleves?' I asked. It was the first time I'd spoken since being introduced.

'Cromwell may push harder for a Protestant marriage,' explained Gertrude. 'Cleves, in Germany, has two marriageable daughters.'

A gloom settled over the room. Clearly, it was the last thing anyone wanted.

'Well, I would wait on a Turk wrapped in nothing but purple sashes – if that is what's required to secure a post as a maid of honour in a queen's household,' Cecily announced. Everyone mock-scolded her.

'I suppose there is no chance of another English marriage?' asked the countess.

'The king shows no signs of such inclination,' answered Gertrude.

'If there were any such candidates, you would tell us, wouldn't you, Gertrude?' pleaded Cecily.

Gertrude's eyes flicked my way and then returned to her other guests. 'I've not been in the king's presence in quite some time,' she said. There was an undercurrent of warning to her voice.

Lady R. laughed. It was a soft laugh, but by no means a pleasant one. 'Does that matter?' she asked. She seemed to assume that Gertrude had special knowledge of the king's wishes and desires.

I felt Lady R.'s grey eyes land on me. 'Mistress Joanna, you do know that we have the Marchioness of Exeter to thank for the ascendance of Queen Jane?'

'That's nonsense,' said Gertrude, even more sharply.

'Why do you deny it?' called out Lady C. 'How could a family like the Seymours ever have managed such a feat?'

Lady Anna shook her head. 'Oh, those Seymour brothers – so dreadful,' she said.

Gertrude inhaled deeply, and then, with a little laugh, let it all out. 'The father was the worst of all – they are terrible,' she admitted, to a roomful of knowing laughter. I tried to hide my dismay. I remembered coming into her receiving room, when she sat with Doctor Branch, and hearing them speak of an insignificant girl from a terrible family. She must have referred then, and now, to the late Queen Jane Seymour.

The spite in this room, the jabs and drawling mockery, it was not what I'd hoped for and certainly not what I enjoyed. The cakes came in a moment later, borne on silver trays. Gertrude's confectioner had triumphed. One of the hired musicians sang an exquisite story of love for a distant lady, while the guests listened, nibbling on their cakes.

The exceptions were Gertrude and Lady R., who talked together quite intently, oblivious to food or music. Gertrude was questioning her about something. I heard one word through the song: *Londinium*.

The music ended. Gertrude rose to join her other guests. To my dismay, Lady R. beckoned to me with a finger. It was my turn to make conversation with this strange woman. I picked up my half-empty glass of spiced wine and sat in a neighbouring chair.

She leaned over. A fragrance of dry violets encircled me.

'I've served all three queens, did you know that?' she said.

'No, my lady.' I shrank from the scrutiny of those eyes. Not grey at all, I realised now. Palest blue, with dark circles around the pupils.

She continued, 'I was a lady-in-waiting to Katherine of Aragon the day that you arrived to be her maid of honour in 1527. Such a long, long time ago. I have a good memory, but I do not recall you, I'm afraid. So interesting that you only served her as queen for a single day.'

The air fled my body. I struggled to find breath, to feel my heart pumping blood. There was nothing. Nothing. I could not believe that this woman knew I'd attended the court for that one day so long ago. Gertrude Courtenay didn't know it, or if she did she'd never mentioned it. How was this possible?

'Forgive me,' I stammered, 'but I did not hear your full name when we were introduced. What does the *R* stand for?'

She leaned closer still. Our faces were inches from each other.

'Rochford,' she said. 'I was wife to the late Lord Rochford. But when you were at court, he was not yet a lord. He was known by his Christian name – George Boleyn.'

11

Dearest Joanna,

I had not wanted to disturb you during your visit with family. Your letter from the Red Rose was filled with cheer. I am glad that you are united with these good Christian people. But neither did I want you to think that you could ever be forgotten. Brother Edmund and I speak of you every day. We pray for your good health and for Arthur's.

All is well in Dartford, although I recognise our excitements cannot compare with those offered by the city of London. Brother Edmund has treated the injuries and illnesses of new townsfolk, and one of his patients even paid for a remedy with coin. He works so many hours a day that I worry for him, but you know my brother and how much contentment he finds in healing. I hope I am improving in my efforts to assist him.

I put down my letter from Sister Winifred. Closing my eyes, I envisioned Brother Edmund, bending over a flustered villager struck with fever – the butcher's apprentice, say – and calling for cosset ale. How Sister Winifred would rush about, gathering the required lettuce and sorrel and violet leaves. With a touch to her quivering arm, he would take over the mixing of the cosset and then administer it to his grateful patient.

With all my heart and soul, I wished myself in Dartford.

Gertrude had kept her promise. She'd not dragged me to the king's court. But earlier today the court had come to me: shallow and selfish and, as Jane Boleyn's twisted smile flashed in my thoughts, dangerous. Did Lady Rochford know what her husband did to me – how he violated a sixteen-year-old girl? She seemed to know *something*. Would she tell others?

And just as disturbing: How could Gertrude trust a Boleyn? The

Boleyns had destroyed the life of Katherine of Aragon. Anne Boleyn had famously threatened to undo the Lady Mary. It was only her execution that prevented it. Yet Gertrude was a close friend of the sister-in-law of Anne Boleyn? It didn't make sense.

I was struck wordless when Lady Rochford revealed the identity of her dead husband. I could manage but few words to anyone for the remaining moments I was trapped at Gertrude's party. Afterward, I fled to my room and remained there. Alice brought me dinner on a tray, but I had no appetite. Fortunately, she also carried the letter from Sister Winifred, which delivered sustenance of a more important kind than food.

Across the room, a tiny tearing noise filled the air. Alice ripped off threads and then knotted them. She was mending one of my skirts by the fire in my bedchamber. I resumed my reading:

There is news from the house of the sisters of Dartford. I do not know if you recall the gentleman who mourned his wife in Holy Trinity Church that morning before you left. His name is Master Oliver Gwinn. Sister Agatha tells me that Master Gwinn was grateful that Brother Edmund and the rest of us sought to ease his suffering. He now goes to the house of the sisters regularly and sees to repairs that were much needed and advises them about their livestock. Sister Agatha said that the heavy cares of the sisters are eased by his goodness.

Also the presence of Geoffrey Scovill, our new constable, is welcomed everywhere I go. He is every day on the High Street, acquainting himself with the people of Dartford and listening to their business. His first matter is to relocate the shambles to a place farther from Holy Trinity Church. I remember how many times you said that it should be done as well. Now it will be.

Master Scovill came by the infirmary yesterday afternoon to ask if I had received word from you. I passed on the news that you are prospering. I hope that was well done of me, Joanna. His intentions seemed benevolent.

Written in the town of Dartford,
Sister Winifred Sommerville

Only a few seconds after I'd finished the letter, I removed a sheet of drawing paper from the shelf and began to write.

Dear Geoffrey,
    You were right in what you said and I am sorry we quarrelled.
I wish to return to Dartford as soon as possible. A family
engagement requires my presence at the home of my cousin, the
Marquess of Exeter, on 4 November. After that duty is discharged,
Arthur and I will come home.
    Written in the manor of the Red Rose in the city of London,
    Joanna Stafford

Once the ink had dried, I folded the paper twice. I held the bottle of sealing wax over my candle, passing it back and forth. After it had softened, I poured the wax over the closing fold of the letter. I pressed down the seal so hard, the red wax squeezed out into long hard bubbles along the edges, like a fresh wound.

'Alice,' I said, 'I want this letter carried to Dartford. It's very important that it go out with the next batch of correspondence.'

Delighted to have a task of importance, Alice seized my letter, the red wax still warming the paper, and hurried away. Soon the letter would pass out of her hands, and by the end of the day I expected it would begin the journey to Dartford. I felt a stirring of worry. Perhaps I should have slept a night before sending Geoffrey Scovill such a letter – the first one I'd ever written him. I pushed down the qualm.

Alice soon reappeared with the news that my letter had been dispatched and she had an answer to my request to Father Timothy as well.

I'd asked my maid to send a message to the Courtenay chaplain. And the answer had arrived: Father Timothy would be available to hear my confession at dawn the next day, before Mass. The cleansing powers of the sacrament of penance should help steady me.

I was awake well before dawn. I dressed and waited, impatient, for the first lightening of grey outside the windows. At last I glimpsed it – the night was in retreat. As I hurried down the dark corridors, a candle in my hand, noises stirred from the far corners. I knew that downstairs, in the kitchen, buttery, and pantry, Courtenay servants began their duties early indeed.

'Ah, Mistress Stafford, I appreciate your promptness – it looks to be a busy day for me,' said Father Timothy, standing in the doorway to the elegant private chapel. A row of fresh tapers flickered at the altar behind him.

I set down my candlestick in a stone nook and dipped my fingers in the chapel's stoup. Father Timothy opened the door to the confessional, a freestanding, well-glossed oak chamber. He eased inside. I heard the sound of the door sliding in its groove, as Father Timothy took his place behind the grille.

I followed him into the confessional. There was almost no light inside, just the faintest gleam emanating from the silver crucifix that hung from the top of the dense wooden grille. I couldn't see the silhouette of Father Timothy's head. But I could feel his warm breath through the grille. And I smelled the faint odour of onions, too.

'I will hear your confession,' he said.

'Bless me, Father, for I have sinned,' I said. 'It has been five days since my last confession.' I paused, to gather my thoughts. Where to begin – how to frame my offences?

The voice of Henry Courtenay boomed, no more than ten feet away: 'I wonder if Joanna will join us at Mass this morning.'

I jumped off my narrow wooden bench. I hadn't heard anyone come in. But now the Courtenays were in the chapel. I should have emerged from the confessional at once. But the mention of my name rooted me to the bench. On the other side of the grille, Father Timothy, too, was silent, unmoving.

'I expect she will continue to sulk in her room,' said Gertrude.

'I don't want you to speak of her that way,' said Henry, in a sharper tone than I usually heard.

'Oh don't worry, husband. I won't trifle with your prize.'

My cheeks flamed with embarrassment. How could I step out of the confessional now? Why did Gertrude call me a 'prize'? I needed to know what Father Timothy thought we should do, but he was swallowed up in darkness. I knew, however, that he, too, was distressed, by the quickening of the warm onion-scented breath that puffed through the grille.

Henry said, 'I must ask you not to pass Father Timothy private requests for little sermons on the importance of fortitude, courage, and sacrifice, Gertrude.'

His wife responded, 'Don't worry. I've abandoned hope of your choosing such a course.'

A boom echoed through the chapel. As if, incredibly, Henry had slammed his fist against a wall. Or kicked something. Tears sprang from my eyes. This was like a nightmare, for my kind cousin to behave so – and in a sacred space.

He hissed, 'It's not going to happen, Gertrude. Can't you understand? It isn't just Henry. *Hear* me. It's Cromwell and Cranmer and Suffolk. And Norfolk. Never forget Norfolk. Those men surround him.'

The door to the confessional slid open. Father Timothy was revealing himself to the Courtenays. I should have done the same but was too terrified to move.

'Father Timothy, this is outrageous,' Gertrude cried.

In his most soothing manner, the priest apologised and reassured them that all the words he had indeed heard would be kept in strictest confidence.

'But why were you sitting in the confessional this entire time?' she asked.

'I was preparing it for the day, my lady,' he answered.

'You were not hearing someone's confession, were you, Father?' she asked. 'I see a candlestick left by the door. Pray tell me, whose is it?'

Father Timothy said nothing. Of course he would not lie to his patrons.

I slid to the far side of the bench in the confessional. With both hands, I felt my way to the top of the wall. Was there a latch? A door on the other side? I could not face the Courtenays after hearing what was just said.

But there was no other way out of the confessional.

'I will see to it, Gertrude,' said Henry Courtenay. I heard footsteps. Getting louder.

The confessional door swung open. The body of the marquess filled the narrow opening. Barely any light penetrated around him. He saw me – of course he did. I could not read his expression.

After a few seconds, he stepped back. The door shut with a bang.
'There's no one there,' Henry said. 'And now, Father, it's time for
Mass.'

12

I wore my own clothes, a plain dark kirtle I put away after that first day, when Gertrude forced her finery on me. But I wouldn't wear her clothes on the afternoon I left the Red Rose. For, by the time the sun rose to its highest point in the sky, I had made my decision. Danger was closing in, and Arthur and I must leave at once.

When I reached the children's study, it was empty except for Edward Courtenay's French tutor, a grave university student named François.

'The boys are having a lesson in the courtyard, mistress,' he said. A frown deepened his wide young brow. 'Are you well? You look … different.'

'I am quite well,' I told the tutor firmly.

His eyes flicked past me, to a point over my shoulder. I turned. It was James, the quick-witted twin.

'Master Edward and Master Arthur should be back upstairs before supper,' said James. 'Don't you want to wait and see them then, mistress?'

'No, I don't,' I snapped. 'I will see my cousin now.'

I turned and hurtled down the corridor. When I reached the first turn, I heard footsteps behind me. Both François and James followed.

'I know the way,' I called back. 'No need to accompany me.'

One more stretch and I reached the main stairs. It was hard not to run down them. But panic would not serve my intentions. I was halfway down the stairs when I heard a clatter of feet above. I looked over my shoulder. François and James still followed. My maid Alice was with them, as well as a male servant whose name I did not know.

As I turned the last corner, it sounded even louder, the footsteps of those behind me. More servants must have joined them. Why did they trail me so? I wondered, furious.

It was cool in the courtyard that morning. Layers of grey clouds covered every bit of sky. The two boys brandished flat wooden swords in the centre. Arthur waved his weapon at me, smiling. Young Edward Courtenay bowed, but his face showed confusion. I looked over my shoulder. The servants who'd followed me had grown to half a dozen. They inched forward tightly, all together, like a single body with many heads and arms.

Struggling to ignore them, I said to Master David, the head tutor, 'Good morning. After the lesson is finished, I will need to have Arthur prepared for departure. We return to Dartford today.'

'No, Joanna, no!' wailed Arthur. 'Don't want to leave.'

'I'm sorry, Arthur. This must be.' I reached out, but Arthur shrank from me.

'Mistress Stafford, I haven't received word about this from the marquess,' said Master David.

'Arthur is *my* cousin,' I said. 'The visit is at an end. I am a guest here, not a prisoner.'

Arthur ran to Edward Courtenay, and threw his arms around his waist. 'Edward, want to stay,' he wept. The older boy comforted him quietly.

'No one said you were prisoners,' Master David said stiffly. 'I apologise if I gave you that impression, Mistress Stafford.'

I silently cursed my rudeness. Fear had frayed my nerves. 'Forgive me, you did not give that impression,' I said. 'Arthur, please. Come with me for a moment.'

'No, no, no,' Arthur sobbed, clutching Edward. The Courtenay heir glared at me. He drew Arthur toward the side of the courtyard whose wall abutted the great hall. The servants shuffled forward and then spread out. They now served as a barrier between my little cousin and me.

Master David said, 'Mistress Stafford, I can send word to the marquess, and ask for instructions on change of plans. Nothing is done at the Red Rose without an authorised plan.'

I said, 'There is no need for that – I will speak to the marquess tonight myself.' It would not be an easy conversation. But it should be done. To leave in the middle of the day was cowardly, after all. We'd leave tomorrow.

James, the twin, said, 'You can't speak to him tonight. The

Marquess of Exeter will not be back at the Red Rose until November third, the day before his dinner for Baron Montague.'

'What?' I said.

'The king has moved with his privy council to Greenwich,' said Master David. 'When he is at Greenwich, my lord stays at court lodgings.'

I stared at the men, these favoured servants of the Courtenays. I was shocked that Henry had not told me of this. But, after all, I made myself scarce yesterday. When would he have had the opportunity?

There was no way around it – I'd have to make my departure arrangements through Gertrude. This course of action promised to be more unpleasant but had the advantage of Gertrude's not knowing I'd heard her words while I hid in the confessional.

I said to Alice, 'Please alert the marchioness that I am on my way to see her.'

Before she could answer, James spoke up again. 'My lady is unwell. After Mass she went straight away to bed. She sees no one but Constance when she is in this condition. You won't be received today.'

Rain spattered on our heads. I wiped a splotch from my eye as I took in everything that had been said and done here. No one sought shelter from the rain. The only sounds were the tapping of fresh rain-drops on the bricks of the courtyard and Arthur's wordless whimpering.

Darting between two servants, I ran the short distance to Arthur, my arms outstretched. 'Come with me, *now* – let's go,' I cried.

Arthur broke away from Edward Courtenay, reaching for me. But seconds before our hands touched, I was jerked back, roughly. Someone pinned my arms behind my back.

'You, too, are unwell, Mistress Stafford,' James hissed in my ear. 'You need to rest.'

My arms ached from his grip. 'This is monstrous – unhand me,' I shouted.

Master David held up his hand. I expected him to order James to release me.

But no.

'Take her to her room at once,' he said.

James hauled me toward the doorway, my shoulders burning. I could not say anything to Arthur, who was crying again, loudly. I caught a glimpse of Alice. She, too, had tears in her eyes.

'You will be sorry for this,' I told James, as he pushed me into the corridor.

'I don't think so,' he grunted. 'I believe you are the one who will be sorry.'

We passed a few wide-eyed servants on the way to my bedchamber. There was no mistaking the force that was being used. James had his hand clamped around my forearm the entire walk, half dragging me. But no one said anything or tried to help me. One of the highest officers of the household, such as Charles, would surely have asked why I was being treated roughly. But I did not see him before being shoved into my room. The door slammed shut.

I sat on the edge of my bed, rubbing my sore arms. James's grip would leave large bruises. At first I was full of rage. But then it gave way to mounting fear. James was no fool. He would only have acted this way if he were certain there would be no consequences. He must have been ordered to prevent me from ever leaving the Red Rose. I should have employed more cunning in extricating Arthur. I'd made the mistake of announcing my intentions, of being obvious. Issuing orders to people who had no cause to obey me.

I couldn't make that mistake again.

After I had calmed myself, I opened the door, to go in search of Charles. But standing guard in the hallway was James. He didn't speak, just shook his head, his muscular arms folded across his chest.

I said, 'You have no right to hold me here.'

He made no reply.

'I want you to tell the Marchioness of Exeter that I must speak with her at once,' I said.

James answered, 'My lady is unwell, Mistress Stafford. I told you that. She cannot be disturbed.'

I fought down an impulse to scream, scream so loudly that the people walking by on Suffolk Lane would hear. But to act like a madwoman wouldn't get Arthur and me out of the house. I had no choice but to go back into my room.

Shortly after, Alice arrived with dinner on a tray, her eyes red and puffy. I sensed that my maid would help me, if James knew nothing of it. But he watched us closely. Alice left and I ignored the food. Instead, I scribbled a short note, asking her to go in search of Charles and bid him come to my aid. Next time I saw her, I'd slip her the message.

But Alice never returned. I walked the floor, turning my note over and over until its corners frayed. There was no stirring on the street at the return of Henry Courtenay – he truly must have transferred to Greenwich. After the afternoon shadows lengthened into darkness, it was Joseph, the slow-witted twin, who brought a tray of supper. His expression was so wary, I knew it hopeless to try to persuade him of anything.

The flames faltered to embers in the fireplace. I did not call for help nor stir it myself. I sat in the dark. The room's chill spread, swallowing up the last islands of warmth. 'I am a guest here, not a prisoner,' I'd informed Master David. I was wrong. For I was a prisoner of the Red Rose just as surely as in the months I was confined in the Tower of London.

Eventually the room grew so cold, I crawled under the thick blankets. I did not change into my shift. Instead, fully dressed, I curled up, my knees drawn toward my chest. How I prayed for an answer. I needed to trust in Christ to show me the path.

I was in the middle of a dream when a candle warmed my face. I opened my eyes.

A man's face loomed over me. He held a candle high in a dark room. It was Henry Courtenay, Marquess of Exeter, and he was sitting on my bed.

13

I cried out, but the marquess clamped a wet, cold hand over my mouth. 'Hush, Joanna, please,' he whispered. 'They'll hear you. I'm not going to hurt you. Please. I must talk to you.'

I nodded, and he removed his hand. His clothes, his hat, even his face, were wet. I glanced at the window. It was thickest black outside.

'What are you doing here?' I asked. 'James said you were at Greenwich.'

'I was, but when the messenger brought word from Charles that you'd been confined to your room, I rode home. I can't stay long. I have to be at court this morning.'

'How did Charles know what happened to me? I tried to get him a message but I failed.'

'It is my house. Do you think my people do not know what occurs? It is just a matter of the proper action.' He grimaced. 'I should not be surprised you sought to leave, after what you overheard in chapel. I've told him to make sure that you are not confined tomorrow. You will have complete freedom of movement.'

'Henry,' I said, 'why wasn't I allowed to leave the Red Rose?'

My cousin walked over to the fireplace and bent down, using his candle to ignite a flame. 'Such a cold night,' he muttered.

After a moment he stood up again.

'Joanna, I need your help,' he said.

'*My* help?'

He walked over to the window facing the lane and peered into the blackness. What Henry Courtenay needed to tell me would not come easily.

'I love Gertrude,' he said finally. 'So much. No one can ever know what I feel for her – and she for me.' His voice trailed away. I churned with emotions: embarrassed and impatient and confused, yes, but moved as well.

'Gertrude's mother died when she was a child,' he continued after a moment. 'Lord Mountjoy was Queen Katherine's chamberlain. He didn't send her away. He brought her up close, near the queen's rooms always. So Katherine of Aragon was in many ways a mother to her. And the Lady Mary was like a sister.'

Still looking out the window, he said, 'Are you familiar with Sister Elizabeth Barton?'

My fingers turned to talons, gripping the side of the bed. 'Yes,' I whispered. How grateful I was that he did not see my face.

He said, 'Gertrude went to see the nun or the nun came to her, several times, three at least, beginning in 1529. I think those trips Gertrude made to Canterbury are when her obsession with prophecy began. She went to solicit Elizabeth Barton to see into the future, see what would happen to the king and to our family.'

He turned to look at me. My horror must have been written large on my face. *Gertrude had been a follower of Sister Elizabeth Barton.*

Henry said, vigorously, 'That's not what Gertrude admitted to, of course. She said she sought out Sister Barton to ask if she would ever have another child. But I know there was more. When they examined Sister Barton for treason, when they searched her papers and possessions, the Saint Sepulchre records, that's when Gertrude's visits became known. She had to write a letter to the king, confess to grievous mistakes in judgement, and plead for royal mercy. I feared the letter would not be enough. It was. My wife did not go to trial.'

What if they knew of my visit with my mother to Saint Sepulchre? I thought, horrified. Aloud, I said, 'You should have told me this before you invited me to stay here.'

Henry lowered his head. 'Yes,' he said. 'You're right.'

Now I had to know everything.

'Gertrude went to great lengths to find me and bring me here. Now she prevents me from leaving. Why?'

Henry paced before the fire. 'The idea did not come from her,' he said. 'Before this past summer, she never spoke of you. Then suddenly she bought your name up again and again, insisting we must go to Dartford to seek you out.'

'Was it the Lady Mary who bade her do it?' I pressed.

Henry threw up his hands. 'I don't know, Joanna. It is possible, though I can't think why.'

He was right. It didn't make sense for the Lady Mary to push for me to go to London. But I couldn't think of anyone else.

'In truth, it is not your presence here that worries me most, Joanna. It is what interests Gertrude now pursues. She swears to me that there are no more conspiracies. But I fear that her reverence for Katherine of Aragon and the empire of Charles the Fifth – those passions override all.'

'Wait,' I said. 'No *more* conspiracies?'

'Gertrude has passed her own messages to Eustace Chapuys, the ambassador to the Emperor Charles. And she has gone to see him, in disguise, to tell Chapuys what she knows of the king and council. She promises me that she no longer meets with him, but I am not sure I believe her.'

I gripped the bedpost. She had supplied a foreign ruler with information. 'And have you conspired against the king?'

The marquess straightened before me. 'I support the true faith of the Catholic Church and the monasteries – as does everyone from the old families. I grieved for Katherine of Aragon and I love her daughter. But I am loyal to my anointed sovereign.'

'Then you must stop her,' I said. 'You *must.*'

'I will,' he said fervently. 'After the dinner on November fourth, I will find an excuse to go west with my wife. I will get her under control.'

'Why does this dinner mean so much to you?' I demanded.

Henry said, 'Why must it be a matter of suspicion that I choose to dine with my closest friend?'

He sat next to me on the bed. It creaked under his weight.

'Only one week remains until the dinner for Montague,' he said. 'Don't leave. Please, keep watch over Gertrude. She cannot conspire with you present. Stay close to her side.'

I said, 'But I can do nothing to stop Gertrude should her will be set on a course. Especially not while she is surrounded by her personal servants.'

'You can send word to me through Charles.'

I sank forward, my head in my hands. 'You're asking me to spy,' I said into my palms. I remembered my impotent fury when Bishop Gardiner forced me to spy for him, when I searched the priory for the Athelstan crown. It was a dishonourable, sordid business.

Henry said, 'I'm sorry, Joanna. There's no one else who can help me in this way.'

The fire popped and sizzled. I watched his weariness shade to anguish.

'Prophecy,' he whispered. 'I've begged her to stay clear of its lure. To imagine and compass the deposition and death of the king is treason.'

He paced the floor again. 'It's not just Gertrude – the whole kingdom has gone mad. When I was a boy, there were no seers people rushed to pay, no revelations passed around. But now every village crone spouts predictions. They claim they're received wisdom from the Celts, from Merlin's scroll dug up out of the ground. It's rubbish – and worse.'

'There is nothing I detest more than prophecy,' I said.

He nodded rapidly. 'Then you'll find a way to dissuade her, should she make a plan in the next week to visit a seer?'

'I will do my utmost.'

He took a step toward me. 'And if you can't dissuade her, Joanna, then you'll go with her? And then tell me what is said?'

'*No* – that cannot be!' I leaped off the bed. 'Henry, I cannot go near anyone who spouts prophecy.'

'I ask too much of you,' he muttered. 'I humbly ask forgiveness, Joanna. It's just that I'm so … afraid.'

He stared at the floor for nearly a moment, and then said in a rush, 'Don't you see? If something were to – were to – *happen* to me – when I think of Edward in the Tower, without me, I can't endure it. He'd be so frightened in there. All alone. I can't bear the thought of it, I can't—' Henry's voice broke. 'O Christ in Heaven, preserve him.'

He turned away from me, his right arm thrown over his face. Muffled gasping sounds filled my room. It was as if he were trying to swallow his own sobs.

A single knock on the door made Henry stop. 'Just a minute, Charles,' he called.

'Henry,' I said, 'know that I will do everything I can to help you here. I will stay close to Gertrude. I will try to influence her – as much as it is possible for me to do. And then I will go.'

'Bless you, Joanna,' he said, not quite meeting my eyes. And he hurried out the door.

I did not go back to sleep. I did nothing but pray for strength and wisdom. After the sun came up, Alice appeared, wide-eyed. I said nothing to her about leaving the Red Rose. Instead, I asked her to fetch me food and clothing. She happily complied.

Gertrude was not alone that morning. A strange man sat next to her. They looked down at something, in her lap. A large box. Gertrude's back was turned toward me, so I could not quite tell. My observation of her must now begin.

'Good morning,' I said. My voice sounded natural.

Gertrude whipped around. Her face was drawn – perhaps the illness was genuine. But then a smile warmed her features. 'Joanna, how sweet of you to visit.' She darted toward me and kissed me, enveloping me with her exotic scent. She must have just bathed. 'Please share in this beauty.'

She gestured to her guest and he tilted the box in his lap. It was piled with fabric samples, all colours and textures. Velvets and brocades and silks.

'Show her the one,' Gertrude commanded.

What he unwrapped gleamed like the shimmer of a waterfall.

'Cloth of silver, from the finest merchant in all of Brussels,' Gertrude said. 'I've decided. Garments shall be made for you for my lord's dinner. My favourite dressmaker should finish in time, with this material.'

'I am to wear this?' I said.

Gertrude said, 'Baron Montague is of the blood royal. He was the heir presumptive to the throne, until the birth of Prince Edward. We must look our best.'

She folded her hands. Waited for my protest, for my refusal to accept it. That is what would have been expected.

'Thank you, Gertrude,' I said.

And so it began. Three days of forever being in Gertrude's company. There were no noteworthy guests. She did not pay any calls. We embroidered, we read, we listened to music. One evening I sat by her bath and read from a book of Christian lamentations. We saw Arthur and Edward twice a day. The boys seemed to have forgotten the scene in the courtyard, and no one made any reference to my demand to leave. The king was never mentioned, nor his daughter Mary – nor her cousin, the Emperor Charles. It was all so benevolent, so free of conspiracy, that there were moments when Henry's pleadings to stand watch over her receded. But I did not forget.

And then, on the last day of October, I experienced a jolt.

Coming down the main passageway, Alice right behind me, I heard a shout ahead. Servants carried chairs and boxes and trays. Once I'd come closer, I realised to where: the main doors of the great hall yawned open.

'What are they doing?' I asked Alice.

'Preparing for my lord's dinner for Baron Montague,' she answered.

Gertrude, I learned, was in the kitchens, and I hurried there. The time had come to reveal my visions in the great hall, for I could not possibly dine in that room.

The cooks had hung an iron pot over a large fire. Gertrude peeked into it, an apron tied around her brocade skirt. A sweet musky smell reached me from across the kitchen.

'Joanna, come and see,' she called out gaily. 'This will show the Lady C.!'

I peered into the pot – it bubbled with an orange liquid, pulpy and marked with seeds.

'I'm making a gift of quince preserves to her. Everyone's doing such presents this season. Lady Carew's preserves are superb. I must do better.'

She shrugged and laughed, in that winning way she had of saying, yes, isn't this frivolous but I'm doing it and don't I do it well. I was no longer seduced by Gertrude's charm. But I acknowledged its potency.

'Is it necessary that the dinner be held in the great hall?' I asked.

Gertrude stirred her preserves with a long spoon. 'That's where we always have it. The room is only used for the yearly dinner for Montague. The men enjoy feasting there. They call it "playing Plantagenet".'

'But it's so huge and we are a small party,' I said.

'Not *that* small,' she answered. 'There'll be Henry and me, and you, and Father Timothy. And then there are Baron Montague, his sister-in-law, and Sir Edward Neville. Neville comes to these dinners, too – if he is in London. Which he is.'

I was baffled. 'Why does Baron Montague bring his sister-in-law and not his wife?'

A frown line danced between Gertrude's eyes as she stirred.

'Baron Montague's wife died early this year, Joanna. I assumed you knew that.'

'No, but I am sorry for Baron Montague's loss,' I said. Still confused, I asked, 'Who is the sister-in-law?'

'Christine is the wife of Godfrey Pole.'

'But Godfrey isn't coming himself?' This dinner did not make sense.

Gertrude's eyes flicked up, at me, and then back into the pot of quince preserves. 'Godfrey is in the Tower.'

Just the word *Tower* weakened me. The steam heated the kitchen. But my rush of memory – those months in a cell, trapped behind walls so thick that no cannon fire could make them tremble – left me chilled.

'Why is Godfrey Pole held there?' I asked.

'I believe he is being questioned about his brother, Reginald Pole, who is in Rome, writing papers against the king, his divorce from Queen Katherine, and his break from the church. We have all disowned Reginald, of course' – Gertrude stirred faster – 'but the king's men want to be certain of loyalty.'

'How long has he been confined?'

Gertrude said briskly, 'It is for my husband to answer all such questions – it is his dinner, not mine.'

There was no question now of voicing my fears of the great hall. I backed away from Gertrude and her simmering pot.

The rest of the day, I could not concentrate on needlework or conversation. That night I was not the least sleepy, so I read by candle for a long time, but restlessly. I had no idea that the king's suspicions of those with any trace of royal blood – those who could conceivably make a claim to succeed him – had led to imprisonment. I wished I had not submitted to Henry's pleadings to remain here. Everything about the dinner, now four days away, was wrong.

I don't know what time it was when the horse whinnied. Hoofs slammed on cobblestone. Another whinny. Leaving my candle by the bed, I went to the window.

There were four horses on Suffolk Lane, all of them mounted. One gave his rider trouble. A single torch blazed in a fixture next to the entranceway, affording me enough light to recognise the auburn-haired rider as he spun around: Joseph. And yes, his twin brother, James, rode a grey. With a start, I realised two women accompanied them. Joseph finally got control of his horse, and James signalled that it was time to go.

I strained to see the women. They weren't ladies, that was obvious from their drab clothes. Their faces were obscured by long hoods. Could they be fellow servants? How would the Courtenays feel about the twins, trusted servants, riding out late, into the wicked dangers of the night, with women?

The foursome rode up the street, away from the Thames. The woman who was second from last pulled on the reins, reached up and adjusted her hood. The torchlight danced on her. She had long, slender fingers. I knew this hand, this quick but elegant movement. The fingers were long. There were usually gold rings encircling two or even three of them – but not tonight.

Those were the hands of Gertrude Courtenay.

14

I stood at that window long after the four of them disappeared. How easily I'd been fooled. Gertrude conspired, and it must be a dangerous cause indeed for her to ride disguised into the streets of London at night, defying curfew. She took bold advantage of her husband's absence.

I determined I would stay awake until they returned, no matter how late the hour. And then I'd make a report to the marquess through Charles, as I had promised.

I had no timepiece in my room, so I never knew how long Gertrude and the others were gone from the Red Rose. It seemed like most of the night. Several times I nearly surrendered to exhaustion. But I fought off temptation.

I'd again splashed water in my face when I heard a faint noise. I crept to the window. The torch had been extinguished outside. There was no moon. But I could just make out four riders coming down Suffolk Lane. Two of them dismounted and approached the entryway. The others rode to the stables. Gertrude was home.

I fell asleep the instant I lay down. It had been a gruelling night. What felt like moments later, someone gently shook my shoulder.

Alice said, 'I'm sorry, mistress. I knocked. But you didn't answer. The dressmaker is here.'

I'd forgotten the fitting. I couldn't rub the weariness from my eyes. I could not seem to assemble my thoughts. I lamented such thick-headedness. I'd need all my wits now.

'Tell Charles that I will have a message for him this morning,' I muttered.

I did not want to be pinned and pinched by dressmakers. Or to be in the presence of Gertrude.

To my surprise, the Marchioness of Exeter did not appear weary at all. As the dressmaker and her apprentice pulled me this way and that,

Gertrude watched closely. The precious cloth of silver, which looked so light in the merchant's box, weighed heavy on my limbs.

Yet as I studied her, a difference became apparent. Her smiles, her laughter, her pointing – all carried an extra degree of animation. I remembered when we met, in Dartford, and she'd shown that same brittle excitement beneath her courtly words and gestures. I thought it her normal manner then. But while in the Red Rose, she calmed herself; the excitement lessened. What had revived it? It could only be what happened last night.

When the fitting was over, Gertrude insisted I remain.

'You looked beautiful in that cloth of silver, Joanna,' she said. 'It sets off your colouring.'

I said nothing.

In that same false tone, Gertrude said, 'My confectioner is trying a different mixture, employing the new sugars of the islands across the sea. Tell me how this treat tastes. If you like it, I'll order it for our dinner.'

Reluctantly, I took a seat next to her. The treat made me wince. 'Too sweet,' I said.

'Oh, really?' Gertrude mock-pouted with disappointment.

'I shouldn't be the one you ask. I don't much care for treats.'

Gertrude shifted in her chair and tilted her head. 'Joanna denies herself all pleasures, even a sweet.'

I could not bear her teasing any longer. Once again, I made to leave. And once again she detained me. This time she rose from her chair and stood before me, her hands on her hips.

'Joanna, whatever is the matter?' she asked. 'Are you ill?'

'No.' I started to edge around her.

'Did you have trouble sleeping?' she pressed.

There was not a trace of anything but affection in those large brown eyes. Try on these clothes, eat a treat. Yet she plotted and lied, putting her husband and son – and myself and Arthur – in the greatest danger.

'No,' I said slowly. 'I did not sleep well.'

It was darkly thrilling, this decision I had just made. No more dissembling. *I shall confront her*, I thought. *I am not afraid*. Anger sent strength into my bones and cleared my mind of confusion. From a distance rose the image of Brother Edmund, shaking his head, pleading with me to curb my anger. But he was not present to dissuade me.

'Why not?' she asked.

I answered: 'I was awake for hours, waiting for *you* to return.'

The corners of her mouth twitched. But Gertrude did not flinch.

At that very moment, Constance opened the door to say, 'My lady, Charles is here. He wants to speak with Mistress Joanna. He said she has a message for him.'

Without taking her eyes off me, Gertrude said, 'Tell Charles to wait.'

After we were alone again, she said, perfectly calm, 'Aren't you going to ask me where I went? You wouldn't want your message to my husband to be incomplete of facts. That is what you arranged, isn't it? When he came in secret to your bedchamber – that you'd send messages through Charles? I think I should be the one questioning *you*, Joanna. About your light conduct with my husband.'

'You know that is not true,' I said, furious.

'Do I?' she said. 'I suppose so.' She laughed.

Her laugh made me even angrier. 'Yes, my lady, I will send word to the marquess of your leaving the house last night.'

I made for the door. But before I took three steps, she seized me by the wrist, just as she had in Dartford. Her grip was stronger this time.

'We didn't travel far, Joanna. I had an appointment with a man. A hard man to find. But I finally found him and made arrangements to go to his secret place, and on the most propitious date and time of the year for his particular business.'

I pulled free my wrist but did not move toward the door. If Gertrude was of a mind to reveal herself, I would discover it all.

'What is his name?' I asked.

'I don't know his real name. He has taken the name Orobas.'

'Taken?' I repeated impatiently. 'What does that mean? What sort of name is "Orobas"?'

A nerve danced on the side of Gertrude's slender throat. 'I believe it is of Latin origin. As to why he took it, I think it is because Scriptures say the demon Orobas serves as the chief oracle in Hell.'

I made the sign of the cross.

'A *demon*?' I cried. 'You are consorting with those who worship demons? It is the worst sort of blasphemy. You have gone mad, Gertrude.'

'I am not mad,' she said, 'Orobas is not a demon worshipper. It's just a name. I am not sure what the description is. I will settle on "seer". And I do not consort with him. I pay him, and I pay him well, to divine the future. Last night he shared with me a prophecy I've waited a long time to hear. I must perform one more task and then I will learn the rest. He has sworn it.'

I dropped to my knees before Gertrude Courtenay and clasped my hands. 'I plead with you – I beg you – do not proceed. Do not seek out prophecy. It is so dangerous to you and your family, to all who love you. In the name of the Virgin, I implore you to stop.'

She looked down at me, entirely unmoved. 'It really doesn't suit you, Joanna. To beg on your knees. Which is rather amusing, when one remembers you were almost a nun.' She yanked me to my feet. Our faces were inches apart. 'I must know – what did she say to you? What did Sister Elizabeth Barton say to frighten you this badly?'

I ripped myself from her grasp. I backed away from her so fast I stumbled over a table.

'You know I went to Canterbury,' I stammered.

'I know that in October in the Year of Our Lord 1528, Sister Elizabeth Barton informed you that you would come after if she should fail to stop the king of England. She told me that herself. But the precise prophecy that concerned you? She shared it with not a soul. I don't believe anyone knows it but you and Sister Elizabeth, and she's dead.'

Gertrude bore down on me again, her eyes afire, like a hunter who is seconds from killing long-sought prey.

'Sister Elizabeth Barton recanted,' I said. 'The prophecy meant nothing.'

'You know that's not true,' Gertrude said. 'And you know why she gave a false recantation. I am certain that I know the reason that Sister Elizabeth Barton broke down in the Tower and begged to deny her prophecies. Her gift of prophecy was genuine – given by God. She must have falsely recanted because it was the only way to stop their questions before they forced your secret from her. She did it to protect *you.*'

'No, no, no,' I said, covering my ears. 'I won't hear this.'

Gertrude wrenched my hands away. 'Stop it,' she hissed. 'You're not a child. You are the key to our enterprise, you are the one who could deliver us from Henry Tudor and restore the true faith to England. *But you won't.*'

'I don't know what you imagine can be done,' I said, shaking my head violently. 'The king has dissolved the monasteries, the churches are stripped. We have no choice but to conform.'

'Conform?' she cried. 'When our souls are in peril, you of all people counsel us to conform? Just weeks ago, the king took his latest step against the true faith, the most blasphemous of all. He sacked the shrine of Saint Thomas Becket in Canterbury. All of the jewels and precious objects were carted to the royal treasury. All that is left now are the holy bones of the saint himself.'

In a dozen steps, perhaps less, I could reach the door. Charles was just outside. Gertrude was strong, but if I could get around her and run for the door, she could not prevent me from escaping this room.

I began to move, but Gertrude thrust herself directly in front of me.

'If you don't get out of my way, I will scream,' I said.

'No, you won't,' she said. 'There will be no message for Charles today. And not only that. Tomorrow night I am going back to see Orobas, and you will come with me. You must come of your own free will and unconstrained.'

It was a savage blow, to hear those words again. So the letter *did* concern me. I now saw that everything she said or did in this house was to drive me toward the next stage in the prophecy.

'I will never agree to that,' I said.

'Give us what we want, Joanna,' she said, her voice thick with desperation.

'Us?' I repeated. 'Who told you to secure me from Dartford? Who tells you to take me to a seer now?'

Gertrude said, 'I can never tell you that.'

Enraged, I said, 'I will not go with you tomorrow or any other day, Gertrude. I shall send a message to the marquess and then leave this house.'

Her lower lip trembled. Red patches flared in her hollow cheeks. 'Don't you care what I tell my husband about you after you've gone?'

'No.'

'That his precious Joanna Stafford secretly met with Sister Elizabeth Barton, just as I did? That you are a liar and a traitor too?'

I flinched from her ugly words but said, 'Tell him anything you want.'

'Oh, I don't believe that. There is one thing you don't want Henry or anyone else to know, something that has nothing to do with prophecy.'

The door swung open and Constance reappeared. 'Charles is most insistent, my lady. He said he must speak with Mistress Stafford.'

I moved toward Constance, and Charles waiting behind her, but Gertrude suddenly had me by the shoulders.

'And what if I tell others that you were once the whore of George Boleyn?' Gertrude whispered in my ear.

I could not find my voice, could not breathe. *This is what it is like*, I thought. *This is what it is like for the world to end.*

Finally I managed three words: 'Shut the door.'

Constance slipped back out. There was a muffled conversation and then the sound of footsteps walking away.

'You should sit down, Joanna,' said Gertrude. Her desperate tone was gone. She was all solicitude. 'You are not well.'

I turned my back as I struggled to control myself. Finally I said, my voice hoarse: 'Lady Rochford lied to you.'

'Oh, Joanna,' Gertrude said. 'It is obvious that she told me the truth.'

Tears coursed down my cheeks. 'I was sixteen years old.'

Gertrude shook her head. 'If it's any comfort to you, just before he was executed, Boleyn told the crowd he was a sinner who deserved death. Perhaps he was thinking of you and all the other girls he hurt.'

I made fists and pressed them against my eyes, to stop the weeping. But it did not work. The tears seeped through my fingers. 'Who else knows?' I said.

'No one,' said Gertrude. 'And I will never tell a living soul, I swear to you before God – *if* you go with me tomorrow. The seer said he would not complete his prophecy without you being present. He stipulated that you must come of your own free will.'

For so long I had feared that the second prophet would divine my future and bring me closer to a terrifying destiny. Nearly as great was my fear that George Boleyn's crime against me would be revealed. I did nothing to encourage him and struggled to get away from him when he trapped me in the curtained corner of his sister's receiving room, but he was too strong. I knew that women were never believed. I'd always been afraid of how people would at once condemn me and my family if his attack on me were known. Now my fears had intertwined, and by doing so become so powerful that I was crushed to nothing.

I would do what Gertrude asked. She knew that. I could not live with the sordid truth being exposed.

Then a new fear took hold. 'But how can you be sure of Jane Boleyn, that she has told no one else what her husband did to me?' I asked. 'Or that she will remain silent in the future?'

Gertrude said nothing. I lowered my fists from my eyes and turned to face her. I expected to see a woman gloating. But it was the opposite. Hers was a visage of aged sorrow. The faint lines crisscrossing Gertrude's face had deepened. In the last ten minutes, she had truly aged ten years.

'Tell me,' I said, louder. 'Set my mind at rest that in return for going with you I shall never be shamed before the world. How can you be this sure of Lady Rochford's silence?'

Gertrude sank into her chair. Her hands trembling in her lap, she said, 'Because Jane Boleyn never told me anything. She is ignorant of his actions against you. I saw how you reacted to meeting the widow of George Boleyn – and the whole court knew of his nature, of his predilection for despoiling girls. I wagered that that was what happened to you. It was a gamble. And I won.'

PART THREE

15

The doors of the Red Rose were always locked after sundown. The servants finished their duties sometime after seven o'clock and found their beds by eight. But that night, at ten, there was a tapping at my door. It was James, dressed in a threadbare coat and breeches. Without a word, he held out his hand, palm up. I took it, though to do so made me shudder. He pulled me out of my room and into the darkness.

He used no candle to light our way. James was familiar with each turn of the corridor, every length of step, and he made his way forward, his left hand running along the wall. With his right he pulled me after him, but gently. I was not dragged through the house, as when I attempted to flee with Arthur. Tonight I was precious cargo.

Off the larder was a door that led to a back passageway connecting the Red Rose to a narrow passageway leading to the street. In moments we were on the street. I could smell the dank waters of the Thames as we made our way to the Courtenay stables.

'Don't let her leave,' James told his twin once he'd deposited me inside, and then hurried back. Joseph grunted. He watched me, fingering a rope with both hands, as if he ached to tie me.

I ignored him as I waited. I listened to the horses chew and move in their stalls. And every moment I thought about Sister Elizabeth Barton. Could it be true, what Gertrude said? Had Sister Elizabeth falsely recanted the messages in her visions to put a halt to the interrogations and so prevent the king's men from learning of me?

'You are the one who will come after . . .'

James led in Gertrude, herself dressed in humble bodice, kirtle, and cloak. Constance was nowhere to be seen. Four would ride out again, but this time I would complete the quartet.

We rode to the top of Suffolk Lane and turned onto a wider street, lined with two-storey wood and plaster buildings. Not a single candle glowed within any of them. The curfew had been rung long ago; all decent folk were asleep. London days were shrill with noise – bells and shouting and laughter and screams – but this night was deathly still.

At a curve in the street, James suddenly leaped from his horse and whistled, in short, sharp bursts.

Two ran out of an alleyway. They carried something in a long bundle between them and offered it to James. An acrid smell filled the air, and then golden light soared. The boys brought torches for our journey.

More dark figures slipped out of the alleyway. They were men this time, six of them. One by one, the men grabbed the coins offered by James. The torchlight revealed the blunt clubs and sharpened sticks in their grip.

We formed a group, with Gertrude and I in the centre, led by James and the torch carriers, and surrounded by hired ruffians. Joseph came last.

Gertrude spoke to me for the first time. 'It takes more than two linkboys to see us through the parts of London we must travel tonight. These men are being paid more coins than they would otherwise see in a year to keep us safe.'

After a moment I responded, 'I pray to God they fail in their task so we never reach our destination.'

Gertrude nudged her horse to ride closer to me. She did not remove her hood; I could not see her face. But I heard every word. 'Joanna, you are someone who has suffered more than most because of the policies of the king. Your uncle beheaded, your cousin horribly burned. Your family fortune robbed. And then, your priory, your spiritual and temporal home, destroyed. And yet you will do nothing – nothing – to fight back.'

Her defiant words bewildered me. 'Fight back?' I repeated. The notion of it was bizarre. Henry VIII was served by men of utter ruthlessness. He had broken the church leadership; men of arms took orders only from him. But it was only his power that held his subjects in fear.

I said, 'The king is our anointed sovereign, we are bound by God to obey him as his subjects.'

'Are you certain of that?' Gertrude asked.

For the first time, I questioned the sanity of Gertrude Courtenay. 'Henry the Eighth is the *king*,' I hissed.

'Perhaps not for much longer,' she retorted. 'The pope wrote a bull of excommunication two years ago. His Holiness made many efforts to bring England back into the fold, but with the latest abominations, the sacking of the holy shrines, he is now close to publishing it. Henry the Eighth will be excommunicated from the Catholic Church.'

Excommunicated. The word made me tremble, as it would any Christian. Our family chaplain, to tame the unruly Stafford children, liked to wield the word like a weapon, drawing out each syllable. I could still hear his shrill voice all these years later: 'To be ex-com-mun-i-cat-ed is to be banned from God's grace; shunned, unable to take sacrament. The rite of bell, book, and candle would be summoned – the candle to be snuffed at the end because the offender is *removed from the light of God.*'

'How could a king rule after being excommunicated?' I muttered, more to myself than to Gertrude, but she took up my question with vigour.

'He couldn't,' she said. 'And it will be the *duty* of other Christian kings to depose him. We his subjects could not rally to the defence of King Henry. Not if we wished to remain faithful to the Holy Father.'

If this were true, it changed all. Yet could I put my trust in Gertrude's account? After a moment, I said, 'You haven't been waiting for the pope to sanctify your actions up to now. What treason have you already committed against the king?'

Gertrude snorted. 'No acts of treason. Although, yes, I have delivered the kingdom from a certain source of torment. I removed the Boleyns. You have me to thank for that bit of business.'

'*You* did that?' I was struck by how Gertrude used the word *remove* to describe the arrest, trial, and execution of Anne and George Boleyn.

'While many men of the court hated the Boleyns, they did little but complain. The Duke of Norfolk tossed a few bonny sluts at the king, to distract him and weaken Anne's hold. But it didn't work. I've watched King Henry all my life – I know his way with women. We had to find a woman who was the opposite of Anne Boleyn. I was the one who secured her. Jane Seymour had served Queen Katherine, she had been at the court for years. She was so unimpressive, no one had ever courted her. But Jane had one quality that was more important than any beauty or wit. And it is the same quality you singularly lack, Joanna. She was *ambitious*. She followed my instructions precisely in how to capture the love of the king.'

Amid my disgust at Gertrude's pandering, I had to acknowledge the boldness of such a scheme – and its success. Yet I realised something. 'You made her queen and annihilated the Boleyns – to what end? The king has turned his back on Rome. The monasteries still fell. Queen Jane did nothing to prevent it.'

'Queen Jane tried to save the monasteries, you have no notion of the risks taken,' she insisted. 'If she'd lived, as the mother of the heir to the throne, she would have had great influence.'

'It is easy to say that now,' I retorted. 'The truth can never be known.'

Before our quarrel escalated further, we were interrupted. A bearded man stood before the head linkboy, gripping a long staff with one hand.

'I am the nightwatch of the ward of Dowgate – declare your intent,' he growled.

James was the one who jumped off his horse to address the watch. They spoke for a moment; a small, bulging bag disappeared into the man's frayed coat and we were waved on.

James hurried back to Gertrude. 'The watch for the next ward will demand twice as much coin, my lady. But we must have his protection past the gaming houses. We dare not proceed without him.'

'So be it,' she said.

We rode down two more long dark streets. At the second corner, James paused at a much narrower – but cobbled – lane that sloped down a hill. At the end of it, I saw flames flicker before a low building. I also heard men's shouts – and, amazingly, the faint tinkle of music.

'We must tarry here, until the next night watch walks past, and then enlist him,' said James.

But Gertrude declared that our personal guard would more than suffice. James argued with her:

'If a mob should assemble, I cannot best them with just a handful of men, and poor and hungry specimens at that.'

'Oh, there won't be a mob – that is ludicrous,' she said. 'We cannot cower here for hours, the appointed time will pass. We ride forward. Now.'

Shaking his head, James mounted his horse. A ripple of fear moved among the half dozen men who encircled us. But no one could dissuade the Marchioness of Exeter.

Down the lane we went in a single line, very slowly, the horses' hoofs clattering on the uneven stones. For the first time I realised that the man who walked beside me was malformed, with one shoulder higher than the other. I said a quick prayer for him.

It was such a narrow lane that if I stretched out both arms I might have touched the walls of the silent houses we rode past. When we had reached the bottom of the lane, it opened onto a wide street. A bonfire blazed in front of the building closest to us. That is what I had seen from afar. Around it men stood, warming their hands, in disregard of city curfew. Inside the building flickered dozens of candles. The dark silhouette of heads crowded the long, cracked windows on the first floor. It must have been close to midnight, and the building groaned with men. So this was a gaming house. I tensed in the saddle.

I was now near enough to see the hard young faces of the men slouched over the bonfire. And to inhale its surroundings: charred wood, ale, and vomit. It was all so ... *ugly.* Yes, I had glimpsed the darkness of the soul before – but sinful cravings were usually concealed by pretence, a veneer of morality. Here there was no pretence.

The men at the bonfire peered over at us without interest. My shoulders began to ease. We would not be interfered with; James's fears had been unwarranted.

A door swung open on the side of the building. A man staggered out, his arm slung around a woman whose breasts spilled out of her bodice. They stopped short at the sight of us. I looked down, quickly, and shook the reins to signal my horse to keep going.

The woman screamed, 'What's this?'

Still I kept my head down.

'Ye taking new whores to the market?' she screeched. 'Southwark's across the river.'

Her companion laughed. Then there was a crackling noise, much nearer. One of the young men at the bonfire lurched toward me. James turned his horse around to head him off. He called out, 'We want no trouble tonight – let us pass.' He tried, without success, to keep his tone light and friendly.

'If ye want no trouble, then why do ye come here?' the whore's companion called out.

'Let us pass,' James repeated.

Out of nowhere, more people appeared at the bonfire. There were now at least ten young men outside of the gaming house, with more tumbling out the door. We were outnumbered.

16

I had told Gertrude that I hoped we would be attacked before reaching the second seer. How foolish. With one hand I gripped the reins of my horse, but with the other I fumbled for the Rosary that hung from my waist.

Gertrude was ahead of me, with five of the hired men and the linkboys huddled around her. Joseph was by her side, too, scowling.

James tried to save me. He had clearly meant to wedge himself between me and the gathering crowd, to move me to the other side of him, with Gertrude. But the men had already reached the street and blocked James's horse. He could not go farther without knocking someone aside. I saw his eyes dart up and down, as he considered dismounting. He did not.

Now just the crook-backed man stood between me and the drunken gamesters. 'Get back,' he shouted, waving his cudgel.

Someone laughed. While I watched, helpless, another man hit my protector in the face. He collapsed. I could no longer see him. But I heard his screams and grunts as the mob took turns kicking him. The cudgel flew up in the air, and they tossed it back and forth, like a toy.

A man with hair hanging past his shoulders shoved his way past the violent, seething circle. He reached up with one hand out, as if to help me dismount.

I desperately wished for a horsewhip at that instant, but I never carried one. 'Go away,' I said, like a child.

He lunged forward with both hands, trying to get them around my waist. I tried to kick him, but my foot was fastened into the stirrup.

At the top of his lungs, James shouted, 'Men of London, we want no trouble. Here – for your troubles—'

James flung a fistful of shillings in the air, to the side of the street. The light of the bonfire made them shimmer like a shower of gold.

The man who had been trying to drag me away whirled to join

the scramble for money. The mob jostled for it. With the street clear of human obstacles, I kicked the sides of my horse as hard as I could. James, Gertrude, Joseph, and I charged up the street. At the first turn, James signalled for us to follow him around. We rode until the cries of the gaming-house ruffians had died away behind us.

James held up his hand to wait for the hired men and linkboys to catch up to us on foot. Once they'd reached us, panting and sweat-soaked, James made a count.

'We've only lost the one,' he announced.

A tall hired man spoke up; it was the first time he had addressed us. 'We need to go back. I know the man and his mother, they be in my parish. He can't be left there. He's badly hurt – he may die. They'll all go back inside and then we can retrieve him.'

'No!' Gertrude said quickly. 'There is no time for that.'

I heard one of the men mutter an oath.

'What is the man's name, sir?' I asked. Gertrude made an impatient noise beside me.

'Owen, my lady,' muttered the man.

'I shall pray for Owen,' I said, 'for he received his injuries in defence of me.'

James cleared his throat. 'After our night's business is finished, and we are close to Suffolk Lane, you can retrieve him. My brother and I will assist.'

There was hesitation in their ranks. Hope surged in me. If the men refused to continue, this insane journey might well end. But after a moment they took their original positions. James nudged his horse to lead, but not before shooting Gertrude a glare of resentment. She did not see it. I did, and it sent my thoughts in a new direction: Could James possibly be pried loose from the Marchioness of Exeter?

We rode on, deeper into the darkness of London. All was quiet.

The linkboy walking in front stopped short. There was no visible sign of anything amiss, yet he looked fearful. James leaned down from his horse to say something to him.

'They've lost their nerve, Gertrude,' I said. 'They realise you care naught for their lives.'

Gertrude said, 'No man's life is more important than our mission tonight.'

'What about you?' I burst out with. 'Would you give your life so that I would hear prophecy?'

Before she answered, there was a strange muffled cry. We both turned. It was Joseph. He had stopped riding and held his head in his hands.

'What is it, brother?' called out James.

'Not right,' moaned Joseph. 'It's not right.'

My horse, so obedient up to now, shook his head and backed up a few steps. James's horse started turning in a circle, and he angrily pulled on the reins to regain control.

The first wind raised my horse's mane. The air had been sour and still from the moment we left the stables of the Red Rose. But no more. A loose shutter flapped on the building closest to us. There was a sense all along the street of something stirring. Something that had been sleeping and was now awake.

My throat closed in fear.

James had made it to Joseph's side. But he was unable to calm his brother. 'It's not right,' he said, over and over.

'Do something – he's frightening the horses,' Gertrude cried. Her own mount rocked nervously.

'He is not the cause,' I said.

Now Gertrude turned on me. 'What do you mean?' she demanded.

'We don't have much time,' I said. 'It will be a wind without rain, a terrible wind.'

Without another question, Gertrude ordered us to hurry onward. The linkboys led our group, as they struggled to keep their torches from being extinguished by the wind. At the second corner, Gertrude called, 'Halt!'

She pointed triumphantly down a street that branched off from ours. At first I saw nothing. Then the clouds eased off the moon and a building came into view. I gasped at the sight of it: a huge stone structure, four storeys tall, with a number of soaring stone columns spaced elegantly in front. Rows of windows stretched across each floor. The steeply pitched roof rose so high it seemed possible it would meet the clouds.

'That is where you are taking me?' I said in disbelief.

Gertrude laughed shortly. 'Not exactly. That is the Guildhall. The Lord Mayor of London and his council rule from there.'

We dismounted, and the hired men were ordered to a stable nearby. Horses and men would wait there for us to return. Only James and Joseph would escort Gertrude and me the rest of the way.

The wind gathered in strength; each fresh burst made Joseph shudder, as if it were causing him physical pain. It was so strong that we lost the torch flame for good. But the moon was not obscured; we could see enough of our surroundings to keep moving.

'Now – let's go,' said James, and he darted out into the street once more, Gertrude and Joseph right behind.

I followed them to a small wooden building across the street from the Guildhall. A sign with the words *Coneyhope Tavern* was visible. It was long after curfew and no businesses were open, but James peered up and down the street before waving us forward.

In seconds, we four were pressed against the rough wooden door of the building.

Just then the clouds covered the moon. I could no longer see the street, the stone buildings behind us, or the Guildhall soaring above. Someone yanked me inside a gaping door. Candles were lit. For the first time that night, I could see Gertrude's pallor. She was ashen. I could not think of any reason why we would go to such dangerous lengths to gain entry to a closed, common tavern.

Nothing could calm Joseph. He huddled in a corner, sobbing, 'It's not right, it's not right, it's not right.'

After a few minutes more of this, Gertrude said, 'James, take him out of here.'

'Where?' said James.

'If Joseph can't be calmed down, he has to go,' she said.

James stared at her, incredulous. I saw my chance and took it.

'Listen to me, James, you know very well this is madness,' I said quickly. 'We must all get back to the Red Rose.'

He looked from me to Gertrude and back again. Then, with a snort, he poured himself an ale, downed it in one gulp, and grabbed Joseph. The twins staggered out into the howling blackness.

I felt my face flush hot as I sat on a stool, in this miserable tavern. I expected Gertrude to lash out at me for trying to recruit James to flaunt her. But instead she studied me with pride. 'You said the wind would be dangerous, and you said that there would be no rain,' she said softly. 'They were right – you do have powers. If only you would stop fighting me every step of the way, Joanna, and *use* them.'

'Who are "they"?' I demanded.

Not directly answering me, she said, 'There are certain things you need to know before we proceed. Only you can deliver us from the destruction and the evil.'

I snapped, 'Sister Elizabeth Barton talked about deliverance from evil, too, and she is dead.'

Gertrude took off her cloak and hood. From the same tankard James opened, she poured ale into a chipped mug. The first sip made her wince, but she forced it down. 'This tastes wretched, but we need to fortify ourselves,' she said. 'You must drink, too.'

'I don't want it.'

'You had nothing to eat today,' she said, struggling to control her temper. 'It serves nothing to weaken yourself.'

'Gertrude, just tell me what is going to happen to me now.'

She took two steps toward me. 'Orobas is one of the most gifted seers in all of England – in all of Christendom, I wager. He knows the ancient rites that others have forgotten. To practise his art at the highest level, he must come here.'

I peered around the tavern in disbelief.

She said, 'Joanna, we will soon make our way to a very, very old chamber far below this tavern. It was once a crypt for the dead.'

'We are going to a *crypt*?' My voice cracked.

'Orobas can obtain a vision of the future only under certain conditions.' Gertrude hesitated, as if trying to decide how to phrase something she knew I would not like.

'Orobas must have contact,' she said. 'He must have contact … with the dead.'

Necromancy. My knees weakened and I sank to the floor.

'Christ, forgive me, oh, please forgive me,' I whispered.

'Orobas believes that we will see very clearly tonight,' said Gertrude, determined to pretend that I did not presently kneel on this filthy floor. 'We will know what lies ahead, how long the king will rule and how to prepare the way for who comes after.'

I clasped my hands in front of me and closed my eyes.

'Lord have mercy on us, Christ have mercy on us,' I prayed.

A floorboard creaked. But unless Gertrude had somehow moved

across the room, she did not cause it. I swallowed and forced myself to continue.

Again, there was that creak. And a second later, the sound of walking from another direction. Without a doubt, there were now three people in this room.

I stopped praying and opened my eyes. Inches away from me were taffeta skirts of deep maroon. As I rose to my feet, I looked at the woman who stood before me. Her bodice was cut low, almost as low as the woman's at the gaming house. Long brown hair fell loose on her shoulders, even though she was no girl. She must have been in her thirties. Her eyes flickered with excitement, the same sort I'd seen in Gertrude's eyes but more pronounced.

'So you brought the bride of Christ, and just at the appointed time,' she said. 'He will be pleased.'

'Yes,' said Gertrude. 'I've done all that was asked.'

The woman's stare never wavered from my face. She dipped a shallow curtsy. Her lips parted, and her pink tongue whirled in a tiny circle between her teeth.

'My name is Hagar,' she said. 'Welcome to Londinium.'

17

Hagar picked up a candle and turned away. Behind the bar, in the farthest corner, was a door. She pushed it open and stepped into a narrow walkway. Gertrude tapped me so that I would follow.

About ten feet down the walkway was another door. Inside was a small storeroom with empty barrels lining a shelf. Opposite was a box heaped with bits and scrapings of rotted cabbage, carrots, and leeks. Tiny insects spun and dove into the pile.

Hagar squatted in the middle of the floor. After a few seconds she found a chain and pulled it hard with both hands. A trapdoor shuddered. She scrambled to her feet, yanking it open. I glimpsed steps going straight down. Hagar clambered in.

Gertrude pushed me forward. 'You go next.'

The top steps were broken, uneven. I took two steps and then paused. I did not want to steady myself by touching Hagar. My head ached, whether from thirst or weariness, I wasn't sure. I rubbed my eyes. The brightness of Hagar's candle made my vision swim.

'Let me tell you of our destination, Bride of Christ,' said Hagar, who stood on her step, waiting for me to gather myself. 'In the city of London, there are places that people are drawn to for certain purposes. Celt, Roman, Saxon, Norman, all are compelled to this ground, century after century. Do you know why?'

'No,' I said, faintly.

Hagar said, 'They come to this ground, over and over, to pursue justice. Today, in the Guildhall, sit judges and lawyers. They pass laws. The guilty are sentenced to prison or to hang. It was always so. In the beginning, when Brutus the Trojan founded this city, he tamed two giants of Britannia, Gog and Magog, and forced them to guard it. Then the Druid priests held their ceremonies here. They could be very precise with their knives, very cruel indeed. But nothing compared to the Romans.' Hagar pointed. 'Beyond this wall of dirt was a gigantic amphitheatre. They held the Roman games there, where condemned criminals were torn to pieces while thousands cheered.'

As grotesque as her stories were, they drove back my dizzying weariness. The passageway we crept down had changed. The steps were made of quite different material. Pale, smooth stone. Much older, yes. And fashioned with definite symmetry of length and width.

'Not much farther, Bride of Christ,' murmured Hagar. 'I heard the Marchioness of Exeter tell you we were going to a crypt. That is not strictly true. It began as a shrine. The Romans built this room off the amphitheatre to honour the goddess Diana with prayer and sacrifice. The virgin Diana.'

Hagar snickered. I hated her mocking of chastity.

The steps had ended. We clustered in a shallow, hollowed-out area, a sort of cave that fronted a stone wall. It was made of the same light grey stone as the lower steps. Hagar gestured toward an arched opening to her left, its sides chipped and crumbling. 'Bride of Christ, before you is the entranceway to Londinium,' she said dramatically.

'It is not necessary to keep calling me that,' I said, irritated. 'I am no longer a novice at Dartford Priory. My name is Joanna—'

I placed it in that instant, between my given and my Christian name. I knew I'd heard the word *Londinium* spoken in the last weeks. The person who said it in a feverish whisper, at Gertrude's party, was Jane Boleyn.

'No,' I cried, turning on Gertrude. 'I can't.'

Gertrude took a step back. 'What's wrong?'

'This is the place Lady Rochford told you about – it's where the Boleyns summoned up their sorcery,' I said.

Gertrude remained mute. I turned to Hagar. She stood perfectly still; her face a blank. It was all the confirmation I needed. Orobas once served the Boleyns.

'I don't care what you do to me, Gertrude,' I said. 'Tell your husband, tell the world whatever you want about me. I'm past caring about that. I won't enter into the same devil pact as the Boleyns. I won't.'

'She was to come of her own free will,' Hagar said to Gertrude. 'You were carefully instructed.'

Gertrude shook her head, violently. 'Joanna, no, no, no.' She seized me by both shoulders. 'I realise that you hate me. I've lied to you and tricked you. But only because I had to. Please, please come with me. I won't let any harm befall you. I am a Christian, the same as you. I love the true Faith – just as you do.'

'Yes, I follow the true Faith, and I cannot think it is God's plan that I should be subservient to evil,' I shouted. 'It's impossible.'

Her eyes filled with tears. 'We have to find out how to defeat the king, Joanna. I know you're afraid, but you are the last hope of our cause. Think of my son, and of my husband.' The tears streamed down Gertrude's anguished face. 'This is the only way – the only way. To commit a necessary act that will save the souls of so many, can't you put your fears aside?'

Gertrude's grip loosened on me. She stumbled forward, burying her head on my shoulder. 'I beg you,' she moaned. 'I beg you.'

I extricated myself from Gertrude. 'I will go with you into this room, but I have a condition that must be met.'

Her face went slack with relief. 'Name it, Joanna.'

'Henry plans to take you and Edward and the rest of the household west after his dinner for Lord Montague. You must leave London as soon as possible, and swear to me before God that you will not conspire, not put your family's lives at risk.'

'But the cause I fight for, that's why I've brought you here,' she stammered. 'I must learn what is to be done.'

'No matter what we hear tonight, *you* must do nothing,' I said. 'If you don't agree, I will not take another step.'

Gertrude took less than a moment to decide.

'I agree,' she said, resigned.

I pulled the crucifix dangling from my dress. 'Swear on this,' I commanded her.

Gertrude bent down and pressed her lips to my crucifix.

'Now I'm ready.' I turned to Hagar. 'I come *de libero arbitrio.*'

I glared at Gertrude to make sure she understood. I knew of her conspiracies, her secret letters. She had forced me to this dark and Godless place, but I was no fool.

Hagar led Gertrude and me through the arched entranceway. There's still the third seer, I told myself. No matter what happens here tonight, I don't have to do anything until I hear prophecy from a third – that is what Sister Elizabeth Barton said. And I will never do that.

The shrine was about twenty feet long. It had not been well kept. The walls were damp and chipped. A pillar lay in pieces on the floor. A

statue next to the door had long ago been toppled – only a pair of slender women's feet remained, rooted in mid-flight to a block of marble.
One candle flickered in the corner. Hagar used hers to light two more.
The stronger light revealed painted figures on the walls: wide-eyed
people wearing capes and carrying shields stared back at me. Strange
words were scrawled over their faces. There were two shallow circular
pits carved out of the floor. A rectangular stone pressed against the far
wall – long enough to contain a body.

But realising that this tomb contained human remains was not
the worst aspect of this room. It was the smell: sour and rotten, like a
butcher yard. This place carried the odour of fresh death, yet the crypt
was hundreds of years old.

At the far end of the room were two pillars equal distance apart.
Between them was blackness. But then the blackness moved and
turned into a wide column of its own.

I froze where I stood.

The black column moved forward, into the candlelight. A shin-
ing white head loomed atop it. I was looking at a man wearing a loose
black robe, like a friar's unbelted cape. And yet there were strange rippling movements beneath the loose robe. It was as if he were unfurling
himself.

The man opened the front of his robe and a boy emerged. He was
no more than eleven years old. The boy stumbled forward, his eyes as
blank as Hagar's had been when I said the name *Boleyn*.

'Come with me, Son,' said Hagar. She kissed him on the cheek and
turned him toward the door.

'Gertrude, no,' I said hoarsely. 'This is monstrous. It can't be borne.'

She whispered, 'It's too late now, Joanna. We cannot leave.'

A man's deep, gravelly voice said, 'Have you come to preach to me,
Bride of Christ?'

The tall man moved toward us. This could only be Orobas. He
was a truly terrifying sight. There was not a hair on his skull. He had a
high, narrow forehead; his nose jutted out in a proud beak. Even in the
candlelight, those eyes brimmed with contempt.

'That is not a woman's place, to preach,' he said. 'It is the place of
the priests and friars you serve. Don't you know that they would burn
with desire for Hagar's son?'

I fought down my urge to flee from this room. 'You are wrong,' I said, forcing strength into my words. 'You don't know anything about those good men. And I don't serve anyone but God and the Virgin.'

He smiled, revealing a line of fine white teeth. 'And me – tonight,' he said.

'No,' I said.

'Ah, so full of righteous fury. You think you saw something, Bride of Christ, but your perceptions, formed in such a narrow and dark little world, are inadequate to your surroundings tonight. It was not what you thought.' He gestured dismissively toward the mother and son in the doorway, and they left the chamber.

'Hagar's son is of an auspicious age and so I was drawing on his power, nothing more,' he said. 'In the ancient world, only boys such as him could look into a bowl of shimmering liquid and read the portents of the future.'

Gertrude shifted next to me. 'The future is what we seek here,' she said, impatiently.

He nodded. 'And you shall have it. All is in alignment now for the visions. The handmaidens of Christ, the two who took the veil within the walls of chastity, will come together in this place, a shrine to Diana.'

I wasn't sure I'd heard him correctly. 'Gertrude was never a nun,' I said.

Orobas made his way to the stone tomb. 'But she was,' he said, spreading his hands over the tomb in a way that was oddly tender. 'My most precious girl. Ethelrea. So unlike you in the end. But for a time she was exactly like you. A nun of Dartford.'

'That's impossible,' I retorted. 'No sister of Dartford could possibly be interred here.'

'Why not?' he asked, tilting his smooth head at me.

'This is a room built by Romans, and they were gone from here more than a thousand years ago. My priory was built two hundred years ago.'

He bent down and ran his fingers along the top of the crypt. 'This is not a Roman tomb. It's Saxon. When the Saxons occupied London, the amphitheatre was still here, the shrine was still here. They made use of it. Such a practical people. A shrine became a crypt for a seventeen-year-old girl.'

'She was a Saxon nun?' I said, wonderingly. And then I remembered

that there had been a nunnery on the hill, hundreds of years before
Edward the Third built a priory for Dominican nuns. The stone foun-
dation was all that remained. The first nunnery burned down in the
tenth century, when Viking warlords attacked them. 'The Order of
Saint Juliana,' I whispered.

'You're not stupid.' He walked back to the two columns on the
other side of the room. 'That's rare in a female.'

Ignoring his insult, I said, 'I still don't believe it. There were nuns
at Dartford in the time of the Saxons, yes, but why would one be
buried here, in London? And placed in a shrine to a Roman goddess?'

Orobas returned to the tomb, carrying three small urns. He set
each down with care, arranging them in a row.

A surge of protectiveness rose in me. 'If you are correct, and the
woman in this tomb was a nun in life, you must not desecrate her
remains with necromancer tricks.'

His head shot up. 'I don't like that word,' he said. 'Necromancers
are fools. Clipping fingernails from children and using them to
summon the spirit who will find buried treasure. Or asking questions
of a corpse's head with a mirror. I do not perform tricks. The ceremony
I perform reaches back ten thousand years.'

Gertrude pulled on my arm. 'Be careful, Joanna,' she pleaded.

I shook off her hand. 'What should I call you, then?' I persisted.
'Besides the name of the demon oracle you've assumed?'

'I took the name Orobas for the same reason that a bastard named
Giulio de' Medici adopted the name Clement the Seventh once he
finagled the papal election,' he said with a shrug. 'It's good for trade.'

My first reaction was outrage at his disrespect for a Holy Father.
But then I thought, *He's practically admitting he is a charlatan.* My fear
over the imminent ceremony lessened.

'In response to your question, I am an evocator of souls,' he said.
'We can begin as soon as you both let down your hair.'

I was certain that he was no evocator of souls. I was full of cold rage
at Gertrude for forcing me to endure this sacrilegious rite. All I wanted
was for it to be over. Although it was distasteful to show my hair to this
man, I removed my hood and unfastened my plaits, as did Gertrude.
The candle picked out the white strands in her black hair. My hair had
grown out since it was chopped short at the priory, now reaching my
shoulders.

Orobas dipped his fingers in the first urn and made a circle around the shallow pit closest to us. Every second step he sprinkled a few drops of liquid onto the floor of the crypt. I tensed. Could this be the source of the foul odour that still turned my stomach?

'It's water,' Gertrude mouthed to me. I nodded in relief.

In a singsong voice, Orobas said, 'Heaven-born son of Laertes, you have to make another journey and find your way to the halls of Hades and dread Persephone, to consult the blind Theban prophet—'

'That's Homer – the story of Odysseus,' I said.

Orobas's eyes widened. He was as surprised by my knowledge as Gertrude's physician had been, but he hid it more swiftly. 'So you've been taught the ancient stories,' he said softly. He put down one urn and picked up another. 'The great philosophers of Greece and Rome understood that the dead are always within our grasp. They spoke to them, just as Odysseus. Most of the dead are witless, that is the problem. They see and hear very little. But a precious few, when the soul is detached from the flesh, know a great deal about what has happened and what will happen.'

He walked the circle again, sprinkling liquid from the second urn. This wasn't water. It was white, like milk.

'To find out what they know, the dead must be brought closer to the living, and the living brought closer to the dead,' he said. 'It is an extremely dangerous thing to attempt, you understand? I am the master of the rite.'

Repelled by his arrogance, I said, 'Sister Elizabeth Barton did not evoke the dead.'

Orobas had finished the second pacing of the circle. He picked up the next urn. 'Your first seer was something else. She had a genuine gift for prophecy, but she was untrained. She made mistakes in interpretation – always a risk in our world. And you both saw how she suffered because of her visions.'

Gertrude asked, 'Why did you not help her?' She sounded indignant.

He smiled. 'And reveal myself to the men who serve the king? Am I a fool? From the day she first spoke in public against the king's divorce, she was closely watched. You should know that, Marchioness.'

He sprinkled liquid from his third urn as he walked the circle. It was dark this time. I caught a whiff of it – a rich, sweet wine.

'Now the two of you must come to this part of the crypt,' he said, beckoning to the far pit. Gertrude squeezed my arm. It was a gesture of both support and warning.

Orobas picked up a large cylindrical object, covered in a cloth. It was no urn. He set it down on the other side of the pit. The foul smell was strongest here, but I couldn't see why. The candles were far away; the pit was dark.

He whipped the cloth away in one swift move. It had covered a wooden cage. Something lay motionless at the bottom of the cage. I was certain the animal was dead, but then I heard a weak flapping noise. The cage contained a bird.

'What are you doing?' I called out, my heart hammering. He did not answer, nor did he look in my direction. Instead, he opened the door of the cage, and pulled out a grey bird with a long tail, a swallow. It had a hood tied around its head. At the touch of Orobas's hand, the poor creature beat its wings harder.

With one hand, he gripped the swallow tightly around the neck in a way that prevented pecking. With his other hand, he produced a long knife.

'Stop,' I said. Everything in me rebelled against witnessing this cruel pagan act. Gertrude threw both arms around me, to hold me in a tight embrace. 'He must make the sacrifice, Joanna,' she said. 'Without it, the soul cannot see or speak.'

Orobas plunged his knife deep into the breast of the swallow.

18

The swallow squawked just once, and then went limp. Blood gushed out of the feathered creature and dripped in a heavy stream into the second pit. Now I knew what the smell was: the blood and flesh of sacrificed birds.

'No, no, no, no,' I sobbed. I wriggled in Gertrude's arms, but she would not let me go. I felt as if I were the one gutted over the pit in this ancient tomb. My chest burned.

Orobas flung the corpse down and then reached up with both hands. Blood trickled down his wrists. He bellowed, 'I conjure you and call you to witness. That you come in a benign form. That you should have no rest until you come to me.' He paused for a few seconds and then repeated the invocation.

I don't know how many times he said his conjuring chant. My head throbbed from it. Fear fought with doubt in my mind. Next to me, Gertrude panted for breath as she held me tight.

Suddenly the words died in Orobas's throat and his face went slack. His knees buckled, and in a slow, slithering movement, he collapsed. Gertrude darted over. She knelt by his side to peer closer.

'Is he dead?' I asked.

Gertrude said without looking at me, 'No. But this is the most dangerous point. It's when some go to join the dead instead of pulling them to our side.'

The minutes crawled by. I couldn't help but wonder if it wouldn't be better for us – for the world outside as well – if this man died. But then I was consumed with shame for such thoughts. Every man and woman was worthy of redemption.

There was a stirring on the other side of Gertrude. Orobas pushed himself up with one hand. He did not stand. He sat on the floor, slumped forward, his chin resting on his black-robed chest. His pale head gleamed in the candlelight.

'Ethelrea?' Gertrude whispered.

'Why am I called here?' Orobas said. His voice was different. It was still low and gravelly, but subdued, without any scorn. 'Who is responsible?'

'I did it. I am Gertrude Courtenay.'

Orobas raised his head. His shoulders were rounded; his face was slack. His eyes found Gertrude. 'I see you,' he said. 'I have spoken to you. Why do you summon me again?'

Gertrude beckoned for me to come closer. 'I brought the other one,' she said. 'The bride of Christ.'

I did not move. Orobas turned his head, to the left and to the right. He stopped when his dull grey eyes fastened on me. 'I see her. She must come closer.'

Gertrude beckoned for me again.

This is all a sham, I told myself. *Orobas is pretending to be a dead Saxon girl to dip deep into Gertrude's purse. I'll make a show of believing, and then we'll depart.*

I made my way over to them. I knelt next to Gertrude. Orobas studied me, and then shook his head. He stuck out his lower lip, as would a child. It was a good performance, I thought, but only that – a performance.

'She is no sister of Christ,' Orobas said. 'I see no habit or veil.'

'They were taken from her,' Gertrude said. 'Her Dominican priory of Dartford was dissolved.'

Orobas lifted his chin. His eyes rolled up in his head for a few seconds. Gertrude reached out and gripped my knee, next to hers.

'Yes,' he said. 'All the monasteries ... swept away. It is a sadness.'

'But they will be restored?' Gertrude prompted. 'When the true Faith returns, the monasteries will be restored?'

Orobas shook his head. 'I don't want to converse with you. Only to her. I will speak tonight of Dartford.' He turned to me. I edged a little closer.

'My father had a farm near Middlebrook,' he said. 'We had a house. He built it with his own hands. It stood on a hill. From the door I could see the river split into three fingers.'

A chill swept down the back of my neck and tingled all the way to my fingers. I still fought against belief, though. It would be possible for anyone to learn the land and rivers of Dartford.

'Why did you take the veil?' I asked. It would not be easy to affect a convincing knowledge of the life of a Dartford nun.

'It was a vow of my father's. He had three daughters; I was the second. And one son. Just one son. When I was fourteen, my brother sickened with a fever. The priest gave him up for dead and said the words. My father made a vow that if God spared Caedwalla, he would send over his most beautiful daughter to the Order of Saint Juliana. And Caedwalla lived – he lived.'

His smile faded. 'Vanity is a sin,' he said dully. 'We are punished for our sins. Always.'

'Were you happy with the sisters of Saint Juliana?' I asked.

'They were harsh. They beat me when I was slow to do the chores. There was more work to do there than at the farm. I was always tired. When I wanted to rest, they said I must pray. They made me repeat the prayers after them. There were so many to learn.'

'What book of prayers did you use?' I asked.

'No one had the reading gift. The nuns said that if I recited the prayers I'd learned, if I suffered without much rest or food, it would bring me closer to understanding Saint Juliana. For the first year, I understood nothing but that I hated being a sister.'

It was getting harder to doubt the words that poured from Orobas's mouth. *He is clever*, I thought weakly. *The priests say the devil is very clever.*

'Why were you buried here?' I persisted 'It's far from Dartford. Did you run away? How did you reach London?'

'My life ended here,' he said.

'When you left the nunnery, you came to London?'

His shoulders slumped further. 'It was wrong. It was sin.'

This was all so confusing.

He said, more rapidly, 'There were three hundred ships. The Norsemen pillaged Canterbury, then they turned on London. Everyone who did not flee London was put to the sword. I was one who did not flee.'

'Was it Orobas who discovered you?' Gertrude asked.

There was no answer. He looked weary, as if he wanted nothing more than to sleep again.

'We are honoured to hear your story,' said Gertrude in her brittle voice. 'But now I must plead with you to turn your sight to the future.'

'If it must be.' The sulking tone had returned.

'Two nights ago, you saw the Lady Mary wear the crown of queen of England,' said Gertrude. 'But will it be with the help of foreign soldiers? Will the troops of the emperor invade?'

I grabbed Gertrude's arm. 'That is treason,' I whispered.

Gertrude whispered back, 'How else could Mary take the throne?'

'I see many ships,' whispered Orobas. 'They sail for England.' But he blinked several times, frowning, as if unsure about something.

'Are they Spanish?' Gertrude demanded.

Orobas nodded.

'When? When will they sail? That is what I must know.'

Another moment crawled by, as he rolled his eyes, searching through the visions. At first he shook his head, as if confused. Then he burst out: 'I see Mary as queen. She walks with a man in cardinal's robes. And a bishop, too. There are priests with her and nuns and monks. The true Faith is restored.'

Gertrude threw herself in my arms. I could feel the tears of relief rolling down her face. I should have been as happy as she was. This was the best future I could conceive of. And yet something felt wrong.

Orobas moaned and shuddered. A bubble of sweat shivered on his brow.

'I see a different vision,' he said. 'The king has a second son. Henry VIII will die. Edward will die. Cromwell stands behind the boy who is king now, he rules the land.' Orobas trembled again. 'The Lady Mary is in a prison cell; she is abandoned. Cromwell and the boy king are feared by all.'

Gertrude shrank from him, covering her face with her hands. 'No, no, no,' she wailed.

'How can there be two futures?' I demanded.

For the first time, Orobas moved a limb. He raised his right arm and pointed at me. 'You are the key to all. You will set the path the future must follow.'

'How?' I asked. 'That is impossible.'

Orobas continued to point at me. 'When the raven climbs the rope, the dog must soar like the hawk.' I covered my face with my hands – it was unbearable to hear the words of Sister Elizabeth Barton, words I'd never shared with a living person, pour from his lips.

'Look to the bear to weaken the bull,' he then said. 'Look to the bear to weaken the bull.'

I had not heard that before. More instructions – but they too meant nothing.

'I don't know what to do,' I cried. 'I can't choose a future. Your words don't mean anything to me. They're as useless as Sister Elizabeth's.'

'The third seer will tell you exactly what you must do,' Orobas said faintly. 'It is over.' His eyelids fluttered; sweat poured down his brow.

'Wait!' Gertrude shoved her way forward again. 'You saw a cardinal and a bishop walking with Queen Mary. But what of my husband and my son? What of the Courtenays?'

'Let me go, let me go,' said Orobas.

'No, tell me,' she ordered. 'You must. I will pay you more. Much more. *Anything.*'

'Ah, poor Henry Courtenay,' he finally groaned. 'The reckoning is coming.'

I shook with fear. Those were the words screamed by the madman John, when I left Dartford with the Courtenays.

'Why do you say that?' Gertrude was completely frantic. 'Why?'

A thick gurgle of saliva oozed out of Orobas's mouth. He collapsed and said no more.

19

So began my time of torment. Was Orobas genuine – did he reach into the underworld and grab hold of a long-dead Saxon girl who could glimpse into the future? On the face of it, that was both blasphemous *and* absurd. But when I thought of how Orobas described the river winding through Dartford, or gave voice to the tumultuous feelings of a young nun, my instincts told me I heard truth. And he spoke the same prophecy as Sister Elizabeth, which forced me to accept the fact that I did have a crucial role to play in the future of our kingdom. Some act I performed would change everyone's lives. It was an unearthly responsibility that I shrank from just as violently as when I kneeled before the writhing Sister Elizabeth Barton. How would I ever make confession of this, what possible penance could I receive?

Gertrude and I rode back to the Red Rose in exhausted silence, accompanied by the twins and the other men. It was nearly dawn when we reached Suffolk Lane.

Gertrude said in a low voice, 'I will keep my word to you, Joanna. I'll go west with Henry. He must never know what was said tonight.'

I could see how deeply the prophecy about her husband had frightened her.

I nodded. 'And I'll take Arthur back to Dartford and seek a quiet life.'

But first I must endure the dinner of Henry Courtenay.

The Marquess of Exeter came himself to accompany me when the hour approached, two nights later. It was the first time I'd seen Henry since he asked me to spy on his wife. He smiled as he held out his arm. 'I will escort you, Cousin Joanna,' he said.

While we walked to the great hall, we spoke of small matters until, with a half glance at the servants close behind, Henry asked, 'So, all has been quiet here in my absence?'

It was the question I'd been waiting for. 'Yes,' I said, without missing a step.

I heard an exhalation of breath – he was relieved to hear it. Henry did not press me. That almost made me falter. I came so close to pulling him into the alcove off the stairway landing, away from the servants, and telling him what had happened two nights ago. To plead with him to get out of London as soon as possible – now, tonight.

The reckoning is coming.

'Ah, they've lit all the candelabras – excellent,' boomed Henry. I followed his gaze. The stairs were indeed afire with golden lights, fixed every few feet. The walls and steps never gleamed so bright. The servants must have polished the surfaces for hours. All this hard work, preparing the house for what was, after all, an insignificant dinner for a few friends. How could this be important when the darkness was closing in?

I couldn't bear it any longer. I had to warn Henry. But as I opened my mouth, Henry stepped back to examine me in my cloth of silver at the top of the landing, against all the lights. Wearing it was a trial for me, the fabric was so heavy and rough against my skin. But evidently it had a different effect on the beholder.

'You are truly beautiful,' he said, clapping his hands twice. 'It's an honour to escort you to your dinner.'

The time for revelation had passed.

'My dinner?' I said. 'But Baron Montague is the guest of honour.'

Henry smiled again. He was in the best of moods. 'Of course he is. Of course. Come, we don't want to keep him waiting.'

In minutes we would be in the great hall. I wasn't afraid. The strange visions I had twice seen couldn't possibly frighten me after what I had endured in the presence of the second seer.

But Henry did not escort me into the great hall. Instead he led me to the music room. When I asked why, he didn't answer but hummed a tune.

There was one person waiting for us, the room now alight with candles like all the others. He had his back to the door, hands clasped, as he scrutinised the frieze carved into the wall. Slowly he turned around.

It was Baron Montague, but how he had changed. I hadn't seen him for at least five years, when he visited his sister Ursula at Stafford

Castle. As the eldest of the Pole siblings, he was the one responsible for the family after the death of their father.

Those visits of his always caused a stir. For one thing, Baron Montague was a great nobleman of the land, as much a childhood companion to the king as Henry Courtenay. But it was more than that: I knew that some women considered him handsome. I had never thought so, nor found him memorable in conversation. He seemed cold and haughty, avid for gambling, indifferent to books. In short, the perfect aristocrat.

Montague was somewhere in his forties. His black hair was heavily salted with white; a cobweb of wrinkles had deepened around his eyes. His face was almost gaunt. He wore a black doublet unadorned with the jewels or chain of office he doubtless owned. He was like a dark wraith stalking toward us.

He kissed my hand, with a bit of the courtly flourish I remembered, and said, 'Buckingham had such a passion for music.'

'Yes, my lord,' I said, though I wasn't sure why he brought up my father's eldest brother. But then Montague was always a great favourite of his. My looks must make him think of the Stafford duke.

'He had a company of incredible lute players,' Montague said, reaching for the memory. 'There was one who played like an angel, though he grew fatter every year.'

'Oh, yes – that was Robert,' I said. 'My uncle had a special tailor brought in to make alterations to his livery. The tailor once stayed up all night sewing so Robert would be presentable for a feast day.'

Montague chuckled and, to my own surprise, I laughed too.

How delighted Henry Courtenay was. 'You see?' he said. 'It is possible, my friend, to enjoy life.'

Montague grimaced. For some reason, the marquess's happy words embarrassed him. An awkward silence filled the room.

Thankfully, Gertrude appeared just then, beautifully dressed in deep-green velvets. She took her husband's hand and pressed it to her cheek. It was one of her pet gestures, but I thought it a touch more fervent than usual. She and I locked eyes for an instant. We understood each other perfectly once more. Tonight was Henry's night; we would both endeavour to make it a pleasing one for him.

Baron Montague escorted me to the great hall, with the Courtenays walking behind us. 'I must offer you my condolences on the passing of your wife,' I said. I regretted how stiff my words sounded. It did not seem quite the best moment, but better now than in a hall filled with food and drink.

He thanked me, just as formally. 'How sorry I was to hear of your father's death,' he said. 'I knew Sir Richard Stafford my whole life. He was never anything but honourable and generous.'

'We've both lost people we love,' I said as we approached the entranceway to the great hall.

He said nothing to that. My comment seemed to pain him, just as Henry's exhortations had earlier. I was so wretched at this, at entertaining others with conversation. I should not have brought up the death of his wife. Behind us, the Courtenays laughed at each other's jokes.

The two other guests waited for us in the lavishly decorated great hall: Sir Edward Neville, a portly man with a warm smile, and Baron Montague's sister-in-law, Lady Christine Pole. She was a little older than I, with the fair hair and pink-and-white skin that an admired Englishwoman should possess.

'Oh, my, cloth of silver!' she exclaimed. 'Is this how nuns dress now?'

My face turned hot. Gertrude swiftly explained that though my tastes were modest, she had insisted on presenting the dress as a gift to me.

'How nice to have such friends – you are the luckiest woman I know,' said Lady Pole, clutching her goblet of wine. Her nails were bitten to the quick. '*Very* lucky.'

There was some meaning behind her words I did not understand – and did not like. I remembered that her husband was confined in the Tower of London. That was a great trial; how well I knew that. I fell into the same silence as Baron Montague. He'd wandered away from the rest of us, to examine the walls and artwork of the room.

Everyone else made his or her way to the last place I wanted to be: the huge fireplace. I stood by the table, alone. Gertrude gestured for me to join them. I pretended not to see.

'Montague, bring Joanna over here,' Courtenay called out.

Again Montague held out his arm and escorted me. I tried as hard as I could to affect nonchalance. *Don't be foolish*, I told myself.

Taking a breath, I looked at the fireplace and at the stone lions that crouched above it.

A sickening dread stirred in my belly.

'What is the matter, Joanna?' asked Baron Montague.

'I'm sorry, I'm sorry,' I murmured, closing my eyes.

With a tug on my arm, he pulled me a few feet away, so that my back was to the others. 'Does being here again disturb you?' he said in a low voice.

'Yes, it does,' I said. My eyes sprang open. 'How would you know?'

'Because it disturbs me, too, a little,' he said. Baron Montague's huge dark eyes were filled with a mournfulness that matched my own.

'Do you see the visions, too?' I blurted. His sadness made him trustworthy.

'Visions? What sort?'

Haltingly, I told him what I had seen and heard twice when I gazed at this stone fireplace. The boy dressed as a cleric and the frightening giant. The sound of mocking adult laughter all around me.

Baron Montague pulled me even farther from the rest of the party. 'Joanna, those aren't visions – those are memories. You were here, in this room, as a small child. Perhaps six years old. The Christmas feast. That was Buckingham's party.'

'Why would my uncle give a party here, in the Courtenays' home?'

Baron Montague shook his head, as at something he found difficult to believe. 'Because it didn't belong to the Courtenays then. It was the London residence of the Duke of Buckingham. The king gave your uncle's house to Henry after the execution and attainder. Christ's blood, didn't Henry or Gertrude tell you that?'

I could not speak, overwhelmed.

Baron Montague said, 'The duke loved to host Christmas parties in the old tradition. For many, many years, it was the custom to dress a boy like a bishop and have him administer blessings, and to hire a giant for good luck.'

'And the sense I had, of flying up?'

'You really *did* fly. Buckingham noticed that you were afraid of the giant, and so you were lifted up to face him, so to speak. But the giant was a bit simple, and he was more afraid of you than you of him. I do remember how everyone laughed. That was unkind, yes. I fear the party guests had had a great deal to drink. It was the third day of Christmas festivities.'

After a moment, I said, 'I am surprised my father would do that to me. He was always sensitive to my nature. The last thing I'd ever want to be was the centre of attention.'

'It wasn't your father,' said Baron Montague and rubbed his temples. 'Ah, Joanna, don't you remember? It was *me*. I lifted you up as high as I could.'

As I stared at him, the memory was complete. It was a handsome dark-haired man in his twenties, laughing, who whipped me off my feet. Now I knew why I'd always felt this antipathy for Baron Montague.

'I am so very sorry, Joanna, for frightening you,' said the sombre man who stood before me now. 'Permit me to atone? Can we go to the fireplace now and banish those memories?'

We walked together, to gaze at the stone lions. That is all they were now, just lions that grimaced like gargoyles on a cathedral. I was overwhelmed with relief – my visions weren't real, but simple fragments of memory. Though now I saw Henry Courtenay with new eyes.

'I should have been told the true history of the Red Rose,' I said.

Baron Montague answered me in the same hushed tone: 'Please do not blame him. Henry may have assumed you knew and did not want to broach the delicate topic. Or else he was ashamed to benefit so by your family's fall. It is hard for him, the shifts we must make in these dangerous times.'

A woman's voice cried out, 'So I see all is going very well indeed.'

I turned to see a smiling Lady Pole bearing down on me and Baron Montague.

Gertrude Courtenay said, warningly, 'That's sufficient, say nothing more.'

But Lady Pole laughed. 'Why all the pretending? These two aren't children. None of us are children.'

I truly did not care for this woman. 'What are you trying to say?' I asked.

'Henry Courtenay has decided you would make an excellent second wife for his closest friend, and by the look of it, my brother-in-law agrees.'

Nothing inspired more scorn in me than heartless party games. And I did not appreciate being the object of a joke. I opened my mouth to say as much to Lady Pole when I realised something. Everyone in the room was miserable. Gertrude and Henry glared at Lady Pole.

Sir Edward Neville appeared to wish he were elsewhere. And Baron Montague's face was rigid with embarrassment.

'This is impossible,' I stammered. 'Impossible.'

Henry Courtenay hurried toward me. 'Joanna, I'm sorry. I wanted you to meet Montague again, for you to see each other, and then to see if you wished to proceed.'

Baron Montague stepped forward. 'And I should not have allowed Henry to arrange this. He was thinking of my happiness – and yours, too. But you should have been told.' His eyes shone with even more regret than when he admitted his role in the Christmas party.

'Yes,' I said, embarrassment mingling with anger. 'You're right. I should have been told about a great many things in this house.'

Across the room, Charles cleared his throat.

'My lords, there is a disturbance with the children, I regret to inform you. Master Arthur Bulmer must see Mistress Stafford. It has something to do with a child who is a guest. The tutors and servants are unable to calm Master Arthur.'

'That would be my son's doing,' Baron Montague sighed.

I held up my hand. 'I will attend to this,' I said.

Gertrude said, 'This is my house, I must accompany you and make matters right.'

'I go alone,' I announced to the room with some ferocity.

Once I was out of their sight, I picked up my skirts to move faster, up the stairs, across the landing, and down the passageways. From outside his room, I could hear Arthur crying. I burst open the door. Arthur was flailing in the bed, while Edward Courtenay stood by, worried. I learned that Baron Montague's fourteen-year-old son had teased Arthur relentlessly until Arthur exploded and had a full-fledged fit of temper. Servants separated them; I did not know where the other boy was now.

'Arthur, hush, all will be well, Joanna is here,' I said, cradling him in my arms. His cries subsided into hiccups.

'I'm sorry I didn't defend Arthur better,' said Edward Courtenay. 'That beast Montague is our guest. He kept mocking the way Arthur speaks. I wasn't sure what to do.'

I patted Edward's arm. 'You did your best, you are a good boy.'

Once Arthur was calm, I straightened my skirts. I had to return to the party, although it was the last place I wanted to be. As I walked along the passageway, I thought of Baron Montague. I was not the only one embarrassed tonight. I did not want him to think that when I cried 'Impossible,' it was because he was unacceptable. Baron Montague had shown sensitivity in how he handled the Christmas party of the Duke of Buckingham. And he had also spoken well when his sister-in-law exposed this plan. Pole marrying Stafford, on the face of it this was a natural solution. His sister was the wife of my cousin. And I did not dislike him. Quite the opposite. But I could never marry anyone.

I'd reached the landing when a man whispered, 'Joanna!'

I turned, confused. A servant would never address me by my given name.

But it was a man dressed in Courtenay livery who emerged from the alcove at the top of the landing. He kept his face from the full candlelight. With a quick movement, he beckoned for me to come to him.

'Sir, I will not go with you,' I said, offended and a little frightened. 'Shall I call for the others?'

The man took another step and the light fell on his face. It was Geoffrey Scovill.

I froze.

He charged the rest of the way, grabbed me by both hands, and pulled me into the darkness of the alcove.

'Why are you here?' I choked.

He held me an arm's length away. 'By God's good grace, *look* at you,' he said. 'I've never – in my life – seen anyone as lovely.'

Whether it was the shock of seeing him amid my mounting fears of everything in London, I will never know. But I stepped forward and laid my forehead against his chest. Tears burned my eyes.

'Geoffrey,' I said.

In an instant, his arms were around me. So tight I thought he would grind the costly, rough fabric into my skin and incinerate me. But I burrowed even tighter into his embrace.

'Joanna,' he whispered, his lips on my ear and then my throat. 'Joanna.'

It was the same as before, at the priory last spring, when he came to give me the last piece of news. My eyes closed, I sought out his lips. I kissed him with as much fervour as he kissed me.

I felt the first sharp twist of shame at my weakness. My eyes fluttered open and I caught the shimmering outline of the candelabra at the top of the landing. I tore myself out of Geoffrey's arms.

'Are you here because of my letter?' I said. 'But why disguise yourself like a servant, why come here tonight? I am leaving tomorrow, with Arthur.'

Geoffrey shook his head. 'No, Joanna. You must leave here tonight – within the next few minutes. I am here to get you and Arthur out. The king is sending men to the Red Rose, they should arrive within the hour. They have warrants for arrest. The charge is high treason.'

20

'But Henry Courtenay is no traitor,' I told Geoffrey, once I'd found my voice.

'Nonetheless, they are coming for him,' he said. 'And Courtenay's is not the only name written on the arrest warrant. Pole and Neville are to be taken as well. By coming together in private here, away from the court – members of three families with royal blood – they stir much distrust. God knows the king and Cromwell were already suspicious.' Geoffrey shook his head, exasperated. 'There could be no cause important enough for them to sup together in secret now, when His Majesty fears conspiracy at home and invasion from abroad.'

I covered my mouth with my hand.

Geoffrey took me in his arms again. 'The name *Stafford* isn't on the warrants, Joanna.' He kissed my forehead. 'If I get you out now, there's a chance you won't be drawn into the investigations. It's a slim chance – I won't lie to you. But it's your only one. You can't be here when the king's men pound on the door.'

I pulled back. 'If there are to be questions tonight, then I must present myself, to speak for Henry and the others. I can explain why the guests are here. It has nothing to do with any treason.'

He shook his head. 'The man who comes to arrest them is Lord John Dudley. He's a soldier. And a seeker of the king's favour. He won't listen to the explanations of a woman. And not a woman named Stafford, for certain. He's ambitious enough to throw you into the Tower on his own authority, because you're from a traitor family.'

The thought of returning to the Tower of London made my stomach turn cold and sick. But I managed to steady myself.

'No, Geoffrey. I can't run away. You don't understand – this is all my fault. The reason that—'

But he would not let me finish my sentence. 'That's nonsense,' he said. 'Nothing is your damn fault. Joanna, why must you always fight with me?' Frustration – and fear, no doubt – turned his voice to anger. I took two steps back from Geoffrey, leaving the protection of the alcove. I felt the glow of the candlelight warm the back of my head.

'Joanna, is that you?' cried a man's voice from below.

Geoffrey raised both hands, slowly, in a calming gesture. In the faintest whisper, he said, 'Say nothing to anyone.'

'I have to warn them,' I mouthed back.

Alarm flickered in his eyes. 'No. Get rid of him and come back.'

Geoffrey must be protected, there could be no question of that.

Baron Montague was halfway up the stairs, his forehead creased with concern. I rustled down the stairs, to head him off.

'How are the children?' he asked.

'All is well with them, Baron Montague,' I said stiffly.

'But not with you.' He shook his head. 'Ah, Joanna, you are so upset. I am deeply sorry for what happened here tonight.'

'There is no need for you to apologise.' I peered past Baron Montague, to the bottom of the stairs leading to the entranceway of the manor. Would Lord John Dudley pound on this door? How much longer did we have?

'There is every need in the world,' said Baron Montague, turning to look in the same direction I'd peered in. 'We are alone here, Joanna. And here is where I will say what must be said.'

'No, no, no.' I rushed down the rest of the way. I was so frantic to prevent Baron Montague from speaking, I covered his mouth with my hand. He removed it. But he did not let go of me. His hand was cooler than Geoffrey's.

'Henry is my oldest and closest friend, and he sees me through those eyes,' Baron Montague said. 'He actually believes that to be the wife of Baron Montague is a happy station. While I am certain it is quite the opposite.'

'My lord, I must implore you to rejoin the others,' I said, growing desperate. 'We can speak of this at a later time.'

'No.' He still held my hand. His mournful eyes hardened with determination.

'I bear a great name and I have my title, but my purse is not full, like Henry's. No great fortune came to *me* at my father's death. And the troubles of my kin are beyond compare. My mother depends on me for every matter. My youngest brother is imprisoned. You can see what it is like to keep company with his wife, though she, too, is my responsibility now. My other brother is the greatest enemy of the king's. I wrote to Reginald, at His Majesty's request, and chastised him for his disloyalty. Not that it would make the slightest difference to Reginald, who has never listened to me. He places us all in the greatest peril, but insists he must follow his conscience.

'Then there are my children.' His mouth twitched. 'Their mother was everything to them. My oldest boy – who was tormenting your cousin, no doubt – tells me he wishes I were dead instead of her. It's ridiculous what he expects of me. I have brought him up as my father did me, as all sons are brought up in our families.' He winced at his own words. 'I must begin anew with him – I *will* – if it's not too late.'

I was torn between deepening sympathy for Baron Montague and anguish over how he would react if he knew someone beside myself were listening.

But nothing Geoffrey had heard so far could compare to what followed.

'I tried to dissuade Henry from this enterprise of his,' said Baron Montague. 'But he kept insisting that you could be my helpmate as well as my wife. He wanted me to see you again, in social surroundings, without obvious pressure. I asked Neville to come, too – he is my late wife's brother and a fine man. My brother Godfrey's wife invited herself. She is under great strain because of his imprisonment. Try to forgive her rash words if you can.'

I nodded, though my view of her was unchanged.

He continued: 'I admit that I did not see this fiery spirit he described – until you ordered us all back in the great hall and insisted you would attend to the children alone. I saw the Stafford in you then.'

There was nothing haughty about him any longer. A spark of hope, of dawning affection, softened his features.

I simply could not let it go any further.

'Baron Montague, I have to—'

Again he cut me off. 'Allow me the courtesy of finishing what I mean to say. Then we can proceed to make our plans or I can leave and never trouble you again.' He turned my hand over and cupped it in both of his. 'Perhaps Henry knows me better than I think. For you are the perfect woman for me. I could not take up a match with a silly young girl who has no experience with the harshness of my world – she would be but another burden for me. But I am also, and I admit it, an exceedingly proud man. I couldn't marry a widow, couldn't bear to take into my bed a wife who'd known another.'

I was so distraught about Geoffrey Scovill listening to this proposal, to Baron Montague's most intimate thoughts, that my arms shook.

'Ah, you are trembling,' he said tenderly. 'This cannot but frighten you. After all, you expected to live as a nun. I promise you that I will—'

'Enough!' cried Geoffrey Scovill from the top of the stairs.

Baron Montague was simply incredulous. 'Who are you?'

I turned around. Geoffrey, already on the third step down, strode toward Baron Montague, his lips set in that determined line I knew all too well.

'I need to explain some things to you, my lord,' he said.

'You will explain to *me*?' His voice, his bearing, every bit of Baron Montague quivered with indignant fury. Here stood a Pole of the House of York, the descendant of kings.

Before I could say or do a thing, Baron Montague had sprung up the steps and was moving incredibly fast toward Geoffrey.

'Wait!' I cried, running after him. My voluminous skirts slowed me. Before I could intervene, Baron Montague had reached him.

Geoffrey said, 'My lord, this concerns you and the Courtenays and Neville, too – not just Joanna.'

'You use her name?' Baron Montague said. 'God's blood, I will teach you manners.'

I'd reached them by then. 'Geoffrey, let me speak,' I pleaded.

Baron Montague whirled around. His mouth parted in shock. 'You are familiar with this servant?' he demanded of me.

'I'm not a servant,' said Geoffrey, his hold on his temper fraying.

'Baron Montague, listen, please,' I said. 'He has something important to tell you.'

He stared at me, confusion warring with pain. And then rage swept everything from its path.

'I will thrash Henry Courtenay for this,' he said. 'For pushing me toward a woman who plays the part of a lady – who even wore a novice habit, for the love of Christ – but who whores with commoners.'

'Don't talk about her that way,' said Geoffrey, tightening his fists. He took a step closer to Baron Montague.

'You were having your way with her up at the top of the stairs, weren't you?' said Baron Montague. 'And I thought she was seeing to the needs of children.'

To my horror, Geoffrey slammed the heel of his palm into Montague's chest. 'That's enough,' he said.

Baron Montague stumbled back but righted himself quickly. A mirthless grin twisted his features. 'Yes, it is – quite enough. For you have laid violent hands on a peer of the realm, and now I have the right by law to kill you.'

He reached deep into his doublet and pulled out a knife.

'Stop,' I cried. I reached out for Geoffrey, to push him out of the way. But Geoffrey pivoted and then pulled a knife from his own green doublet.

'You're not going to kill me, old man,' he said.

The grin vanished from Baron Montague's face. His hand tightened on the knife handle so hard that his knuckles turned pure white. 'You will die tonight, be assured,' he choked.

'This is madness,' I said. 'I will get Henry – I will get all the others.'

They circled each other, their eyes flicking up and down, searching for a point of attack. Geoffrey was the younger and fitter man, but Baron Montague's knife was longer. Its blade gleamed in the light of the candelabras. And Montague moved with calculated agility up and down those steps, like a dark cat preparing to pounce.

I peered up and down the stairs. Still there was no one else in sight. I was the only one who could stop this before it came to blood.

'There's no time for this,' I said. 'Geoffrey's a constable of Dartford who came here to warn me. The king's men are on their way. They have warrants for arrest. Yours and Henry's and Sir Edward Neville's, too.'

Baron Montague's eyes flickered. 'I don't believe you.'

Geoffrey stopped circling him. He took a deep breath. He turned the knife around and offered it, handle first, to Baron Montague.

'Everything she said is correct,' he said. 'I am a constable of Dartford. I must apologise for striking you, my lord, and I do disarm.'

My heart pounded so hard I thought I could hardly bear the pain of it. I waited, as did Geoffrey, to see what Baron Montague would do.

Slowly, very slowly, he lowered his knife. He waved off Geoffrey's.

'Who bears the warrants?' he asked quietly.

'A man named Lord John Dudley has the king's charge in this matter,' Geoffrey replied.

Baron Montague bowed his head. 'There was never a doubt this day was coming,' he said. I realised he spoke not to either of us but to himself.

He straightened his shoulders and returned his knife to his doublet. 'I must return to my friends – we will prepare,' he said.

'But not her?' Geoffrey said quickly. 'Her name is not on the warrants. I came here and took this livery as disguise to remove Joanna and Arthur from the Red Rose.'

Baron Montague's face was made of stone. He said, 'For the love and respect I bore your father and your uncle, the Duke of Buckingham, I will see to it that your name is not mentioned.'

He started down the stairs.

'My lord, wait,' I said.

He turned, wary.

'Geoffrey's name must not be mentioned either – you must not say who gave you this information,' I said. 'Do you agree?'

'As you wish, Mistress Stafford,' he said dully.

My throat ached as I watched him walk down the stairs, his head held high. Geoffrey took my arm and hurried me up the stairs. He had endangered himself to come here. In the fight with Baron Montague, my fears had been for Geoffrey's life. I'd kissed him with shameful passion just moments ago. Yet now I could not bear to look at him.

'We must get Arthur without delay,' I said, leading him down the corridor.

We hadn't made it twenty steps when men's voices could be heard ahead, from around the corner. I recognised the deep voice of Charles. I grabbed Geoffrey, to pull him out of sight.

'Do not fear – I've walked past other Courtenay servants tonight and no one stopped me,' Geoffrey whispered. 'It's such a large household. They see the livery and that is enough.'

'But Charles is the steward,' I said. 'Also, he came with the Courtenays to Dartford – I believe he saw you there.'

Geoffrey stopped, and with a curse, he returned with me to our place of concealment.

The voices of Charles and the other servant did not grow louder. Nor did they die away. I realised they must have stopped to talk. I edged out so that with one eye I could peer around. Yes, I could see them at the end, chatting. There was no way to move past without their getting a direct look at Geoffrey.

I whispered, 'Why did you do this, wear Courtenay livery? Why not just send me a message?'

'I attempted to,' he answered. 'And was attacked by twin men. One of them said he must break the seal of my letter and read it first. It was devilish hard to pull my note – and myself – away from him after I refused. This household is like a fortress.'

'Then how did you get this?' I pulled on his jacket.

Geoffrey grimaced. 'Best not to ask.'

Charles's laughter rang down the corridor. How much longer would they tarry there? Geoffrey gnawed on his lip.

'You knew it wasn't safe for me to stay with the Courtenays weeks before these arrest warrants – how?' I asked.

'The Marquess of Exeter has royal blood, and the king hates all rivals for the throne, no matter if they are family or if they swear loyalty to him,' said Geoffrey. 'It's well known that the Courtenays are in a difficult position.'

But not known to me. My loathing of the court had made me ignorant of the court, and this was where wilful blindness led me. And Geoffrey.

It came then. The pounding at the door to the front entrance of the Red Rose was so loud, I cried out in fear. Geoffrey wrapped his arms tight around me, more to silence than to embrace.

Charles rushed past us and down the stairs.

'It's too late,' I whispered to Geoffrey.

'No,' he said, determined. 'Their attention will be downstairs for a good while. We can retrieve Arthur as soon as they move out of sight. We may have to go out a window on the Thames side.' His eyes flicked over my dress. 'We'll have to secure a cloak to throw over this dress.'

The front doors swung open. Charles had the keys, of course.

'I bear orders from His Majesty King Henry the Eighth to arrest several persons who are now within this house,' declared a man's voice.

Charles stammered that he would fetch the Marquess of Exeter and hurried away.

Geoffrey pulled me deeper into the windowless alcove. We were hidden from view of anyone on the stairs. But there was no door to close and bolt. If someone were to take one step inside the alcove, we'd be seen immediately.

After a moment, two other men's voices were heard. I recognised them at once. Henry Courtenay had come with Baron Montague to the front entrance.

'I shall see the warrants before anything else is done,' said Henry. He sounded calm. Montague must have had enough time to prepare everyone. While papers rustled at the bottom of the stairs, I thought of how Henry's arrest would devastate Gertrude and Edward and everyone else here. I prayed that there would be a proper investigation and fair trial. How could evidence exist? Henry had participated in no plots, I would swear it with my life.

I heard the scornful voice of Baron Montague. 'Dudley, why do you force your way in to harangue us after dark, when we are dining? It is scarcely proper.'

'This supper is one of the reasons I've come,' answered Lord Dudley. 'It reeks of conspiracy. We shall learn exactly what was said here by all parties and what plans you've formed.'

'This is a strictly social occasion,' said Baron Montague. 'Our discussions are none of your concern, nor could you grasp much of what is said or done in a house such as this. You are the son of a condemned traitor. It was in poor taste for His Majesty to dispatch *you* to arrest us.'

I winced. Why did Montague bait him like this?

'It hardly matters who was sent,' answered Dudley, his voice level. 'Questions will be posed and answered as to why you convened here tonight on Suffolk Lane.' There was silence for a few seconds. 'See to the searches.'

'What are you doing now?' demanded Baron Montague.

'We have warrants to search certain rooms,' answered Dudley.

Geoffrey and I stared at each other in the dim alcove as the boots of a half dozen men pounded up the stairs. In seconds we'd be pulled out. Exposed.

But the king's men swiftly headed down the corridor without stopping to search our alcove. We were safe for a few moments longer.

'This may help us,' Geoffrey whispered. 'There'll be chaos and disruption. It could provide cover.'

Among all the men's voices around us, I heard Henry Courtenay speak again. His self-assurance was gone. His voice panic-stricken, he said, 'No, no. This cannot be true. These warrants – all the names. This can't be possible, Dudley.'

His fear undid me. I went hot and cold with the waves that rippled through me: terror and confusion and disgust. How could I scurry away, fretful for my own safety, and abandon Henry and Montague to this? When they worsened their situation every moment by refusing to tell the king's man the true reason for this dinner tonight – me.

'They will move off very soon,' murmured Geoffrey. 'Then we'll take our chance.'

I stared at him in the shadows of the alcove. Why had Geoffrey done this – endangered himself again? I regretted it, and regretted that he had such a powerful feeling for me. He was a man who deserved a sweet and comforting wife, not a difficult woman beset with dangers. I did not see how the two of us could possible succeed in escaping from this house together. The king's men combed the Red Rose. As long as he was with me, he would be subject to questioning. Alone, Geoffrey might stand a chance.

A new question stabbed me. The prophecy of the seers could be true. What if I were meant to exonerate Henry and Montague and whoever else was on the warrants? It was up to me to choose the path of the future, Orobas said. I had struggled against the prophecy because it seemed so frightening and impossible – if not ludicrous – that I could stop King Henry from doing anything he set out to do. But what if this were not about directly confronting His Majesty? The prophecy could revolve around another sort of action. If I said nothing tonight, these blameless men could well be destroyed, the king made even more powerful, poised to breed a second son who would succeed him. But what if I pushed my way forward to explain that the reason all were convened was for me to meet Baron Montague? I could save their lives – and, by saving them, set England on the other path.

I stepped away from Geoffrey, and toward the light.

'Joanna?' he whispered, alarmed.

'Get out of the Red Rose without delay,' I urged.

He reached out to tug me back, but I was too quick. I ducked and then slipped out of the alcove once more.

At the top of the stairs, it came close to overpowering me – the shimmering candlelight and the sight of a dozen men, most of them strangers, standing at the bottom. The words died in their throats. All attention turned to me.

I threw my hand up in front of my eyes, to shield them from the bright light, and kept walking down, as steadily as I could. It was silent behind me. Geoffrey did not follow. The smell of roasted meats filled the air – squab and venison. The great kitchens of the Red Rose had finished cooking the feast. Servants were ready to serve it. How confused they must be, huddling in the kitchen and corridors with platters of food no one would eat.

'And who comes before me now?' said the voice of Lord John Dudley, which I could now match to the man himself. I lowered my hand.

Dudley looked to be about five years older than me – tall and lean, with a precisely trimmed beard. He stood with his hand on his hip, waiting.

I glanced over at Henry Courtenay, saw his face reddened with distress. He mouthed, *No*.

Next to him stood Baron Montague. His eyes were filled with sorrow and pride and something indefinable.

I reached the bottom of the stairs and walked straight to Lord John Dudley.

'My name is Joanna Stafford.'

21

'Sir, I fear there is some confusion over the purpose of this dinner,' I said with all the politeness I could muster. 'You are mistaken if you believe anything untoward occurred. My cousin the marquess had proposed a marriage between Baron Montague and myself. This dinner was set for us to make our plans.'

I waited for Dudley's cold hostility to thaw. It did not.

'You are a Stafford?' he asked. 'Whose daughter, the Duke of Buckingham's?'

'My father was the duke's youngest brother, Sir Richard Stafford,' I replied.

Dudley nodded. 'The treasonous families make new alliances with each other.'

'We have committed no treason,' said Baron Montague, thrusting himself forward.

Dudley's eyebrow rose again. 'So speaks the brother of Cardinal Reginald Pole,' he said.

Cries came from the corridor upstairs. Was this because of the search? Geoffrey had predicted chaos. I glanced at the alcove at the top of the steps. Geoffrey was still safely hidden. I wondered if he could hear my attempt at intervention – which so far had done no good at all.

Two of Dudley's soldiers strode past the entrance to the alcove. To my relief, they turned to head down the stairs. A group followed them. First came a grave and fearful Edward Courtenay. Behind him walked a black-haired boy, perhaps two years older than Edward. He could only be Baron Montague's son and heir. 'You have no right to take me anywhere,' the boy shouted. As he twisted and turned, we could see his hands were tied behind his back. Two soldiers prodded him down the steps. I looked for Arthur, but thankfully he was not among the horrific procession. Yet what if it had awakened him, and he was frightened and confused?

Henry Courtenay cried out. I turned toward my cousin. His hands outstretched, helpless, he watched his frightened young son being led down the steps.

My focus then shifted to Montague, also watching the approach of his child. His dark eyes blazed in his thin face. His right hand groped inside his doublet. I knew well what weapon he sought. Dudley, too, watched Montague carefully.

I flew to Montague's side. 'Don't do it,' I whispered. 'That's what Dudley wants. He seeks to provoke you.'

Montague did not acknowledge that I'd spoken to him. But he withdrew his hand from his doublet.

Montague's son was held back from going to his father. The soldiers announced that the younger Pole had resisted them upstairs, and so would be restrained. Two men stood between the baron and his son.

But the soldiers did permit Edward to join his father. 'I don't understand this,' he said in his high child's voice, not yet broken. Henry caught him up in a tight embrace.

'You can't arrest *children*.' The words were out of my mouth before I could stop them.

'I have warrants signed by the King's Majesty to do just that,' Dudley said.

'But this is terrible – an act of infamy,' I said.

Dudley said, very deliberately, to Baron Montague, 'If I were you, I'd get my betrothed under control.'

With the greatest of difficulty, I held my tongue. But Montague did not. 'Tell me, Dudley, how old were *you* when they came to take your father to prison?'

So there was another element to this business for Lord John Dudley.

Montague's taunt found its mark. The muscles of Dudley's jaw tightened. 'Five,' he said, and then turned in the other direction, toward the corridor leading to the great hall. 'Ah, here they are.'

With soldiers right behind, Sir Edward Neville and Gertrude Courtenay appeared, each struggling to hide their fear. So she was to be arrested as well. The entire Courtenay family would be conveyed to the Tower of London.

I will never forget how Gertrude reacted when she saw her son in her husband's arms. She swayed, blinking, her face turning white as ivory. I thought she would collapse. But somehow she pushed forward, past Baron Montague and me, not even seeing us. Her fragrance of orange and chamomile and rosemary drifted in her wake as she staggered to her family. Henry reached out and took her in his arms. Edward cried harder now that his mother held him. The Courtenays clutched each other so tight, they were like a single tree with three trunks.

'Not her – not Lady Pole,' said Dudley. He pointed at wide-eyed Christine Pole, who had found her way to us. 'She is the one who cannot be arrested, no matter what.'

'Why is that?' demanded Baron Montague.

Dudley said, 'It was evidence given by her husband, Sir Godfrey Pole, that persuaded the king that grounds exist for a treason inquiry into all of your activities.'

Lady Pole cried, 'No, no, no,' and then began to weep.

'That's impossible,' said Henry Courtenay, still clasping his wife and son.

'Have you put my brother to the pain, Dudley?' said Lord Montague, his face darkening. 'If you have, I swear by the Virgin, you will pay.'

But still Dudley kept his cool. 'I am no torturer, Baron Montague. I was made vice admiral of the king's fleet last year. I command ships and companies of men, not the scum of the Tower. In answer to your inquiry, these statements were given freely by Sir Godfrey Pole.'

Baron Montague made a sound of disgust.

Lady Pole's crying escalated. Dudley pointed at Father Timothy, who huddled in the opposite corner of the room with Charles and Ralph. 'You – priest. Take Lady Pole out of here and keep her out.' The way that Dudley spat the word *priest* left no doubt in my mind that he was an enemy of the Catholic faith. He must relish the task of arresting Catholics.

More of Dudley's men strode down the stairs. They carried books and papers – the fruits of their search. Constance, Gertrude's lady-in-waiting, trailed the last soldier, greatly distressed. As they came closer, I realised what that particular soldier carried. It was the small brown box that contained Gertrude's letters.

My heart beat in a painful, jerky rhythm. What correspondence did it contain? That evening I came into her bath unexpectedly, she had tried to hide a letter from me, one written in Latin. This was what the king's men sought. They knew of Gertrude's conspiring. They did not come because of news of a private supper. It would never have mattered what I said.

I felt someone's eyes on me. It was Dudley. With all the commotion going on around him, I was the one he watched for a reaction to the sight of Gertrude's box. A tiny, satisfied smile hovered above his beard.

Constance made her way to him at that very moment. 'Sir, I must attend the Marchioness of Exeter – I cannot be left behind.'

'Don't you understand where she's going tonight – where they are all going?' Dudley said, as if speaking to a small child.

'Yes, my lord,' answered Constance. 'But where the marchioness goes, I go. Always.'

He shrugged and turned to the older man who now held the documents of arrest. 'On my authority, take this woman to the Tower as well. And Mistress Joanna Stafford.'

It took a few seconds for me to comprehend what Dudley had said. I'd heard the words but could not take them in. I did not scream or weep like Lady Pole. It was if I were being swept out of the room, out of this city, by a huge dark wave. All of the voices around me dimmed and the lights began to swim in a golden haze. The points of the candles were meeting in a circle around me.

Somehow I tore free from the glowing numbness and joined in the furious argument going on before me.

Baron Montague demanded, 'How could she play a part in *anything*? She's only been in London a month.'

'But the last month has been quite an eventful one – particularly in this house,' said Lord Dudley. 'And I suspect that Mistress Stafford is involved in it up to the hilt.'

I stared at the floor. I vowed to say nothing to my interrogators. But what if they put me to the rack, as they had Sister Elizabeth Barton and, years later, my father? Would I have the strength to stay silent?

All of those terrors were reduced to nothing when a new realisation dawned.

'Arthur,' I choked. 'What about Arthur?' I turned to Dudley. 'I have charge of a cousin, Arthur Bulmer. He's asleep upstairs. There's no one left here to care for him if you take me away.'

Dudley replied, 'This house is full of servants.' He gestured toward Charles. 'I'm sure someone is competent enough to make arrangements.'

The thought of Arthur waking up to find me gone as well as Edward and the Courtenays was unbearable.

I stepped toward Lord Dudley, my hands clasped before me. I would do anything to prevent Arthur's suffering. 'I beg you, don't do this. He's so little. He's five years old – the same age *you* were.'

There was not a trace of feeling in Dudley as he gazed at me. No sympathy, no anger at my mention of his own childhood tragedy. Nothing. He turned away, to give his orders.

'Bring them to the wagons,' he commanded his men. 'Do it in small groups. All must be kept orderly.'

I looked up the stairs, at the alcove. What would Geoffrey do now? If he escaped this house, that would be something – one comfort I could cling to. I'd destroyed my own life, but his would continue.

'Have you searched the alcove at the top of the stairs?' asked Dudley. I flinched. Again Lord John Dudley watched me and seemed to pluck the thoughts from my head, better than any sorcerer.

A soldier bounded up the steps.

I willed myself to say and do nothing. But in my mind I pleaded with Christ to spare Geoffrey Scovill.

'No one is here, my lord,' reported the soldier after a few seconds in the alcove.

Prayers were answered. So Geoffrey must have slipped out some time ago. Wearing the livery of a Courtenay servant was the perfect disguise – no one would suspect him of anything. Geoffrey was clever, far more than I. He had warned me that if I revealed myself I could be arrested, just as last month he'd warned me of the dangers of staying at the Red Rose.

A hand seized my arm. Baron Montague moved to escort me out the door of the Red Rose. He said nothing. I glanced up at his profile, grim and haughty. Was it two hours ago that he had exorcised me of my childhood fears? Only one hour ago that he told me I would make him a perfect wife?

Now Baron Montague said in a low voice, 'You should not have done it.'

'What?' I asked, miserable.

'You should not have come downstairs. You should have hidden in the house with your lover.'

I said, 'Geoffrey Scovill is not my lover. No matter what occurs tonight, my lord, I must insist that you keep a courteous tongue.'

Baron Montague's expression shifted from disapproval to amusement. A bark of a laugh escaped his lips.

The sound of it made every man's head turn. Dudley frowned, as in disbelief.

But Montague was anything but abashed. Blood pumped into his ashen cheeks; his eyes sparked with new life. 'Dudley, you bear the warrants, so let us be off,' he declared. 'What did you expect from me? Weeping? I am well prepared for you to do your worst.'

Lord Dudley and Baron Montague stared long at each other. Such palpable hatred. Walking out the door, my hand gripping Montague's arm, was welcome to me, for it meant escaping the scrutiny of Dudley.

The sun had dropped below the horizon. A sickly grey light lingered, soon to be extinguished by darkness. I smelled burning fish. The boatmen were roasting their supper over fires along the riverbank.

Two long, empty horse-drawn wagons waited for us on Suffolk Lane. A dozen more soldiers stood by them, watching us. Dudley had brought many men with him. Behind them a crowd gathered. There was a low murmur coming from the Londoners. It was a sombre sound. No one jeered or shouted a word. In a flurry of arm movements, I saw an old woman make the sign of the cross. A younger man standing next to her pushed her out of sight immediately afterward. Perhaps she was his mother.

The Courtenays and Sir Edward Neville were brought out after us. Dudley came last. He split us into two groups. Henry, Gertrude and their son and Constance, the marchioness's lady-in-waiting, would ride in the first wagon; I would accompany Lord Montague and his son and his brother-in-law, Sir Edward Neville, in the second.

When they walked past us, Courtenay paused for a few seconds to gaze at Montague. Whatever he found in the face of his oldest friend seemed to bolster him; he took a deep breath and continued on, his arm around his son's shoulders. It was me that Gertrude looked at. Those large brown eyes were full of pleading. Then she passed by, leaving Montague to peer sideways at me, perplexed. Well he might wonder why the Marchioness of Exeter sought help from Joanna Stafford.

Never had the seers' prophecy seemed more mistaken than tonight.

A soldier beckoned for me. I was to be the first in the wagon. I made my way forward without hesitation. It was often said at Stafford Castle that the third Duke of Buckingham exhibited no fear from the moment of his arrest to the time when he kneeled before the executioner. It was small comfort to his fatherless children, but it was something.

I found it hard to climb up into the wagon, wearing this kirtle and bodice. The cloth of silver caught on a plank of wood. I felt a pull and then heard a rip. The dress was ruined. It did not matter. I found a place on the narrow hard seat running alongside the wagon. The others silently shuffled in to join me.

Dudley huddled with two of his senior men near the door. Montague seized the time to speak to his son. Sitting close together in the wagon, even in the fading light, the resemblance was marked. I quietly rejoiced to see his son listen so closely to Montague. In these moments together, they were father and child.

'No! No! No!' shouted a man.

Someone charged toward the first wagon. He wore Courtenay livery. It was Joseph, his arms outstretched to Gertrude. Dudley said something, and his two men threw themselves in Joseph's path. He was easily tackled and hurled down. He screamed when his back slammed into the cobblestones with a horrific crunch. The simple-minded twin was no longer a threat. But the soldiers did not move on – they kicked Joseph in the side and in the shoulders and, to my horror, in the head.

James surged forward but not to attack. I could see Charles had him by the arm. He would not let James be beaten, too.

'You're killing him – for the love of God, you're killing him,' James screamed.

Lord John Dudley watched the attack without emotion. His face was the same smooth blank as when I pleaded Arthur's case. At one point, a soldier, his face glistening with sweat, looked over at Dudley for a signal. He did not get one. The kicking resumed.

At last, after how many moments I do not know, Dudley raised his hand. 'Halt,' he said.

James ran to his senseless brother and knelt next to him. He reached down and cupped Joseph's bloody head in his hands, lifting it off the ground with extraordinary gentleness. 'This cannot be,' he said.

In the Courtenay wagon, Gertrude slumped forward in a faint. Her husband on one side and Constance on the other held her up. Edward Courtenay wept. It was silent on Suffolk Lane except for the sound of the boy's crying.

My stomach coiled. I closed my eyes, for fear I, too, would faint or sicken.

The wagon lurched forward and my eyes flew open. We were leaving the Red Rose.

22

Although curfew had been called, clumps of Londoners silently watched us go by. Somehow word had spread of who huddled in the wagons closely guarded by the king's soldiers. Perhaps it was the boatmen, for they knew everything first.

Dusk had turned to darkness. But it took only a sliver of moon in the November sky to reveal our destination, rising above the houses and shops and churches of the city: the square castle keep of the Tower of London.

I couldn't see Lord John Dudley. He rode with most of his soldiers in front of the first wagon, the one carrying the Courtenays. A single soldier on horseback followed our wagon. Two other soldiers walked briskly behind, bearing their pickets on their shoulders.

Behind them, a discreet distance, rode one more man. He did not wear a soldier's uniform. Because I hated the sight of the looming Tower, I fixed my attention on this last man. He had to be under the command of Dudley – I could not think why anyone else would accompany us. Certainly no one of the Courtenay household would dare, not after Joseph's savage beating. But why did he ride so cautiously? It was as if he followed but did not intend to appear to be doing so.

As I watched, the distance narrowed between the man and the two soldiers on foot. Because of the lit torches on this stretch of street, I could see him a bit better. He shook the reins of his horse on his left side and tapped his right leg impatiently. Those two familiar movements jolted me with such intensity that I jumped off the hard wooden seat of the wagon.

The man who rode behind was Geoffrey Scovill.

'Don't make such a show of staring at him,' Baron Montague murmured, inches from me. He seemed preoccupied. His eyes darted around the wagon, at his son and brother-in-law sitting across from us, and then at the men who rode and marched behind.

'This is foolish,' I lamented, my hands clasped. 'Why does Geoffrey do this?'

'That is an idiotic question and you are not an idiotic woman,' Baron Montague replied. 'Be very still. You must not turn again. Don't draw attention to him.'

Baron Montague leaned forward, sliding his hands down until they rested on his knees. His movements slow, almost casual, he looked ahead, past our wagon driver to the wagon and soldiers ahead. And then he peered behind. After a few seconds Baron Montague nodded, as if in response, and then sat back up. With me sitting between him and the back of the wagon, he shifted so that one arm angled behind me, and out of the wagon. I felt his arm twist and then tense, as if he were gesturing. Giving some sort of signal.

'What are you doing?' I asked.

'Helping you escape, Joanna.'

I said in the same furious whisper: 'This is madness. What about the soldiers?'

'Constable Scovill and I are both armed – you know that better than anyone.'

'So you will go with us?'

Baron Montague said: 'I could never leave my son or the Courtenays. And we can't *all* get away. The element of surprise should be sufficient for one to escape.'

'But that will make it even worse for you,' I protested.

'Nothing can save me,' Montague said calmly. 'I will die in the Tower.'

I shook his arm. 'Don't say that. There will be a trial – you will be heard. How can you be sure that no hope exists?'

'Because I know Henry Tudor,' he answered. 'In truth, this is something of a relief, Joanna. I have lived in the shadow of the axe for many, many years, not because of anything I've done, but for who I am. I am the House of York. Henry the Seventh exterminated many of our line. Now the son finishes his father's work.'

I couldn't insult his intelligence by arguing further. Tears filled my eyes, and I gripped Montague's arm tighter. Across from us, Sir Edward Neville nudged Montague's son and they moved up the wagon, out of earshot.

Baron Montague smiled and wiped a tear from my cheek.

'I don't want to leave you in this way,' I whispered.

He wiped a tear from the other cheek and then cupped my face in his hands. 'Ah, Joanna, you can't fall in love with a dead man.'

Montague glanced behind our wagon once more. 'Scovill must act soon; we will be at the Tower moat in minutes.'

I started to turn, but Montague said, 'No.' He slipped his arm around my waist and squeezed. 'I will jump over you when he breaks the line and try to get the best of the soldiers. Be ready to run to Scovill when I give the signal.'

The road was veering closer to the Thames. We were almost there.

'Closer, closer,' Montague muttered, his head turned away from me. His body was taut, ready to spring.

Part of me still fought against this plan. It seemed crazed. Where would Geoffrey take me – where would we go? Dartford would be the first place they'd search for me. And what of Arthur? Would I be able to retrieve him with soldiers in pursuit? But, oh, how I ached to run to safety. The Tower terrified me like no other place on earth.

'Oh, no,' said Montague, his voice bitter. 'Not this.'

I heard a thundering of hooves. Geoffrey was close behind the two soldiers who marched behind our wagon. But coming up fast on either side of him were at least ten men on horseback. One of them carried a blazing torch as he rode, one bright enough to reveal his livery. He didn't wear Tudor colours, nor those of the Courtenays. The man wore a black doublet with a golden figure stitched on it. A golden lion.

Black and gold. Howard colours.

Thomas Howard, Duke of Norfolk, surged forward on his grey horse. His men swiftly parted to clear the way for him.

'Dudley,' he bellowed, rising up in his stirrups. 'Get back here, Dudley!' His voice split the air like thunder. There was not a louder man alive.

All was confusion as our wagon slammed to a halt. Horses wheeled and turned as Howard men overtook the king's soldiers commanded by Dudley. Soldiers ran this way and that. I couldn't see Geoffrey any longer. He'd disappeared amid the chaos.

Montague withdrew his arm from around me. He leaned forward to speak to Sir Edward Neville in a low but urgent voice.

Lord John Dudley trotted past my wagon to meet the Duke of Norfolk.

'I am officer in charge, Your Grace,' Dudley said, all confidence. 'Do you need to read the commission?' He pulled a paper from his black doublet and waved it at Norfolk.

'I know that you are the one Cromwell picked,' said the duke. 'At his supper, His Majesty bade me go as well, to see that all was done properly in the arrest. And it appears far from proper to my eyes. I've just come from Courtenay's house. God's teeth, there's a man lying half dead in Suffolk Lane and twenty servants weeping.' He gestured toward the wagons. 'These are high nobles – you can't round them up like thieves and toss them into wagons. You are not fit for this responsibility.'

Dudley's back was to me. I could not see his reaction to the duke's scorn, ladled out in front of all the men – and us prisoners, too.

Without waiting for an answer, Norfolk flew off his horse and stalked toward our wagon. In the torchlight his face was scored with even deeper wrinkles than I saw a year ago. He still moved like a young man with the face of a death's-head.

'Baron Montague, Sir Edward, have you been mishandled?' he barked. 'Who is the woman with you?'

It wasn't until he was near enough to touch the side of the wagon that he recognised me.

'Christ's blood, not you,' he howled. 'Joanna Stafford, what are you doing here?'

Dudley dismounted and the two of them stood inches from me, quarrelling over my inclusion in the night's arrests. Dudley was plainly in the wrong – my name was not on a warrant and I'd not said or done anything to incriminate myself. But for that very reason he stood his ground most stubbornly.

Norfolk did not ask me a single question. All of these men talked about me – my putative engagement to Montague, my stay at the Red Rose, even my former service at Dartford Priory – but not to me. I found it all most confusing. Why would my fate matter to the Duke of Norfolk? If anything, he should rejoice in my arrest. Last year he'd led the interrogation into my possible treason, pursuant to the execution of my cousin Margaret. Norfolk even struck me in the face when I did not break under questioning.

'I will take personal responsibility for her – it will be on *my* authority,' Norfolk said, spittle flying from the corner of his mouth.

'But she's not a member of your family,' Dudley said.

'Are you not even aware that my wife's a Stafford, and this girl her first cousin?' Norfolk retorted. 'My brother-in-law, Lord Henry Stafford, has given me charge of the Staffords' welfare as well as the Howards'.'

'That is not true,' I said, but no one heard me but Montague. He said warningly, 'Say nothing – it's better Norfolk than the Tower.'

I shook my head. 'They are close to the same thing.'

But in the next moment, it was decided. These courtiers of the king rescinded my arrest. I was to be released at once. Norfolk pushed his way on to speak next with Henry Courtenay. Dudley mounted his horse to retake his place at the head of the party. He aimed one final look at me, full of loathing, as he trotted past. I turned my back on him and peered at Baron Montague.

All words seemed inadequate. He was going to the Tower while I had, inexplicably, won my freedom. And what were we to each other? Nothing. Everything.

'I shall pray for you,' I said finally.

His lips curved into a smile. 'Ah, yes, you were nearly a nun. A woman whom two men were ready to die for tonight. Most incredible.' He took my hand and kissed it.

The Duke of Norfolk's men stepped forward, helping me out of the back of the wagon. I left it with a good deal more care than when I went in. The duke himself returned at that moment, shouting, 'Find her a horse.' He walked over to his own mount, dispensing more orders to the scrambling Howard retainers.

'Good-bye,' I whispered to Baron Montague.

He nodded, and then called out to the Duke of Norfolk, 'A word, Your Grace?'

Although Norfolk was about to mount his horse, he walked to the back of the wagon to hear what Montague had to say. I'd never seen him show anyone such respect before – except for Bishop Gardiner and, I assumed, the king.

'Now there's no one left but you, Howard,' Montague said. 'Be ready.'

The duke flinched very slightly – only Montague and I could have detected it – and then bowed. A whip cracked on the back of the horses pulling the Poles' wagon. Norfolk's hand shot out. As the wagon surged away, he clapped the side of the wagon with such force, it almost yanked him off his feet.

Montague did not look back. He sat in profile, his head held high. That vaunted pride of his – a pride taken as arrogance by so many – would carry him through, I hoped. It was all he had now.

I peered over at Norfolk, standing inches away. He seemed fearfully tall until one got close to him. At this moment, his aged face was twisted into a grimace.

He realised I was looking at him and treated me to a scowl. 'Let's be off,' he said.

'Off where?' I asked.

One of Norfolk's men, sporting a red beard, stepped forward. 'Your Grace, a man has come forward who—'

'Richard, can you not handle anything yourself, man?' the duke demanded, his anger mixed with a profound weariness. The sight of the Poles, the Courtenays, and Neville rumbling away had truly shaken him.

'It concerns her.' Richard pointed my way.

Geoffrey. On the other side of a line of men wearing black-and-gold, he stood under the torchlight.

He bowed deep to the duke and then said, his voice strong yet respectful, 'Your Grace, bearing on the matter of Mistress Joanna Stafford, I—'

'Stop!' Norfolk held up a hand. 'You are familiar to me.'

My heart sank to the ground. How was it possible that the duke recognised Geoffrey from less than an hour of questioning that took place more than a year ago? The duke struggled for the memory as Geoffrey and I waited, not daring to look at each other.

'Yes, yes, it was in a Tower cell and ...' Norfolk whipped around, to look at me. 'He was arrested with *you* at Smithfield. You said he was nothing to you, a man in the crowd. I think you described him as an insect.'

I flinched. Yes, I had denounced Geoffrey. It was a desperate attempt to remove suspicion from the young constable. I'd succeeded in freeing him, but my words had wounded Geoffrey deeply then.

'What is going on here?' asked Norfolk.

I spoke first. I would not denounce Geoffrey again. 'Constable Geoffrey Scovill is my friend,' I said.

The Duke of Norfolk stared at me, incredulous. The other men looked at me too, clad in my torn cloth of silver gown, and then at Geoffrey, wearing the garb of an ordinary man.

'By Christ's holy wounds,' the duke said, and laughed. How he seemed to relish this, uncovering our connection. His grief over the arrests of his fellow noblemen was swept away. I hated his blasphemy as much as I hated that rough, mocking cackle.

'I gather Montague had no notion he'd be sharing you with this young buck?' the duke jeered.

'I will not respond to such an unseemly question,' I shot back.

'You call *me* unseemly?' the duke said.

Struggling for dignity, Geoffrey said, 'Your Grace, I am a legal representative of the town of Dartford, where Mistress Stafford resides, and in that capacity alone I ask to escort her and her cousin Arthur Bulmer to their home.'

The duke frowned. 'Arthur Bulmer?'

'Margaret's son,' I said. 'He is at the Red Rose now, sleeping in his room upstairs. I have charge of Arthur now that his parents are dead.'

The duke's salacious laughter died. He was the one who had arrested Arthur's parents in the north of England, as commander of the king's forces during the rebellion. He brought them down to London for trial. And Margaret was his wife's half sister.

The duke thought for a moment. 'Arthur Bulmer will be returned to Dartford. The constable can take custody. But you, Joanna Stafford, are coming with me.'

'But why?' I demanded. 'You told Lord Dudley I was guilty of no crime, that my name had never come up in the treason investigation.'

'If you heard that, then you also heard that I make decisions for the Stafford family now,' Norfolk responded.

I protested his decision – and Geoffrey made another attempt to intercede. But the Duke of Norfolk had set his mind.

I turned to Geoffrey. 'Arthur will be wild, he will cry and scream,' I said. 'Even if he remembers you from the priory, it will be hard.'

'I can handle him, Joanna,' he reassured me.

'Please take him to see Sister Winifred and Brother Edmund at once,' I continued, frantic.

'Joanna, I will arrange everything; Arthur will be cared for.' His voice dropped to a whisper. 'And he and I will be with you again very soon.'

The Duke of Norfolk bellowed to his men that we were about to depart. A man led a mare forward and helped me onto her.

'I have one more thing to say,' the duke announced, gathering his reins. 'You, Geoffrey Scovill, must not come after Joanna again. My wife's cousin has a taste for commoners. I have been lenient with the two of you tonight, for it's a taste I share. But that's at an end now. There can be no more scandals in the family.'

The highest-ranking nobleman of the kingdom pointed at Geoffrey. 'If I see you again in her company, it will be your hanging, Constable. Do you understand?'

I could not see Geoffrey's face. But I heard his voice. It was low, subdued. 'I understand, Your Grace.'

'Very good.' The duke slapped the flank of his horse. It bolted forward, and the rest of the horses surged after him. I barely needed to rattle the reins, my animal was so well trained. Norfolk moved fast, and his men and their horses knew how to keep the pace.

I twisted this way and that in the saddle, but there was no sign of Geoffrey. He did not follow me any longer. No sane man would, after the duke's warning. I was now at the mercy of the Duke of Norfolk.

23

My thoughts churned as I followed the duke along Lower Thames Street. How would I manage it – how would I possibly free myself of Norfolk? There had to be a way to return to Dartford without endangering Geoffrey's life. My closest friends, my dreams of independence – I could not abandon them for Stafford Castle.

Norfolk trotted to the Thames, and I heard the cry go out for a boat. We would make a night crossing. The duke's destination must be Howard House, in Southwark. I'd been to his large London establishment once before with Brother Edmund, a fateful day indeed.

The boatmen helped me onto their craft. Only three of us would be ferried across the river: the duke, his servant Richard, and myself. I watched the rest of the men gallop for the bridge and wondered why we had been split into two groups.

I said, 'Your Grace, may I inquire—?'

'No, you may not,' Norfolk said, roughly. 'I'll brook no questions, no women's pleading or caterwauling. Let me think, damn it.'

And with that, we eased away from the north shore. There was no sound but the boatmen's grunts as they pulled hard on the oars. It was not an easy journey; the tides were strong and against us. I could not imagine why Norfolk wanted to do this – surely it made more sense for us all to ride across the bridge to Southwark.

The wind blew cold on the dank and choppy river. I wrapped my arms around myself and bent over, shivering. The water in the boat bottom thoroughly soaked my borrowed velvet slippers. A hand tapped my shoulder, and Richard handed me a rough blanket he'd secured from the boatman.

'Thank you,' I whispered.

He nodded, his careful eyes on the duke hunched over at his seat at the bow.

Our boat finally reached a large wharf on the south bank. Freshly lit torches soared above it. Four men swarmed down the steps to the landing.

'Welcome, Your Grace,' one called out. It was not surprising that Southwarkers knew the Duke of Norfolk on sight, for he was a famous nobleman. Still, these did not seem like the type of men who'd find a livelihood on a river wharf. Where were we? A high wall hid what lay beyond.

We climbed the narrow stone steps to the top of the riverbank. The frigid wind whipped off the river, making my eyes sting and my nose drip. My feet had turned numb in my damp slippers.

An opening in the wall led to a narrow lane through a wooded park. At the other end was an arch; a large building rose behind it, though the trees obscured much of it. This wharf served a single prosperous establishment. It wasn't Howard House, though. I remembered that Norfolk's London manor house stood at least one mile from the river.

I followed the duke and Richard up the dark, well-swept lane. Trees lined both sides; their leafless branches met and mingled above our heads like a lattice.

The line of trees ended. I stepped into the clearing – and came face-to-face with a pale, staring woman. I stumbled back and fell on the cold ground. It took me a moment to realise that she was a statue. A white marble statue of a woman dancing, or perhaps an angel fleeing the earth. I was suddenly tempted to flee, too. The duke had passed through the arch ahead without stopping for me. I could hide in the woods or run back to the wharf.

But a night breeze made me shudder anew. I would freeze to death without shelter tonight or the means to secure it.

The moment I walked through the archway, my breath quickened. I'd entered a bustling courtyard lit with torches. Horses stood waiting on one side, with a half dozen finely dressed attendants standing by. Not Howard retainers – these served some other high-ranking noble-man. Two young servants crossed the courtyard, gingerly carrying glazed stoneware jugs.

On the far side of the courtyard rose a castle with a slanted-roof hall and a church steeple. Lights flickered in the windows of all three floors. This was a castle fully occupied. But whose?

Norfolk bounded through the castle's main entranceway, the initial *W* topping the doorway. Richard turned and beckoned for me to follow, and then he scrambled to keep up with the duke.

Inside the duke shouted for me to wait as he hustled into a room at the far end.

I half fell into the first chair I found in the warm gallery. My feet began to thaw. The smell of sweet herbs filled my head, emanating from the rushes strewn across the floor.

Sitting in a gallery such as this began to restore me, to stir my curiosity. What first caught my interest was a large painting of Our Lord Jesus Christ. It pulsed with vibrant golden light. Our Saviour gazed out of the painting with directness, a tender immediacy that I'd never experienced before. It was as if he gazed right into my eyes, if not my soul. This vivid work must have been painted in Rome by one of the Holy Father's most cherished geniuses. Now that I thought about it, the lifelike statue in the park was exquisitely fashioned, too. I felt humbled to be in the presence of such artistry. That was one of the most tragic aspects of the Reformation – its leaders' virulent hatred of art.

A young man dressed in velvets, carrying a rolled parchment, nodded to me as he walked past. After a moment I heard the murmured conversation of two more men strolling down the hall. By their collars and dark garb I immediately knew them to be priests. Once the two reached Richard, they fell into pleasant conversation.

What was this place? Neither palace nor cathedral, and, while religion was woven into much of my surroundings, it was certainly no monastery. This seemed like the residence of a prince of the church. A cardinal, perhaps. *But there are no cardinals left alive in England*, I reminded myself. There would never be another papal legate in the land.

Frustrated, I gazed at the painting once more. As impossible as it may seem, Christ's expression had altered. With a chill, I realised what filled His eyes when He gazed upon me. Pity.

A bishop. The letter *W*. A person close to the Duke of Norfolk.

This was the residence of the bishop of Winchester. Stephen Gardiner no longer served the king as chief ambassador in France. Gardiner, my nemesis and my master, the churchman who I had spied for against my will, had returned.

I was on my feet. I had no plan – only panic. Two words repeated in my head: *Get out. Get out. Get out.*

'Mistress Stafford, what are you doing?' Richard's voice echoed down the long gallery. I could hear his steps as he rushed after me.

I didn't turn around. I pushed open the door with all my strength, but the young page slammed it shut and jumped in front of me to bar my way, his smile gone.

'Do you serve Bishop Gardiner?' I asked.

He nodded but was puzzled, as if he could not understand why I would ask such an obvious question.

'This is Winchester House,' he said.

The next voice I heard was Norfolk's, ordering Richard to bring me down the gallery. Richard took my arm roughly, with an accusatory glare.

As Richard forced me to the end of the gallery, I remembered the last time I'd been in the presence of Bishop Gardiner: at Dartford Priory, on my very last day, when he'd flattered and badgered me to press me into continuing my spying – unsuccessfully. *'Defy me, and you shall bitterly regret it, as shall all my enemies.'* So this was why the Duke of Norfolk worked so hard to wrest me from Lord Dudley – to return me to the grip of the bishop.

When we reached it, Richard knocked twice on the door and then pushed it open. I tried to rid my face of all feeling. It was always a mistake to show fear to Gardiner.

I expected to encounter two people inside this room: Gardiner and his chief ally, the Duke of Norfolk. And indeed, those two men were present. Norfolk stood by the mullioned window, sombre, his hands clasped behind his back. Bishop Gardiner sat in a plush high-backed chair on a platform, his white robes grazing the floor. In Winchester House he wore on his head the bishop's mitre – the base of the imperious cone sparkled with gems. Gardiner had not changed. I felt those same light-hazel eyes on me, scrutinising me, probing for weakness.

But there was another chair next to his on the raised platform, and on it perched a third person, a small and forlorn figure, someone whom I had not expected for a single second to see.

It was the Lady Mary Tudor.

24

I curtsied low to the king's eldest daughter, a formal slide to the floor that my mother taught me before I learned to read.

The Lady Mary looked ill – no, worse than ill. Her luminous white complexion had turned chalky and loose. Her eyes were rimmed with red.

The princess held out her arms. I stepped up to the platform to embrace her, and it was like enfolding a frail child, not a twenty-two-year-old woman. The jewel-encrusted crucifix around her throat pressed so hard I thought it would pierce my flesh.

'I thank the Virgin that you at least are safe,' she whispered before letting me go. And then, louder, 'I will always be grateful to you for what you've accomplished tonight, Norfolk.'

The duke made a stiff bow. So this was why he'd extracted me from the wagon, not for belief in my innocence but to gain favour with the princess.

The Lady Mary looked at me expectantly and then at the bishop by her side. My stomach clenching, I took two steps over to stand directly before Gardiner. I knelt and then bowed my head.

From under lowered lashes, I saw the hand extend. What I had done thus far was not enough. The bishop was determined to wring every last form of obeisance from me. To obey readily and never contradict your superior – those were core principles taught at Dartford. I must perform them.

I kissed Gardiner's ring, a golden one set with amethyst. My lips grazed that smooth white hand, and I forced myself not to shudder.

Very slowly, the bishop withdrew his hand and I rose to my feet.

'*Benedicte*, Sister Joanna,' he said in a mild voice.

'*Dominus*,' I answered automatically.

'My most faithful bishop is recalled to England after three long years,' the Lady Mary said with a tremulous smile.

'You honour me with your trust and favour,' Gardiner said.

Fingering her crucifix, she declared, 'You are a great counsellor of the realm and purger of the faith.'

The words of Orobas from two nights previous echoed in my mind: *The Lady Mary wears a crown, she walks with a cardinal and a bishop.* Would Gardiner help Mary rule?

Aloud, I said, 'My lady, I believed you to be at Hunsdon House, far away in the country.'

'Cromwell said it was best I return to London,' she said. 'The Lord Privy Seal has me watched more closely than ever. He still reads every letter I write and receive.' She squinted into the farthest corner of the room as if searching there for spies.

'Your privacy is assured in this room,' Bishop Gardiner said soothingly. 'There is no danger for you in Winchester House. Norfolk and I are the king's most loyal servants.'

Gardiner, a most loyal subject? When he had forced me to search my priory for a mysterious relic that could have halted the king's Reformation? With deep frustration, I accepted that I'd never be able to penetrate the depths of the bishop's deceptions and discover whom he really served: the king, the Lady Mary, the pope, or simply himself.

Lady Mary said, 'I do not know why Cromwell wanted me close to court now – he gave no reason and I know better than to question him.'

'It must be the arrests tonight,' Norfolk said, pacing the room. 'If there was any question of upset, of citizens rising in rebellion, Cromwell wanted you within reach, my lady. Not in the country, where he fears you could rally the discontented.'

Bishop Gardiner asked, 'Did you see any signs of such discontent, Thomas?'

The duke shook his head. 'London is loyal to the king. They would never take up arms against him. Courtenay and Pole have no popular support.'

I burst out angrily, 'There was no rebellion planned. Those men are loyal.' I turned to Norfolk. 'What evidence could Sir Godfrey Pole possibly give Cromwell? Dudley said his information was freely given. Is that true?'

Norfolk stopped his pacing to snort. 'Godfrey was taken to the

Tower and questioned over and over, by men who are skilled in such matters, and he broke. Then he tried to take his own life. I'm told he stabbed himself but the knife was too blunt to do the fool serious damage.'

I made the sign of the cross as did the Lady Mary, fresh tears swelling in her eyes.

Bishop Gardiner patted the princess's arm protectively and said, 'We need not press into the sad details of this matter.'

But press on I did. 'Forgive me, Lady Mary, but I still don't believe this.' I pretended not to see the bishop's icy stare. 'I would swear on my life that Henry Courtenay never conspired against the king. I cannot imagine that Baron Montague or Sir Edward Neville did either.'

Dabbing her eyes, the Lady Mary said, 'Well, Norfolk? What are the grounds for arrest?'

'I've just heard rumours – no one knows but Cromwell and the king,' Norfolk said, his face darkening. Plainly he hated being kept in ignorance by the Lord Privy Seal. 'Of course, Montague's greatest crime is that Cardinal Pole is his younger brother. I heard there wasn't much to what the other brother supplied in the Tower but grumbling. Montague once said the king was served by knaves and heretics. Courtenay has been heard lamenting the changes in religion the king made.'

Stunned, I said, 'Is that all?'

Gardiner said, 'A recent Act of Parliament states that it is high treason to maliciously wish, will, or desire by words or writing, or by craft imagine, invent, practise, or attempt any bodily harm to be done or committed to the king's most royal person. Almost anything can be bent or stretched to fit such a definition.'

The Lady Mary dazedly twisted a long strand of dark red hair that had escaped from her Spanish headdress. 'My poor friends,' she said. 'Such good people. The Poles were the English family my mother loved above all. Sir Edward Neville is a gentle soul. Gertrude Courtenay has done more for me than any other lady dared, and Henry is so kind, always so kind.'

Bishop Gardiner said, 'They have royal blood in their veins, my lady. They are a threat to the House of Tudor. The French ambassador told me today that the king said he long wanted to destroy Montague and the rest of the Poles, for they were of the House of York.'

It was almost word for word what Baron Montague said earlier this night. Bishop Gardiner studied me. I bit the inside of my cheek, desperate to quiet my humours.

The bishop said, 'As long as Emperor Charles and the king of France stand against England, the king can brook no grumblings in his court. Should there be invasion and war, a disloyal group of nobles could join forces with Emperor Charles.'

A distant look came over the Lady Mary. With her dark red hair, blue eyes, and white skin, there was nothing outwardly Spanish about her. My colouring marked me as far more foreign than hers. Yet, at that moment, seized by such aloofness, she was the granddaughter of Queen Isabella of Castile and King Ferdinand of Aragon. What would happen if the emperor, her cousin, set out to conquer England? I knew that that was what Gertrude dreamed of. Was it possible that she had ever discussed such dreams with the princess?

The Duke of Norfolk cleared his throat. 'Lady Mary, I counted these men among my friends, too, but it must be admitted that their removal would make *you* more secure.'

'Do not say that to me,' she said, her voice deepening into command. 'I would never wish for a blood sacrifice of good Christian men so that I could sleep safer in my bed at night.'

Suddenly she sagged in her chair. 'Oh, you cannot know what it is to be the cause of such suffering,' she moaned. 'No one ever could but my mother. Men martyred themselves; they went to the block rather than abandon her cause. How could this be happening to me now?' Tears slid down the princess's ravaged cheeks.

Gardiner said that the Lady Mary had endured enough for one night. Norfolk left to order her party to prepare for the princess's departure.

She held out her arms to me again, for an embrace. 'I do not know when we will see each other again, Joanna. Please, please, please exercise better caution from this day forward.'

I gently freed myself from the Lady Mary. 'Forgive me, I don't follow,' I said. 'Better than what?'

She sighed. 'It was not wise to stay for weeks on end with Gertrude Courtenay. I love her dearly, yet she can be ruled by reckless passions. I must admit, I was surprised to learn you had become such close companions. I thought you happy in your lodgings in Dartford.'

I said slowly, 'Weren't you the one who sent Gertrude to Dartford to find me and take me into her home? That's what she told me.'

The Lady Mary was even more startled. 'Why ever would I do that? I corresponded with Gertrude over the past year, yes, but I wrote of no other friends of mine in those letters. To do so would be most unwise.'

I had no opportunity to say more, for Norfolk reappeared with the princess's retinue. She turned to me a last time and said fervently, 'Joanna, we must have faith in Almighty God the maker and redeemer. Pray to the pure and blessed Virgin for the safety of our beloved friends.'

I promised to do so, and she left.

The men who had been waiting outside burst into the room: Norfolk's Richard and the two priests of Winchester House. The bishop took papers from the older priest.

'I wonder,' he mused, as his eyes travelled down the sheet of paper, 'who it was that told Gertrude Courtenay to find you in Dartford and bring you to the Red Rose.'

Keeping my voice as calm as possible, I said, 'It's possible I made a mistake.'

Bishop Gardiner handed the first sheet of paper back to his priest attendant and beckoned for a second. 'Yes, I do know you are very capable of mistakes,' he said.

I must not let myself be baited by Gardiner. It was far preferable that he think me incompetent than learn that I had never told him the full truth of what I had found at Dartford Priory.

As Gardiner's eyes travelled down the second paper, the room was silent. Norfolk and Richard had left without my noticing. Had the Duke of Norfolk departed from Winchester House entirely? That possibility made me go cold, despite the roaring fire.

The bishop leaned back in his huge chair. 'You aimed high in trying to match yourself with Montague,' he said in that mild, musing voice. 'Some people thought he had a claim to the throne. Did you fancy yourself worthy to be queen of England?'

'I'm a loyal subject of the king, just the same as you,' I answered.

A smile stretched across his face. 'Last year, when I suggested that you marry someone for the sake of appearances to better assist the cause of the true Faith, you shouted at me in your usual rude manner. I had no idea you were saving yourself for a prize like Montague. And such a worldly man, not the husband I'd have envisioned for you. Not that it matters – you'll never be a baroness now.'

Something was abundantly clear to me.

'You don't care what happens to Montague, or the Courtenays, or Neville,' I whispered.

'They are dispensable,' he said calmly. 'As are you, Sister Joanna. I'd not care a whit if you were back in the Tower but for the fact that you have ingratiated yourself with the Lady Mary. As long as His Majesty's daughter cares about your welfare, then so do I.'

'I have no need of your solicitude,' I said. My desperate hold on my temper was fraying. Soon it would be gone.

Gardiner studied me in silence for a moment. 'Do you know, I am not even sure of the legality of a union between a man and a woman who has taken vows of chastity advisedly. The king has quite pronounced views on the matter. I will discuss it with him during my next audience.'

To my great relief, Norfolk reappeared. He huddled with Gardiner for a moment, and then beckoned for me. 'Time to go,' he said.

'Wait, Thomas,' said Gardiner. He murmured something to one of his minions, and a moment later a cloak was borne into the room on a page's outstretched arms. It was black velvet with the letter W embossed in gold.

'We wouldn't want the Lady Mary's protégée to sicken from the cold,' he said.

'I thank you, Bishop Gardiner,' I said between gritted teeth, and wrapped myself in the heavy cloak.

'*Di te incolumen custodiant*,' he responded, the Latin pleasantry trilling off his tongue.

At nearby Howard House, a tall torch flickered outside the entrance to the sprawling manor. A man slumped next to it, deep asleep. Norfolk jumped off his horse and kicked him in the leg. 'Wake up, cur!' he shouted.

Servants rushed out the doors in a panic. Others scrambled from around the house to take our mounts to the Howard stables.

Richard helped me off my horse. My legs, my arms, my feet, my neck and shoulders, even the tips of my fingers, ached with weariness.

'How long am I to stay here?' I asked thickly.

Richard shrugged.

Norfolk heard my question and said, 'As long as it takes to make arrangements to bundle you up to Stafford Castle.' He turned to a hard-eyed female servant. 'Find her a room.'

My quarters that first night at Howard House were shabby by most standards. The bedding wasn't clean; unwashed goblets littered a table. But all I could think of were the new prisoners at the Tower of London and what cells *they* huddled in tonight. I blew out the smouldering candle stump and stumbled into bed, still wearing the cloth of silver Gertrude had commissioned for me and the heavy cloak Gardiner forced onto my shoulders. I'd brought nothing with me. It was either sleep in these absurd garments or be naked between soiled sheets.

I should have lost consciousness at once. But they crowded before me, whether my eyes were open or shut: Gertrude, her eyes pleading. Henry Courtenay, clutching his weeping son. Baron Montague, masking his terror with a show of arrogance. Geoffrey, struggling to pull me to safety – but never quite able to. And finally James, lifting the bloody head of his twin brother off the street. Each vision pierced me in a different way.

I'd told Baron Montague I would pray for him; I'd promised the Lady Mary as well. And pray I did. Whispered pleas filled my dark, dirty room. But they were all but drowned out by the noises in my head. Screams and sobs. Horse hoofs on Lower Thames Street. The slap of oars on the Thames. And one man's voice, Stephen Gardiner's, saying a single sentence over and over.

'I wonder who it was that told Gertrude Courtenay to find you in Dartford and bring you to the Red Rose.'

25

'Wake up, Joanna,' said a woman's voice. 'Ah, you're still one of the hardest people to rouse in the morning.'

I opened my eyes to a small room flooded with sunlight. Sitting next to me on the bed was a long-faced woman in her middle years: my cousin Elizabeth, the Duchess of Norfolk.

Her presence in the house of her husband made no sense. The marriage of the Duke and Duchess of Norfolk was the unhappiest in all of England. Their mutual hatred often erupted into shouting and even blows, until my cousin ceased sharing a roof with the duke five years ago. She'd lived alone in the country ever since, refusing to grant the Duke of Norfolk a divorce or reconcile.

Elizabeth gathered a fold of my cloth of silver dress in both hands, holding it up to the light 'Where did you get this dress?' she asked.

'Gertrude Courtenay gave it to me,' I muttered. My throat ached and my head spun from lack of nourishment. 'Do you know what happened last night?'

She sat back down on the edge of the bed. 'Yes, it is all most upsetting,' she said calmly. 'I will order that food and drink and suitable clothes be brought to you. If this were my father's house, it would all be here within minutes. But it's a Howard house and I've only been back a week. I've not yet got the staff in hand. So it may take an hour.'

She made for the door. She wore a sombre, square-necked dress, the sort my mother favoured years ago.

'Wait – Elizabeth,' I cried. 'What's to happen to me?'

'You're to be sent up to Stafford Castle as soon as possible. The Howard secretary writes a letter today to my brother. When the duke returns from court, the letter will be signed and dispatched.'

Pulling myself up in the bed, I said, 'But I have a home in Dartford. Arthur must be there by now. My friends are there – my life is there. Please, you must help me.'

Elizabeth frowned. 'Don't be tiresome, Joanna. It's all been decided. Arthur will be sent up to Stafford Castle, too, when the time comes. But he can't stay at Howard House. The duke won't hear of it.'

She opened the door. 'You can attend me in my receiving room later, but not if you intend to harangue me. Your tantrums always made my head ache.'

With a swish of her dark skirts, she was gone.

The Duchess of Norfolk was correct, it took nearly an hour for a chunk of bread and mug of weak ale to arrive. But that gave me time to think. And once new strength flowed into my body, I was ready to attempt a plan.

I was not going to be sent anywhere but Dartford. I would do whatever it took to find a way home.

Elizabeth and I had never been close. She was seventeen years older. Among the females of the Stafford family, she, the eldest daughter of the Duke of Buckingham, reigned at the top of the heap. My place was near the bottom, if not *the* bottom. But Elizabeth's young half sister, Margaret, was the closest companion of my childhood. After the Duke of Buckingham was executed, Margaret went to live with her unhappy sister. I saw them both on visits, and Margaret wrote me many letters besides. I knew something of the moods of Elizabeth.

I could hear the duchess's sharp voice from outside her receiving room. 'Must I go through this *again*?' she demanded. 'Do you remember nothing of what I taught you?'

I eased inside.

Elizabeth stood, arms folded, mouth set in a severe line, in front of a table. There were a few objects set upon it: pewter plates, cups, tiny mounds of salt in dishes. And a large knife. It was a strange assembly and yet familiar too.

On the other side of the table quavered a girl of about sixteen, short and verging on plump, with long auburn hair. She was not the duchess's daughter. The only other time I had been inside Howard House, at a masque party given by Elizabeth's oldest son, the Earl of Surrey, I met this girl. Catherine Howard. She was one of the many nieces of the Duke of Norfolk. I remembered her as giggling and lovely, with deep dimples. She most definitely did not exhibit dimples now. Catherine was frozen in indecision, her hand hovering over the knife.

'You must prostrate yourself three times before you touch it,' said Elizabeth.

'The knife – or the salt?' she whispered.

Elizabeth threw up her hands. 'See what I must cope with, Joanna?' she demanded, seeing me enter the room. 'My husband said I am to train her for court service. The Howards are making her their candidate for maid of honour. Catherine is the only one of the right age and bonny enough to qualify. But she knows nothing! Her only talents are lute playing and dancing. The Howards haven't taught her anything serious – she can barely read – and yet they expect her to wait on a queen brought up in Paris or Brussels? *Ridiculous.*'

Catherine, scarlet with shame, peered over at me. Recognition flickered in her eyes – she remembered me too.

I moved toward the table. 'You curtsy as low as possible to the knife,' I explained. 'You rub the plate with some of the salt. Then, you put a tiny mound of salt on the knife.'

'I am most grateful for your kind help,' the girl said to me, a smile restoring the prettiness I remembered. 'But how do you know all of this, mistress?'

'My mother taught me how to prepare dinner for the queen's presence chamber,' I said.

The duchess said approvingly, 'Joanna's mother was trained in Spain, where they have the highest standards of all for court ladies. She and I served the queen together; I waited on Katherine of Aragon for sixteen years.'

Catherine said timidly, 'Your Grace, it might help me if I understood why this is done. *Why* must the plates be rubbed with salt?'

'It has to do with the threat of poison,' Elizabeth said.

Catherine's eyes flickered with interest. 'Has anyone ever tried to poison a queen of England?'

'Not to my knowledge,' Elizabeth admitted, 'but the Borgias were not so long ago, with their poisoners.'

'Who are the Borgias?' asked Catherine.

Elizabeth groaned. Once again, I stepped in to explain. It was not easy. The Borgia crimes always made me uncomfortable. Some people claimed the Borgias were in some part responsible for igniting the firestorm of heresy that now threatened to engulf Christendom.

After I'd finished, Elizabeth marched over to a stool pushed against the wall. She snatched up a piece of needlework and waved it at me. 'This is all that Catherine is capable of.'

Even from across the room, the stitches looked primitive. I stole another glance at Catherine. She rolled her eyes at me – I was relieved to see she had spirit – and then dipped a curtsy. 'I apologise for all my shortcomings, Your Grace.'

'When is the new queen set to arrive?' I asked.

'Oh, nothing is decided yet,' Elizabeth answered, 'but the field is narrowing.'

My cousin nibbled on a fingernail and then said, 'Catherine, I've endured enough of you. Leave me.'

The young Howard girl scampered out of the room.

'Will *you* wait on the queen?' I asked my cousin. 'I'd imagine you would be the principal lady of waiting.'

'It's possible.'

'Then you will need all sorts of new garments to wear to court,' I said, with a single clap of my hands. I wanted it to seem as if the idea just occurred. 'I want you to have that cloth of silver dress, Elizabeth. It can be easily mended. And all the rest of the fine dresses the marchioness of Exeter gave me – you should have them as well. We are of the same size.'

My cousin's face lit up. She tried at once to dampen it – she realised its unseemliness. She said, 'If it can be managed to secure them from the Red Rose, then, yes, I could make a place for them here. Are you quite sure, Joanna?'

'Oh, I want you to have the clothes,' I said. Which was true enough. I would never wear them again.

Elizabeth suddenly flung herself across the room. Thin arms encircled me. 'It's kind of you, Joanna. Most kind. If there's anything I can do—'

I counted to five and then said, 'You can speak to the duke about my returning to Dartford, not Stafford Castle.'

She rapidly withdrew from our familial embrace. 'No I couldn't,' she said. 'The duke would never, ever agree. Joanna, this is your fault. You shouldn't have taken lodgings in Dartford with that child in the first place. It was not fitting – no one approved at the time.'

'"That child", as you call him, is Margaret's own son,' I said.

Elizabeth said, 'I know – yes, of course I know of the poor boy.'

For the first time I glimpsed the caring heart that Margaret always insisted that Elizabeth possessed. 'I've wanted to see Arthur for a long time – I wanted to be by Margaret's side at the end. Impossible. I'm the highest ranking lady in the land after the king's wives and daughters and Lady Margaret Douglas, but I have no power at all.'

Elizabeth had always raged over our sex's inferiority. Other women submitted to slights if not abuses every day. Not Elizabeth. That was one of the reasons she had taken the shocking step of leaving her husband. She was unwilling to submit to him after she felt wronged.

'Why have you returned to Howard House?' I asked.

'I had no choice,' she said. 'My husband would not give me a proper allowance after I left him. I have no money of my own. No one would visit me, not even my children. They took their father's part. Gertrude Courtenay, your great friend, abandoned my cause like everyone else. I asked my brother Henry if I could return to Stafford Castle and live with him and his family – and do you know what he did? He wrote to my husband that he did not want me – he did not even write back to me at all. There's too much scandal attached to my name.'

'Perhaps cousin Henry won't want me either,' I said hopefully.

Elizabeth waved a hand at me. 'I'm the Duchess of Norfolk, and you're a nobody. It's not the same.' She sighed. 'It was Cromwell who brokered this reconciliation. My condition was he not strike me or humiliate me by keeping his whores under the same roof. In return I will take his households in hand again, though it is not easy. My husband wants to keep Christmas in grand style. *Ridiculous.* Everyone in the family comes and goes, the accounts are in chaos. The Howards are a bad lot. I told my father that when he forced me to wed. Father laughed at me – but I was right.'

Looking at her mournful face, I had another idea.

'Let me help you, cousin,' I said. 'I can teach Catherine needlework and the other things she needs to know to be a proper maid of honour. I will assist with all the preparations for Christmastide.'

Elizabeth brightened. 'Would you do that for me, Joanna?'

I felt a twist of guilt over my deceit but forced myself to say yes. Southwark was so close to Dartford, two hours by horse. If I managed to make myself indispensable here, I could yet find a way to manoeuvre home. If I were forced to return to Stafford Castle, it would be much, much harder.

Elizabeth interceded with her husband, and I was permitted to remain through Christmas. But while here I'd need to adhere to certain rules, for the duke plainly did not trust me. Arthur Bulmer was never to be permitted inside the house. I must not correspond with anyone. I could not discuss the arrests of the Courtenays, Baron Montague, or the rest inside the walls of Howard House. I was not to read any books. The last rule left me stunned. Elizabeth explained that her husband detested reading and was certain that book learning had ruined the kingdom. Literature and theology and politics were all forbidden topics at Howard House.

Everyone fearfully complied with the duke's edicts except for one member of the Howard family – the Earl of Surrey, Norfolk's twenty-one-year-old son and heir. Surrey broke every rule.

On my fourth day there, he materialised at dinner with his wife, Frances. Like Catherine Howard, when prompted, he recognised me from the party last year. But he was not preoccupied by festivities now. The treacherous politics at court were his chief concern. 'There's no specific evidence of treason against Courtenay and the rest,' he declared. 'They may serve long terms in the Tower, but the king won't let Cromwell kill these good men based on no evidence at all.'

I ached to question Surrey, to learn more about how my friends fared in the Tower. Elizabeth, knowing my mind, shook her head warningly at me.

Surrey leaped to his feet and threw a goblet at the fireplace. It shattered. 'Cromwell wants no one but low creatures like himself around the king,' he roared.

My next encounter with Surrey was more personally troubling. I was asleep when the words of a bawdy tune exploded down the passageway outside my room.

I opened the door a crack to discover the cause of the disturbance. Surrey clung to the wall, his mother at his side.

'You!' he shouted. 'You are the one who hates my father.'

He lunged into my room, pushing the door open with such force that pieces of wood split into the air. 'I will speak to your cousin,' he said.

Now that he was close, I smelled the vomit on his clothes. The earl's face was reddened and shiny. Men drank too much wine – I knew that. But there was a horror to this level of drunkenness.

'She's your cousin too,' Elizabeth pointed out, worried for me.

'I don't want to talk to *you*,' he growled. 'I want to talk to Joanna Stafford.'

'Then do so,' I said, disgusted. 'Speak your piece and leave me be.'

Surrey pushed his mother out and closed the door. 'I know what people whisper behind my back. That my father was a pimp for Anne Boleyn. It's a damn lie. The Boleyns never listened to him. They did what they wanted always. What did we get out of that marriage? Nothing. She talked to him worse than she would a dog.'

A memory stirred. A few days before he died, my father told me the most sordid story about Norfolk. When Queen Anne was with child, the king caught sight of my beautiful cousin Margaret and lusted for the daughter of the man he'd had killed. He wanted Margaret brought to his bed. Norfolk tried to force her to comply, thinking his sister-in-law could prove a mistress of benefit to him. When a revolted Margaret fled the court, my father hid her from Norfolk until she could go north.

Perhaps the duke ended up loathing his niece Anne Boleyn, but I suspected that in the beginning he'd pushed for that dalliance too. The doubt must have shown in my face. Surrey redoubled his efforts to persuade me of his father's worth.

'Why does it matter to you what I think?' I asked wearily.

'I want you to know the truth – I want everyone to know the truth,' he said. His face whitened, he covered his mouth, and he stumbled out the door. I heard him coughing and spitting outside my room. Elizabeth, who had been waiting, spoke soothingly.

'Oh, Mother,' moaned Surrey, and began weeping. Childish wails filled the passageway. They grew fainter as he retreated to his room. Unhappy Howard House fell silent once more.

26

I kept my promise to Elizabeth, training Catherine Howard in the skills she'd need for court. I helped with the planning of Christmastide, the ordering of meats and mince pies and sweets.

But I longed for the company of my friends in Dartford as never before. Within these walls, there was no one remotely like selfless Brother Edmund – or his devout sister, Winifred. As for Geoffrey, thoughts of him were never far away either. In the middle of the night, tossing sleepless in my bed, I saw Geoffrey emerge from the shadows of the alcove at the top of the stairs. He'd press me into his arms so tightly, my cloth of silver burned my flesh. But, come morning, I always felt deep shame at my weakness. Geoffrey Scovill would be best off without me. I had brought him little but trouble, and if we came together in the future, it could mean his death.

Then there was Arthur. Worry bored into me like a wasting disease. My father had entrusted him to my care – and I had failed. Who was looking after him? How was he faring? It was so cruel that Norfolk had forbidden Arthur to come to me or for me to send word to those who cared for him. It was the duke's guilt over Margaret's death, I suspected, that made him take such a stance. My cousin Elizabeth felt nearly as miserable about Arthur, I knew that. But there was little she could do – her own position was precarious. One night, after a quarrel with the duke, Elizabeth wept in my arms for hours.

'What was your quarrel about?' I asked.

'He wants to match our daughter Mary with Thomas Seymour, a lout and wastrel. But I know Mary loathes Seymour, and I tried to take her part. She has refused to marry him and stays away from London. How he cursed at me.'

I tried to comfort my cousin, but I was terrible at such a task. Margaret would have talked with her, pressed compresses on her forehead, brushed her hair, prayed with her. I tried to do those things, but my own mood was so fraught, it was difficult to lift her spirits. In addition, she steadily refused to help me make my way home to Dartford, not Stafford Castle. 'Don't harangue me about that now!' she always implored me, rubbing her forehead.

It was Catherine Howard who noticed my deepening sadness, much as I tried to hide it, at needlework one morning. She had shadows to her own nature, and was far from the 'pretty simpleton' that Elizabeth dubbed her. Catherine rarely spoke of her past, but I learned that her childhood had been one of hardship. No grown member of the Howard family cared what happened to her until the duke thought her fit for court. Even now, her happiness was of no importance – all that mattered was the possibility she could do well enough to advance the clan. It had been made clear to her she must find a husband with enough coins in his pocket to take her off the Howards' hands.

'If you are unhappy here, why don't you return to Stafford Castle?' Catherine asked.

'I made a life for myself in Dartford with friends and a little boy who needs me,' I said. 'I mean to start a tapestry business. At this moment, my loom sits, unused, in a building office on the High Street.'

'I can barely keep my stitches straight, and you can create whole tapestries?' she asked, awestruck.

'Catherine, your stitching is far better than you give yourself credit for,' I said, pointing to the work in her lap. 'You've improved, without question.'

The smallest compliments had such an impact, for she was so starved of them. She said, 'I have an excellent teacher,' a dimple appearing in her soft cheek.

It was the end of November and quite cold when everything changed one morning. I had not broken my fast, for I was determined to go without sustenance all day. It had been too long since I fasted. There was a soft tap at the open door. Catherine beckoned for me, her face flushed. 'You must come with me now,' she said, and pulled me out of the room.

'Why?' I asked as we hurtled along. But she wouldn't answer.

Shortly I found myself walking down the long passageway on the main floor, and I watched, surprised, as Catherine removed a key from her pocket and began fiddling with a door at the end.

'What are you doing?' I asked.

'Shhhhh,' Catherine said, and then burst out giggling.

'I am glad to see you in better spirits, but I must insist you tell me what we're about here,' I said firmly.

Catherine whispered: 'There's a man come to see you, and I've hidden him in here.'

Geoffrey. He'd been unable to bear our separation any longer. I felt a flash of joy, swiftly swallowed up by fear. How incredibly dangerous to come to the Duke of Norfolk's own house.

As soon as Catherine got the door open, I pushed in ahead of her. It was a dark storeroom, filled with chairs and trays.

Brother Edmund stepped out of the corner.

'Sister Joanna,' he said, 'I've come to take you home.'

27

B rother Edmund said, 'Won't you speak to me, Sister Joanna?'
But I couldn't, for it was too impossible to believe that he stood before me, after all these weeks. I soaked in every detail: Brother Edmund's ash-blond hair, grown long because he never wanted to take the time to cut it. His sensible dark brown doublet, the one I had helped him order from a tailor after we were forced to put away our white habits and black cloaks. His sturdy shoes, caked with dried mud. He must have walked the entire way from Dartford to Howard House.

'It's you, ah it's you—' I burst out.

He stepped forward quickly to comfort me. It was not the same sort of embrace as Geoffrey Scovill's. He squeezed my shoulder with one hand and gently patted my back with the other. 'I am here, hush, I am here,' he said.

'You are my friend,' I said, as if I were a small child. Brother Edmund smiled and said, 'Did not your favourite Dominican, Thomas Aquinas, say, "There is nothing on this earth to be prized more than true friendship"?'

'Yes,' I said. 'Oh, yes.' I turned to Catherine. 'Thank you for this.'

She explained that she saw Brother Edmund walking up the path from her window this morning. She recognised him from when we both came to Howard House last year; she was the one who greeted and conversed with us before we donned our masks. She'd rushed down to find out why he'd come. A few sentences persuaded her that Brother Edmund best be brought inside and hidden until I could be secured.

'How is Arthur?' I asked.

'He is well, Sister Joanna, do not be troubled. He lives with me and Sister Winifred.' Brother Edmund shared the precious details of Arthur's arrival and subsequent activities. 'Of course Arthur misses you, as have I.' He added quickly, 'And Sister Winifred and Sister Beatrice and all the rest – Sisters Eleanor and Agatha and Rachel. We all miss you.'

I asked, 'How did you know I was here?'

Brother Edmund explained that when he brought Arthur to Dartford, Geoffrey Scovill relayed the news of the Red Rose arrests. Geoffrey said that the Duke of Norfolk forced Lord Dudley to rescind my arrest and then commandeered me. 'Master Scovill said that though he did not have knowledge of your whereabouts, you knew where he was and would send word when the time was right. He advised waiting.'

So Geoffrey did not tell him of the duke's warning to hang him if he were found with me. A significant omission.

Catherine said, 'But you didn't wait.'

'No,' Brother Edmund said. 'I didn't wait.' His cheeks reddened slightly. 'I remembered Howard House from when we came here, Sister Joanna. It was my first destination.'

Catherine had already told Brother Edmund about the duke's shifting plans for me.

'I am prepared to speak to His Grace on your behalf as soon as he returns and make a case for your coming back with me to Dartford,' Brother Edmund said.

Catherine and I exchanged a look of horror.

'The duke won't listen to you, Brother Edmund,' I said. 'I appreciate your wanting to do this, but it will only succeed in bringing his wrath down on you.'

Brother Edmund was silent. He peered out the window, the corners of his mouth turned down. I knew what this meant – his supple Dominican mind turned the problem over.

'I don't see where the Duke of Norfolk's authority originates from,' Brother Edmund said. 'He is not your father or husband or brother – you don't have any. Being married to your cousin Elizabeth does not give him the right to determine where *you* should live and what you should do. It'd be different if you were accused of some crime and he had legal powers granted in the matter. But that is not the case. You simply wish to pursue a life he disapproves of.'

'Everything you say makes sense,' I said. 'But all he has to do is issue commands and everyone around him obeys.'

'At Howard House, yes, but I would like to move this matter to a different sphere,' said Brother Edmund. 'I think it is time we found you legal counsel in London.'

Again I was rendered speechless. It was ludicrous to think a lawyer could get the better of a nobleman, and especially one who commanded armies.

'I see you are sceptical,' said Edmund. 'But do not rule out the possibility of a legal solution. In the last twenty years, lawyers have become a force to be reckoned with. Didn't the king turn to the law of the land when denied his divorce by the pope?'

'This is hardly a matter of the same magnitude,' I said. 'But I agree it's a plan, and the only one that could possibly work.'

Catherine was eager to assist. She and I would leave the house together, saying we sought exercise. Brother Edmund would meet us down the road, and he and I would then make our way through Southwark to London Bridge. Since the Duke of Norfolk was sure to send men to Dartford to search for me, we would find lodgings at a London inn until legal discussions commenced.

In no time at all, Catherine and I were out the front door of Howard House. When I said good-bye to her at the bend in the road, while Brother Edmund waited by a leafless oak, she pressed a purse of coins into my hand. I knew it was all the money she had, and so I tried to give it back, but she wouldn't allow it.

'I will miss you, Joanna,' she said, her voice trembling. 'You're the only person who's shown me kindness without expecting anything in return.'

We embraced, and then, my arm encircling Brother Edmund's, I walked quickly up the road. Every time a horseman trotted past, my stomach leaped. I feared seeing the gold-and-black livery and hearing my name shouted once again. But no one seemed to pay us any notice. The streets grew more crowded, the manor houses disappeared. We entered the rougher part of Southwark, then, finally, reached London Bridge.

It was a fantastical sight from the south side of the Thames. Houses and shops, painted all different colours, crowded on top of the stone bridge. I'd heard that bookmakers, merchants, and artists throve in their homes perched atop the Thames.

'Oh, there's a line of people waiting to walk over,' said Brother

Edmund, regretful, pointing at a string of men and women standing to the side of the wagons and horses that streamed into a dark, narrow opening, more like a tunnel than a bridge. 'This could take longer than we'd wish.' He glanced at the door we stood in front of – a solid bench was nailed to the ground next to the doorway, out of the main thrust of the street. At the end of it began the throng of taverns and whore-houses that surrounded Winchester House.

'Why don't you sit here?' asked Brother Edmund. 'I'll make inquir-ies. You look fatigued, and we have a way to walk yet before we reach Lincoln's Inn.'

I sat down. As I watched Brother Edmund hurry the rest of the way to the bridge, I had to admit that it felt good to rest.

A strange guttural roar sounded from across the busy street, fol-lowed by men's cheers. It seemed to come from the other side of a high wall of wooden planks, tied together to form an enormous circle. The guttural sound rose up again – it was not like any other noise I'd heard. But I could see nothing but the wooden circle.

An old man standing by the bench noticed my straining to see what caused such an unearthly noise.

'That's the bears, mistress,' he said.

I stared at him. 'There are bears in Southwark?'

'They are hard to find but men capture them far away and bring 'em to Southwark for bear baitin',' he said. 'People save pence for months and months to pay for a trip to the baitin'.'

I swallowed. Something disturbed me about these bears.

A gang of young men led in dogs to the bear-baiting arena. The dogs were large. I knew they were to be used against the captured beast but not quite how.

Then I remembered, with an icy rush, what it was about bears I feared. I heard the voice of Orobas, channelling the spirit of a long-dead Saxon nun: '*Look to the bear to weaken the bull.*'

Next the prophecy of Sister Elizabeth Barton hurtled into my thoughts. Why would these words all descend on me now, unbidden, in the midst of loud, dirty Southwark? I did not know, and yet I could not suppress it: '*When the raven climbs the rope, the dog must soar like the hawk.*'

I felt Gertrude Courtenay's eyes boring into me from the wagon conveying her to the Tower of London. *Do something*, those eyes screamed. Yet I'd never for a single moment understood what it was that I could do.

'Sister Joanna?' Brother Edmund had already returned. 'What's wrong?' he said. 'You look terrified.'

'Nothing,' I said. 'It's the bear baiting. Nothing.'

He stared at me. 'Bears frighten you?'

I leaped to my feet. 'Can we now cross the bridge?'

Brother Edmund explained that because the bridge was so narrow and the horse and wagon traffic so heavy, all who trod across it on foot must walk carefully, in a single file. We'd have to wait our turn. We might not be across the Thames for another hour.

'That's fine,' I muttered, still thinking about the screams of the bears.

'Wait, Sister Joanna.'

Brother Edmund stopped walking. His arms were folded across his chest, his frown running deep. 'I must know what has happened to you,' he said. 'Something *else* has shaken you.'

I could not say a word to Brother Edmund.

'If you tell me what's happened, I can help,' he prompted.

I said, 'Brother, we need to cross the Thames.'

In tense silence we walked those last yards to London Bridge. My mind worked frantically with every step. I thought about how Brother Edmund had helped me in the desperate search for the Athelstan crown. How valuable his intelligence was. And, just as important, his integrity and compassion.

I stopped short of the line to cross the bridge. I pulled Brother Edmund away, finding a place where no one else could hear us: a filthy, narrow alleyway between shops. He was not startled, nor did he pull away from me. He knew full well that I would tell him what he wanted to know.

'When I was seventeen,' I said, 'my mother took me to Canterbury.'

PART FOUR

28

Brother Edmund listened to my story – my experience of twice hearing prophecy that pushed me toward an unknown fate – in rapt silence. The only time he interrupted was after I told him that Sister Elizabeth Barton repeated the words of another seer, Mother Shipton of Yorkshire: 'When the cow doth ride the bull, then priest beware thy skull.'

'I've heard that,' he said. And then: 'Continue.'

When I'd finished, he was silent for a good while. He stared at the filth-covered wall of the alley, faint crinkles deepening around his eyes. Then he turned to me.

'Do you believe it?' he asked.

I took a deep breath. 'I have asked myself that question many times, considering everything: Sister Elizabeth's recanting, and then Gertrude's explanation for why she recanted. The possibility that Orobas was a fraud after Gertrude's money. This is what torments me – I am not sure. I go round and round and round.'

I laid my hand on his arm. 'Tell me, Brother Edmund, you must tell me what *you* think. Can such prophecies exist?'

'Oh, prophets and seers and witches and necromancers abound, all of them claiming to divine the future,' replied Brother Edmund. 'As to how much of it is genuine, it's impossible to know. Certainly tricksters excel at extracting coins from the gullible. But your experience, what you've seen and heard, makes me believe …'

To my amazement, Brother Edmund smiled. I'd expected him to be frightened for me, not react like this. 'Sister Joanna, I do believe this could be genuine.'

I was taken aback. 'And you think it welcome?'

'It's frightening, yes, and most mysterious, but just think, if it be true, then you would be the one,' he said.

'The one?' I repeated blankly.

He seized both my arms and shook me, not in anger but with excitement. 'You would be the one to restore the *monasteries*.' Our faces were inches apart – his was transformed. Longing poured from him. He'd lost his life as a Dominican friar, though his calling remained. We'd all been forced to abandon our dream. Yet now, because of what I'd revealed, a restoration was possible. Why didn't I surge forward, snatching at my place in prophecy, eager to bring back our way of life? But I couldn't. I moved away from him, bumping against the brick wall.

A man laughed at the end of the alleyway, and his companion shouted at us, 'That's right, my lad – take her where ye can get her. Up against the wall!'

Brother Edmund immediately stepped back. I blushed at such crudity.

Still laughing, the two men walked away.

I cleared my throat and said, 'None of it has ever made sense to me. All those descriptions of birds and animals – I don't understand why the prophecy has to be delivered in such an unclear manner.'

'Prophecy is dangerous,' Brother Edmund said, calmer now. 'The king knows this and that is why he fears and hates it among his subjects. He's proclaimed it "devilish". A prediction of what may come to pass could inspire men to commit desperate and violent acts. Do you know anything about codes?'

I shook my head.

'Foreign ambassadors and statesmen – and the spies they employ – often write in code to protect their meanings from anyone who would steal or misuse their communications. Animals, birds, plants, insects – they can symbolise certain people or events. But a code works only if both parties understand the meanings: the sender and the receiver.'

'But that's my point,' I said. 'I *don't*.'

'They are not always difficult to decipher,' Brother Edmund said. 'What Mother Shipton said – "When the cow doth ride the bull, then priest beware thy skull" – has been widely interpreted as what happened to us all when Anne Boleyn ruled over King Henry.'

It was as if a door opened.

'The bull is the king,' I cried. 'But Orobas said, "Look to the bear to weaken the bull." That animal must symbolise the man or woman who will weaken King Henry. So who is the bear?' I winced. 'Could the bear possibly be *me*?'

Brother Edmund thought for a moment and then shook his head. 'I don't have any idea.'

'Why me at all? Why would I be chosen to perform some sort of act? Sister Barton said, "You are the one who will come after." Gertrude said I would be the salvation of the true Faith in England. And Orobas suggested that the future of the whole kingdom depends on something that I do. But I have no power, no influence over anyone. I'm not even courageous.'

Brother Edmund smiled. 'I would beg to argue that point.' Then he bit his lip. 'I can think of two reasons why you would be chosen. First is your Stafford birth, your connections. I know you deplore your noble blood, but it does put you into the court and near the king and Cromwell, should you wish it.'

'I don't,' I said sourly. 'What is the second reason?'

'You are a Dominican. Perhaps when you met with Sister Elizabeth Barton, it was known by her, with her talent for seeing into the future, that you would profess vows to our order.'

'How does being a Dominican make me a more likely tool of prophecy? There are other orders that delve deeper into such mysticism.'

'There is a deeply mystical side to our order,' he insisted. 'We are engulfed by God. Knowledge comes to us, wisdom and understanding, that is not knowable through the intellect. A part of that knowledge is glimpses into the future.'

'So any Dominican can become a prophet?' I asked, taken aback.

'No, no, no,' he said. 'Very few possess true prophetic powers. If only I had access to the books of a Dominican monastery. We could try to find the keys to unlock these predictions. Without knowledge, there is only fear.'

Brother Edmund was right. It was time to stop trying to escape from the prophecies. If I could decipher their meanings, at least I would gain some advantage in knowledge.

But there was a serious obstacle.

'If the monasteries are all destroyed, so are their libraries,' I pointed out.

Brother Edmund said, 'The greatest of them all – Blackfriars – was just surrendered to the king. The library may still have its books.'

'Are you familiar with it?' I asked.

He nodded. 'I was a friar professed there for four years. Today we could go to Blackfriars and then on to Lincoln's Inn. The two are not far from each other.'

Full of new purpose, we took our place in line waiting to cross the Thames on the sixty-foot-high London Bridge. After paying, we shuffled slowly across the river, the wagons and carts rumbling so close to us in the narrow passageway that they sometimes brushed against us.

The moment I stepped out into the light on the north side, we heard, 'Where are ye bound? Do ye need a horse? A riverboat? For a few pence, I can find ye anything!' The offer was made by a hunchback who greeted the foot travellers as they emerged.

'I thank you, sir, but we travel by foot to Blackfriars,' answered Brother Edmund.

The hunchback laughed. 'No one goes on foot to Blackfriars,' he said, and moved on.

'What does he mean by that?' I asked.

'You'll see,' said Brother Edmund, looking rather pained.

And so I did. Blackfriars is the largest Dominican house in England and the wonder of Christendom. For two centuries, its friars answered to no English rulers, king or clergy, only to the pope. Despite its fame, I had never seen the monastery with my own eyes. Brother Edmund was surprised by that – like many others he believed being a member of a noble family denoted intimate knowledge of London. But there were many parts of London I did not know. After we arrived, I stepped through an enormous arch – carved into it the revered Dominican crest, with its stars and white lilies and the word *Veritas* – and into a cobbled courtyard, as large as the one at Winchester House. To the left stood a gatehouse and, behind it, an enormous windowed castle and churchyard and supporting buildings set within high stone walls. One would come on horseback or litter to such a place, not humbly on foot.

We found the porter, a red-faced man in his forties, sitting alone in the gatehouse, singing.

'This is Master John Portinary,' Brother Edmund said. 'For many years, the tireless porter of Blackfriars.'

'And proud of it, proud of it,' the man shouted, slamming his fist on the table. 'Ah, it's a mercy you weren't here when the cowardly prior surrendered us to the will of Cromwell. Only sixteen friars left at the end – can you believe it? Sixteen. When once there were hundreds. But they drifted away. Like you, Brother Edmund, you transferred to

Cambridge, I know, and after that one was dissolved, you were sent to Dartford?'

'That's correct – I am honoured you've followed my progress,' Brother Edmund said. 'We've both come from Dartford Priory.'

'I always kept up with the friars who showed the most promise.' The man peered at me. 'Ah, so this is she. I remember you telling me about your sister in Dartford.'

I waited for Brother Edmund to correct him, but he did not. When we travelled to Malmesbury last year, we'd passed as brother and sister to attract less notice. Perhaps it was best to take up that pose again, though I hated to deceive.

'I thought we would walk in the monastery tonight, to pray and see the library,' said Brother Edmund. 'Would that be possible?'

'Possible?' He brightened. 'I say to you as porter of Blackfriars, it is possible for you to walk through the monastery – and even to sleep here tonight – but only if you drink the prior's malmsey with me.'

Brother Edmund tried to refuse, but the man would not hear of it. He filled goblets high, for both of us. Sipping the rich, sweet malmsey sent a warm current coursing through me. I had not eaten a thing and this was far more potent than the watered-down strawberry wine I sometimes consumed.

Glancing over at Brother Edmund, I saw his cheeks flush and knew he was experiencing its heady strength, too.

'We only have an hour or so left of daylight and other tasks that must follow,' Brother Edmund said, standing up. 'So I thank you for the malmsey but—'

'Stay with me a while,' pleaded Master Portinary. 'I've not spoken to anyone from the good days for so long. Tomorrow is my last as porter – we will part, never to see each other again, I expect. One more drink?'

Brother Edmund's heart softened. He sat with the porter and talked of shared times, when Blackfriars was a power unquestioned.

Finally the porter stood up, rattling his keys, to unlock the cloister doors. I was filled with wonder as we strode under sweeping arches and past thick columns. Candlelight revealed lofty ceilings, painted and gilded. Here I could feel more powerfully than anywhere else the prestige and reach of the Dominican Order. Our leaders counselled kings of Europe. Our scholars translated the ancient Greek and Latin documents that uncovered the wisdom of a lost world, opening eyes to the thinking of Aristotle, Virgil, Livy, and Pliny. Our priors sponsored architects and musicians, designed intricate gardens, funded the work of the finest artists the world had ever seen. Leonardo da Vinci's *The Last Supper* was painted on the refectory wall of a Dominican monastery in Milan.

We stopped at the dining hall for the friars. The porter wanted to show off the refectory's windows. The room was ten times the size of Dartford Priory's refectory. I was humbled by its sweeping grandeur, topped by row upon row of windows set in the west wall. Through them filtered the last gasp of dusk, a greyish-purple light of melancholy humour. Sixteen friars? The room could fit six hundred.

I caught sight of one small object on a far table. It was a wooden bowl, half filled with mixtum, the breakfast for all who live in a monastery. As I stared down at the hard, dried lumps of bread, I realised that I was looking at the last meal of Blackfriars. I could imagine it: one of the older ones was too heartsick to eat all of his meal. He pushed this bowl away and then left the cloister forever, carrying his only possessions across the cobblestone courtyard.

'Sister, aren't you coming?' bellowed the porter from across the refectory, interrupting my reverie. 'We're bound for the great hall next.'

Naturally, this room in Blackfriars dwarfed every single great hall I'd been in, including the ones of the Courtenays and Howards.

'Parliament met in this room twice, and this was where the divorce proceedings were held for King Henry and Queen Katherine, before the two cardinals,' said Brother Edmund.

'All gone, all gone,' said the porter brokenly. 'The unbreakable Blackfriars is broken, and by the great-grandson of a Welsh groom.'

Brother Edmund said immediately, 'No, no, Master Portinary, you must not speak such of the king. Buck up your spirits.'

The porter nodded. 'You were always a fine friar, Brother Edmund. They said you could be one of the greatest Dominican scholars in all of England. And look what's happened to you – an apothecary practising in a small town of no distinction. It's a damnable tragedy, and yet you comfort *me*.'

Brother Edmund stood very still. There was not enough candle-light for me to read his expression, but I didn't need to. I'd always known that within him burned a desire for achievement. Although he insisted that healing others was a true calling, that being an apothecary was sufficient, I sadly doubted it.

Master Portinary caught an inkling that he'd wounded Brother Edmund. 'What am I saying? Too much wine, too much wine. I must to bed.' He stumbled toward the entranceway of the great hall. 'I shall see you on the morrow, Brother, and your sweet sister, too. I will lock the cloister. No one will disturb you.'

The next thing I heard was a ditty, hummed by the porter in a distant room. It slowly faded to silence.

Brother Edmund and I were alone in Blackfriars.

29

'Should we truly stay here?' I whispered.

'The rooms may not be too comfortable, but I can think of no place safer,' he answered. 'Certainly we cannot seek out a lawyer tonight. They've all left their chambers. But we have time to work in the library.'

Holding his candle, Brother Edmund led me deeper into the cloister. On our walk through London, from the bridge to the monastery, he'd told me of the riches of the library and scriptorium. People came from all over Europe to see the Blackfriars collection: the illuminated manuscripts, the ancient scrolls, the collected philosophies.

Yet the moment we stepped inside the library, we saw that all was amiss. Some shelves were empty; others still held books, but they were turned upside-down or jammed together haphazardly.

For Brother Edmund, this was acutely painful. 'All the illuminated manuscripts – taken,' he choked. 'Do you know how long a man would spend creating one? His entire life. And it wasn't only to serve God – it was to provide spiritual sustenance for the man who would come after. We are a chain, Sister Joanna, honouring who's come before and help-ing the ones yet to come. That's why we take vows, to become part of something bigger than ourselves. What do we do when the chain is severed – destroyed – by our king?'

I could think of nothing to say that would comfort him. The sack-ing of the monasteries was a wound that would never heal, for any of us.

As Brother Edmund looked through the books left behind, I moved toward a stone statue of Saint Dominic. It stood next to the doorway to the scriptorium.

I approached the image of our founder slowly, reverently. A large stone dog sat faithfully at his side, a torch between its teeth.

Saint Dominic's mother had a dream when she was pregnant with him, that a dog would emerge from her womb carrying a torch. When, fearful, she approached her priest, he told her that that the torch would set the world on fire through preaching the word of Christ. That was a prophecy that came true – and the dog became our symbol.

When the raven climbs the rope, the dog must soar like the hawk.

'Brother Edmund,' I cried, 'I may understand one of the codes.' Pointing at the statue, I said, 'If the dog symbolises the Dominican Order, then there can be no doubt that I am the dog.'

'Yes, Sister Joanna, yes,' he exclaimed. 'I should have thought of it already. But what of the raven? What does it represent? Sister Elizabeth Barton was a Benedictine, and their symbol is the olive branch, for their pursuit of peace. I wonder who the raven could be.'

Another memory stirred.

'At Saint Sepulchre, I saw their book,' I said slowly. 'I believe it was one of the illuminated manuscripts you spoke of. There were olive branches on the pages, but a bird too, perhaps.'

'Saint Gregory's life of Saint Benedict is found in every convent library – we will search for one,' vowed Brother Edmund. He took one half of the room and I took the other.

We searched for at least an hour, perhaps two. I did battle with weariness, rubbing my eyes in order to see clearly. When I doubted I could read the words on another cover, I paused to watch Brother Edmund. He stood over a table strewn with books. The candlelight gave birth to a glow pulsing around his long blond hair. He never paused; he worked furiously to find answers in this forlorn library.

Brother Edmund is my guardian angel, I thought. A fierce tenderness flooded through me.

I shook my head. I must get hold of myself. Such thoughts were not seemly.

'I have it!' he cried, holding up a small book with a leather cover.

Brother Edmund and I turned the pages together, translating Latin at the same speed.

I gasped when the turning of a delicate page revealed a large black bird. 'Yes,' I cried. 'I knew I saw that same bird in the book.'

Brother Edmund and I ran our fingers along the sentences eagerly. It was a story from Saint Benedict's early days in the wilderness:

At mealtimes a raven used to come out of the nearby wood and take bread from Benedict's hand. This time, when it came as usual, the man of God threw down in front of the raven the bread that the priest had handed him that had been poisoned, saying, 'In the name of the Lord Jesus Christ, take this bread and drop it somewhere where no one can find it.' Again and again the man of God told him to do it, saying, 'Pick it up, pick it up. Do not be afraid.' After hesitating a long time, the raven took the bread in its beak, picked it up and flew away. Hours later it came back, after having thrown the bread away, and received its usual ration from the hands of the man of God. And so the raven and Benedict in the beginning were intertwined.

'The raven *was* a symbol of the Benedictines in the beginning,' I whispered. 'And if this is the fulfilment of an ancient prophecy ...' My voice trailed away.

A more disturbing realisation followed.

'Sister Barton was hanged, was she not?' Brother Edmund said. 'So the raven did "ride the rope", I'm afraid. Which means that the time of the raven is finished and now it is the time of the dog, a dog who becomes a hawk.'

'But what does the hawk symbolise?' I asked, deeply frustrated that unlocking each riddle only left us with more.

Brother Edmund paced the floor, deep in thought. At last, he turned to me. 'In this case, it may not be what it is but what it does. Hawking is the favourite sport of kings, and hawks are incredible killers. The bird is famous for hiding and then, when it sees its prey, moving fast – swooping down.'

I snatched up my rosary and gripped it so hard it hurt my palm. 'You think the hawk symbolises me and it means I have to *kill*? Please, Mother Mary, let that not be true. I could never kill anyone. It is a mortal sin.' I stared up at Brother Edmund. 'And neither could you. You could never take a life.'

'No, Sister.'

Something in his voice sounded strange. I stared at him, waiting.

Finally, Brother Edmund said, 'My life has been dedicated to service, to learning and teaching, healing, and helping others. That is the way of those who take holy vows. Peace.'

His lips twisted. 'And that is why it has been so easy for the king and Cromwell to crush us,' he said.

'We don't fight back,' I whispered, echoing Gertrude's plea the night we went to Londinium. Heavy with dread, I said, 'Do you think yourself capable of committing an act of violence, in service of a greater good, Brother Edmund?'

'I don't know,' he answered. 'That is the truth.'

Perceiving my confusion and fear, Brother Edmund said, 'The intent of the prophecy may not be harm. Perhaps you actually *save* someone. Or prevent something terrible from happening. The smallest act, at the right time and the right place, can have profound effects.'

I slumped in a chair and held my head in my hands. The room spun around me.

'We are in need of prayer, of spiritual guidance,' Brother Edmund said firmly. 'Let us go to chapel.'

In the exquisite chapel of Blackfriars, I knelt before the altar. Brother Edmund knelt beside me. It felt odd to be so close. At Dartford Priory and at Holy Trinity Church, men and women sat separately.

His voice firm and clear, Brother Edmund began the prayer for the Dominican dead, 'Out of the depths I cry to you, O Lord. Lord, hear my voice!' He paused and looked at me. With a start, I realised he wanted me to say the prayer with him, at the same time. He was not going to preach to me. We would say the prayer together.

And so the words unfurled from our lips, overlapping: 'Let your ears be attentive to my voice in supplication. If you, O Lord, mark iniquities, Lord, who can stand? But with you is forgiveness, that you may be revered. My soul waits for the Lord, more than sentinels wait for the dawn.'

When we'd finished, I rose and we walked together, in silence, down the nave of the chapel. It had been stripped of all valuables. But beneath the last pew, by the light of the candle I carried, I spotted a plain wooden cup.

I stopped walking.

'The chalice,' I said.

Brother Edmund frowned. 'What?'

'I didn't tell you – I'd nearly forgotten – but the very last thing that Sister Elizabeth Barton said to me was, "The chalice".'

'Chalices can be used simply for drinking, but the chalice also holds first place among sacred vessels, for it is used in celebration of the Mass,' Brother Edmund said slowly. 'Perhaps the prophecy must be followed in order to protect the chalice – and the Mass.'

My heart thumping, I said, 'I don't think that is what she meant. I can't tell you anything except that it felt like a – a warning.' And then I cried, 'Oh, Brother Edmund, I'm afraid. I don't want this to happen to me. I've never wanted it.'

Brother Edmund nodded. 'And Jesus said, "Father, if you be willing, take this cup from me."'

'Gethsemane,' I whispered.

Brother Edmund continued. 'There Christ prayed, for he was full of fear over what he knew would come. God appeared and Jesus said, "Father, if you are willing, take this cup from me; yet not my will but yours be done."'

I turned away from Brother Edmund, overcome.

He laid his hand on my shoulder. 'You must know that I will do everything in my power to help you. I don't want you to go through this alone, Sister Joanna. You will have me, always.'

'Yes,' I said.

'Everyone has said that you must learn the prophecy of three seers – the third one will tell you exactly what you must do. But you can only hear it of your own free will and unconstrained. So if you choose not to learn more, it stops now.'

A look of hunger seized Brother Edmund. I flinched. I knew how passionately he longed for a return to our old lives. Yet still I recoiled from my destiny. Anger rose – why must this burden fall upon me?

As if he could read my thoughts, Brother Edmund said, 'You have been chosen for a great task.' He paused. 'But it's not just because you're from a noble family and you took vows to become a Dominican novice. It's *you*. You are a woman unlike any other, Sister Joanna. I've tried to define this quality that sets you apart. I've never quite been able to.'

I gazed at Brother Edmund, and I trembled with emotions I did not understand.

Saying we were exhausted and would resume our discussion the next day, Brother Edmund took me to the *calefactorium* off the chapel. Every monastery had one – it was where fires were lit, but only between All Hallow's Eve and Good Friday, to warm the faithful. While I waited, he gathered wood and a pallet for me to sleep on. He proposed that I spend the night here, near the fire, and he in a room down the passageway.

Brother Edmund slipped the kindling into the shallow square in the centre of the calefactory floor. I heard that first sigh of fire catching and then the eager whispers of new flames. They popped and crackled. Golden spears flickered as they devoured the wood. The room now pulsed with light.

Sitting a few feet away from him on the stone floor, I watched the shadows leap across Brother Edmund's face.

He leaned back, nodding, and half turned to me. 'You shall be safe and warm here, Sister Joanna.'

'Yes,' I said.

'I will be nearby.' He stood up. 'No one will be able to get to this room without passing mine first.'

I stood up, too. He reached for my hands and squeezed them. When he started to step back, I gripped those hands tight.

'Don't go,' I said.

He looked down at me, his brown eyes uncertain. 'Do you wish me to stay a little longer?'

I was silent. I knew I must send Brother Edmund away now. But I couldn't part from him.

'Stay with me.'

I could not draw breath. It was as if I still wore one of Gertrude Courtenay's bodices, too tight for me to inhale. He did not take back his hands, but I could feel his whole body stiffen.

'I'm not sure what you want of me, Sister Joanna,' he said.

I looked into his face. There was surprise there and a new wariness. But his lips parted as if he, too, could not easily draw breath.

That it was sinful was never in doubt. But I slipped my arms around him. I reached high, and higher, feeling his smooth back. I turned my face up to his and, in terror, closed my eyes. I had thought Brother Edmund's body would be cool, but it wasn't. He was warm and lean, and tense as a strung bow.

I waited, with eyes shut. After I don't know how long, his lips pressed against mine, but so gently I almost doubted it was happening. I had never felt a touch this tender. I ached for more from him.

The next moment he pulled away, abruptly. I stood alone. My eyes were still shut as I wove in the air.

'This is wrong,' he said. 'Remember that night at Malmesbury Abbey? I made a vow to you then before God. I said that I would never violate your faith and trust in me. Tell me you haven't forgotten.'

'I haven't,' I said.

'We've learned so much today, together, about things that may come to pass,' he continued. 'The monasteries could be restored. It is part of the prophecy. Sister Joanna, how could we rejoin our brothers and sisters, take our place beside those who trust us, if we succumb to this? We took vows of chastity – and so we would be unclean.'

I nodded and turned away. My eyes were blinded by humiliation.

'Don't cry, please; you mustn't cry,' he said, anguished. And then, 'I will go now – I *must* go now.' And without waiting for me to speak, Brother Edmund left the *calefactorium*.

After a few moments, I made my way to the pallet that he had dragged in for me. The fire crackled high and merry, in a mocking conflagration. I stared into the twisting yellow flames. What I did was so weak, despicable. I couldn't believe that it happened.

Now I understood evil – I was able to grasp the cunning power of the devil. What other explanation could there be for how I had offered myself to Brother Edmund than that my body and spirit were seized by the devil? And to do it *here* – in a place that was until weeks ago a renowned monastery – was doubly horrific. I longed for the Sacrament of Penance. On my knees, I would confess my desires and seek absolution. If grace were restored to my soul, then I could resist sin.

But I must also beg Brother Edmund's forgiveness. And there must be no reoccurrence. What happened this night must never happen again. I simply could not survive without Brother Edmund's friendship. That was the most important thing. *There is nothing on this earth to be prized more than true friendship*, he said to me at Howard House. I would prove myself worthy.

After I'd made my resolution, my eyelids grew so heavy, I slumped onto the pallet and found sleep.

The next thing I felt was hands dragging me from my pallet. I was pulled to my feet and shaken, my legs flailing helplessly above the floor.

The Duke of Norfolk slapped my face hard. I heard a small *rip* at the same instant that hot pain ripped through me, from my scalp to the tip of my shoulder.

'By my trowth, you are a wayward bitch,' the duke roared. His spit drenched my forehead.

A half dozen men crowded into the room. Behind the duke stood Bishop Gardiner. There was no sign of Brother Edmund.

'You think you're clever, don't you?' said Norfolk. 'Corrupting that fool Catherine into aiding your escape with a miscreant friar. But my men aren't fools. They saw two ladies leave and one return. Once I was informed, I had my men combing Southwark and London and Dartford all night – *all night* – to track you down. It wasn't until we found this crookback at dawn that we learned of the fair man and the dark woman headed for Blackfriars.'

The hunchback who'd offered to help us with transport when we emerged from London Bridge edged out from behind another man. He pointed at me. 'That's the one, that's her,' he said.

'Of course it's her,' the duke said. 'Give this stunted foot-licker a shilling and boot him.'

My left cheek stung from the slap, but it was nothing compared to my neck. I couldn't even stand straight but bent over, clutching my shoulder. I managed to ask, 'Where is Brother Edmund?'

Bishop Gardiner said calmly, 'He has been taken to Winchester House, to await my judgement.'

Norfolk seethed: 'To come here, the two of you, lying to the porter, claiming you're brother and sister, and then to soil this monastery – I thought I had seen all matter of depravity in my life a person could commit, but this ... this ...' He couldn't finish his sentence.

'We committed no crime,' I said.

'You brought that friar here to fornicate,' Norfolk shouted. 'You may fool others with your novice guise, but I know what a whore you really are, Joanna Stafford.'

'No,' I said.

It took every bit of strength I possessed to stand up tall through the haze of pain. I looked to Bishop Stephen Gardiner, not the duke. 'We came to Blackfriars to learn,' I said. 'To pray. That is the truth.'

Something flickered in the bishop's eyes. It could have been pity. Or contempt. He opened his mouth to say something – but was drowned out by the duke.

'To *learn*?' The Duke of Norfolk's contempt was savage. 'But you don't learn – ever. You were arrested last year, your priory was dissolved this year, any woman with sense would understand that the time for nuns and friars and monks is finished. It's *over*. There are no more monasteries. Everyone must accept it or be crushed to dust. The end of the year will bring the last destruction.'

'What more can be destroyed?' I asked bleakly. 'Everything is gone.'

Norfolk said, 'You're wrong, as always. The king has already stripped and closed the shrine of Thomas Becket, and on the night of December twenty-eighth, men will go to Canterbury Cathedral and remove the bones of the saint. When those last pilgrims arrive the next morning, on the anniversary of Becket's death, they will find nothing but a wrecked shrine. The king wants the bones burned. So end all men of the cloth who defy their anointed king.'

I had never even conceived of anything so monstrous. It was agony – far worse than the fleshly pain dealt by Norfolk – to know that our most beloved and revered saint would be so molested. To steal the holy treasure of a saint and close the shrine to the pilgrims who needed him was already a tragedy. But to defile his remains?

My hands shaking, I made the sign of the cross. Then I peered over at Bishop Gardiner. His face was white marble. This must be as horrifying to him as it was to me, but the bishop revealed not a hint of feeling.

Norfolk said, 'You're going to Stafford Castle, to rot there for the rest of your life. God's teeth, if I have to tie you over a horse myself, you are going. But first you have a duty to perform.'

'Duty?' I repeated.

'The Marquess of Exeter and Baron Montague were tried and found guilty yesterday of high treason. It is the king's pleasure that they be beheaded on Tower Hill. Their last request, which His Majesty granted, was to die together. I will attend. And you will, too, Joanna Stafford. The Lady Mary wants you to represent her at the execution, and so you shall. You and I will see this through to the end.'

30

When I was a prisoner confined in the Tower of London, I could not see the moat from my cell. But the morning of the executions, I stared at it for hours: a ring of dank muddy water, fringed with dead branches. On the other side of the wall, all was scrupulously maintained. There must be a meaning behind the neglect – there was a reason for everything at the Tower – but I couldn't discern it.

The rain started falling before dawn. By the time I stood on Tower Hill, the downpour had turned steady. The Earl of Surrey cursed behind me. He'd worn his best cap, topped by an ostrich feather, but the rain wilted the plumage. Like many young men, Surrey most feared looking ridiculous.

The rain streamed down the lined face of the Duke of Norfolk. It turned his white furs sodden; but his chain of office, his gold medallion, still gleamed defiantly on his chest. When I mounted a horse at Howard House, he said, 'Keep your head down. Shut your eyes if you can't bear it. I won't have woman's weeping.'

'I won't weep,' I said. 'This isn't the first time I've seen someone die before the mob.'

We stood on the hill that swelled beside the Tower. Behind us lay the city. All Hallows Barking Church and a cluster of houses straddled the border between London and Tower land. Many men came to crowd around the tall, straw-covered platform where Henry Courtenay and Baron Montague would soon die. I saw other chains of office and furs. This was nothing like the raucous mob that gathered to cheer on Margaret's burning. These did not laugh or cheer, but I did not imagine for a second that they mourned.

I ignored them, one and all, to concentrate on prayer. Henry Courtenay had been found guilty of plotting to overthrow the king and marry his son Edward to the Lady Mary so they could rule together. I knew it to be a foul lie. Gertrude was not tried, but neither she nor her son was released. As for Baron Montague, guilt lay in his supposed sympathy with the anti-monarchical ideas of his brother Cardinal Reginald Pole.

I stood straighter. I'd not falter today – I'd not fail Courtenay or Montague. I would represent the Lady Mary as best I could.

Nor would I fail Brother Edmund. I had a plan to free us both from the bondage of Norfolk and Gardiner. It had a small chance of success. As terrible as things were for me, this plan could well make my lot much worse. But I would attempt it before I left Tower Hill, no matter what the cost.

I heard someone speak French to Norfolk. I turned and at once recognised Eustace Chapuys, the ambassador to the Emperor Charles. And according to Henry Courtenay, a man who Gertrude once confided secrets in.

'His Majesty must take steps to punish traitors – yet such occasions as these can be mournful,' said Chapuys. I waited for him to remember the maid of honour who attended Katherine of Aragon in exile during the last weeks of her life. But he merely half bowed with the imperial courtesy shown to an unimportant woman of gentle birth, and then he moved on.

Behind me a group of men talked louder and louder. 'Blessed be the God of England whose instrument you are in freeing us of these foul traitors, my Lord Cromwell,' said someone.

Cromwell.

I was a fool not to have prepared myself. He was the king's chief minister and the architect of these arrests. If I turned around to look at Cromwell's face, it might weaken my fortitude. And yet, I felt a great burning desire to see the enemy of all that was good.

Clutching my crucifix, I turned around.

A half dozen eager courtiers surrounded a short, broad-shouldered man of middle years wearing plain black clothes. At first I could not see his face, but then a man shuffled to the side, and the minister was revealed. He was but ten feet away.

How ugly Cromwell was. He possessed the thick white skin of someone who rarely ventures into the sun, but he was no ascetic. A double chin nestled on his collar – this was a man who gorged on food and drink – and above it creased thick lips. His close-set grey eyes rested steadily on the clergyman then addressing him.

I did not deliberate the thought; it came surging up from my soul, like a pure stream bubbling from the earth:

I curse you, Thomas Cromwell. You are a murderer and a heretic and a destroyer. But I pray to God that somehow, someday, I shall be the one who brings you down.

It shocked me, the force of my hate, but it fuelled me as well. Would that I could decipher the last part of the prophecy, to know if I would be the one to bring an end to Chief Minister Thomas Cromwell.

Just as Norfolk lunged to spin me back around, Cromwell's gaze shifted from the clergyman to me. It was as if he'd heard my vicious thoughts. Our eyes met for three seconds at the most. But in that fleeting span, those grey eyes assessed me with such incredible acuity that the air rushed out of my body and Tower Hill tilted beneath my feet.

'Stop staring, you fool,' hissed the Duke of Norfolk when I once more faced the scaffold.

I took a deep breath and regained my balance.

It was not Cromwell who ambled over a moment later to find out who I was. Master Thomas Wriothesley – a thin man with a long red beard – chatted with Norfolk and Surrey while awaiting an introduction.

'This is Joanna Stafford,' Norfolk finally said, without grace.

'Ah, yes,' Wriothesley said. The husband of the guest at Gertrude's party stood before me, waiting. When I remained silent, he made a bow and left.

'He's gone back to Cromwell to make report,' muttered Surrey.

Norfolk's angry oath was swallowed up by a ripple through the crowd. All heads turned toward the Thames. There it was – a pole with a flag attached sauntering above the wall that lined the walkway to Middle Tower. A moment later, I saw a group of yeoman warders emerge. And then, at last, appeared Henry Courtenay and Baron Montague. A group of other men came down to meet them – I gathered they were the sheriffs of the city, and they, not the keepers of the Tower, would officiate. I would be spared the sight of the fearsome Sir William Kingston, at least.

As they climbed the path up Tower Hill, I could see what a month in prison had wrought. The marquess, who came first, had lost much weight. He had not been permitted to wear a doublet, despite the cold. He was dressed only in dark hose tied with rope around his waist and a white chemise. His shirt was already drenched with rain, making it cling to his skin. Right behind him walked Baron Montague, wearing a similar chemise shirt and hose. His face was so gaunt he seemed a spirit floating up the hill. As he came closer to me, I saw his chemise was torn in front, exposing a chest of grey hair. It was sickening to see them so attired.

A priest walked up the stairs of the scaffold first, followed by two sheriffs. The fourth man stomping up the stairs was the executioner. I had never seen him who wields the scaffold axe before. He was burly, wearing all black, as well as a mask that fitted over his head except for two slots for eyes. Like the spawn of a fevered nightmare.

Now it was time for the two men to ascend.

Henry Courtenay mounted the stairs, slowly, as hundreds watched. Three steps from the top, he halted. Baron Montague climbed quickly to follow. He tapped his friend on the elbow. Henry nodded and resumed his climb, though his hand shook hard on the railing when he reached the scaffold's top.

I thank God and the Virgin that Gertrude is not here to see this.

Courtenay and Montague handed the executioner their coins – for a man must pay to be killed on the block – and took their places at the front of the scaffold.

I sucked in quick shallow breaths. Snatches of prayer careened through my mind. I had tried to steel myself. Yet now that it was happening, I struggled to control the waves of fear and pain and sorrow.

Henry Courtenay, my cousin, stepped forward.

'See me, Henry,' I whispered. But his glassy gaze skipped over the crowd.

He coughed and then said, 'Good Christian people, I come hither to die and by law I am condemned to the same. Pray for the king, your just and merciful sovereign lord. And trust in God, to whom I now commend my soul.'

No one ever declared innocence or spewed bitter words at the end – that was unthinkable, moments before meeting eternity. And I knew why Henry, in particular, would praise the king. He sought to protect Gertrude and Edward.

Henry Courtenay knelt and put his head on the block.

To my shame, my eyes closed. I was a wretched coward. Beads of sweat sprang out on my forehead.

There was a *thud*. The axe struck Henry's neck so hard that the ground shivered below my feet.

'Jesu,' whispered the Earl of Surrey behind me. 'Thank Christ it took only one swing,' his father responded.

I opened my eyes. The headless body of Henry Courtenay lay next to a blood-drenched block. The yeoman warders carried it to the back of the scaffold and lowered it into a long box. A second empty box stood next to it.

A man lifted a burlap sack to the edge of the scaffold and pulled the severed head into it. As the man turned around, cradling the sack, I saw it was Charles, the Courtenay steward.

I looked up at Baron Montague. He did not weep nor tremble.

A sheriff said something to him, but he did not move.

Now it was his turn to die, and I understood everything. Henry was the kinder man, a better man if all were considered. But Montague was stronger. I had no doubt that he had insisted Henry die first. To have to watch that butchery knowing you would follow – it called for a toughness that I doubted many men possessed.

Montague finally stepped forward. His eyes roamed until he found Norfolk – and then me. We locked eyes and in that moment my breathing calmed; the sweat dried on my brow.

I knew my purpose.

I did not recite a psalm or mourning prayer for the dead. I opened my mouth and it was the Dominican daily blessing that emerged: 'May God the Father bless us.'

Montague nodded as if he could understand me.

'May God the Son heal us,' I said, louder.

Norfolk turned toward me, his hand was out, but I stepped forward quickly. I headed straight for the scaffold. The duke did not follow.

'May the Holy Spirit enlighten us and give us eyes to see with, ears to hear with, and hands to do the word of God,' I continued, my voice ringing out.

Men parted to make way for me as I drew closer to the blood-soaked scaffold. 'Feet to walk with, and a mouth to preach the words of salvation with,' I said. I knew they must have all been watching: Norfolk and his son, Cromwell and Wriothesley, Ambassador Chapuys, and the whole wretched court. I didn't care.

I was just a few feet from him now; I tilted my head back as far as possible so I could look into the face of Baron Montague.

'And the angel of peace to watch over us and lead us at last, by our Lord's gift, to the Kingdom,' I said.

The blessing was finished.

Baron Montague looked past me, at the crowd. The rain had stopped. A breeze stirred his hair.

'Long live the king,' Lord Montague cried, so loudly it echoed across the hill.

The crowd waited. But there was no more.

Montague whipped around and in one graceful move was on his knees. He laid his head on the block. His eyes found me again, and he said to me, as if no one else were at Tower Hill, 'Joanna, look away.'

31

B aron Montague closed his eyes, but I did not close mine. The executioner lumbered forward. I could see his eyes through the hood
– darting this way and that as he picked a spot. He planted his feet and
lifted his axe high over his head. Its bloody edge glinted in the dull
light. The axe crashed down in one sure arc.

What I saw next was seared into my soul forever.

Afterward, a stranger gathered Montague's severed head. Guards
dragged the body to the back of the platform. The stair boards creaked
as the sheriffs and the priest and the executioner all descended. Other
men went up, to collect the boxes with the headless bodies. I knew
that it was all happening around me, but it was at a distance. I felt
like one of the grey gulls that banked and soared above the Tower of
London.

Charles, the loyal Courtenay steward, nudged me. 'Mistress
Joanna?' he said. From the tone of his voice, it was apparent he repeated
my name.

I could not speak.

'We'll be burying them now. We've received permission from the
sheriff. Do you wish to come?'

'What?' I said.

'The church back there' – he pointed in the direction of the city –
'All Hallows Barking. That's where they will rest for a time.'

With all the effort I could summon, I nodded.

Surrey was the next person to speak to me. 'Joanna, we need to –
Christ, you've got blood on you.'

He drew me a few feet back from the scaffold and searched
his doublet for a cloth. The young earl cleaned my face myself, his
eyes full of pity. Behind him, men stared at me, in horrified fascin-
ation. Whispers encircled us; I heard someone say, 'Stafford.' He
ignored them, wiping the blood from me. If I had been able to feel

anything, I would have regretted what I was about to do to Surrey.

'Let's be off,' shouted the Duke of Norfolk from twenty feet away. 'No,' I said.

The duke approached with reluctance. I saw his eyes flick up at the scaffold. The boxes were being brought down the stairs, containing the headless bodies of Courtenay and Montague.

Norfolk said to his son, 'I go to court directly. The king must see me present. Take her back to Howard House, then join me.'

'No,' I repeated.

The duke said, 'You'll do what I say. Tomorrow my men take you to Stafford Castle.'

I reached for the Earl of Surrey's slashed brocade sleeve. 'I need to tell you something, my lord. It's about your aunt, about Margaret Bulmer. You in particular must know this. There is a reason she went north. It has to do with your father.'

Norfolk dragged me a short distance away, waving off Surrey.

'Have you gone mad, bringing up her name now – and *here*?' he said, quivering with rage.

'Your son hates it when people whisper that you're a procurer,' I said. 'How would he feel if I tell him you tried to force Margaret into the king's bed, to become his mistress – that that is why she fled the court.'

The horror written large on his face must have been very much like what I exhibited when Gertrude Courtenay said the name of George Boleyn.

'Untrue,' he said.

My poor father told me Margaret's secret, days before he died. But I would not speak his name to Norfolk now. Keeping my voice steady, I spun my falsehood.

'I had a letter from Margaret telling me of it,' I said. 'I never showed it to anyone, I wished to protect her memory. But I will make its contents known if you do not leave me behind today.'

The Duke of Norfolk actually smiled at me – such a dangerous smile. The grief in his eyes over the executions that occurred moments before had turned to murderous rage.

'That was why the king commanded such a merciless death for Margaret,' I continued, forcing down my fear. 'But none of it would have happened but for you. She'd never have gone north, become involved in the Pilgrimage of Grace, if it weren't for you. You killed Margaret before she ever rebelled against the king. And I think your son – and your wife – should know that.'

Norfolk leaned over to say to me with utter clarity, 'Do you not know whom you're opposing?'

I looked at him, at the duke who led men to battle. He'd ordered the deaths of men and women – and, yes, even children.

I said, 'To make me come with you, you'll have to beat me and then drag me, Your Grace. But is it wise to draw attention to you when the high nobility of this kingdom is under suspicion? Montague said it. You are the last.'

Norfolk's lower lip shook. It took tremendous control for him not to kill me with his bare hands. Over his shoulder I could see his son watching us.

'I will never tell your son or any living soul the truth about Margaret – you have my word before God on that,' I said. 'But only if you leave me here. I will attend the burials. And then I will go to Dartford. You will not see me again. I'll have no further dealings with your family again, nor with any of the noble houses or the court.' I paused. 'But I will stop at Winchester House first and collect Brother Edmund. You must send word to the bishop he is to be released today.'

The Duke of Norfolk turned to look at his son and then back at me. He said, very quietly, more quietly than he had ever spoken to me before, 'This is not over.'

With that, he left, snapping his fingers for his son and heir to follow. Surrey went with him. I always knew that he would.

I made my way through the thinning crowd to All Hallows Barking Church at the edge of Tower Hill. There were a dozen Courtenay servants there. A trio of men who'd served Baron Montague had gathered as well. No relations or friends for either man attended, apart from myself. This was the place where traitors of esteem were first buried: Cardinal Fisher, Sir Thomas More. Sometimes, after his vengeful rage had cooled, the king would grant permission for families to inter their loved ones elsewhere. Sometimes he wouldn't.

A melancholy priest said a few words over the two fresh graves.

I bade the mourners farewell and I left Tower Hill. At London Bridge, the hunchbacked man who offered help with transport, the one who took coin to betray me to Norfolk, did not notice me today. I paid my pence and shuffled across the bridge, hewing to the side of the horses and wagons. The vigorous churn of the water below my feet sounded strange; the shouting and laughter of the other passengers was alien to me, too. There was no triumph over freeing myself of Norfolk. I felt a choking sadness that I must live in a world so dark and pitiless.

I never entered Winchester House. I planted myself outside the courtyard, on the Southwark street that led to the bishop's palace. I told the boy posted there my name and nothing else.

No one came out for a long time. The rain fell again, softer. I did not seek shelter from the sodden drizzle. Men who came to do business at Winchester House edged around my immovable body to enter.

Finally a priest walked halfway across the courtyard, his face stony. He looked me up and down and then turned to give a signal.

Brother Edmund appeared in the entranceway, under the stone arch carved with the letter *W*. He walked slowly across the cobblestone courtyard to the street. My dark haze lifted at the sight of Brother Edmund, though guilt clawed as well. I regretted pulling him into my troubles – but most of all I regretted shaming myself that night at Blackfriars.

'Sister Joanna,' he said when he reached me.

'Brother Edmund,' I said.

His face was pale with deep shadows under his eyes, but he appeared unharmed. As his eyes travelled down my dress, he winced.

'Is it blood?' he asked.

I looked down. I had not noticed until now, but there were dark red splotches on the left side of my cloak.

'They died this morning,' I said.

He nodded, took my arm, and led me away.

'How is my freedom made possible?' he asked.

'I threatened the Duke of Norfolk that I would disclose something that he does not want disclosed if he did not release both of us,' I answered.

Brother Edmund stopped walking. 'You *threatened*?' he asked, startled. And then, 'What was it?'

'I can't tell you.'

His voice lowered, he said, 'It has nothing to do with the prophecies?'

'Of course not. I would never say a word.'

'I think you should take me into your confidence, so I am better prepared, Sister Joanna.'

'I can't,' I answered. 'I took a vow before God that I would tell no one.'

Brother Edmund nodded. 'Ah, then, we shall speak of it no more.'

We resumed our walk. At the mouth of the street I saw a gang of ruffians pummelling a beggar.

'Bishop Gardiner questioned me himself,' said Brother Edmund. 'I told him nothing, but I fear that he suspects that something deeper than a need for prayer led us to Blackfriars.'

My heart jerked faster. This was something I had not anticipated. The bishop was so cunning and knew Brother Edmund and me so well, he of all people had the ability to find out about the prophecies and my role in them.

Brother Edmund gasped, but it was not due to fear of the formidable bishop. His attention was on the ruffians' fighting. Before I could say anything, he sprinted toward them.

'Stop!' he cried. 'Leave that man alone.'

I ran after him, confused. Why, at such a time as this, would my friend hurl himself into a street brawl?

A large ruffian who had the beggar folded under his arm, like a sack of wheat, said to Brother Edmund, 'What – are ye a pope lover?'

It was only then that I focused on the beggar. But he was no beggar. That was the hooded habit of a Cistercian monk.

The ruffian tore his victim's hood off and I saw the chalk-white face of Brother Oswald. He was half conscious, blood trickling down his chin.

'Do ye know this freak?' demanded the ruffian.

'He is a monk – a man of God,' Brother Edmund said. 'You must release him at once.'

'We don't bow to monks no more,' howled the ruffian. 'They be nothin' but hypocrites, sorcerers, and lazy creatures.'

I'd heard such terrible descriptions of monks before, and each time it was like a blow.

'He's a Papist,' roared the man, 'and we know what to do with Papists, eh?'

The crowd cheered. There were ten of them, at least. I'd sometimes told myself that it was only the king's and Cromwell's minions who hated the old ways and the men and women of the monasteries. This sadistic assault proved me wrong.

'He is defenceless, you need not prove your strength on a man such as him,' insisted Brother Edmund.

The ruffian dropped Brother Oswald onto the ground. The Cistercian groaned. Brother Edmund darted toward him but the monk's attacker stepped into his path. 'How 'bout I prove it on a man such as ye instead?' he jeered.

'No!' I cried. 'Stop this now.'

Now the ruffian turned to me with a leer. 'Ye brought a girl for sportin'?'

Brother Edmund pushed me behind him. 'You will not harm her, or anyone else.' He lifted his right arm, the fist clenched. Brother Edmund was not easily angered, but when he was, the consequences could be fearsome.

With his gang amassing behind him, the ruffian strutted toward Brother Edmund and me.

I heard footsteps behind me. Two dozen men ran down the street from the direction of Winchester House. Some of them waved long sticks.

'Be off with you – be off!' shouted a silver-haired priest.

At once the ruffians retreated. At the bend in the road, their leader shouted at us, 'We won't soon forget it, that yer Bishop Gardiner took the side of *Papists*.'

'This man is Brother Oswald, a former monk of the Cistercian Order,' I told Gardiner's priest. 'He's been injured – we must bring him inside Winchester House for treatment.'

'Absolutely not,' the priest retorted. 'We've done all we can. Either leave him on the ground or take him with you. But I recommend you leave this place before those men return in greater numbers. Which I assure you they will do.'

And with that, Gardiner's men retreated as quickly as they'd advanced. Brother Edmund knelt next to the bleeding monk. He lifted his head with caution. 'Brother Oswald, do you hear me? Do you remember me? It's Edmund Sommerville – from the pilgrimage to Stonehenge.'

The Cistercian's eyes fluttered. 'Edmund ... yes,' he said. 'I remember.' He blinked a few times. 'Is that Joanna with you?'

'Yes,' I said.

'We're going to take you to a place of safety now,' said Brother Edmund.

'Bless you,' said Brother Oswald. 'God the Father and Redeemer has delivered me.' His right hand flopped in the mud as he tried to make the sign of the cross.

'I doubt he can walk,' I whispered to Brother Edmund.

'Are you alone?' my friend asked him. When we first met Brother Oswald, he led a dozen other displaced monks on a journey across England, seeking answers through prayer and pilgrimage.

'The others wait for me near the river,' Brother Oswald said. He winced and rubbed his side, then coughed. 'There are five of them. Near a – a bear-baiting pit. We are on our way to Kent, to the Aylesford friary.'

'Dartford is on the way to Aylesford,' I said.

Brother Edmund scooped up Brother Oswald in his arms, to carry him. His face flushed with the effort.

'I wish we could bring them all to Dartford,' Brother Edmund said through gritted teeth.

I felt a rush of excitement.

'We *can*,' I said.

'How? Even with help, a wounded man can't be carried such a distance by foot.'

I tugged on the front of my bloodied cloak. 'We will hire a wagon,' I said. 'I have the coins in here. Catherine Howard gave me a purse with a little money. It should be enough.'

'And this is how you wish to spend all the money?'

'Yes,' I said. 'Before God I see no higher purpose.'

He nodded, his brown eyes hardening with determination.

'To Dartford,' said Brother Edmund.

32

'Janna! Janna!' Arthur shouted in the doorway of the Sommervilles' house. An instant later I almost toppled from the force of his strong little body hurled onto mine. Laughing, I held him as tight as I could while I watched Sister Winifred weep in the gentler embrace of her older brother.

'Hush, I'm here now – I'm here,' Brother Edmund said. 'All will be well.'

After a day of tears and more embraces, I gratefully slipped into my own bed. But that night I was seized by night terrors without end. The next morning found me weak and thick-headed. But I forced myself to go to the Building Office to at last secure my loom.

Jacquard Rolin, the young reformer from the Low Countries, led me to the storeroom. Sure enough, there was the second long wooden bar along with the roller that fitted between and the pedals for three weavers.

'Brussels does fine work, *n'est-ce pas?*' said Jacquard, proud of what had been created in his countrymen's workshops.

Jacquard told a boy to run and summon four youths for the duty of conveying the loom. A moment after the boy scurried away, an older man paused in the doorway to the storeroom to stare at us.

'Can I be of service, Master Brooke?' Jacquard asked.

I tensed. So this was the husband of Mistress Brooke, who had tormented me that last day in Dartford before I left for London. He was the one entrusted with the hiring of all men to oversee the construction of the king's new manor house on the rubble of the priory.

'Timothy will be ready when the bell strikes four,' Master Brooke said.

'I will be present – there is nothing that could prevent it,' Jacquard said.

After the man left, Jacquard informed me that Timothy, the eldest of the Brooke children, had two months earlier returned from school an enthusiastic preacher of Reform. He climbed onto a tree stump in the pasture next to the family house and proclaimed God's word to anyone who came to listen.

'A tree stump?' I asked. Few things baffled me more than the Reformers' contempt for a beautiful cathedral or monastery church – adorned with stained glass and statues and jewelled plate and chalices – in favour of worshipping in a pasture or a plain gathering room.

'He is most inspiring in his views of the Scripture,' Jacquard said. His rather delicate features strengthened as a fierce glow emanated from within – the glow of a true believer. 'Every time Timothy speaks, more people appear and join in the discussions of Gospel.'

The four youths appeared, and Jacquard insisted on leading the way to my home. The High Street was fairly crowded that afternoon. I did my best to appear unconcerned as I walked beside Jacquard, but in truth I was unnerved to repeat that unfortunate trip. It was ridiculous to fear the simple townsfolk of Dartford. Yet I could not quiet my riotous nerves.

But the man I walked beside was much more the attraction than I was. Jacquard cast a spell on the females of Dartford. I noticed young women – and then a woman not at all young – gape at him in the street.

'You are popular, Master Rolin,' I observed.

Jacquard laughed. 'In the most modest of ways. Now should we see Constable Geoffrey Scovill walk along the High Street, *that* has a most profound effect on the women of Dartford.'

Hearing Geoffrey's name on his lips – and in such a frivolous context – made me tense again. I had not seen Geoffrey since my return. I should have sent word to him at once, but I wasn't sure yet what to say.

When Jacquard began chatting about my tapestry enterprise, I was grateful – at first.

'It is remarkable what you plan to do,' he said. 'I have seen your design, and I admit to some surprise at your choice for the first tapestry.'

'But my design was wrapped and sealed,' I said. 'How do you know my plan?'

Jacquard made a deep, apologetic bow. 'For the ledgers, I must make record of all purchases coming in to Dartford, it is part of my royal commission. I examined it briefly only for that purpose and then resealed it.'

Perhaps he did have that right, but his poking into my affairs disturbed me.

Aloud, I said, 'What surprises you about a mythical bird?'

He smiled. 'For one, the ambition of the artistry. The phoenix is one of the most brilliant creatures. You will have to employ many, many different colours and shades. Then you've chosen to depict the phoenix at the end of its life, when, after one thousand years, it rests on its nest of twigs, only to ignite and burn – and a new, young phoenix will, we presume, emerge from the ashes. How will you suggest flames?'

'With goldwork threads,' I answered. 'As for the ambition of it, I must create something impressive for my first. A tapestry series that tells a story commands the most money, but I have only a three-weaver loom. It would take more than a year to create a series. So I selected one image, and a beautiful one, that could be appreciated at a single glance. If I find the right purchaser, and it is shown in a prominent place, the phoenix tapestry will bring me more customers.'

Jacquard stopped in the street. 'But – but you have thought this through in every detail and conceived of a brilliant plan,' he said.

'It is no matter,' I said, embarrassed. 'But is that all? You said, "For one." Is there something else about my choice of design that surprises you?'

He tilted his head, his liquid eyes studying me. 'I wondered if you gave thought to what some people might perceive the phoenix represents, in particular if it is woven by women who once professed in a priory.'

'It's just a *bird*,' I protested. 'The myth of the phoenix comes from Herodotus, who lived in the fifth century before Our Lord Jesus Christ. It has nothing to do with the Catholic faith.'

Jacquard said, 'The phoenix lives for one thousand years. And the Catholic monasteries have existed one thousand years. Could this death and possible rebirth not be seen as a symbol? Symbols can be powerful.'

The men carried the loom to my door. I led the way inside, struggling to hide my dismay. Could this have been my intent, in some half-understood way, to declare to the world my ache to be reborn from the ashes of our faith? But I had no wish to create controversy in my weaving – that would serve no good purpose at all.

Sister Winifred played with Arthur in the front room. Thrilled by the men's arrival, he peppered me with questions about the loom.

In the kitchen, my serving girl Kitty served dinner to two of the men who had followed Brother Oswald. All of the men slept at the infirmary. Brother Oswald was badly injured, and three of the others were likewise too sick or weakened to go about the town, and Brother Edmund cared for them there, day and night. Once they'd sufficiently recovered, their plan was to travel to Aylesford, to a recently suppressed Carmelite friary where a man wanted to join them.

Looking at the bedraggled monks as they devoured fish pie, I realised how strange they might look to Jacquard. Their worn habits revealed that they once served in monasteries. I did not want the afternoon's prayer meeting to turn into a dangerous gossip session about the monks come to town.

But just as I opened my mouth to bid him farewell, Jacquard announced, 'I shall direct the assembling of the loom.'

'That is not necessary,' I protested. 'You've done more than enough.'

Sister Winifred said, 'You should take Master Rolin up on his kind offer, Sister Joanna. It would be so difficult for us to do it – won't this save you time?'

Jacquard said, very earnestly, 'I wish to help in any way I can.'

And so Jacquard plunged to work. While overseeing the loom construction, he ruffled Arthur's hair, made courteous conversation with Sister Winifred and me, even called out teasing remarks to a blushing Kitty. Of the two silent monks in the kitchen, he seemed to take no notice whatsoever, not even when they left my house to return to the infirmary.

Once the loom was completed, Jacquard departed with a last courteous bow.

Sister Winifred came over to lay her head on my shoulder. 'It is splendid,' she whispered. 'Now we will resume our work at the priory – we will create works of beauty. Oh, Sister Joanna, I will spend every moment I can helping you weave.'

'Will you?' I said. I wrapped my arm around her tiny waist. I was so grateful for her friendship – and that she had overcome her trepidations about my tapestry business.

The door swung open. At first I thought it was Jacquard returning, but there stood Geoffrey Scovill and Sister Beatrice.

They came in together. Yet there could not be a greater contrast in demeanour. Geoffrey Scovill moved stiffly and said nothing beyond 'Good afternoon.' While Sister Beatrice, her green eyes glittering, proceeded to babble.

'I was so beside myself with happiness – so beside myself – to hear of your return, Sister Joanna. It's been two long months, and we've all missed you greatly. Your absence was keenly felt. Geoffrey did not believe me when I found him today, east of town, to tell him you were back. I said, "Let's see for ourselves." And here you are. With your loom – at long last!'

She turned to Geoffrey and slipped her hand around his arm. 'Doesn't she look well? Doesn't she?' Sister Beatrice's voice was edged with panic as she clutched his arm. Geoffrey did nothing but look at me, a hundred questions in his eyes. I did not feel well and was sure I did not look it either.

Suddenly everything began to wobble around me.

'Are you sick?' asked Sister Winifred.

'No, no,' I said, sucking in a deep breath. And then: 'I have something to say.' I looked at them in turn, at Sister Winifred, Sister Beatrice, and Geoffrey. 'I thank you for looking after Arthur when I was unable to. To have friends such as you is a great honour, and I am grateful to God the Father for you. I am unworthy—'

My voice broke, and my shoulders heaved. To my mortification, I began to cry.

'She is so tired – she has suffered through so much – we must let Sister Joanna rest now,' said Sister Winifred firmly. 'I will take care of Arthur for the rest of the day. I think you should both go now.'

'Perhaps that would be best,' I murmured. Without looking at Geoffrey or anyone else, I turned to find the stairs leading to my bedchamber. I crawled into bed. I was more lost than ever, damaged by the horrors I'd seen and without much hope for a future of any grace or purpose. Exhaustion claimed me. I knew nothing for the rest of the afternoon and slept on through the night, as if I were seeking escape through dreamless slumber.

I woke up feeling somewhat stronger. It was Saturday, and I set out for the market directly after morning Mass. I'd put Kitty to work churning and pickling – baking bread was beyond her skills, and I hadn't the oven for it in any case. Rather than wait for Kitty's mother to get to it, I'd decided to purchase loaves and as many other foodstuffs as I could carry. Until Brother Oswald was ready to journey to Aylesford, there were many mouths to feed.

The Dartford Market House jutted out into the street. The market teemed inside with Dartford townsfolk, all talking and laughing and calling out to one another. I filled my basket with bread and then carrots, dried peas, beans, onions, and more. I found much to buy. Doing these ordinary tasks felt pleasant. Perhaps I would, in time, feel a part of this town.

I was picking through a barrel of apples when Geoffrey Scovill eased into a place next to me in front of the fruit stalls.

'Joanna, may I speak to you?' he said.

'Certainly,' I said, my rising spirits now in collapse. I continued to examine the apple I'd picked. It was firm and red on one side but had a soft brown bruise on the other. I balanced it on the edge of the stall, so no one else would buy it.

'You look haler today, I am glad of it,' he said.

'Thank you,' I said.

His eyes studied me. 'I'd like to know why the Duke of Norfolk permitted you to return to Dartford and under what conditions,' he said.

I stopped sorting through apples. Geoffrey pulled at a button on his doublet with his left hand as he waited for me to answer.

'This isn't the place to discuss it,' I said, moving away from the fruit stall.

'I know of none better,' he said, following. 'It's the loudest spot in town. No one can follow what we say.'

After a moment, I said, 'The duke didn't exactly *permit* it.'

Geoffrey groaned, 'I knew it. Oh, Joanna, what you have you done?'

'His Grace will not pursue me,' I said. 'We spoke at Tower Hill, after which I told him to leave without me, that I would be returning to my life in Dartford. He left.'

'But were there any terms or conditions?' Geoffrey pressed.

I said fiercely, 'I stood inches from the scaffold, with the blood of Baron Montague upon me – it wasn't the time to haggle over terms and conditions.'

Geoffrey stared into the distance. 'Montague was a brave man, and I was very sorry to hear of his death,' he said.

I regretted speaking so harshly to Geoffrey. 'I'm sorry, too,' I said.

We shared a moment of sorrow. Around us the townsfolk jostled and made jokes, oblivious.

Geoffrey then stepped closer to me. Leaning down, he said, 'What you are suggesting then is that there is no impediment.'

'Impediment? To what?'

'To us, Joanna,' he said, his face alight with hope. 'To coming together – finally.'

I stared at Geoffrey, in disbelief. 'What about Sister Beatrice?'

He shook his head, pulling at the button so hard I expected him to tear it off. 'It's not the same. I realise she is very … very fond of me, but—'

'She loves you, Geoffrey.'

He reddened but said, 'No promises have been made.'

'I never thought to hear you be cruel,' I said, and marched toward the doorway to the Market House.

Geoffrey was at my side again. 'This is far from fair, Joanna. Aren't you using my friendship with Beatrice as an excuse? I believe Sommerville has worked away at you again. You are the one making the promises – to him. Do you think I don't know you came back to Dartford with him?'

I pushed my way out onto the street. I nearly crashed into a fishmonger bending over his cart. My sack of beans tumbled out of my basket and spilled into the dirt of the High Street. But I was too upset to care.

Once again Geoffrey loomed over me. I could not get away from him.

'He crept out of Dartford to find you without telling me,' Geoffrey said, seething. 'He knew very well where you were – he just waited until I was safely occupied with town business and then ran to be the one to rescue you. Just remember, Joanna, you didn't write to Sommerville when you were trying to find a way out of London. You wrote to me. You wanted *me*.'

Now Geoffrey shouted. Heads turned to see what was causing such a commotion.

'Stop this,' I said desperately, pulling him to the other side of the High Street, outside the cobbler's storefront. 'This jealousy demeans you – it demeans me. Brother Edmund isn't like that at all.'

Geoffrey slammed his hand against the wooden wall. I'd never seen him lose control of himself like this.

'The worst of it is, I know what binds you to him. He's just as crazy as you are. He doesn't try to talk sense into you. He encourages every wild idea you've ever had. His are even worse! Such as going to Blackfriars after it was suppressed by the king.'

'How do you know about Blackfriars?' I demanded. 'And how did you know that the arrests were going to happen at the Red Rose that night? You've never told me.'

'A constable hears things,' he retorted. 'I may not be a scholar like your noble "Brother Edmund", but I'm no fool. And at least I'm honest with you. He's pretended all along that he is above earthly desires – that he doesn't want you. Can't you see the deception?'

I was so angry I could hardly breathe.

'You *are* a fool, Geoffrey Scovill,' I said, the words pouring out. 'You don't know a thing about him or me. He doesn't want me the way you do, the way other men would. At Blackfriars, I was the one. I wanted him. I offered myself to him – and he said it was wrong. He refused me.'

I will never forget the look on Geoffrey's face. How anger and disbelief collapsed into deep pain.

'I never thought to hear *you* be cruel, Joanna,' he said thickly.

He turned to walk away from me.

'Geoffrey,' I called after him. 'Wait. Stop.'

But he didn't turn around. Instead he walked faster and faster, until he was running away from me up the middle of the High Street.

33

At Mass on Christmas day, there was not an empty space to be found in Holy Trinity Church. The church had been stripped of its adornments, its beautiful images painted over and rendered much darker, but something significant was added: long wooden pews. As Father William Mote told the story of the birth of Our Saviour with as much vigour as he was capable of, I sat in a pew halfway down the middle of the church, next to Arthur and Sister Winifred, with Brother Edmund on her other side. We were no longer relegated to the chantries chapel and the ramblings of Father Anthony. During my time away, Father William allowed the former residents of the priory to join the larger congregation. This should have been a blessing but for one serious drawback.

The chain.

As Father William expounded, he stood next to it – a platform nailed to the altar and, attached to that altar by a long and heavy chain, an English translation of the Great Bible, written by Myles Coverdale. 'I am exhorted by Lord Cromwell to gently and charitably exhort you to read this Bible for yourselves – the king would have you examine it using sober and modest behaviour,' Father William had announced to all of us two Sundays ago. The parishioners looked at one another, baffled. Not one man in seven in Dartford was able to read at all, and far fewer women. These numbers were unlikely to increase at any near time, since priories and abbeys, long the centres of education, were no more. The rich could afford private tutors for their children. But the minor gentry and merchants no longer had a place to send their sons and daughters to learn letters.

Ironically, the only parishioner who made it his business to study Coverdale's Bible was Brother Edmund. 'I do not fear the Scriptures and shall not be corrupted by misinterpretation,' Brother Edmund reassured Sister Eleanor, who begged him not to put himself at risk.

Faulty translation, leading to heretical belief, was what we Catholics feared. After a few days of reading, he commented, 'Coverdale acquits himself reasonably well – he was an Augustinian, after all.'

My problem was not the book itself but the chain. Every time I looked at it, I felt as if I were being pulled back to London, to the court and prison and scaffold of King Henry the Eighth. As I listened to Father William's sermon, I put both hands around my throat and closed my eyes.

When Mass was finished, Brother Edmund pulled me aside. 'Sister Joanna, could I have your assistance in the infirmary for a short time?'

'Of course,' I said. Arthur, smiling, went with Sister Winifred.

And so Brother Edmund and I left church together. No one took notice of it – not even Geoffrey Scovill. He sat near the back with Sister Beatrice, giving her his complete attention. They were always together now. Geoffrey had not spoken to me since that day at the market. I had decided to do nothing to heal the breach, though it hurt me. Geoffrey was better off without Joanna Stafford.

Brother Edmund's small infirmary, tidily kept and stocked with potions, pills, plasters, and herbs, was empty. As Brother Edmund lit a small fire in the back, it occurred to me that it was unlikely someone from town would require an apothecary on Christmas Day – or that he would need my assistance.

'Sister Joanna, I must speak to you in confidence about something important,' he said, gesturing to stools set next to his oak worktable.

'Of course.' My breath quickened. I wanted to be important to Brother Edmund.

He pulled his stool closer to mine so that we were but inches apart. I had not been this near him since I took his hands in the *calefactorium* of Blackfriars.

Brother Edmund said, 'Have you noticed anyone following you?'

I drew back, surprised. 'What do you mean?'

He ran his hand though his ash-blond hair. 'I believe that someone watches me. I see a shadow in this doorway and turn – the shadow is gone. It could be anyone, not a man following me. But the last time it occurred, when I heard the footsteps, I slipped between two shops and waited. No one appeared for a very long time, and then it was the butcher and his son. The man had been clever enough to know what I was doing and turned back.'

I stared at Brother Edmund, struggling to take this all in.

'Are you absolutely sure no one watches you?' he asked.

'I cannot be sure, of course, but no – I've not noticed anything like that,' I said. 'Do you have any idea who this person could be?' I asked. Before he could answer, I sat up straight on my stool.

'Oh, no,' I cried. 'It's a spy sent by Gardiner and Norfolk.'

Brother Edmund bit his lip. 'That is a possibility. There is another.'

He hesitated, as if mulling over how to put it to me. I heard the madman John shouting gibberish outside – his particular demons provoked him again. I hoped that someone would take John in for Christmas dinner, though it was a daunting prospect.

'Sister Joanna, have you given more thought to who must have sent Gertrude Courtenay to find you?' he asked. 'Do you have any idea who was directing her when she forced you to see the second seer?'

Of course. Brother Edmund was haunted by the prophecy. He *wanted* someone to seek me out – to take me to the third seer. This was the only reason he asked to speak to me in private.

'I don't know who it was beyond that it was not the Lady Mary,' I said, concealing my disappointment. 'Perhaps I will never know. Certainly Gertrude cannot be asked.'

Just then, someone banged on the infirmary door.

Brother Edmund opened it to Jacquard Rolin and Master Oliver Gwinn, the widower whom we'd comforted in church the day I left Dartford.

'You see?' Jacquard said. 'I told you Brother Edmund was open for business in the infirmary. I noticed him and Sister Joanna walk in this direction after church.'

'I don't want to trouble you,' said Master Gwinn, his left hand wrapped in a rag. 'It's all my own fault. I was so clumsy.'

Jacquard said, 'Our Master Gwinn was hard at work at the barn at Holcroft early this morning when he had a mishap.'

Holcroft was the name of the house where the six sisters of Dartford Priory lived. I'd read in Sister Winifred's letter that Master Gwinn spent a great deal of his time helping them, and heard more about it since.

'Let me see your hand,' said Brother Edmund. After examining Master Gwinn, he said, 'The wound is not serious, but it requires cleaning and a salve of herbs to prevent it becoming so. With your permission?'

'Of course, Brother Edmund,' he said. 'I am most grateful.'

While my friend busied himself with the remedy, Master Gwinn turned to me. 'When you were at the priory, was Sister Agatha your novice mistress?' he asked.

I nodded.

'I can well believe that,' he said, his mouth twitching in a shy smile. 'She would excel at teaching and looking after younger women. But, by my trowth, she would excel at anything. She is the kindest, warmest, most thoughtful person. And she makes me laugh – no one call tell a story like Sister Agatha!'

His tone was nothing short of rapturous. Master Gwinn seemed besotted with Sister Agatha. It occurred to me that Sister Agatha could be the one among us to marry. It was happening across England: former monks, nuns, and friars finding someone to marry. When I first heard this, I felt upset. But slowly, as with other things, I was getting used to the idea.

'This *is* good care – very good care,' Master Gwinn said. 'What the others say is wrong.'

I asked, 'Who are the others?'

'The people in town,' said Master Gwinn. He peered at Brother Edmund and then at me, realisation dawning. 'Do you mean you don't know? Now I have made a muck of things.'

'I know that in the last two months, I've seen very few people come to this infirmary for treatment, beyond my friends who were passing through,' Brother Edmund said quietly.

This greatly surprised me. Why hadn't he told me?

Master Gwinn sighed. 'It's Brooke's boy – the preacher Timothy.'

'The one on the stump,' I muttered.

'He speaks against the sisters and you even more so, Brother Edmund,' Master Gwinn said. 'Said good Christians should mistrust your popish remedies. I'm very sorry to have to repeat such slander.'

Brother Edmund applied the herbal salve to Master Gwinn's hand and then bandaged it. 'Please do not feel badly, Sir,' he said. 'I have suspected it.'

'It's not just Timothy,' Master Gwinn said. 'It's all built up from months of what Father William used to preach to us, too. He doesn't say it now, of course, when you sit among us, but he used to say that if the monasteries fell, then King Henry would never have to impose another tax on the people, because the treasury would be full for the rest of our lives.'

I cried, 'That is a most vicious thing for a priest to say to his flock.'

Brother Edmund raised his hand. 'Do not blame him entirely, Sister Joanna. Two years ago, Archbishop Cranmer sent directives across the kingdom, giving priests those exact words for the pulpit.'

Master Gwinn made a face of misery. 'It's wrong – and I am so, so sorry.'

After the widower shuffled from the infirmary, Brother Edmund cleaned his wooden bowl and pestle while I sat at the table, my head in my hands. The tears spilled down my cheeks. This roiling hopelessness was so painful, I couldn't bear it. Would I live the rest of my days in the grip of despair?

'If I knew who the third seer was, I would go to that person now – today – to receive the prophecy,' I blurted. 'I must do *something* to take charge of my life.'

Brother Edmund was silent for a moment. I could not discern his feeling.

Then he said, softly, 'When the raven climbs the rope, the dog must soar like the hawk.'

He had been turning the prophecy over in his mind, all these weeks. While I struggled to push it from my thoughts, he had done the opposite.

'Perhaps we could piece the prophecy together ourselves,' I said. 'We made a start of it at Blackfriars.'

'Perhaps we could,' he nodded. 'But Christmas Day is not the most propitious of days to do so. We must calm ourselves before we meet the others.'

I wiped away the tears as best I could. How worried Sister Winifred would be if I appeared at her Christmas dinner in a wrecked state. I must rally to ensure that Arthur had a pleasant day, at the very least.

Brother Edmund reached over and patted my hand, but with a certain tentativeness. I remembered his comforting embrace at Howard House and, later, how it felt to slip my arms around him in Blackfriars. I fought off my longing to feel that again.

The sound of singing drifted into the infirmary. The townsfolk were making their way up the street with their serenading. Their words of cheer and friendship were not for us but we heard them nonetheless:

On Christmas five and twenty
Fum, fum, fum
Comes a most important day
Let us be gay, let us be gay.

Brother Edmund carefully withdrew his hand from mine and turned on his stool to stare out the front window of his infirmary.

'I was promised to the monasteries when I was eight years old,' he said slowly. 'I can't remember a time when I thought to be other than a man of religion. I accepted that I would never be a husband or father. Of course, those things mean nothing to a child.'

My breathing quickened. He had never confided in me like this before. Was Brother Edmund attempting to explain why he turned away from me at Blackfriars?

The singing continued, fainter and farther down the street:

Oh, a child was born this night
So rosy white, so rosy white
Son of Mary, Holy Virgin
In a stable, mean and lowly ...

Neither of us spoke. The tension in the room had become unbearable. I couldn't help but wonder if he was waiting for me to fumble toward the unspoken question.

'Brother Edmund,' I said faintly, 'have you ever had doubts about celibacy?'

Staring down at the table between us, he replied, 'Scriptures say, "A man who governs his passions is master of his world. We must either command them or be enslaved by them."'

I felt a sharp pang, which was ridiculous. I knew very well how Brother Edmund felt, how could I expect anything different? He did not seem angry at me, at least. To steer the conversation back to safer ground, I said, 'But you became a friar, not a monk for the monastery.'

Brother Edmund said: 'What was important to my father was that I take vows, whether it be monk in the cloister or friar among the people meant nothing to him. I was the one who asked to be a friar of the Dominican Order. He agreed to it.'

There was something odd about this. Seeing the question on my face, Brother Edmund continued, 'I am the second son. My brother Marcus is ten years older than me. My father had some money, but not a great deal of it. He didn't want to divide between us. Everything must go to Marcus. I must not divert from him in any way. My father himself was a second son. You would expect my father to have sympathy with the position of second son. But it was just the opposite.'

This was not at all how I imagined the family of Brother Edmund. Yet while telling this story, his face remained neutral. He did not seem upset, and in truth, it was not unheard of for a father to regard his boys so.

'What was it like for Sister Winifred?' I asked.

After a moment, he said, 'There are three sisters besides Marcus and myself. So there were several dowries to pay for. Winifred was a sickly child – I heard him call her the "runt". Father feared he'd never be able to marry her off without a dowry. He borrowed the money to endow her at Dartford as a novice and that was that.'

The creases deepened in his forehead. Their father's scarce love for Sister Winifred bothered him more than his own treatment.

I asked, 'What does your father think now that the two of you are no longer at Dartford?'

Brother Edmund said, still staring out the window, 'He passed into God's hands seven years ago.'

After a moment, I said, 'But what of your brother now? Perhaps he never wished for these sorts of actions to be taken. He may regret your father's stance, and wish to form a bond with you.'

Brother Edmund finally turned to face me. 'How is it possible,' he said, 'that after all you have been through, all the losses suffered, you can still see the best in people, Sister Joanna? It is so very remarkable.'

For the first time in weeks, I felt a warmth, a steadiness, rise inside me. Yet, as welcome as his praise was, I winced, too. Why did a kind word from Brother Edmund transform me so? It was time I acted as a grown woman, not a weak and adoring child.

Brother Edmund jumped to his feet and put his arm around me. But my exhilaration swiftly shifted to fear, for his face was full of alarm. His act was one of protection. I looked toward the door, to see what he saw.

Jacquard Rolin stood just inside the infirmary. He had somehow opened the door without either of us hearing it.

'What are you doing here?' I said angrily.

Jacquard said, 'I came to make inquiry about my friend Master Gwinn.'

Brother Edmund cleared his throat. 'He left some time ago. The poultice should speed the healing.'

'That is good,' said Jacquard. But he did not turn to leave.

'Is there anything else, Master Rolin?' asked Brother Edmund.

'I have received such interesting news,' Jacquard said. 'It has the potential to change everything in the kingdom of England.'

'What is it?' I asked.

'Pope Clement has decided to issue the bull against King Henry the Eighth. Your ruler is now formally excommunicated from the Catholic Church.'

34

After Jacquard left, Brother Edmund put out the fire in the infirmary, and I thought about what this news meant. Papal excommunication was rare and serious. Extraordinarily serious. The last person to be cast out of the Catholic Church by the Holy Father was Martin Luther, in 1520.

I remembered what Gertrude said on our ride to Londinium: '*It would be the duty of other Christian kings to depose him. And we could not rally to the defence of King Henry. Not if we wished to remain faithful to the Holy Father.*'

During our time in the infirmary, it had got colder outside. A damp fullness hung in the air, the sort that suggested snow. The serenaders were nowhere to be seen. Almost everyone was indoors now, fires roaring, as they enjoyed Christmas dinner.

When we reached the High Street, I saw a group of people at the top of it, walking toward the centre of town but very slowly. To our shock, it was Brother Oswald and his followers. We hadn't expected them to return.

The Cistercian was so exhausted, I feared he would collapse in the street. His followers looked just as bad: dirty, bruised, and dishevelled.

'What has happened?' I cried.

'All is well, Sister Joanna,' said Brother Oswald faintly.

'I see no new face – did you find the friar you seek in Aylesford?' asked Brother Edmund.

No one answered.

Arthur burst out of the Sommerville house, outraged by my lateness. I hurried the coatless boy inside. It took a few more minutes for Brother Edmund to join us, leading in the new guests for his table.

I'd rarely been so proud of Sister Winifred as when she serenely greeted Brother Oswald and his followers. While I served each of the men a cup from the wassail bowl, she transformed a dinner for four into ten. Every guest had a bit of roasted goose with a slice of mince pie. It was a wonderful pie, with the mutton seasoned to perfection and not too many raisins.

Arthur was ecstatic over Christmas. I wondered if he remembered the one that came before: a day spent with grieving relatives in the North of England, an orphan no one wanted until my father came looking, and brought him south. And what memories did he hold of a Christmas two years ago, spent with loving parents? I prayed that Margaret would think her son well treated, that I was not failing her memory. Yet what would she think of me for turning her painful secret into barter so that I could force my way home to Dartford? My throat clenched with remorse. I should have won my freedom another way.

But today, at least, Arthur was happy, and his smiles and curiosity and laughter pleased everyone else at the table, though the monks said very little. Brother Edmund asked no questions; he quietly saw to their comfort, as would any host. But I knew him well enough to see he was as perplexed as I. Something went wrong in Aylesford. What could it be?

Kitty materialised, to clean up the dinner. I asked Sister Winifred if she would mind looking after Arthur for a short time, so that I could show Brother Oswald my new tapestry loom.

The Cistercian inclined his head. 'If it would please you, Sister,' he said.

The monks examined the first weeks of stitching on the loom, greatly interested. No one made the connection that Jacquard had – that the phoenix might resemble the rebirth of the monasteries.

In the privacy of my home, I felt freer to urge them, 'Please tell us what happened in Aylesford.'

The same sadness settled over the group. All peered at Brother Oswald, awaiting his decision. At last, he said, 'If it would please you, Sister Joanna,' and he sat on the floor. That was his way – Cistercians were so profoundly humble.

'Aylesford Friary was so beautiful,' began Brother Oswald. 'When we arrived, it was twilight, and to see it so, ah, it was like a dream. Three hundred years old, built in the time of the Crusades ...'

Brother Oswald's faltered as he stared at the candle smoking in front of him. I could see that the wound on his face dealt by the ruffian in Southwark had not healed.

'We found Brother Paul. He had been living there, in hiding. He could not light a fire for cooking or for warmth, for fear of discovery. Brother Paul said he took it as a sign from God that we came when we did – that all was not lost. We prayed together and then found places to sleep. How comforting it felt to be together in that room, as if we'd found a religious house once more.'

Brother Oswald bowed his head. 'The next morning we could not wake Brother Paul. He died in the night.'

I now regretted I'd pressed him for answers.

Brother Oswald straightened his shoulders. With great effort, he said, 'We will not despair – no, we will not. God has a purpose. I think that our next pilgrimage will reveal God's will. Yes, I am sure of it.'

'Where do you go from Dartford?' Brother Edmund asked.

'To Canterbury Cathedral, to kiss the relics and make offerings at the shrine of blessed Saint Thomas Becket on the morning of the anniversary of his death,' answered Brother Oswald. 'It is in four days.'

'No,' I cried. 'Oh, no.'

I never told Brother Edmund what the Duke of Norfolk said would happen on the night before that anniversary. I had not forgotten it, of course – but I had pushed it from my thoughts, like a vile nightmare.

My heart pounding, I said, 'The king plans to send men to the cathedral, the night before the anniversary, to remove the box that contains the bones of Saint Thomas.'

'Why?' choked one of the monks.

I said faintly, 'His Majesty means to have the body defiled – the bones burned and the ashes thrown onto the ground – to make example of a man of God who defied a king.'

Brother Oswald's eyes squeezed shut and he made the sign of the cross. The others clutched one another, in sorrow and pain.

I felt a hand grab my arm. It was Brother Edmund. 'Why didn't you tell me this – why?' he demanded. 'When did *you* learn it, Sister Joanna?'

'At Blackfriars,' I whispered. 'From the Duke of Norfolk.'

Brother Edmund said, 'Yes, this is why the king has been excommunicated. I knew it had to be some sort of terrible desecration that would force the pope to finally issue the bull. If Norfolk knew, and told you, then others must know at court. This horrific act may have been planned months ago. The word travelled to Rome – and Pope Clement had no choice. A saint cannot be defiled this way.'

A new noise filled the room. It was Brother Oswald, kneeling in the middle of the floor and sobbing. The others were thrown into a panic at the sight of their leader's distress. Another monk knelt before Brother Oswald and said, 'Maybe we can stop this. We could go there now, before the king's men, and convince the prior to let us take Saint Thomas to safety.'

Brother Edmund said, 'I'm afraid the prior of Canterbury Cathedral would never allow that. He won't dare defy the king.'

'*We will go!*'

It was Brother Oswald. The Cistercian had ceased weeping. 'We will be there the same night that the king's men arrive,' he said, rising to his feet. 'We will wait for them to emerge with the box – the sacred feretrum – and then we will take it from them.'

'Yes! Yes! Yes!' the others cried. They all agreed at once to a plan that seemed to me highly dangerous. Yes, I could understand their wanting to do it. The king's indomitable hatred caused despair and great pain. This plan removed the pain. Hope was restored. But how could they get the better of the king's soldiers? I looked at Brother Edmund – he must talk them out of this.

'I shall go with you to Canterbury,' Brother Edmund declared.

I rushed to him, saying, 'I beg you to listen to me. Haven't we been taught, "Arm yourself with prayer, rather than a sword; wear humility, rather than fine clothes"?'

He turned to me – I saw that his eyes, like Brother Oswald's, glittered like hard gems. 'We have been humble too long, Sister. See what has become of us as a result. I *must* go.'

'But Brother Edmund, they'll kill you – all of you,' I said. 'None of you have seen what the king's men are capable of. Not as I have.'

'And if I should die in this attempt – an attempt to prevent an act of hate and blasphemy – then my life at last has been infused with meaning, Sister Joanna,' he said passionately. 'You of all people know what it cost me to take the Oath of Supremacy to King Henry five years ago. I denied the Holy Father. I haven't known grace since, not the true grace of God. I was weak; I feared torture and death; I swore the oath. I cannot live with that any longer.'

'And Sister Winifred?' I asked.

'If we succeed in Canterbury, then she can be proud of me,' he said. 'And if I fail, she will take pride in knowing that at last I showed courage when courage was called for. As will you, Sister Joanna.'

'I am proud of you, Brother Edmund,' I said. 'Now, tonight, and always.'

He stared at me, wildly, and for an instant I thought I'd won. But then he backed away, to join the others.

Helpless, frightened, I watched them talk together, their faces flushed with purpose. They were in the grip of a destiny now, one they had chosen for themselves.

Destiny.

There is a destiny one creates. And there is a destiny ordained.

I walked slowly, toward the middle of the circle of men. Everyone stopped talking and waited for me to speak.

'I will go with you to Canterbury,' I said.

35

The fire of purpose, once ignited within me, did not falter. When I ran to the doors of Canterbury Cathedral, three nights later, Brother Oswald had already wrested the feretrum from the soldiers.

The oldest soldier, grey-haired, stood between me and Brother Edmund, tall and vengeful, waving his cudgel. I screamed at him. I felt like a Queen Boudicca, driven mad by rage.

The old soldier backed away from the both of us, retreating into the cathedral and past the dazed prior. We frightened him. Within minutes, we'd be able to spirit away the remains of our dead saint to a place of safety.

I felt a powerful excitement coursing in my blood. I was fulfilling my destiny. But it was even more than that. For the first time I, Joanna Stafford, a novice trained in peaceful contemplation, understood why men chased after wars and sought the honour of the field. The unity of purpose with Brother Edmund, Brother Oswald, and the five other monks, our shared devotion to the service of God, no matter the personal cost . . .

The sound came from behind me, from the top of the wide street. It was a roar, not unlike the one inside my head when I fought for consciousness outside the monks' graveyard, but a hundred times louder.

'No, no, no, no,' said Brother Edmund, in a chant of anguish.

At least twenty soldiers in royal livery galloped toward us. As the first line reached us, the men flew off their horses and swarmed up the steps. Silver flashed in the torchlight – they carried swords. These were not frightened boys or old men. Two of them wrested the feretrum from the monks. But my attention was not on the remains of England's revered saint.

Our leader, the poor, pious Cistercian Brother Oswald, lay still, his ivory head smashed open on the street, just below the bottom step.

Snowflakes touched down in the dark red blood curling around the stones.

A helmeted man on a huge black horse, its mouth foaming, blocked our escape. He called out orders to his men to seize us all. The orders were instantly obeyed. Rough hands grabbed my friends, pulling their arms around their backs to restrain them.

I could not take it in, could not believe this was happening. To succeed and live – that was always a possibility. To succeed and die was more likely, and I had accepted that and prepared for it. But to fail at our mission *and* to live? This was impossible. Dread rose in me as I realised I was once more made a prisoner.

'Get them out of sight as quickly as possible,' cried the helmeted commander on the black horse. Two burly soldiers picked up the limp body of Brother Oswald, as callously as slinging a bag of meal to market.

The man in charge removed his helmet – Lord John Dudley. Not two months earlier, I'd watched him order a far different group of people gathered for imprisonment.

One of the soldiers grabbed Brother Edmund and spun him around, tying his wrists together behind his back. He winced with pain, crouched over. His eyes searched for me and found me. The friar apothecary straightened as best he could, struggling to hide his pain.

I stepped out of the shadows of the door. I could not bear to be separated from Brother Edmund now.

Dudley nodded at the sight of me. There was absolutely no surprise.

In that moment, I understood. We were betrayed. And I knew who it was who had betrayed us.

And so our pilgrimage ended. It began in hope, faith, and courage. It concluded in death and in failure. We did not even possess the unquestioned dignity of a holy mission. Lord John Dudley tried to take that from us, too.

'Did you do this because you thought the king's men came here to defile Becket's bones?' Dudley demanded of me as he walked us through the dark streets, away from the cathedral. It had stopped snowing. A thin white layer clung to the street – I walked in the sharp hoofprints of Dudley's horse.

He continued: 'That is a baseless rumour, spread by Papists who would blacken the king's good name throughout Christendom. The king stripped and closed the shrine, yes, but only to prevent superstitious practices. The bones were to be moved somewhere safe, to prevent just such criminal actions as you took tonight.'

I said nothing. It was impossible to know if any part of that were true.

But of one thing I could be sure – it was nothing but hubris to think that I could change anything in the kingdom. Christmas night in Dartford, I'd thought that perhaps this action was the one I was meant to take – I did not need to wait for instructions from a third seer. But either the prophecies were false or I had grievously misinterpreted them.

'When the raven climbs the rope, the dog must soar like the hawk ... Look to the bear to welcome the bull.' I was further from understanding these words than ever before.

A frustration raged in me as never before. Why had I been cursed with this? It had brought me nothing but pain and confusion. If by some miracle of God's grace I evaded trial and prison – if not execution – I wanted nothing but a quiet life filled with prayer and repentance.

I wished I could speak to Brother Edmund. We walked side by side, our wrists bound behind our backs. Dudley rode just ahead of us, half turned to taunt. A dozen soldiers separated us from the followers of Brother Oswald. All I could remember was the Cistercian's dashed head on the steps of the cathedral, the snow touching his blood. I prayed that someone would take his poor body away, for Christian burial.

Dudley nudged his horse to the side of the road and signalled to a young soldier to receive orders. The soldier nodded, turned, and grabbed Brother Edmund and me, to push us off the road, closer to Dudley.

The others marched on, led by a boy carrying a torch, the soldiers surrounding the five followers of Brother Oswald. As they passed us, one monk called out, 'God protect and keep you.'

Dudley made a hissing noise of disgust.

After they'd disappeared from view, Dudley kicked his horse to start again, but down a different street. His one soldier walked behind us, prodding Brother Edmund with his halberd periodically. We had nothing but the weak moonlight to guide us.

What did it mean, that we had separated from the others and went with only Dudley and one other man to a different destination?

We walked for at least an hour, perhaps two. All the buildings we passed were dark. The citizens of Canterbury obeyed their curfew. No one watched us go by – there would be no witnesses to our fate.

We walked through an opening in an ancient low stone wall. I ached with weariness, with grief and dread. But my mind stirred. I was on the brink of memory.

Fewer buildings stood on the other side of the wall. There was a barren forest, the snow clinging to naked branches like bandage strips on withered limbs. My gaze shifted to the left side of the road, where a group of buildings loomed, a church spire stretching to the frozen sky.

Dudley has taken us to Saint Sepulchre.

A young bearded man ran from the gatehouse of Saint Sepulchre. It was not the porter I remembered from when I was seventeen, that was for certain. The bearded man took Dudley's horse.

Saint Sepulchre was only half standing. The new owner of the convent, whether it be king or Reformer bishop or favoured courtier, had ordered the beginning of the destruction. The church had been torn down as well as that first room, where I'd seen the painting of Saint Benedict. But the work had halted, no doubt because of winter's arrival. The wing containing the prioress's chambers and the dormitory still stood.

The bearded man who took Dudley's horse reappeared with a lit torch. He and the soldier led us down the sole passageway; Dudley did not follow. He hadn't seemed to grasp the significance of this place, of my having been brought here before. But if Dudley knew nothing of my history, why bring me here?

The two men stopped at the dormitory where I remembered the nuns of Saint Sepulchre slept. Keys rustled, a door opened. Brother Edmund was shoved into the room without benefit of candle.

Before I could say a word to him, the door slammed shut again.

'Over here,' grunted the bearded man, and pointed. I was to be imprisoned in the next room, the very same room where I'd received prophecy from Sister Elizabeth Barton.

I recoiled. I leaped in the other direction. 'Not there!' I cried. The soldier seized me at once.

'Open it,' he commanded, his hands tightening around my wrists. I yelped in pain.

The other man opened the door. The soldier flung me in. I fell flat on my stomach, my bound hands flailing behind me. A mound of old straw broke the fall or else my face would have been bloodied.

The door slammed shut. The room was black. As I well knew, there was no window.

'Help me, Mother Mary – help me, Lord God,' I pleaded, wriggling in the straw.

But there was no help for me. I pulled my knees up to my belly and wept, like a terrified child. This was the room where I watched a young nun writhe on the floor; now I did the same. 'You are the one who will come after,' she'd moaned. Was it true what Gertrude Courtenay told me – did she falsely recant in order to protect me? She must have faced torture terrible indeed to make her take that step to keep safe the secret. How would I stand up to the pain when it was my turn?

'Sister Joanna, Sister Joanna!'

Had I gone mad? Whose voice was this – Sister Barton's perhaps. My entire body convulsed with terror. But then I realised it was a man calling out to me. Brother Edmund.

'Can you hear me?' he shouted.

'Yes!' I shouted back.

'Follow my voice – follow it,' he said. 'I will keep talking until you reach the wall.'

I got to my knees and inched forward to him. I could not feel my way forward with my hands. As Brother Edmund spoke, I made my way to him, until I hit the brick wall. The pain in my head was so sharp, I thought I would faint. I sucked in breath after breath, until the pain subdued enough for me to sit. His voice emanated from a hole in the bottom of the wall.

I thanked God and the Virgin for it. I huddled above that hole, my cheek pressed against the rough, cold brick.

'This is Saint Sepulchre, isn't it?' he asked. Now that Brother Edmund was so close, he no longer needed to shout.

'Yes,' I said.

'Sister Joanna, listen to me,' he said, his voice urgent. 'I don't know how much time we have. You must stay calm. Tell them nothing about the prophecies. We may yet find a way to freedom. The important thing is – do not panic.'

I said, 'How could we possibly win our freedom now? We are going to be roughly questioned – one or both of us may be put to the pain. Or perhaps they will just kill us here in Saint Sepulchre, before sunrise.'

Brother Edmund was silent for a moment. 'Yes,' he said. 'It is possible we will be killed. In which case we should both pray for God's mercy and forgiveness.'

I had thought myself fully prepared for martyrdom a few hours ago. Now, with all of my being, I did not want to die.

Brother Edmund continued, 'But it is also possible that something else is about to happen. How could Dudley know of our mission? He rode all the way from London with these soldiers.'

I pressed my cheek even harder against the stone's edge, and said, 'I believe that Geoffrey Scovill told him.'

'*What?*' I could hear the shock in his voice.

The morning that we left Dartford for Canterbury, the morning after Christmas, as I hurriedly packed food, Geoffrey banged on the door of my house. I had made arrangements for Arthur to stay with Sister Winifred for a few days – our plan was to tell them we would join Brother Oswald for a single pilgrimage. Which had the benefit of being true.

Geoffrey pushed his way past Kitty to storm into my kitchen. He took in the slices of bread, the wrapped parcels of portable food.

'What are you doing?' he asked.

'I am preparing meals for some friends who came for Christmas,' I said evenly. 'They are going on a journey.'

'Where?' Geoffrey demanded. His blue eyes narrowed as he studied my face.

'It is none of your concern,' I said.

'I am the constable of Dartford, and so it is my concern,' he said. 'Their destination had better not be Canterbury.'

I was dismayed – how on earth could he know when we had decided less than twelve hours ago?

I said, 'Why do you care where they go?'

'Because there is nothing but trouble for them in Canterbury,' he said. And then, 'Is Sommerville going with them? Are you?'

'No,' I said quickly.

Geoffrey's lips whitened. I did not want to keep hurting Geoffrey Scovill, yet I did exactly that.

'So now you lie to me, is that what we've come to?' he said roughly. 'Joanna, you're a fool. This is madness, and it will change nothing.'

With that, he was gone.

I told Brother Edmund everything, every word of the conversation. When I was finished, he said, 'You should have informed me and the others.'

'Yes,' I said brokenly. 'I have erred, so many, many times. And this error cost Brother Oswald his life, and perhaps ours, too. But we didn't leave for another few hours, and I never saw Geoffrey again. He didn't try to stop us. I never imagined he would go to someone like John Dudley. It is hard to believe that Geoffrey would ever do anything to harm me, no matter how angry he was. And I – I didn't want you to know about this quarrel.'

There was silence for a time. I wondered if Brother Edmund was so appalled, he no longer wished to speak to me.

But then his voice came again, and there was no anger in it.

'Do you remember, in the cemetery, when you asked me if something was wrong?'

'Yes,' I said. 'You looked so distressed.'

'While we were there, I looked over at you, hiding behind that gravestone, and I realised something, Sister Joanna,' he said and then his voice trailed away.

I waited, uncertain. When he spoke again, his voice was even softer.

'I realised that as much as I wanted to strike a blow for our faith, for our blessed Saint Thomas, I wanted something else, too. It's what I've wanted for quite a long time. I have not always understood it; I've felt it and fought it. I always thought my destiny was as a man of God. But I now know that I want it so much that, given a choice between life and death, I believe with all of my heart, that I would choose life – even a life that is strange and difficult for me.'

I slid down along the rough wall. I couldn't see him in the darkness, but I knew his face could not be more than three feet from mine.

'What is it that you want, Brother Edmund?' I said.

'Something is called for at this moment, something profound must be said, but all of my references are from Scripture,' he said, the shadow of a laugh in his voice. 'I can only think of Catherine of Siena and what she said: "The human heart is always drawn by love."'

He hesitated again.

'It's you,' he said. 'I am in love with you.'

Tears filled my eyes and my throat tightened. I willed myself to stop, so that I would be able to speak to him.

'If we are able to free ourselves, Sister Joanna, my only wish is to marry you,' he said. 'I know absolutely nothing of being a husband, but I would give the rest of my life to you.'

'Yes,' I said, and despite everything that had happened, I smiled into the darkness. How incredible it felt, this happiness coursing through me.

But I had no time to tell him of my own feelings, for the door to my cell – to Sister Elizabeth Barton's cell – swung open. The young bearded man, holding a torch, pulled me toward the passageway.

'Good-bye, Brother Edmund,' I called out, wildly, as I was dragged out the door.

Fear rose in me, but joy burned in me too. I was loved. I must do everything possible to survive the night.

At the end of the passageway, the man pushed me around the corner.

I nearly collided with someone who stood there awaiting me.

It was Jacquard Rolin.

I stumbled back and tried to speak, but Jacquard whipped me around and covered my mouth with his hand. He was fast and strong – much stronger than I had ever perceived.

'I don't believe your Brother Edmund can hear through that door, but there is a chance of it,' he whispered into my ear. 'Don't say my name if you desire that he should live.'

I nodded, frantic.

'Very good.' He withdrew his hand. I turned slowly to face him. I was unable to believe that it was truly the Low Countries Reformer who stood before me in Saint Sepulchre.

'Come, let us walk farther and then we can converse,' he said. 'But first, untie her hands.'

The man immediately obeyed. Jacquard was in command of this situation.

We walked as he looked me up and down. 'What a night you've had, Joanna Stafford,' he said, as calm and pleasant as if we had met in the middle of the High Street. 'I heard you lost your courage and cried when they put you in Elizabeth Barton's cell. That doesn't sound like you.'

'How is this possible?' I stammered. 'Are you the one who betrayed us to Dudley?'

Jacquard smiled. Those perfect teeth gleamed in the torchlight.

'Come with me,' he said.

Jacquard led me to the prioress's chambers. He knocked once, pushed open the door, and then gestured for me to go first with a flourish of his palm.

I walked into the room, the same one I'd entered with my mother ten years ago. It was lit with many candles. The oak table was still there. A man sat on the other side of it.

It was Eustace Chapuys, ambassador of the Emperor Charles.

'Hello, Juana,' he said.

This was wrong – so wrong. For a moment I wondered if I were hallucinating. But I could feel my legs and my arms. I drew breath. This was real.

The only thing I could manage to say to him was 'You do know me, then?'

Jacquard laughed behind me. Chapuys smiled too, a wry smile as if I'd said something extremely amusing, but there was a bitter edge to it as well.

I pointed at Jacquard. 'Why is he here, Ambassador? He is employed by the king, and he follows the Reform faith.'

Chapuys lifted his chin and said, 'No, Juana. Jacquard Rolin is a spy in the service of the Emperor Charles.'

The candle light tilted and ran together. I was falling and would have hit the floor, but Jacquard, again moving incredibly fast, caught me. He carried me to the empty chair opposite Chapuys.

The ambassador said: 'Wine. Food. At once.'

A goblet was pressed to my lips. I drank limply. I tried to wave off the chunk of bread, but they insisted. I managed to get the bread down but it was not easy.

'Jacquard infiltrated a party of German heretics and arrived in London in May,' said Chapuys. 'We had to have someone keeping you under observation in Dartford. I have English men and women in my service, but none skilful enough for the delicacy of this important task. I asked for the best – and the best is what I received.'

Jacquard bowed. 'Your praise honours me.'

'Why would you need to observe me at all?' I asked.

Neither man answered.

I turned around to glare at Jacquard. 'You are not a Reformer? But your beliefs – you told me of them yourself.'

Jacquard transformed himself while I watched. His eyes burning, he said, 'Timothy's views on the doctrine of free will are most inspiring.' He burst out laughing.

'Enough,' said Chapuys quietly.

'Lord John Dudley – I don't understand how he comes into it,' I said. 'He cannot possibly be in the employ of the emperor.'

'Dudley believes Jacquard to be a low-level spy for Cromwell, which he in fact is,' the ambassador explained. 'Jacquard has been a valued spy for the Emperor Charles for the last eight years. With his skills, he was able to attract Cromwell's interest just enough so that the Lord Privy Seal would recruit him but had no idea of his true allegiances. He employed Jacquard three weeks after he arrived in London.'

'Not to spy on me?' I asked, horrified.

'No, not initially. Cromwell wants spies everywhere, and Dartford is a town with many inns, a prime place for the gathering of treasonous gossip.' The ambassador grimaced. 'But after the scene you created on Tower Hill, the Lord Privy Seal made it his business to learn who you were and then asked Jacquard to make regular reports of your actions. Unfortunately, you are now someone of interest to him. That will make our work together much more difficult.'

The words *our work together* hung in the air.

'We considered allowing you and the others to carry out your quest at the cathedral, but it was too risky,' Chapuys said. 'We couldn't take the chance you'd be killed or arrested. Jacquard knew that you planned something with the monks, something to do with Canterbury. He alerted that constable, Geoffrey Scovill, hoping he'd stop you. He didn't, unfortunately. And Scovill waited hours to inform Jacquard that you'd left. We lost valuable time. Dudley was told of your group's plan, but only under the condition that he separate you and Brother

Edmund from the others. Jacquard and I came directly here, to await you. The other monks are taken to jail in Canterbury – they will pay the price for what happened.'

'No, they mustn't,' I pleaded. 'Can't you help them?'

'They will be imprisoned, but I don't expect they will be executed – and there will be no trial,' Chapuys said. 'The king will not want to inflame the international situation. His treatment of Saint Thomas's shrine and the shrines of England – this is the reason for his excommunication.'

I still didn't understand why Dudley would agree to leniency for Brother Edmund and me, and said so.

'I told him that my own network discovered this plot of yours, and I wished to save you because of the memory of your Spanish mother,' Chapuys said. 'Also I bestowed on him the largest bribe I've had to issue since coming to this country. Dudley, the son of a traitor, desperately needs money, that is the key to controlling him. Cromwell and the king will be told of six monks who stormed Canterbury Cathedral – that is all.'

'We had to make conditions rough for you here in Saint Sepulchre to placate Dudley,' said Jacquard. 'He truly despises you. There's no question but that you have a talent for arousing hatred in the most powerful men.'

I turned away from him, back to Chapuys. 'What is the king's intent for the bones of Saint Thomas? Dudley said we were mistaken, but I can't believe that to be true.'

Chapuys considered before answering. 'Yes, King Henry hates Becket and wants to make an example of him for his defiance to the Crown. From what I gather, their orders were to remove the box and bring it to London. What will be done then, only the king knows, and he is most changeable.'

So Norfolk's information was, indeed, wrong. How could I have paid him such heed? My stupidity was unending.

Chapuys said, 'I can understand why faithful Catholics would go to Canterbury on a mission such as this one. No matter what the king's intention, his despoiling of the shrine is infamous. But this expedition of yours was very costly and very damaging. We will say no more of it. From now on, there will be no more intermediaries. You can understand why I couldn't speak to you directly before now. If our connection were exposed, we'd both be summarily executed, and war with Spain would directly follow. But I am the only one who can direct your movements from now on.'

Again I was to be controlled – used. I'd thought myself free of this – and a life with Brother Edmund beckoned – but my will could never be my own.

Something about the word *intermediaries*. Of course.

'You were the one who sent Gertrude Courtenay to Dartford to find me,' I said to the ambassador.

'Of course,' said Chapuys. 'She was the best conduit I had. A loyal and hard working operative.'

'Is your connection to her now known?' I asked.

'I'd hardly be here if it were. No, she burned all my letters after reading; I had ordered her to do that, and she followed my command. But others' letters were found in her box, and they added to the case against her husband. Do you know that in the Exeters' Cornwall manor, a painted banner was found, to be raised when the time came to rally the west against the king? How could she do such an incredibly foolish thing? Gertrude Courtenay thought her husband's wealth and title and royal blood would preserve him. I tried to point out to her that those were the very things that would doom him.'

Again I saw Henry Courtenay standing atop the scaffold, and shuddered.

Chapuys, ever perceptive, said, 'I know much has happened to you, and it has been difficult. I regret that, I sincerely do. But for the past nine months, our source of information on you, he … fluctuates. "Send her to London." "Remove her from London." "Bring her to an astrologer." This is not something under my control – or under anyone's control. I very much doubt even he can control what he learns and in what manner of speed.'

My mouth had gone dry. 'What source do you speak of?' I asked. 'Who tells you what must happen to me?'

Chapuys looked at me steadily. 'You will not be able to travel under your own name. Not after Cromwell took interest in you. He sees the names of all the people requesting permission to leave England. This will take time – we must create documents, we must devise a way for you to leave Dartford without arousing suspicion.'

'What are you saying?' I asked.

'Juana, you must now go to the Low Countries, to the city of Ghent. It is the birthplace of the Emperor Charles. It is only there and at the appointed time that you can receive the prophecy of the third seer.'

36

Ambassador Eustace Chapuys was a man famous throughout Christendom for his intelligence, his scholarship, his courage, and perhaps most of all, his calm. But he came close to losing that calm when confronted with my refusal to leave England to learn the third and final part of the prophecy.

'You come from an English family that was destroyed by the king, you served Katherine of Aragon, you prayed at the executions of the Lady Mary's friends,' he said, incredulous. 'This very night you were willing to die to protect the sanctity of England's most beloved saint – and yet you will not take the next step in learning the prophecy that concerns you? The Holy Father has condemned Henry the Eighth. There can be no sin in any act you commit.'

I shook my head.

Chapuys rose to approach me, his sharp features quivering.

'In a few weeks' time, King Francis will reach Spain to renew his peace treaty with the Emperor. I have information, good information, that the pope will implore the Catholic kings of France and Spain to form a holy pact to declare war on the heretical king of England. Every year Henry grows more inhumane and cruel. He must be deposed.'

'*I see many ships – they sail for England*' – those were the words of Orobas.

'If invasion is imminent, it will bring countless soldiers and weapons.' I said. 'How could I possibly make any sort of difference?'

Chapuys shook his head. 'Juana, you took vows of obedience to the Dominican Order, the most esteemed order in Spain, France, Italy – everywhere. It makes no difference that this English king dissolved your priory. You must obey us. Those vows are *unbreakable.*'

I took a deep breath and said, 'I have never sought out this role to play; I've fought it since I was seventeen years old. It has brought terrible things into my life. I cannot be guided by these seers, by these powers. You will tell me nothing of this man and yet I am to leave England? It is too much.'

Chapuys returned to his chair behind the table. He poured himself some wine. His fingers on the goblet, his gaze settled on Jacquard, who had been silent for some moments. Something seemed to pass between them, some silent decision.

The ambassador sipped the wine, then said in his usual imperturbable manner, 'Nothing must be decided now. There is a naval embargo between England and Flanders and the rest of the kingdoms of the emperor. No matter what, arranging travel and the necessary papers will require not weeks but months of effort. And so this plan will go forward. By the time all is in place, you may have changed your mind.'

'Please do not count on that,' I said. 'I cannot think of what could make me do so.'

'In the memory of your mother, a faithful daughter of Spain, will you at least keep the possibility open?' pressed the ambassador.

My mother. How could he know that three years after her death, she had a hold over me like no one else? I'd always felt I was a disappointment to her. How could I be perceived as other than a failure? I'd fled service with the queen, I never married. She died not knowing I'd waited on Katherine of Aragon on her deathbed and then taken novice vows. Perhaps that would have finally made her proud of me.

'I'm sorry,' I said miserably. 'I can't.'

The ambassador remained calm. 'Very well, Juana. We will see that you are conveyed back to Dartford.' He turned to Jacquard. 'Please give the orders for the Dominican friar to join the others in the jail of Canterbury.'

'No, no, not Brother Edmund,' I cried. 'Can't you use your influence to free him along with me?'

Chapuys sighed. 'Even if that were achievable, Juana, I cannot allow for the possibility that you will tell him of our plans, of the existence of the third seer. I know that you have formed some sort of attachment to Brother Edmund Sommerville.'

'I will say nothing – nothing,' I said. 'I promise you that, and I am not someone who breaks promises.'

Jacquard spoke up then: 'You know the most secret plans of the emperor. You are half Spanish and so more trustworthy than the

English. But if your Brother Edmund were to learn anything – anything at all – he would have to be eliminated.'

Eliminated. How casually Jacquard used the word.

The ambassador said, 'If I were to bring about his freedom, Juana, if I could do that for you, can we then agree that not only will you tell him nothing but that when the time comes, when the plan is made, you will at least consider taking your place in it?'

After a moment of agonised indecision, I said, greatly reluctant, 'Yes, I agree.'

I detected it again, that silent, meaningful gaze between Jacquard and the ambassador.

'When you do come back to me, though, should I refuse, then that must be the end of it,' I blurted. 'You cannot force me against my will to go anywhere or do anything. That is part of the prophecy and always has been.'

'Of course not, Juana,' Chapuys said. 'Of course not.'

Dawn broke over the frozen fields when I left Saint Sepulchre with Brother Edmund. We returned to Dartford unimpeded. For weeks and then months, I had no contact with Ambassador Chapuys. I felt free to make plans for my life – to marry, to begin my tapestry business at last.

The winter passed, and the stirring of spring brought with it hope for a normal life. Until one April day when I realised that my life could never, ever be normal.

Most of the day was spent at the loom. Thanks to our tireless efforts, the phoenix tapestry was all but complete. The red-gold body of the legendary bird took shape nicely. Its eagle-like beak had a pride to it; the feathers of violet and green shimmered. But now the bottom quarter of the tapestry must be woven. And this, I feared, was where the entire image could be ruined. Flames curling around a thick bird's nest required precision.

'Concentrate on your weaves,' I urged Sister Beatrice and Sister Agatha, who sat on either side of me on the loom. Sister Winifred read from a martyrology on her stool. I'd tried as much as I could to re-create the working conditions of Dartford Priory. I hated having to admonish them, but both women had a tendency of late to drift in their work. They were lost in daydreams – perhaps not so surprising, since both of them were engaged to be married. Sister Agatha's wedding to Master

Oliver Gwinn was only three days away, 20 April. Sister Beatrice would marry Geoffrey Scovill in June.

My wedding date was set for 16 May, when I would become Joanna Sommerville. After Easter had passed and weddings were once again allowed, three women formerly of Dartford Priory would marry in rapid succession.

Sister Agatha probably should not be weaving at all, with her wedding day so close, but she always insisted on helping. It was her way of thanking me for welcoming her into my home. When she became engaged to Master Gwinn, the other sisters did not take it well. They perceived this vow breaking as a flouting of their commitment to live together as brides of Christ. I understood their feelings – and yet I felt sympathy for Sister Agatha. I invited her to live with me and Arthur until she married and she gratefully agreed. I enjoyed her chatter in our house.

Of the three of us soon to wed, Sister Beatrice was the most altered by impending wifehood. She was, quite simply, radiant. Of course I welcomed her marrying Geoffrey. Under the circumstances, it was the only decent response possible.

There was a happy shout on the street. A moment later, the door opened. Brother Edmund brought in Arthur, returning from the afternoon's lesson. To teach Arthur his letters called for extraordinary patience. No one but Brother Edmund was equal to it.

'It was a good day, a good day,' he said, smiling at me, and then all the others.

I steadied. My fears never disappeared altogether, but they receded whenever I was near Brother Edmund. Edmund. If only I could banish the 'Brother', in thought and in speech. For some maddening reason, it proved difficult.

'I need to go to London with a few men from town,' he said. 'Sister Winifred, could you possibly sleep here, at Joanna's house, while I am away? I hope to be back tomorrow.'

I stepped off the bench of my loom. 'But why must you go?' I asked. From the corner of my eye, I saw my friends smiling at one another.

Edmund said, 'It's John – we've received word that he is in London and in great distress. His cousin has formed a party to secure him.'

The town madman disappeared two months ago. John had gone

away before but always returned in a few days. This time was different, and we had all begun to assume that John died in some sad, lost place.

I said gently, 'John's obsession was you – and yet now you endeavour to return him to his favourite spot for further tormenting.'

'But I must do all I can to help him – you understand that?' he said.

'Yes,' I said. 'I do.'

'John may need medicines,' he continued. 'I'll gather them at the infirmary now before joining the others.' Ever since our return from Canterbury, Edmund's business had blossomed. It was Master Oliver Gwinn. He combated the prejudices spread by Timothy Brooke and his parents. The infirmary was now so popular that Edmund had taken on a skilled apprentice named Humphrey.

'Will you come outside with me for a moment?' Edmund said to me.

The High Street was muddy that afternoon. A furious spring downpour had soaked the ground a few hours ago. The sun now eased out from behind fresh clouds.

Edmund looked up and down the street, his forehead crinkling with worry. 'It's possible that a man has come again to Dartford to observe us, Joanna. I was busy in the infirmary yesterday morning. The butcher's son broke his arm playing and the whole family came with him. But there was this other man: very thin, rather tall, with brown eyes, close-set. He stood in the back, and when next I looked over, he was gone. Today, at Mass, I saw him again in the back of the church. I've made discreet inquiries and no one knew who he was.'

'I've not noticed such a man,' I said, and I hadn't.

'You are rarely alone, I know that, Joanna. But still, please be cautious,' Edmund said. 'Will you promise me?'

'Of course.'

He turned to walk down the High Street. He hadn't made it far when I called out to him.

'Wait, Edmund!' I darted after him, picking up my skirts so that they would not be muddied. Edmund smiled at me quizzically.

'You must promise me you'll be back in time for Sister Agatha's wedding – it will provide a perfect opportunity for you to practise your dancing,' I said.

'Ah, yes, my dancing,' he said, chuckling. Edmund had never been taught to dance as a child. I, on the other hand, had been drilled in dancing for most of my life. I'd taught him steps, to prepare for our wedding, but without musicians, it was difficult to demonstrate.

He squeezed my arm and kissed me, lightly, on the forehead. 'I will be back soon,' he said, and resumed his way down the High Street.

I watched him disappear: that loping gait, the long hair so light and fine it looked like white gold in the sun. He'd have to have it cut for our wedding.

I went back to my house, to tell my friends I'd need time to complete an errand. I walked in the other direction that Edmund had gone in – up the High Street. Now that this buoyant sun had emerged, the street was crowded with townsfolk. All of them were intent on the next task, the next meal, the next embrace.

When I reached the Building Office, Gregory, the one-time porter of Dartford Priory, was alone in the front room.

'I need to speak to Jacquard Rolin,' I said. 'Could you tell him that the tapestry order needs to be adjusted?'

'Of course, Sister Joanna,' he said, and disappeared. For Gregory, as for me, priory habits were hard to break.

How dismayed I was when I discovered, shortly after our return to Dartford, that Jacquard remained. 'If I leave my position as commissioning clerk for His Majesty's Dartford Manor House, Cromwell will want to know why,' he'd said when I confronted him. 'And where else should I go? I cannot return to the Low Countries now.'

Edmund never knew that Jacquard was at Saint Sepulchre or anything about his true mission. I relayed to Edmund the same story that Chapuys had given Lord Dudley: because of his affection for me and my Spanish family, the ambassador bribed Dudley to spare me as well as my friend. Our two names were kept off the report to the king. 'Telling truth mixed with a lie is always preferable to telling a complete lie,' Chapuys had advised me.

That night in Saint Sepulchre, Edmund took our freedom from imprisonment as a sign from God that we should pursue peace and cease the struggle to unravel the prophecy. He mourned Brother Oswald's death, as did I. And he worried about the fate of the imprisoned monks, confessing to me the guilt he felt over not sharing their fate. It was terrible, what had been wrought in Canterbury that night. And for what? The king had the body of Saint Thomas Becket in his possession. Did he defile the remains or bury them in dignity – we did not know which, and might never know.

A smiling Jacquard appeared. 'Good afternoon, Joanna Stafford,' he said warmly. 'I understand you have questions on that order. I do have something to show you.'

I followed Jacquard. These were the exact words he'd given me should I have need of him. After that first confrontation, we'd seen each other in church or at market, but never alone. As part of a group, he'd congratulated me and Edmund on our engagement. Even now, trailing him as he moved through these rooms, it seemed impossible that this slender young man who called out greetings to all we passed was a highly trained spy for the Holy Roman Emperor.

Jacquard strolled into a large room filled with new materials for the king's manor house. The brick walls had all been raised; the floors and roofs were finished. This summer the windows would be installed. It was blinding to walk down those rows of framed glass.

When we reached a corner where tapestries hung, he said, 'So you will now tell me what has occurred. Try not to show any strong feeling. Keep looking at the tapestries with me while you speak.'

I said quietly, 'I thought you should know Edmund believes someone has come to Dartford to spy on us. Or on him, at least. He saw him in the infirmary and in church, too. He thought he saw a stranger watching last December, too.'

Jacquard brushed a bit of a dust from a tapestry. 'Is he tall, thin and dark with eyes close together?' he asked.

'Yes,' I said. 'You know this man?'

'Lower your voice; show no emotion,' he said. 'Yes, this is the third spy sent by Bishop Gardiner. Your Edmund saw the first, but he must not have noticed the second. I did. Gardiner uses a different man each time.'

Gardiner.

'How do you know this?' I demanded.

'I must ask you again to remove all feeling from your voice and face,' Jacquard said, his voice edged with irritation. 'I know everyone who comes into this town and everyone who goes out.'

I swallowed and then asked, as calmly as I could, 'What are you going to do?'

'Nothing.'

I peered sideways at Jacquard. He smiled as he continued to study the tapestry.

'You aroused a suspicion, and Gardiner wants you watched. This spy is sent to observe – and what he observes is a woman weaving at her loom, preparing to marry, dancing with her betrothed. He knows nothing, he reports nothing. Joanna Stafford, I know you wish me to slit the throat of this bishop's spy, and I would love to carve him up for you, dropping him piece by piece into the River Darent, but that would be most imprudent.'

I struggled to keep my voice low as I said, 'I would *never* wish anyone harmed.'

'You wished to harm those soldiers at Canterbury Cathedral, that is beyond question. But then, all Spanish women are bloodthirsty.'

I turned to walk away from him – but Jacquard stopped me. His hand gripped mine. Again, I could not believe how strong he was.

'Look at this one – at the work that went into it,' Jacquard said loudly. Then he murmured: 'I will let go of you now. And we will continue to converse. Understood?'

'Yes,' I said finally. There was nothing for it but that I must submit to his wishes.

After a moment, he said, 'I know you fear Gardiner. You are not wrong to do so. Winchester is the most formidable of the king's men, as treacherous and ruthless as Cromwell.'

I shuddered.

'Something is coming,' he mused. 'No one is sure what. For the first time in two years there will be a parliament. It begins on the twenty-eighth of April. Religious matters will be heard as well as preparations for war. Rumours come without stop. I hear one day that French ships were sighted in the Channel, another that Scotland is readying its forces, to take advantage of the invasion. King Henry has one hundred and twenty ships ready at the mouth of the Thames and thirty ready at Portsmouth. Hundreds of men work day and night on fortifications along the southern coast. Do you know where the funds come from for this?'

Again I shook my head.

'The thousands of pounds that poured into his treasury after the dissolution of the monasteries. He will defend his country from the pope's Holy War with money he stole from the abbeys and priories.'

My throat tightened. I said, 'You are angry that I do not comply with Chapuys.'

'I'm not angry, and neither is the ambassador,' Jacquard said swiftly. 'For the last communication he received said that it was foretold you would now hesitate. When the time is right, you will agree. Not just that. You will come to us and *implore* us to take you to the city of Ghent.'

'No,' I said. 'Never.'

Jacquard pulled a paper from his doublet. 'Have you seen Constable Scovill of late?'

'That is none of your concern,' I said between gritted teeth.

Jacquard sighed. 'Though your amorous entanglements are a source of great interest to us all, that is not the reason I ask. Geoffrey Scovill was issued a command two days ago. He must be quite busy. The command comes from the king's commissioner for Kent. I, of course, have a copy of it.'

I took the paper from his hand. It read: 'All the people must be in readiness should the enemies of His Majesty make any attempt into this realm. Each constable must certify the names of men in his town between the ages of sixteen and sixty and record those names, along with the harness and weapons each possess. For the muster, the men must be assembled, and the most able persons selected, with a small number to be held back to defend their town if needed.'

Jacquard said, 'King Henry plays his part in the great game.'

'*Game?*' I said.

'The wars waged by kings for land and glory,' he said.

I trembled as I shoved the paper back in his hands. 'Between the ages of sixteen and sixty,' I repeated. I envisioned them all: the youths who laughed in the street, the apprentices, the proud young fathers, stout shopkeepers, farmers and fishermen, and grandfathers too. Edmund. Geoffrey.

'There will be much bloodshed, here and throughout the kingdom, if invasion comes,' Jacquard said. He tapped my elbow. 'We've been here long enough. I will escort you out. There is only one more thing you should know.'

'Yes?' I said wearily.

'The emperor recalled Chapuys, just after François recalled the French ambassador. That is always the prelude to a formal declaration of war. King Henry wants to keep Chapuys at the English court; he has lodged a protest. But by the end of June, our ambassador may be gone from this island kingdom.'

Jacquard smiled again as he turned to escort me away from the tapestries. 'If that happens, do not be alarmed, for I will remain here. And my instructions are clear – they come directly from the emperor himself. I'm to use my best judgement in the matter of Joanna Stafford.'

37

Edmund did not return the next day, nor the one after that. The afternoon before the wedding of Sister Agatha, I was too nervous to weave. I'd slept little since going to see Jacquard Rolin. I continued to turn over his disturbing conversation in my mind. Moreover, I couldn't stop worrying about Edmund. Sister Winifred made inquiry and said the other two Dartford men were still away, too; one had sent back word to his wife that they'd not found John in the spot he was originally sighted, and would press on. A fear nagged at me that Edmund's absence and my entanglement in prophecy were somehow connected. He would not have left if he knew all. How I hated keeping things from him. How could we begin our married life with me harbouring dangerous secrets? But this was what I must do to protect him.

Sister Winifred patted my arm. 'Do not be so troubled,' she said. 'You must know that my brother cares more for those who are sick or in need than for any wedding – save for his own.'

'Yes, I know that,' I said and forced a smile.

The next day was the wedding of Sister Agatha. From the moment she woke, she was as flustered as I assumed she'd be. Sister Winifred and I would walk with her to Holy Trinity Church across the street. The rest of the guests, including the other former nuns and novices of Dartford Priory, would meet us there, although it was possible that we'd see some absences. Sister Rachel, I knew, had trouble reconciling herself to this marriage.

Sister Agatha had no living male relatives. But at every wedding a man must give away the bride. The solution reached was a surprising one. A man named Ellis Hancock, a prosperous shipbuilder new to Dartford who had formed a friendship with Master Gwinn, stepped forward to do the honours. After the ceremony, the wedding party would proceed to Master Hancock's home.

Sister Winifred and I placed the bridal garland on Sister Agatha's head. It was woven with daisies, daffodils, and primroses that we picked in the meadows south of town that dewy morning. She wore her best dress: a blue brocade with gold trimming.

'You look lovely,' I whispered.

She hugged me in gratitude, and we led Sister Agatha down the stairs. The clock struck eleven as I opened my door.

Master Hancock waited just outside. Behind him was a throng of townsfolk, wearing their finest clothes. As we made our way the short distance to Holy Trinity, I heard many good wishes. The spirit of the town toward the former residents of Dartford had warmed since Christmas. That should please me, but somehow, it left me sad.

I saw the Brooke family as I walked behind Sister Agatha – that lanky boy with spots on his chin and a scowl could only be Timothy – and, standing next to Gregory, there was Jacquard, too, smiling and clapping with the rest of the townsfolk. Waiting nearer the church were Geoffrey Scovill and Sister Beatrice, arm-in-arm. Geoffrey and I avoided each other's gaze, as had become our unwavering custom. On this morning, I saw everyone at Dartford I knew. But I did not see the person whom I loved and trusted beyond question: Edmund Sommerville. He'd not made it back in time.

Framed in the propped-open church doors, Master Oliver Gwinn beamed proudly. Master Hancock delivered Sister Agatha to him and they stood side by side before Father William Mote at the church entrance. In a loud voice that all on the street could hear, the preacher recited the banns and asked if there were any impediment to the marriage. No one spoke up.

Moments later, Sister Agatha was 'Sister' no more.

The couple exchanged rings, and we shuffled inside the church for the nuptial mass and blessing.

The newly married couple, John and Agatha Gwinn, knelt side by side near the altar, the fine linen care cloth resting on their heads. I sat with Arthur near the back. He sniffled into a handkerchief; he'd woken up feeling rather poorly. On my other side were my closest friend, Sister Winifred, and then Sister Eleanor and Sister Rachel and the three others. They had come to the wedding after all. We exchanged no words, not even a glance. But we shared a feeling. It was not joy. We were wistful for the lost life of a nun, a calling like no other, filled with sacrifice and fulfilment. We'd not been the property of men. We were brides of Christ alone. In a month's time, I would be the one at the altar, kneeling next to Edmund. The group sitting in the pew would be reduced one more in number. Edmund was my beloved, yet I shared the sisters' sadness for a life gone forever. Should I not be as joyous as Agatha for the union ahead? I listened to Father William's benedictions and struggled against my melancholia.

After the ceremony had finished, we all proceeded once more to the street. A warm sun bathed the celebrants. Sister Eleanor and the other sisters of Holcroft slipped away; I could not blame them. To ask one-time nuns to feast and dance at the wedding of one of their own was too much. But Sister Winifred, too, began to edge toward the houses across the street, not to proceed to the festivities.

'Will you not come to the bridal dinner?' I asked.

She put her hand on Arthur's shoulders. 'This boy is getting worse by the moment, and must to bed.' Arthur wailed in protest, but she was right: his eyes were glassy and his cheeks flushed. Despite his eagerness for entertainments, Arthur belonged home. I promised to save some treats for him, to share tonight.

I walked in silence, alone, to the house of Master Hancock. People greeted me as I went. Now that I, like Agatha, turned away from habit and veil to assume the part of wife, people were prepared to accept me.

'Constable, is your muster complete?' a man said behind me.

Geoffrey's voice came next. 'Yes, I've sent the list. We are well prepared should foreigners enter the realm. We will be ready to serve His Majesty on an hour's notice.'

The first man said, 'The muster for London must be very long?'

Geoffrey answered, 'I'm told the king himself read through the lists given by the London constables. Next week he travels to Dover to inspect the new defences.'

They began to talk of the bulwarks, blockhouses, and fortifications made along the sea coast. I quickened my pace, so that I was just short of running, to escape from that conversation. Ahead of me walked two young drummers of the wedding march. I much preferred the sound of their eager pounding to the talk of the war muster. I passed the budding apple orchards and the farm fields. The soil had been turned over for planting barley and wheat. The farmers had carved lines into the soil to mark their two or three rows for the season. The smell of the new earth – pungent and sour – poured a bit of strength into me.

At last I turned off the main road. A wide pathway led to the Hancock house. The flowerbeds bloomed and a string of saplings unfurled their pale green leaves.

The house's lush decorations – the garlands of ivy and flowers – put my limp posies to shame. Long tables groaned with food; the wine and ale flowed freely. These newcomers made a great effort to befriend the people of Dartford. There was a determined thrill in the air. Last year saw far fewer feast days and holidays due to changes in religion. Today, in Dartford, we ached to find joy again.

The bridal couple stood in the centre of it. Agatha was surrounded by her new family. My gaze drifted to Geoffrey Scovill, downing ale in a tight group of men. Sister Beatrice was not at his side. I thought she never left it – but now I realised I hadn't seen her since Holy Trinity Church.

In a very short time, a large room was cleared for dancing. The first song played was in honour of the bridal couple. We all clapped when Agatha moved across the floor in her new husband's arms. I'd given her lessons as well as Edmund. Master Gwinn was, truth be told, a rather oafish man. His new wife had never been considered bonny. Yet the beauty they found in each other formed a grace not equalled by anyone else in the room.

The announcement of the galliard followed. It was not a simple dance; many of the guests looked at one another doubtfully and then trickled off.

Master Hancock sought me out, saying he'd seen my father joust when he was a boy and wanted to make Sir Richard Stafford's daughter feel welcome. He proudly led me to the floor and we took first position. His wife stood behind us, partnered with a man I knew to be the most prominent innkeeper in town. Only two other couples joined us.

The musicians launched into the song and we began to move. The galliard called for energetic kicks and turns and leaps while following strictly timed beats. But I did not contemplate the beats. I followed the music with my heart – it was as if no time had passed at all. I turned and leaped into the air; Master Hancock caught me and we spun.

The galliard finished, and a less courtly dance commenced. Everyone surged on to the floor. I curtseyed to Master Hancock and would have retreated, but the innkeeper caught me by the hand and begged for the next dance.

And so began at least an hour of dancing. One after the other, polite gentlemen of Dartford would bow and request me for the next dance. Each time it happened, I was a bit sorry. I should return home, to Arthur and Sister Winifred. But at the same time I was glad, for during the time that I enjoyed the poetry of music, my troubles receded.

Until the moment that Geoffrey bowed before me.

'Where is Sister Beatrice?' I asked.

'She was not feeling well enough to come.'

'I'm sorry.'

All around us, other people were commencing the next dance. We must join them, or get out of their way.

Geoffrey extended his hand with a smile. But there was a mournfulness in the corners of his eyes.

I did not take it.

'I'm not sure it's fitting for us to dance.'

He did not get angry. He said patiently, 'Joanna, you and I are both marrying other people. Can we not be friends today, at least? You've already danced with every respectable man of Dartford. Shouldn't the constable be allowed to take a turn?'

Persuaded, I sank into a curtsy. When I came up, I took Geoffrey's hand. He intertwined his fingers with mine. A quiver ran up my arm. I quickly looked away. I did not want Geoffrey to see how his touch affected me.

We danced together, for the first time in our lives. Whenever I turned, he was in the perfect place. He never held my hand too long or let go too quickly. We were in harmony without even trying. I hoped he would not talk to me again. But of course he did.

'This is a side of you I've often wanted to see,' he said. 'You're smiling here. Even laughing.'

'It's a wedding,' I said defensively. We parted and could not speak for a time. The dance necessitated that I link hands and dance with a partner diagonal. When we were close to each other again, I said, 'So you think me grim?'

'No, no,' he said. 'You mistake me, Joanna. I'm not finding fault. I want you to be happy. It's what I've always wanted.'

'I'm not sure that happiness is my lot,' I blurted.

His eyes widened. The music separated us again. A moment later, he said, very intently, 'That's a strange thing for a woman to say who's getting married within the month.'

I said nothing, just twirled and prayed for the dance to be soon over.

'I've never thought you grim, Joanna,' he said. 'You are – you are—'

The song ended. He should have bowed and retreated, but instead he took a step closer to me, pulling an object from his doublet pocket, a very small cloth sack. He pulled open the strings and carefully emptied its content into his left palm.

It was a glittering dark stone, no more than an inch in diameter.

'Do you know what this is?' he asked.

'No.'

The music began anew. Once again we were going to be in the way.

Geoffrey said, 'Opal. They call it Black Fire. I bought it from a merchant a month after we met in Smithfield, after we went to the Tower together, when I never thought to see you again. I wanted a reminder of you.'

I took a step back, dismayed. 'Oh, Geoffrey, do not show me this. Not here – not anywhere. It's not fitting.'

Geoffrey shoved the opal in his bag and put it back into his pocket. 'I know it isn't.'

Everyone was dancing around us, while we stood in the middle of the floor. Heads turned; I could hear the whispering under the music.

I edged away from him. I'd slip between the dancers and make my way to the other room.

He caught up to me. He grabbed my hand and pulled me to him. It was as if we were back at Smithfield, that very first day. I was always struggling to get away from Geoffrey Scovill. And he was always following. And, God forgive me, there was a part of me that was glad he followed.

'In the barge, when we went up the Thames to the Tower, when I woke up, my head was in your lap. You took care of me. And even though I was in pain – and arrested, God help me – it was something incredible. How you did that for me.'

My eyes filled with tears. 'Oh Geoffrey, no. I'm sorry. I'm sorry.'

'There's one more thing I have to tell you, Joanna,' he said, pulling me even closer. 'The day you went to Canterbury, I knew that if I struck some sort of bargain with the king's men, if I informed, you'd never forgive me. But I also knew that you might be killed in Canterbury, and I couldn't bear that. Even if it meant you hating me, even if it meant driving you so far toward Sommerville there wasn't a prayer for me any more.' His blue eyes shone with tears, something I thought I'd never see. 'I couldn't live if you were dead. That's the truth.'

Suddenly he released my arm. Geoffrey looked over my shoulder.

I turned slowly.

Just a few feet away stood Edmund. He stared at me and then at Geoffrey, his face white with shock. And then he turned and left, pushing more than one man out of his way to get away as fast as he possibly could.

'Edmund,' I cried. 'Stop!'

I hurried after him, dodging the dancers as they leaped and twirled around me. I couldn't see Edmund anywhere. He was lost to me.

I rushed from the dancing room, desperate to find him. The last person I saw, the man standing by the door, his arms folded, was Jacquard. There was a girl with him, wearing a pale green hood. He spoke to her, and nodded as he did so, but his eyes were on me.

38

I searched the crowded rooms but could not find Edmund. After I was certain that he was not inside the house, I rushed outside. Clumps of people spoke on the lawn overlooking the gardens. But he was not there, either. I ran down the path connected to the road, my side aching. I scanned the road for signs of Edmund on the way back to town. Nothing.

Back at my house, Sister Winifred cared for Arthur, unaware of her brother's return. I decided not to tell her of my upsetting encounter – how would I begin to explain it? But I knew that he must at the very least collect his sister. I'd wait with her, here. Edmund was aware that Geoffrey Scovill and I shared a tumultuous past, although it was a subject not discussed. But Geoffrey's future was with Sister Beatrice – and I belonged with Edmund. I'd make him see that.

A note came to my house after supper, delivered by Edmund's apprentice. John had been found and brought back to Dartford; their mission succeeded. But Edmund had subsequently learned that an old friend had need of him and he'd be away for an additional few days. He'd see us both before the next Sabbath.

I sobbed as I held Edmund's cool note, written in his elegant script.

'Sister Joanna, please do not despair so – there is no reason for it,' said Sister Winifred, much concerned. 'Shouldn't he see an old friend now? You two will spend the rest of your lives together, after all.'

The next four days were terrible for me. I expected Edmund to break our betrothal when next I saw him. Perhaps I did not deserve to be his wife – or anyone's. But still, I wanted a chance at redemption.

On a damp Friday afternoon, restless, I went to the infirmary. There was one person in the front room of the infirmary: Edmund stood over his apothecary table, working, as if nothing were out of the ordinary.

I felt as if my heart were turning over in my body as I walked through the door. He was making a fresh batch of pills – next to a bowl of powdered herbs was a smaller one of honey for the mixing. He rolled the pills on a wooden board.

He must have heard my steps on the floor, yet Edmund did not look up from his work. Slowly I walked around, to stand with him on the same side of the table.

Now that I was close, I saw that one of the bowls was almost empty.

'May I refill the honey, Edmund?' I asked. My voice sounded surprisingly normal.

'Yes, that would be helpful,' he said softly.

I took the bowl to the back counter, and spooned more honey into it. My fingers shook with nervousness, and the honey was sticky on the spoon, so it took me longer than it should have to complete the task.

When I walked back to him, I suddenly couldn't bear this any more. 'Do you still wish to marry me?' I said.

Edmund finished pinching off a pill he'd made. He turned to look at me. I saw how tired he was – there were deep lines in his forehead and around his mouth.

'More than anything in the world,' he said.

We were in each other's arms. He kissed me on the cheeks and the forehead as I clutched him. And then he kissed me on the lips, with more passion than ever before. Whenever we embraced, he'd always reined himself in. I could feel it in the tension of his arms, the coolness of his lips. But not now. I felt something new – wild and angry – in how he kissed me. I lost my breath; I thought I would faint from it.

A discreet cough at the doorway made us part. It was Humphrey, returned and hiding a smile behind his hand. We resumed all proprieties. I remained at the infirmary for an hour; Edmund had supper with me later; he gave Arthur a lesson that night. We were betrothed, that had not changed, to my profound relief and gratitude. But there was a new tentativeness between us. I waited for him to bring up Geoffrey Scovill. He did not – and I did not.

I was stunned when my cousin Lord Henry Stafford and his wife, Ursula, and their six children arrived in Dartford. As a family courtesy, I had written to him of my impending marriage, never expecting their attendance. Henry had not left Stafford Castle for years. Henry's adult life had one driving force: to avoid politics and anything dangerous. Travelling south, through London, to Dartford, was unprecedented.

Henry and Ursula looked so much older than when I saw them last, just two years ago. They were stooped, their faces tired and careworn. But Henry said firmly, 'Joanna, I must be the one to give you away at your wedding. I owe it to your father.'

My own house being small, there was no alternative but that my Stafford cousins and their servants reside in an inn. Although I could tell the prospect was distasteful to Henry, he put a brave face on it. The Staffords took up residence in the Saracen's Head Inn – but only for a few hours. News of their presence swept through the town, and by dinnertime, Master Hancock had arrived to insist on housing my relations. It was an invitation graciously accepted. I spent much of my time going back and forth, with Arthur. He was thrilled to meet these older cousins, and they played with him very patiently.

Two days before my wedding date, when the children were occupied, Ursula sought me out. Although we'd never in our lives quarrelled, neither did I feel strong affection for Henry's wife. When I lived at the castle, she gave birth to a child almost every year and was much preoccupied, if not dazed.

But when we were alone, it was with utter clarity that Ursula asked, 'Did you love my brother Montague?'

I decided that she deserved nothing but truth in return.

'No,' I said. 'I cannot say I loved him or would have ever loved him. That was Henry Courtenay's idea, for me to be your brother's second wife. I will say that I felt an – an affinity with him.'

For an instant, I was in the back of the wagon with Baron Montague. I felt his hands cupping my face and heard him say, *'Joanna, you can't fall in love with a dead man.'*

'I know that you prayed for him at Tower Hill in the last moments before his death,' said Ursula, and she gripped my hand. 'He was not an easy man. Undoubtedly arrogant. But he was a loving brother. I mourn him. You don't know how much.'

'I mourn him, too,' I said. 'I am glad that I was able to help him, even though it was so little.'

'It *wasn't* little,' she said fiercely. I looked at Ursula – and I suddenly knew why she and Henry had come to Dartford for my wedding. It wasn't just because of my father's memory. She had made her husband do it, in gratitude for what I did for Montague at his execution.

'The Poles are as much ruined as the Staffords now,' she said. 'My brother Reginald is hated by the king more than any other living man. Godfrey is broken. He's been pardoned by His Majesty but damned by all for giving false testimony. He and his wife have left England – what else could they do? Now my poor mother is under guard in her own home. They question her night and day, attempting to draw her into the Exeter conspiracy. She is nearing seventy years old, Joanna, and *blameless*.'

The king had turned his vindictive obsession for the House of York on an elderly woman. I wished I could think of something, anything, to ease Ursula's torment.

'My friends have written to tell me the worst is over, that it is possible the king will relent and leave my mother alone,' she said. 'Gertrude Courtenay was never tried for any crime; it is possible she will one day be freed, as will her son.'

I found it hard to understand that Gertrude, who did in fact conspire against the Crown, could walk out of the Tower, while her husband, who was loyal, had lost his life. Perhaps they were never able to secure evidence against her besides those flags in the West that Chapuys spoke of.

Ursula said, 'I've heard that King Henry shows distinct signs that he may be tiring of Cromwell's heresy.'

'What?' I said, startled.

'Do you know that on Good Friday, the king crept to the cross from the chapel door like the most faithful Catholic?' she said eagerly.

I threw up my hands. 'Yet here, at Holy Trinity Church, the images of saints are removed as superstition and a Coverdale Bible is chained to the altar.' I found this news of the king's seeming return to the true Faith not comforting but enraging. We were all the victims of his whims.

'Yes,' Ursula sighed. 'The kingdom is in tremendous confusion. They say that in the Parliament just opened, no one can come to agreement on religious policy. We are lost – lost. The only path to follow is to live very quietly and avoid the king and his court.'

I said, 'Yes, and that is exactly what Edmund and I intend to do.'

I learned that Henry had exchanged letters with the Howards. My cousin Elizabeth would not attend my wedding, for she'd once more left her husband. Elizabeth had gone to that same house, to live alone. Negotiations were begun to arrange a separate income for the Duchess of Norfolk. There were no more plans for reconciliation. Catherine Howard still lived in Horsham, the country house of her step-grandmother. There she'd await the arrival of the next queen – if there ever were to be one.

Edmund's people came in two groups. The first to arrive was from Cambridge, a party of three men. Two of them were former Dominican friars. One had become a preacher, the other a tutor. The third man had never been a friar – quite the opposite. He was a Reformer, a young student named John Cheke.

Edmund said, 'He is a very likable person – you will see.'

And I did. For Master Cheke was cheerful and kind and had the liveliest mind – full of curiosity and commentary. He wanted to know everything about my tapestry enterprise and pleaded to see my phoenix, which was nearly completed. Flattered, I agreed.

'Brother Edmund is so fortunate to have a wife this accomplished,' Master Cheke said as he examined the tapestry. Then he reddened. 'I'm sorry, I should not call him "Brother" any more. I of all people should rejoice in the change, but it's difficult for me to adjust.'

'I quite understand,' I said. 'Please do not apologise.'

The second party of Edmund's to arrive was his elder brother, Marcus. He had a large farm in Hertfordshire and a family, but left them behind. He had darker hair than Edmund or Winifred and in fact looked very little like them.

'I don't know whom I should speak to about this, but someone needs to converse about dowry,' Marcus announced to Edmund and me over supper at the inn. He stayed at the Saracen's Head, and no one suggested otherwise.

Edmund shook his head, and they began to argue.

Marcus pointed at me. 'She is from a noble family. How could you agree to this marriage without a dower agreement?'

My body stiffened with resentment.

'None of this has anything to do with you,' Edmund said.

'I'm the head of the family,' Marcus retorted.

'You're not the head of *my* family,' I said, and got up from the table. Edmund rose with me.

'You are welcome to attend the wedding, but we will not discuss this matter any further,' said Edmund, and we left together.

Out on the street, I said, 'I understand everything now.'

Edmund did not answer. I saw what a strain this all was on him – the expectations and demands of family and friends. His religious calling had removed him from such a tumult, but now, owing to his love for me, he was besieged. If I were to suggest, at this moment, that we not marry, how would he respond? In my heart I feared he was a man formed for life as a solitary friar. Straining toward this new role was so difficult. I felt a twist of sharp guilt.

Yet, when he said good night, Edmund kissed me on the lips. 'I love you, Joanna,' he whispered, and all of my doubts receded. Once we were married, and all of these people left us alone, our life together would truly begin.

As unpleasant as the conversation was with Edmund's brother, there was one more left, and this one to be initiated by me.

I went to the Building Office to tell Jacquard Rolin, 'Please make the necessary arrangements to leave Dartford for a short time, for if you stay here, it would be strange should you not attend. And I would prefer that you not attend my wedding.'

I could not bear the thought of a spy who had mused over the 'elimination' of Brother Edmund being among the guests.

Jacquard, who seemed to take no offence, smiled and bowed.

The night before my wedding, only women attended me. Arthur slept with his Stafford cousins at Master Hancock's manor house. Ursula had brought a lovely pale gold dress for me – 'We all know how much you dislike fashion, but this *is* your wedding' – and, with Kitty's assistance, she prepared the dress and worked on the garland to place on my black hair. I felt as if this were all being done to another Joanna, and my true self watched from afar.

While she stripped away some little leaves from a flower for the garland, Ursula said, 'You should let us take Arthur back to Stafford Castle.'

'What – for a visit?' I asked, taken aback.

'Henry and I can raise him. We could even make him an official ward. Your father should not have pressed him on you, Joanna. I don't know why he did that. Margaret's son should be our responsibility. You must devote yourself now to your husband, and to the children you two shall have.'

'I made a promise,' I murmured. 'I couldn't break it.'

Perhaps because Ursula had said Margaret's name, Margaret was in my dream that night, and we were home. She had a secret. She pressed a finger to her lips, as if to silence me, but she was smiling, too. It was a very strange dream because within it I knew that Margaret was dead and that seeing her was impossible. But I was content to have her alive again, in our secret place in Stafford Castle, a room in the oldest wing that no one else ever went to. We were not children, but we talked about the things we loved as children: the stories of Arthur and Guinevere, and those beautiful saints, the Roman virgins who martyred themselves rather than deny their Christian faith. In my dream, we were sure that nothing bad could ever happen to us.

The day of my wedding to Edmund was not as sunny as Agatha Gwinn's, but there was no rain yet. I was up early, my stomach hollow with nerves. I had never liked being the centre of attention. Ursula descended again, to dress me and plait my hair, to drink cider and nibble cakes. I couldn't eat a thing, which made everyone smile.

I, too, left my house as the church bell rang. My cousin Henry Stafford offered me his arm and we trod across the High Street. There were even deeper throngs of people gathered to observe me than at Agatha's wedding. I suspected that it was not fondness for me but curiosity about the Staffords. It was not pleasant to have such sour suspicions on my wedding day.

But as I drew closer to Holy Trinity Church, I saw Edmund at the door, waiting for me. Every qualm and fear and doubt vanished. He waited for me there, tall and proud, his blond hair trimmed above the collar of the fine grey doublet.

He would be my husband. Everything was as it should be.

Friends surrounded Edmund. Master Gwinn nodded, and John Cheke laughed with delight. The two former friars were there, and the former nuns of Dartford. They had come to the wedding of another former sister, and I was deeply grateful.

Father William Mote ushered us all inside. This was something he'd insisted on. Ordinary folk were married at the door. A knight's daughter must be married within the church, with all guests standing between her and the door.

My cousin Henry led me to Edmund and I took his hand. He smiled at me, and the smile carried all the thoughts and feelings and experiences we'd had since the day I met him, the day he rode with me from the Tower of London to Dartford Priory.

We turned to Father William, for the ceremony to begin.

The preacher opened his mouth – and then stopped, peering past us toward the door.

There was the sound of disturbance behind us, out on the High Street. 'Make way!' I heard a man cry. 'Make way!'

Someone was trying to force his or her way into the crowded church.

'Make way for the Earl of Surrey!' cried another voice.

The earl emerged from the crush of guests standing at the back of the church. His face shone with sweat from the hard ride down from London.

'Joanna,' he cried. 'You can't proceed. It's Parliament – as of today, this marriage is illegal.'

39

'That is madness,' I cried. 'Norfolk submitted an act to Parliament in order to halt *my* marriage?'

The Earl of Surrey shook his head. 'It's not only you, Joanna. It's anyone who once served in a priory or abbey. The statute is called "Six Articles: an Act Abolishing Diversity in Opinions".' He pulled a paper from his doublet. 'The fourth article says that no one who has taken vows of chastity can ever marry. To do so would break the law. I only read it today at dawn, Joanna. I swear I didn't know. My father submitted it to both houses at the opening of Parliament, but I came straight here. Friars and monks and nuns – you can't marry. Not ever.'

'No!' cried a woman's voice. It was Agatha Gwinn.

My throat dry, I said, 'Is there anything in the act about restoring the monasteries? Does the king have any intent of doing that?'

'No.'

'So I cannot be a nun, but I cannot marry either?' I asked, stunned.

Edmund stepped forward. 'Let me see it,' he said.

Surrey extended the paper, and John Cheke snatched it and took it to Edmund. They read it standing together.

'Your father writes and submits an act of religious policy?' I demanded of Surrey. 'I find that hard to believe.'

John Cheke read aloud: 'Fourthly, that vows of chastity or widowhood, by man or woman made to God advisedly, ought to be observed by the law of God; and that it exempts them from other liberties of Christian people, which without that they might enjoy.'

'Gardiner,' I gasped. I could hear the bishop's voice in those words.

Surrey would not look me in the eye. On this, at least, I was right. Gardiner wrote the Act of Six Articles, then gave them to the pre-eminent peer of the land, the Duke of Norfolk, to push through Parliament.

John Cheke looked horrified, and not just about my wedding being thrown into disarray. Scanning the paper, he declared, 'This act protects the Mass, the confession, the sacrament of Communion – the core tenets of the Catholic faith. To violate these tenets will be punishable by law. Reform is finished in England. If this act passes, it will take us all backwards.'

The church erupted in confusion. Nobleman and shopkeeper, shipbuilder and nun – all talked at once about the sharp shift the kingdom might now take. Agatha Gwinn wept loudly in her husband's arms. They were clearly terrified that their marriage would be annulled. Father William Mote looked at the altar and the walls of the church, bewildered over what might now be restored. Ursula glowed with pride, shared by her Stafford husband. Outside the church, on the steps, stood Timothy Brooke, flanked by his parents, ranting of his displeasure before a growing knot of Reformer followers.

For a few moments, Edmund and I were simply forgotten.

'What shall we do?' I asked him, the bridal garland pressing down on my forehead.

'I don't know,' he said. Edmund was rarely indecisive. But at this moment he was as frozen as I.

Poor Arthur was beside himself. 'What's wrong? What's wrong?' he wailed, as Sister Winifred struggled to calm him. But how could she give an explanation when none of us had any idea what to do next.

John Cheke was the one to say it first.

'You must *still* marry,' he said to Edmund and me. 'This bill may not pass.'

Surrey heard him and shouted, 'It will pass, sir, have no doubt. This will be law of the land by June. And the punishment will be hanging for those who deny any one of the articles.'

Cheke shook his head. 'Marry today, Edmund. I beg you.'

On every side they descended. My Stafford relations, always wanting to outwardly bow to authority, pleaded for us to delay until Parliament had made its decision. Edmund's brother, Marcus, also said we should wait. But others advised us to proceed and, once the act had officially passed, petition for a legal exception.

The Earl of Surrey said, 'For a nun or friar who marries someone who has never taken vows, there might be some hope of an exception.

Joanna, the fact that you were a novice and never a full nun, that may exempt you.' He turned to Edmund. 'But you, a sworn friar for a number of years – I don't think there could be anything done for you. You'll never be able to marry her, or anyone else.'

'You're not a lawyer,' John Cheke retorted. 'Is there anyone here representing the law? Any justice of the peace or constable?'

'No,' Edmund said sharply. Cheke had turned to address the crowd, and so he didn't hear him. Edmund did not want Geoffrey Scovill to come into this. I began to feel rather sick – please let Geoffrey not be found. I had not seen him in the church. Perhaps he had stayed away today. Considering the feelings he confessed to last month, he *should* stay away.

'Constable Scovill! Constable Scovill!'

The call went out as I silently prayed that he be absent.

But the crowd parted and Geoffrey moved toward us. He had been here the entire time, but away from my sight. There was no sign of Sister Beatrice. Geoffrey's steps were slow, his stance reluctant.

'I cannot enforce an act not yet made law,' Geoffrey said.

Father William Mote said, 'But you must make a judgement here – there are a dozen different opinions. No one knows for sure. Can Edmund Sommerville marry Joanna Stafford today?'

Geoffrey did not look at me. He took a step toward Edmund, then another.

His tone hardening, Geoffrey said, 'No, he can't.'

'And I will never be governed by *you*,' Edmund said. To my horror, he slammed his hand into Geoffrey's chest, pushing him back a few inches. Immediately Geoffrey shoved him back. The jealousy and distrust that always burned in both men exploded in Holy Trinity Church.

'Stop – please!' I cried.

As their fight raged, I was swiftly lifted up and borne out of the church. It was the Earl of Surrey on one side and my cousin Lord Henry Stafford on the other. I tried to turn around, to see what happened to Edmund. There was a thick group of men around him – they had torn him and Geoffrey away from each other.

The townsfolk gaped at me in the High Street, as I was conveyed to my house by Staffords and Howards. There had never been anything like this – no wedding had ever been so disrupted.

Once inside my house, I tore the bridal garland off my head, ripped it into two pieces, and threw them onto the floor.

'Oh, Joanna, don't do that,' cried Ursula, and knelt on the floor to try to put the garland back together.

'Gardiner has made me regret it, he has made me regret it.' I half wept, half laughed.

'Joanna, pray calm yourself,' she said. She placed both her hands on my shoulders. 'Have you even met the Bishop of Winchester? Be reasonable. Why would he take any action against you in particular?'

There was no response possible to her question.

'Edmund,' I said. 'I must talk to Edmund.'

'No,' said Henry. 'Not until the situation is calmer, and we have some clarity on what to do. And your Master Sommerville must cool his temper. He did not act like a gentleman in church.'

'Do not criticise him,' I said. 'You don't understand – you couldn't.'

I made for the stairs. 'Leave me be, all of you,' I said to my relations.

They let me go. I locked the door behind me and lay on my bed. I wept, but with my fist in my mouth to muffle it. Above all, I wanted no one to pet me or advise me. None of them could help me, except for Edmund. We must work our way through this together. Perhaps I was wrong. Perhaps Gardiner did not target me when he included the section forbidding nuns and friars and monks to marry. This was simply part of the larger conservative direction that he meant to take. As John Cheke said, it might not pass Parliament. Or if it did, Edmund and I could obtain some sort of exception.

There were comings and goings downstairs. I stopped crying so I could listen. Edmund would come for me soon – I knew that for certain. I waited for the sound of his voice.

The Earl of Surrey was the first to leave my house. No doubt he would suffer for being gone this long from his father's side. I knew he came to Dartford in fear that I would break the law. But I wished with all my being that he had not done it. At this moment we could have been married, dancing and feasting with friends.

And then would come our first night together, something I feared and desired in equal measure. But I could not let myself think about that, not give way to those vague longings about what it would be like to lie in a bed with my husband.

The afternoon light dimmed; Henry and Ursula remained downstairs. Arthur must be with his cousins at Master Hancock's. I could hear the Staffords' low murmur of conversation. How they must regret coming to Dartford now that all had turned to catastrophe. But they could not leave me alone, for family obligation forced them to act as protectors.

I coughed delicately at the top of the stairs and they looked up, startled.

'I am not so distressed as before,' I said. 'There's no need to remain.' I hesitated for a few seconds and then asked, 'Has Edmund been here?'

'No, he hasn't,' said Ursula.

My stomach turned over. Something was wrong. With every bit of control I possessed, I said calmly, 'I am sure that I will speak to him tomorrow then. As for tonight, I am weary. I will have something to eat, and then try to sleep.'

'Not here,' said Henry. 'You will stay with us at Master Hancock's. The town is too ... volatile. The news of this impending act has them astir. A woman can't sleep in a house unprotected.'

I looked back at the kitchen. Kitty was not there.

'I have a servant girl who can be sent for,' I said. 'I have this company, will you return to Master Hancock's? You have your own family to care for – and you must make arrangements to return to Stafford Castle.'

'We can't leave until the issue of your marriage is settled,' Henry said.

'Edmund and I will settle that,' I said firmly.

Ursula grimaced.

'What is it?' I asked.

She said, 'Henry sent for him two hours ago to begin discussions and Edmund Sommerville was not to be found. His sister did not know his whereabouts, or his brother. We sent an inquiry to that Cambridge student, Master Cheke. No one has seen or heard from Master Sommerville since that unfortunate fight with the constable at church.'

My beloved was in trouble – I had to help him, only I could help him.

Aloud I said, 'Edmund sometimes seeks solitude in prayer. I am sure I will see him tomorrow.'

They finally agreed to leave. A half hour later a wide-eyed Kitty appeared – confirming my suspicion that my doomed wedding was the talk of Dartford – and agreed to sleep at my house that night.

'All shall be well, Joanna – you'll see,' said Ursula as she kissed me on the cheek.

'Shall you have soup, Mistress Stafford?' asked Kitty when we were alone. 'Certainly,' I said, and then I took up a position at the corner of my window.

Outside it was twilight, but people milled about on the High Street, more than was usual at the end of the day. I'd have to wait until it was completely dark outside.

Kitty busied herself in the kitchen. I heard her chopping vegetables and the fire hissing under the soup pot. I regretted having to deceive her. But I hadn't a choice.

I was halfway to the infirmary when I nearly collided with Humphrey in the street. 'Mistress Joanna, I was coming to your house,' he said.

'Did Edmund send you?' I asked.

He shook his head.

'Do you know where he is?'

'Master Sommerville is in the infirmary,' said Humphrey. 'But he's – he's – something is wrong. I think he's sick. I don't know what to do.'

I ran the rest of the way, Humphrey following close behind. Approaching the infirmary, I saw a candle flicker in the window.

I burst in the door, saying, 'Edmund? Edmund?'

There was no reply.

'He's in the back, mistress,' said Humphrey. 'He can't stand up very well.'

I found Edmund lying on a pallet. He still wore his wedding clothes, his light grey doublet and breeches. At first I thought he was unconscious, because he was so very still. There was no candlelight in the back.

I knelt by the pallet. 'Edmund,' I whispered. 'I'm here.'

His head turned, slowly. 'Joanna?' he said, his voice unsteady. 'You've come to me?'

My heart pounded in my chest.

'Humphrey, bring the candle here,' I said.

When he had done so, I held the candle high, so that its light bathed his face. Edmund looked half awake, his expression very peaceful. His eyes were like flat, dark pools. I had not seen his eyes like this for more than a year. And even then, when he was in the throes of his dependence on the red flower from India, the look was never this pronounced.

'I found him lying on the floor next to his worktable,' said Humphrey. 'Forgive me for asking this, Mistress Stafford, but he's not drunk, though, is he?'

'No,' I said. 'He's not drunk.'

My hand holding the candle began to shake, violently, and I placed it on the floor.

'Joanna?' Edmund said, and he blinked twice. 'You're here?'

'Yes, I'm here,' I said. I turned to Humphrey. 'Go to the Bell Inn and ask for John Cheke. Please fetch him. But do not tell anyone else what condition Edmund is in, that's very important. Do you understand?'

'I understand.'

Humphrey rushed out of the infirmary.

I crouched next to Edmund's pallet, on the cool floor.

Edmund turned his head and studied me with those terrible drowsy eyes.

'Are you crying, my love?' he asked. 'Why?'

I said thickly, 'I have no reason.'

After a moment, he said, 'You're still wearing your wedding dress.'

I looked down at the folds of my skirt. 'Yes.'

The stories, the songs and poems, that spoke of heartbreak, they had always left me imagining a mournful, sad feeling. But it wasn't like that at all. The pain was ferocious.

'You look tired, you should lie next to me,' he said. 'Everything will be all right, Joanna.'

'Yes, Edmund.'

I curled up next to him on the narrow pallet. I turned sideways so that my head rested on his chest and my arm lay across his. He stroked that arm, lightly, as the candle's flame burned hot, very close to my back. The tears seeped from my eyes but I did not move, did not quiver with sobs. I didn't want to upset Edmund, although I knew it didn't matter how I moved or what I did. He most likely would not have known.

'You'll see, Joanna – you'll see,' Edmund said softly. 'Everything will be all right.'

40

When John Cheke came to the infirmary, he saw at once what had happened. The terrible concoction Edmund used was known to him. 'There aren't any remedies for this – just rest and time,' said Cheke. 'But let me stay here with him tonight, Mistress Stafford. This has been a terrible thing for you. And I know Edmund well enough to say that he'd be deeply upset to trouble you with his affliction.'

I went home. But it was a mistake. When Edmund emerged from his stupor, he knew that not only had he succumbed to the darkest of temptations – something he had sworn he'd never again do – but I had witnessed his weakness. Perhaps if I had stayed with him through the night, he would not have left me in the morning. I'd have found a way to reassure him of my love. I might have been able to prevent the torrent of self-loathing from consuming him and driving him out of Dartford.

An ashen John Cheke delivered the letter. It was achingly brief.

Joanna:
> *I shall always love you, but your life will be happier if I am*
> *not at your side. You shall not see me again. I ask your forgiveness*
> *for failing you, knowing that I do not deserve it.*
> *Edmund*

I sat alone for a long time, feeling nothing. And then, finally, as I grasped what had happened to us, what the king had done to us, the pain came, lashed with rage. It was like no other anger I'd ever felt. Not hot and uncontrolled, but cold and terrible and filled with certainty.

I knew now what I would do. It was a simple decision. There was no more doubt. I had made a selfish and terrible mistake in seeking to marry Edmund and live a quiet existence. I'd not only ruined my own life but his, too. For far too long I'd recoiled from the prophecy. Perhaps the seers were genuine, perhaps not. But it didn't matter to me, strangely. It was an opportunity to halt the devouring destruction of Henry VIII. If only I could do that, so be it.

I sent for cousin Henry and asked if he would keep Arthur for a while. He agreed immediately, and urged me to come to Stafford Castle as well. I promised him I would follow in a few weeks, after I had settled some affairs.

Telling lies had become effortless.

I went to comfort Sister Winifred, who I knew must also be devastated by Edmund's action, but she was being dragged from her home by her eldest brother. He insisted that she must come to live with him and his family in Hertfordshire now that Edmund had damaged the family name with his bizarre behaviour. She and I wept in each other's arms as Marcus waited impatiently. He was her eldest brother and now exercised his right to order her life. I would have fought for her to stay in Dartford if I hadn't already made up my mind what I must do. Now that I had resolved myself, Sister Winifred should have no further association with me, for her own sake.

And so I left few people behind. There were the nuns of Holcroft. They'd approached me with words of comfort after the wedding that never was. I thanked them and pretended to consider their offer of living with them, just as I had pretended with Henry Stafford.

Finally, there was Geoffrey. He came to my house twice to speak to me, but I refused to see him. Who knew how much of a role he'd played in Edmund's breakdown? That was yet another uncertainty I'd carry with me forever. But I did not hate Geoffrey Scovill. That emotion was reserved for others.

The boat moved swiftly up the Thames the third time I left Dartford for London. The first time had been in secret – just two years ago, but I was infinitely younger then and ignorant of the world. The second time was last year, when I departed in the bosom of a family, noble and rich and a touch arrogant, too. The family had been crushed. And so now I went a third time, alone again and in secret, too, but with no hope of mercy or kindness, much less redemption for what awaited me. All I brought was a little money, a single change of clothes, and Edmund's letter.

The Thames narrowed now that London was close. 'I can't take ye farther, mistress,' said my boatman, an old man with a face like an apple left in the sun and a rough courtesy to match. 'They're making us discharge fares east o' London Bridge. It's to do with the assembly at Whitehall.'

'Assembly?'

'The London muster, Mistress. Every man o' the city must do a march-past today. The king will review his troops. They all reported to the fields between Whitechapel and Mile End at six o'clock this morning. They say there are twenty thousand men in the muster. Can ye believe it?'

'Indeed,' I said.

Heartened by what he perceived as my interest, the boatman crowed, 'The Emperor Charles will be cut to ribbons if he tries to send his cankered Papists onto English shores!' Another boatman heard him and cheered the sentiment. Peering down at me, he said, 'We've never had such a muster in London. The king and Cromwell and all the high nobles, too, will be at Whitehall to survey the muster. The common folk can go watch if they wish. So ye're bound for Whitehall? Ye fancy seeing the king of England, do you?'

Gripping Edmund's letter, I said, 'I would very much like to see the king of England.'

The boatman rowed me to the wharf nearest London Bridge and I counted a shilling into his palm, which was permanently curled from so many years on the pole.

Nothing could be easier than reaching the king's palace of Whitehall. People were going there in a thick stream – women and children and a few men too old to be mustered. On the main street heading west, a short stretch north of the Thames, women crowded their upper-storey windows, holding baskets of flowers. This must be where the route would take the men after Whitehall.

The shops and houses and churches cleared and I reached an enormous field. A rippling sea of men marched across it, toward a distant sprawl of tall stone buildings. I'd reached the end of the muster, the army of Londoners at the king's command. I could not count this moving mass, but it did seem very possible that I gazed upon twenty thousand.

One of the most striking things about the muster was its colour.

The men, incredibly, wore white from head to knee. Thousands of
white caps shimmered in the sun. The order must have gone out to
all of these thousands that on today they should don white caps and
shirts and doublets and hose and breeches. They'd bought the clothes,
washed them, mended and bleached. The Lord God knew that a fair
number of these men had little money. Yet for their king they'd done
it. Was it abject devotion to their king? Or terror of him? Or hatred of
the invaders?

The men progressed slowly across the field. There was a firing of
arms taking place at the front. Smoke puffed above the crowd and then
dissipated. It looked like they moved up in groups and demonstrated
their weapons for His Majesty.

Most of the spectators waited here, but a pack of bold young women
wanted a better look now. They swerved to the side of it all, following
a line of low and scraggly trees that stretched toward the palace. These
women meant to see their king and his councillors.

I ran to catch up with them.

The men of London marched in tight companies of five across,
each man bearing his pike or his bow or just a long knife. There were
some horses in the midst of it, dragging carts piled with munitions.

My forehead was damp with sweat by the time I'd got halfway
across the field. But I didn't care how hot I was, or how tired. Because
now I could see the platform erected in front of the Whitehall gatehouse and the figures of the men who stood on it.

In the centre was King Henry. He was a head taller than everyone else; in the twelve years since I saw him last, I'd forgotten his
exceptional height. He wore a deep blue brocade doublet, its sleeves
slashed deep and trimmed with gold. It swung like a ship whenever
he turned, for the king had become fat. As I drew yet closer, I could
see the hair hanging below his feathered cap. It was reddish-gold, the
same colour as my uncle the Duke of Buckingham. We were related,
as much as I hated to acknowledge it. The king's grandmother and my
grandmother were sisters.

One woman pointed and shouted, 'It's the Lord Mayor!'

A stout man stepped out of the front line of the muster and bowed
to the king and his council. King Henry said something to him in his
high-pitched voice and then gestured to the man who stood next to
him but a little behind.

Thomas Cromwell stepped forward. Once again, the king's chief minister was dressed very plainly.

'Lord Privy Seal, to you the city of London is and shall forever be much bound,' boomed the mayor. 'We stand prepared to meet the forces of that foul serpent, the Bishop of Rome.'

'Thank you, good Sir William,' said Cromwell. It unnerved me how ordinary that voice was. Neither high nor low, aristocratic nor common. It could be absolutely anyone's – and it belonged to the man who had planned and presided over the destruction of the monasteries.

I scanned the faces of the men who stood on the other side of the king. There was the Duke of Norfolk, the man the king picked to lead his army when war came. Today he looked upon the subjects who might very well live and die at his command.

Next to Norfolk, as always, hovered Bishop Gardiner, the undoubted author of the Act of Six Articles. Gardiner glanced over at the king, then down at the Lord Mayor. His attention then shifted to where we, the female observers, stood.

I could not turn around now, nor try to shield myself behind another woman. Any movement like that might catch the bishop's eye. I stood still, and fixed my eyes on the platform floor. I did not look above the shoes of the High Lords of England. I counted to fifty and then slowly looked up again. Gardiner hadn't recognised me in the crowd. I'd once been his favoured spy. But now I was an anonymous face in a crowd of common women.

Six horses pulled up the largest wagon yet, bearing two cannons. Men lowered them to the ground, and then tried to find the best direction to point them in for demonstration.

King Henry pointed down as they did so, crying out, 'Not that way, bring it *this* way!' He walked to the edge of the platform, but his movements were stiff and pained. He moved like an old man, far older than the Duke of Norfolk, who topped the king in age by almost twenty years.

As a dozen scrambled to carry out the king's wishes, I edged to the side of the group. Before leaving Whitehall, I paused a last time to take in the sight of four men on the platform: King Henry, Cromwell, Gardiner, and Norfolk.

I shall make it right, Edmund, I vowed. *I shall bring the country back to grace and faithfulness and obedience to the Holy Father. I won't fail you again.*

I followed the same path I used coming in, along the line of trees through the flat, marshy field. I could hear repeated cannon fire as I hurried to my destination. The sun had lowered in the sky – it was nigh on time for supper – when I reached the street I sought. These prosperous houses were numbered, and it did not take me long to find the one I sought. Three very large men standing guard.

The moment I approached, they surged toward me.

'Be off, girl!' said one of them. Another waved his weapon at me.

'I need to speak to *him*,' I said, pointing at the house behind him.

Suddenly there was a fourth man. I didn't see where he came from. He was older than the others, with olive skin and careful eyes.

'Lower your sticks,' he said to the guards in an accented voice. They did so at once.

He took a step closer to me. 'Forgive them for their discourtesy, but we've had a number of people shout threats and even throw objects.' He gestured down the street, in the direction of Whitehall. 'The king would have it so. He staged quite a display today, purely for the sake of our master who did not attend. It wouldn't have been safe for him.'

'No, it wouldn't,' I said.

The man looked me up and down: my travel-stained dress, the bag in my hand and, finally, my face, with a complexion to match his own and strands of black hair loosened around my hood.

The man said, 'Now, who should I say has come to call on Ambassador Eustace Chapuys?'

'Tell him,' I said, 'that it is the one who will come after.'

PART FIVE

41

I t is not so hard to pretend to be someone else. At least, it wasn't for me.

Two months after I agreed to put myself in the service of the Emperor Charles, I was given a task that possessed some difficulty. Not physical difficulty but requiring subtlety and deviousness. It was a task of manipulation, and Jacquard, the master of the art, felt I was ready, and I did, too. And so I found myself on a very hot July day standing on a London street, talking about marchpane.

My new neighbour, a woman named Mistress Griswold, leaned over in Saint Paul's Row to confide in me. 'You must spare no expense on the rosewater when making it,' she said. 'Too many people worry about the quality of the almonds. But it's the rosewater that gives it that particular taste.'

'Is that it?' I said. 'I wish I could prepare a marchpane that delectable for my husband. It's his favourite sweet.'

'I could have the recipe written out for you,' said Mistress Griswold hesitantly.

'Oh, no,' I said. 'I wouldn't ask so much of you. Particularly if it's a secret.'

'*Don't push*,' Jacquard had instructed me. '*Never be eager.*'

A horseman trotted down the middle of the narrow street, and we stood to the side. She looked back to her own house; she'd part from me in a moment and I didn't have what I needed.

'Of course, I could learn a great deal just from eating a slice of your marchpane,' I said. 'Might I trouble you for a slice the next time you prepare it?'

Mistress Griswold brightened. 'I'm baking today. I will bring you one over this afternoon.'

'No, no, that is too much,' I demurred, so frightened she would take me at my word.

'Consider it my wedding present,' she said and patted me on the cheek. 'I'd very much like to meet your husband. None of us on Saint Paul's have seen him and you've lived among us for weeks.'

'His business keeps him much occupied,' I said, and made a face of wistful regret.

'Oh, I remember what it was like to be a young bride.' Mistress Griswold laughed kindly. I felt my first twinge of regret, then, for what I was doing.

My neighbour turned away, toward her half-timbered house across the street from mine. Then I remembered. How stupid of me. '*You must get her to specify the time,*' he emphasised more than once.

'Mistress Griswold, wait,' I cried to be heard above the din on the street. 'When can I expect you? I will have some spiced beer ready.'

'That would be most welcome,' she said. 'When the clock strikes three?'

'Excellent.' I hurried up the steps to my narrow house. The house-maid Nelly stood just inside. She'd been listening at the window.

'Go and tell him the time,' I said.

Nelly moved swiftly to the back door, which led to a garden and then the street. Although pretty and plump – in some ways she reminded me of Catherine Howard – she was not like most sixteen-year-old girls, who'd be afraid to run alone down the streets of London. The ward north of Saint Paul's Cathedral was not the roughest in the city, but it was not the nicest either. Saint Paul's Row was the sort of street a respectable young married couple with a modest income would be expected to live on. It had been carefully chosen.

I did not leave my house for the next five hours, though it was very hot. This was the warmest July I could remember. If I lived in the country, or Dartford, or closer to the Thames in London, an occasional breeze might venture in a window. But here, in the centre of the crowded, stench-ridden city, there was no relief. Still, I rarely left. The chances were remote that I'd be recognised in this ward. But we could not be cautious enough.

At last the clock struck the appointed time. I was perched at my table, staring at the pitcher of spiced beer. Nelly had just put out mugs and plates. They were unchipped, the sort that a new bride would possess.

There was a timid rapping at the door. Nelly led in Mistress Griswold, clutching her plate of marchpane. She stared with great curiosity at every object in the room while attempting, without success, not to be too obvious.

Nelly poured spiced beer when the door swung open again with a bang.

'Hello, sweetheart!' called Jacquard from the front room.

When he rounded the corner, he stopped for a second, startled at the sight of Mistress Griswold. Then he made his courtliest bow. The heat seemed not to have affected Jacquard. His clothes were fresh; his hair dry.

'This is my husband,' I said, and made introductions.

He turned his most charming smile on her, with predictable effect. Mistress Griswold, flustered, explained that she'd become acquainted with me and thus learned of Master Rolin's fondness for marchpane.

He sat down and ate a piece with delight. He could not compliment her enough.

'It is the best I've ever tasted since coming to this country,' he vowed.

'Yes, I understand you are from Brussels?' she asked, unable to curb her eagerness to learn about this foreigner.

'I left the Low Countries when the truth of the gospels became known to me,' said Jacquard. 'Now I must return, for my father is quite ill and needs me. But I bring with me an English wife.'

He stood up, walked over and slipped both hands around my waist. He bent down – only a few inches, for he was not much taller than me – and kissed me on the lips. I fought it as hard as I could, that impulse to shrink away.

'How sweet,' said Mistress Griswold, averting her eyes, excited but a trifle embarrassed, too. 'Yes, you are certainly a most handsome couple.'

'*My* Catherine is so beautiful,' he said, giving my shoulder a final squeeze.

She fanned her face rapidly.

'I hope that before you leave London, we'll see you both at church,' she said. 'Everyone has been so curious about you, Master Rolin.'

'I would like that very much,' said Jacquard, his sombre gleam filling the kitchen.

After a few more moments of this, Mistress Griswold left.

Jacquard sat down and drank a full mug of spiced beer. He wiped his mouth and said, 'You did well. Now the biggest gossip of Saint Paul's Row will tell all of her friends about us. Should someone come asking questions after we've gone, she can describe Catherine and Jacquard Rolin. She will tell of a nice brown-haired woman from Derbyshire who married the man from Brussels.'

As he said that, I tugged on a strand of the chestnut-coloured hairpiece I wore at all times. It concealed my coal-black tresses, which were unusual.

'I have news from Dartford,' he said. 'Constable Geoffrey Scovill is married.'

I flinched – and could see from the satisfied glint in Jacquard's eye that he'd meant to do that to me, to jab at a vulnerable spot. I'd pushed Geoffrey away so many times; now he was starting his life with someone who truly loved him in a way that he deserved to be loved. I *should* feel nothing but joy at this news.

'It was a wedding much talked about, for the bride had a swollen belly,' Jacquard said.

So Beatrice was pregnant. When did they know it? She didn't attend the Gwinn wedding because she didn't feel well, Geoffrey said. Was it possible that she was with child even then – and yet he declared himself to me as we danced?

I forced myself to shove such thoughts from my mind.

'I know I've asked you this before, but still I don't understand,' I said. 'Why would anyone come here, to Saint Paul's Row, asking questions after we've set sail? No one suspects you of anything – Cromwell thinks you're one of his own.'

Jacquard looked at me for a moment. Instead of answering, he called over his shoulder, 'Nelly, I require supper.' She quickly put together a platter of meats and cheeses. We could say anything we wanted in front of her. Nelly's mother was the English mistress of Pedro Hantaras, the man I met outside Chapuys's house and had seen dozens of times since. Señor Hantaras was Chapuys's most trusted aide; his mistress worked tirelessly for the Spanish cause, and now her daughter did as well.

I knew that Jacquard would answer me eventually. He did not usually sleep in this house; I saw him erratically. But in this guise as a married couple, a guise that often caused me unease, we were thrown together enough that I now recognised his mannerisms.

'I'm not worried about Cromwell,' Jacquard said just at the moment I expected him to.

'But you told me he is the one who examines the licences to leave the country,' I persisted. 'When he sees your name, why would he do anything? You told him you needed to go home and that you took with you a new wife.'

According to Jacquard, Cromwell had, through an intermediary, congratulated him on his marriage, although there had been no gift of money. 'What a miser,' Jacquard had said with a laugh. But Jacquard was relieved. Everyone accepted the forged documents of our marriage. Jacquard and Catherine Rolin had permission to depart from England for the Low Countries. In these times of near-war, to attempt to leave England without permission from Cromwell was punishable by death. Preparations continued: musters of men drilled; ships were outfitted; fortifications built.

As for Chapuys, he had been officially recalled. He awaited us in a house he owned in Antwerp and would escort me to Ghent. The challenge was that there were no ships sailing from England to the Low Countries. Foreign travel was at almost a complete standstill.

Suddenly I knew what troubled Jacquard – why he went to such extraordinary lengths to deceive.

'Gardiner?' I whispered.

Jacquard nodded.

I pushed away the plate of food Nelly had just put in front of me.

'What do you know?' I demanded. 'What have you heard?'

He dipped his chicken drumstick in salt and said, 'I've heard nothing. But it is possible that Gardiner has made it his business also to examine the licences of those leaving England. He rises higher in the king's estimation every day, now that the Act of Six Articles has become law. If the bishop sees my name, he sees the word *Dartford*. Then he sees that I take a wife, and he might make the leap we really do not want him to make.'

'But *why?*' I cried, anguished. 'Why would he do that?'

Jacquard ripped a piece of flesh off the bone and chewed, delicately, before answering. 'I think the bishop has a feeling about you. He knows something is not right. I've had such feelings myself, during past assignments. I learned long ago always to trust them – to pursue every suspicion, examine every shadow.'

In the three days I'd spent at the house of Eustace Chapuys, a plan was formed. Jacquard showed up the first night – apparently, Chapuys had known exactly where to find him. I learned that despite my protestations at Saint Sepulchre, Señor Hantaras and Jacquard had proceeded with forging marriage documents and applying for a licence for a married couple to leave the country. The instant a ship was approved for sailing, we would be on it. No price was too high for the passage. The greatest problem to surmount was me. Where was Joanna Stafford during the time that Catherine Rolin travelled? I could not disappear without explanation. If I told people in Dartford that I was going to Stafford Castle, that was a lie easily exposed, for the Duke of Norfolk was in contact with his brother-in-law and my cousin, Henry Stafford. After hours of discussion, it was decided that I should say I travelled to Hertfordshire, to stay for several months with my closest friend, Sister Winifred. Chapuys posted a spy to watch over the farm of Marcus Sommerville and intercept any letters meant for me. So far none had arrived.

No one seemed surprised that I had indeed offered myself to the cause. Jacquard had said, back at Dartford, 'You will come to us and *implore* us to take you to Ghent.' It chilled me that everything I did followed the predictions of a stranger in another country. Chapuys, Jacquard, and Señor Hantaras shared all plans with me – except for the identity of the third seer. To my frustration, they would reveal nothing except that his powers of prophecy had been confirmed by the Dominican Order.

Now Jacquard was urging me, 'Eat some food – you need to keep your strength up. Then we will practise the *rondel.*'

Ambassador Chapuys suggested it before he left England – I must be trained in certain arts of combat. I'd been dumbfounded at first. Never in my entire life had I heard of a woman fighting. 'If you can learn to dance, you can learn to fight,' said the unflappable ambassador. 'They are not so different. And we must do everything we can to help you protect yourself should the need arise.'

What he didn't say – what he didn't need to say – was that this would not only train me in techniques for protection but also in attack.

In my small bedchamber, I took off my clothes and my ridiculous brown hairpiece. I piled my real black hair high on my head and fastened it. I put on my *rondel* clothes, those of a boy: a loose shirt and hose. Wearing this was unseemly, but I couldn't practise properly in a gown.

Jacquard, dressed similarly, bowed when I entered the room used for our games. He handed me my *rondel*, a twelve-inch-long steel dagger with a blunted tip. He held the same.

I gripped it by its carved wooden handle, and we began.

'Pivot, drop, and thrust; pivot, drop, and thrust,' Jacquard said. After the first round, he said, 'You're improving. You've always been quick of mind. And you're agile. What's lacking is form. Another couple of sessions of this, and you'll be ...' He paused to select the right word.

'Dangerous?' I asked.

'*Précisément*,' he said.

I wanted to be dangerous. That's what hate had done to me. And that is why, deep in my soul, I feared these sessions with Jacquard. They forced me to confront a side of myself that was twisted, savage. I had fallen so low from my time as a Dominican novice. Then I had believed in peace and sacrifice and forgiveness. Now I rarely prayed, except for the courage not to falter when the time came for me to strike.

It was during the third round of practice that it happened. I dropped too low and tumbled to the floor, flat on my back. My hair broke from its pins and fell down over my shoulders.

'Are you injured?' asked Jacquard, kneeling next to me.

I shook my head, though I couldn't get up immediately. I'd had the breath knocked from me in the fall.

Suddenly Jacquard gathered my hair in his hands.

'You *are* rather beautiful,' he mused. 'I wasn't lying when I said that.'

I shrank from him, sliding frantically across the floor.

Jacquard sighed.

'When will you stop being afraid of me?' he said. 'Every time I touch you, you freeze. But we are supposed to be married, and must next persuade others of that on a ship, in close quarters.'

I picked up my dagger and rose to my feet. 'I will convince – but I must ask you not to suggest that there ever be relations between us,' I said. 'That cannot be.'

He walked toward me, slowly, turning the dagger in his hands.

'Why not?' he asked. 'I'd be gentle with you. Don't you think we know you weep at night for your lost friar? I could help you recover from him very easily.'

'I shall never "recover", as you put it,' I said. 'I don't wish to, and certainly not through any of your efforts.'

Without waiting for him to say another word, I left the room, still carrying my dagger. I went straight to my bedchamber on the upper floor and locked the door.

I cannot say that I'd thought this inevitable. Jacquard had never displayed the affection for me – nor the lust – that would lead to a romantic offer. But from the beginning I had feared that playing at marriage would thrust me into inappropriate circumstances. Ambassador Chapuys personally assured me that what had just happened would never happen. 'Your virtue will not be compromised,' he said. But Chapuys was in Antwerp, and I was locked in tense partnership with Jacquard Rolin, a man who'd just suggested lying together as casually as riding together.

Most unwillingly, Edmund entered my mind as I lay there. Now that more time had passed, I saw with greater clarity that marriage was wrong for him. He had a calling to live as a man of God. We had feelings for each other of an earthly nature, but they should have been resisted. All I could do was pray that my mission would succeed – I'd hear the third prophecy and be so instructed on how to stop Henry VIII. After the kingdom was restored, Edmund and I could return to the chaste lives we were truly meant to lead: a Dominican nun and friar.

There was but one small window in my room and the heat did not fade this July night. If anything, it became more airless as the hours crawled by. I lay in bedclothes dampened by my sweat. It disgusted me – I felt more like an animal than a Christian woman. It was completely silent outside. People on Saint Paul's Row observed the curfew. And there were few trees. Not even the sound of night birds' singing drifted through my window.

That is why, when the noises came, I heard them so distinctly.

At first I thought it was a hungry kitten; then, when it changed in nature, grew louder and more desperate, I thought it a wild cat – perhaps more than one. I got out of bed and stood by the door. To my growing concern, this yelping sounded human. It could be a woman in pain. The only other person sleeping here tonight was Nelly – I'd not heard Jacquard walking around in the bedchamber next to mine. She was not really my servant, as Kitty had been – Nelly worked for Chapuys. But I felt responsible for her safety. Wearing only my shift and carrying my dagger, I unlocked the door to seek out the source of the noise.

From the top of the stairs I could tell it was no cat but definitely a woman. Was it Nelly? The sound was like rough panting, a woman in pain, I feared. As I climbed down the stairs, I wondered at its rhythmic nature. The pain did not seem to increase or decrease.

I crept as quietly as I could to Nelly's room next to the kitchen. It was definitely coming from behind the door.

I had my hand on the door, ready to push it open, when I heard another person speak in the room. 'That's it – yes, that's it,' whispered Jacquard.

I dropped the dagger in my haste to get away. I didn't pick it up. I did not want to take the seconds needed to find it in the dark. I did not want to face Jacquard and Nelly.

I locked the door behind me. I stretched out again on the bed sheets and prayed for sleep. Oblivion finally came, and when it did, I found myself sleeping past my usual time.

I heard the sound of men's voices as I dressed. Señor Hantaras discussed a matter quietly with Jacquard, while Nelly served them bread and morning ale. Hantaras came to the house regularly, but usually at night. His dark complexion marked him out as a possible foreigner, and the English were hostile toward those of foreign birth as never before, with talk of war.

'I wish you a good morning,' said Señor Hantaras to me, with his customary courtesy.

I looked at the spot outside Nelly's door. The dagger was gone. Nelly would not meet my eyes.

After Señor Hantaras left, I said, 'Master Rolin, may I speak to you in the other room?'

'Of course.' Jacquard stood up and brushed a bread crumb from his doublet. There was a spark in the corner of those brown eyes.

Once we'd removed ourselves from Nelly's hearing, I said, 'Your behaviour is shameful, and must cease immediately.'

'Which behaviour exactly?' he asked.

'Do not make a mockery of your seduction of a servant girl.' In my exhaustion, my voice was harsh and shrill. 'It's disgusting.' And then: '*You* are disgusting.'

Jacquard slipped his hands in his pockets and bounced back and forth on his heels. 'But young servant girls make not only the best bed-fellows but the best informants of their mistresses' activities, too. Not just here but in Dartford.'

As I realised what he was telling me, the shock was like a blow. 'You seduced Kitty as well. That's how so much was known – how you were aware of everything I did and all my plans.'

He smiled.

'I cannot – I will not – continue this association with you,' I shouted. 'What would Ambassador Chapuys say of your lewd conduct – or Señor Hantaras? Be assured I will find a way to inform them of all that has occurred here.'

Jacquard took his hands out of his pockets. The spark of amusement died in his eyes. 'I've had enough of your virgin caterwauling. Do not interfere with me, Joanna Stafford. I lie with these girls not just to ease my boredom but to better serve my charge from the emperor himself: "To protect Joanna Stafford and guide her to Ghent and to eliminate all those who would endanger her or expose her importance to the Empire." You have no notion – none at all – of that importance, do you?'

'I'm no fool,' I snapped. 'I know it is said that I will be called on to do something that will decide the future of this kingdom.'

Jacquard laughed. '*This* kingdom? This dreary island? Do you think that is why we have gone to so much effort and expense with you? The two most powerful men in Christendom are the Emperor Charles and King François. This king of yours plays a part, a small one – but, yes, unfortunately, a significant one. Henry the Eighth can change the balance of power. And if the balance tips the right way, the cause of the Emperor Charles will triumph. *You* will do that for him. It's been foretold.'

I shrank from this knowledge. The pressures brought to bear on me were already so frightening – such a revelation made my duty ter-rifying. So they believed my actions would not only restore England to the true Faith but change the balance of power in all of Christendom.

'By who?' I said at last. 'If I am so vitally important, then why can't you tell me who the third seer is? Why must I be kept in ignorance?'

'I cannot tell you that,' Jacquard said. 'But what I can tell you is that your Tudor king grows more monstrous with the passing of each day. Perhaps it is his fear of invasion – or his rage at the pope and the Catholic princes for turning on him. Or the pain in his leg that I'm told prevents his getting more than a few hours of sleep at a time. It's hard to know what could turn a man into such a beast.'

An icy dread clamped around my heart.

'What is happening?' I asked.

Jacquard said, 'Despite the fact that the king seems to be veering back to the Catholic church, he lashes out at the monasteries with fresh hatred. The last one left standing, Glastonbury Abbey, became the target of the king's rage. The abbot, an old and sick man, refused to surrender and so he was taken to the Tower. Do you know what Henry the Eighth ordered done to the Abbot of Glastonbury?'

I braced myself for a new horror, but nothing in my experience could prepare me for what I heard next.

'The abbot was taken from the Tower. The old man was dragged on a hurdle by horses to the highest hill in Glastonbury. There he was hanged and afterward beheaded and cut into pieces. His head was fastened to the gateway to Glastonbury Abbey and his limbs were fastened to other places in the four corners of His Majesty's kingdom.'

It was as if Henry VIII plumbed the depths of human nightmare and then made them real.

But Jacquard was not finished.

'I hear other things,' he said. 'Things that have happened in the Tower of London, to those who are not strangers to you.'

I shrank from him. 'Is it Gertrude – or Edward?'

He shook his head, following me. 'They are imprisoned still. Unharmed. For now. No, I must tell you of the family of Baron Montague.'

I could not speak. I closed my eyes.

'The mother, Margaret, Countess of Salisbury, has been carted to the Tower of London and locked in a bare prison cell – though she is seventy years old. But the king shows no mercy for the mother of Cardinal Reginald Pole, the man who defies him in Rome. She will most certainly be executed, as was her eldest son.'

It was then I wept. This would kill Ursula; it would break the heart of anyone who cared for the family of Pole.

'And yet it gets worse than that,' he said.

I could barely see him; my cheeks were sodden with tears. 'How?' I croaked.

'The son of Baron Montague has disappeared. Such a difficult boy he'd been to the yeoman warders of the Tower. One of them was overheard saying someone should strangle this accursed boy in his bed. The last report we've had is that the cell is empty. No announcement of illness or death has been made. But the Pole boy is gone forever.'

I stretched out my hand, toward Jacquard. 'No more,' I begged. 'No more.'

Jacquard took that hand in his. He did not pull me up but knelt on the floor, facing me. He took my other hand in his. His strength was unearthly.

'Joanna Stafford, will you then be ruled by me? I am not here to sully your virtue unbidden; there are a hundred girls for that.' He gripped my hands even tighter. Pain shot up through them to the tops of my shoulders. 'But only you can do what you were meant to do. You must obey me, here and in the Low Countries and for the rest of the time that we are bound together.'

'Yes,' I said. 'I know.'

He released my hands and I collapsed onto the floor, struggling to breathe.

'Then begin to pack,' he said. 'We have a ship at last. Señor Hantaras came to tell me. We leave for Antwerp in three days' time.'

42

On a hot and cloudless morning, a hired barge took me and Jacquard Rolin to Gravesend, east of London, on the south bank of the Thames. This Kent town was where the large ships docked that brought munitions to the king, to be used in his coming war. I had no knowledge of such ships, and certainly none of munitions. I'd never stepped into anything larger than this barge. When we turned the bend, and I saw the half dozen soaring ships anchored at Gravesend, I gasped. It was like a forest sprouting in the water, with masts soaring straight to the sun.

Jacquard smiled at my awe. 'Wait until you see Antwerp,' he said.

Ever since he had extracted a promise of obedience from me, his manner had changed. The elaborate courtesy had receded; his mocking smile was gone. He also had made a point of sleeping in the bedchamber next to mine – alone. Although I did not ask, I assumed that he ceased his attentions to Nelly as some sort of gesture to me. I still felt that I had failed her in not protecting her from Jacquard's predations. When I bade her farewell, I gave Nelly a little money. She was quite grateful, which somehow made me feel even worse.

'Which ship is ours?' I asked.

'The biggest, of course.' He pointed at a massive wooden ship with two masts. It must have stretched two hundred feet from bow to stern. 'It's a galleon,' Jacquard explained. 'Do you see the string of holes in the side for cannon?' Some two dozen men milled about on the deck, preparing it for today's departure. A square hole gaped in the back of the deck, and men lowered large boxes into it. How would such a stately structure overflowing with men and cargo move swiftly across the water? It seemed impossible.

'I look forward to meeting this particular captain, for he's no coward, I'll give him that,' Jacquard said.

'Why do you think him so brave?' I asked.

'He sailed a week from Hamburg to London, in waters full of pirates and spies and outright enemies of King Henry, with a cargo storage full of *gunpowder*,' said Jacquard. 'The only country that would sell King Henry a sizable store of gunpowder was Germany. Imagine what a single lit cannonball could have done – or an arrow dipped in flame?'

Jacquard twirled his hands in a large circle. '*Boom!*' He laughed.

I could not find any comedy in this scenario.

'Is the gunpowder all removed?' I asked.

'Every ounce,' he said. 'The king has distributed it to his many new fortresses. Germany does well by him. He gets gunpowder *and* he gets a fourth wife.'

'The next queen is to be the Princess of Cleves?'

Jacquard looked back and forth to be sure the boatmen could not hear him and then nodded. 'It would seem so. There are two daughters to choose from: Anne and Emilia. The king sent Hans Holbein there to paint both of their portraits.'

As the boatmen rowed us closer to the docks of Gravesend, I tensed. I could not block from my mind the prophecy of Orobas: '*The king has a second son. The prince rules England, with Cromwell standing behind.*'

When our barge reached the wharf, Jacquard hired two boys to carry our trunk to the area set aside for baggage. We had at least an hour to wait, but he steered clear of the clump of buildings near the main wharf. There was no question of going to the town of Gravesend. No, Jacquard led me to the outskirt of those trees, a short distance from the road, and deposited me on a fallen log.

'I must present our papers to the ship captain, and I shall get a better measure of him if alone,' Jacquard explained. 'And the less anyone sees and speaks to you, the better.'

I did not argue with him. I wanted to be alone for a while, to brace myself for this sea journey. Although the trip would be a short one – Jacquard predicted a two-day sail to Antwerp – I had never left England. Never expected to in my life.

My apprehension only increased when Jacquard stalked back to me. I could see in his face that something about the captain troubled him.

'He is a strong man, yes, and deeply corrupt,' Jacquard said. 'The type I can make use of, to be sure, but there are risks as well. I offered him a handsome sum to board this ship – and a small fortune to sail as soon as possible. But should someone with even more gold approach him, he would not hesitate to turn from me. This captain is a man for sale.'

A few seconds later, in a sharp tone of voice, he said, 'What is this?'

A young red-haired man headed right for us, across the marshy meadow and to the trees. Sweeping off his hat, he asked, in French, for directions to the inn called The Black Swan.

That seemed to be some sort of signal. Jacquard shot to his feet. The two of them moved away and spoke together intently for about ten minutes while I watched.

The red-haired man bowed to Jacquard and went back the way he came. When Jacquard again returned to my side, I saw sweat glisten on his forehead for the first time.

'We need to get you on the ship as quickly as possible,' he said.

'What's wrong?'

He said tightly, 'What I most feared has occurred. A spy appeared in Hertfordshire last week, at the farm of Marcus Sommerville. Word of this travelled back to London today and this man rode to warn me.'

'Bishop Gardiner?' I asked, frantic.

He nodded.

'But the man will report that I am not there. The bishop will know that a deception took place.'

'The man will not report back.'

I waited for him to explain, but instead Jacquard offered me his arm; it felt as rigid as iron as he led me to the main wharf.

When we reached the water's edge, I turned to him.

'Bishop Gardiner's man was killed?' I whispered.

Without looking at me, Jacquard said, 'Compose yourself immediately. Of course the man was killed. It had to be done. But this will create new difficulties. His disappearance will be investigated; another man or men will go to Hertfordshire within the month. And I also fear that Gardiner has had us followed here.'

The sun on the water gleamed so brightly, I was blinded and shielded my eyes with my right hand. It began to tremble. Jacquard grabbed it and made a show of kissing it. Then he squeezed my shoulder to lean in close and whisper in my ear, 'This was always a *mission après mort* – and you know it.'

Numbly I shuffled down the wharf. Although it was not Jacquard who had killed the Gardiner spy in faraway Hertfordshire, he had approved it without question. His indifference to the loss of a human life chilled me.

There was a string of small boats rowing out to the galleon. Jacquard lowered me into a rowing boat and clambered into it, planting himself next to me.

Just as our man dipped his oars into the water, a third passenger leaped into the boat.

'Sorry – sorry – hope I'm not intruding,' said the young man, laughing. He was in his mid-twenties with blond hair – almost as fair as Edmund's. 'I'm Charles Adams. I came at dawn to see His Majesty's new fortress. *So* interesting. Don't you think?'

As we were rowed to the galleon, Jacquard chatted with the young man about the newest defences against Imperial invasion.

'You are interested in war, Master Adams?' asked Jacquard, smiling. Because I knew him so well, I detected that the smile was forced. Jacquard suspected Master Adams.

'I'm enrolled on the London muster, if that's what you're asking,' the young man said. 'But the games of war are not for me, alas. I must attend to the family business, that's why I'm headed to Antwerp.'

Just as casually, Jacquard asked him his business.

'We're cloth merchants,' Charles Adams said. 'Adams and Sons have suffered greatly during the embargo. But I take it as an excellent sign that Cromwell granted my request for licence to travel. I must meet with our partners in the Low Countries, and try to repair matters. The trade routes must be reopened.'

'That will be no easy matter,' Jacquard said.

'No – and I'm far from the businessman my father was. But he died last year, and I must do all I can. My mother depends on me.'

I said, 'I'm sure you will do your best.'

Jacquard's hand tightened on mine. He had told me a dozen times not to speak to anyone unless absolutely necessary. But wouldn't it draw more attention to sit rudely silent?

He said to both of us with a proud smile, 'Our cloth business goes back four generations, and the Hapsburgs have attempted to dry up

the English merchant trade ten times at least – and they never succeed! No matter what embargoes they inflict, for reasons of money or
reasons of war, we live on. We're unsquashable.'

Jacquard laughed as if that were the most amusing thing he'd heard
in weeks.

One by one, we were helped onto the deck of our galleon. Jacquard
had paid handsomely to make use of the officers' quarters in the stern.
We would sleep there while on board – at least one night and perhaps
two, depending on wind. We went there directly. Our trunk awaited
us in the narrow cabin.

Jacquard said, 'I have slept in far worse.' And then, with a courteous bow: 'You will have the bed, I can make do with blankets on the
floor.'

The import of our journey seemed to have dampened his lascivi-
ousness. For that I was grateful.

'Must I stay down here during the entire sail?' I asked.

He thought a moment. 'You should be on deck when the captain
unfurls the sail. It would look strange if I were without you then. But
after that, yes, do stay here.'

'I will try not to speak to Master Adams, though I believe him
harmless,' I said.

'I doubt he is a spy from Gardiner, but no one is harmless,' Jacquard
said.

The ship stirred a little – perhaps the anchor was being pulled up.
Suddenly I felt grief over leaving England.

'Jacquard, what will happen if I carry out the prophecy and the
emperor and king of France are victorious?' I asked.

'What do you mean, what will happen?'

'To England,' I said. 'Should Henry no longer be king – if Mary
replaces him on the throne – will everyone then withdraw?'

He smiled. 'Do you think this is why we do this, solely for the support of religion and to restore the Lady Mary's rights to the succession?
I expect the kingdom will be carved up. King James of Scotland, the
ally of France, will extend his border south. I've heard France plans to
claim the West Country. As for the emperor, he will of course control
his cousin the new queen. Not only that, he will finally be unchal-
lenged in the channel and in the cloth trade and other mercantile interests. This is all well worth the fight, wouldn't you say?'

Despite all that King Henry had done to me, it horrified me to hear my country treated in this manner.

'What do you think – wouldn't I make a splendid fourth Duke of Buckingham?' Jacquard asked, oblivious, and then laughed. The thought of Jacquard, spy and murderer, assuming the Staffords' hereditary title was nothing short of obscene.

But I had no choice now. I must press forward. I went with Jacquard back up to the deck.

A short time later we gathered, perhaps a dozen passengers, to see the great sails unfurled. Despite all of my fears, it was a memorable sight. Every man knew his part in hoisting the sails. The chain of commands was shouted across the length of the ship; the men planted on the deck pulled so hard on the ropes that I thought their arms would burst. Others scrambled up and down the masts with incredible ease.

The full triangular sails filled with air with a giant thunderclap. We began to glide east and toward the sea.

An officer approached Jacquard. 'The captain requests the honour of your presence on the bridge, Master Rolin,' he said.

Jacquard glanced up at the highest platform. I followed his gaze, to a tall man sporting a bushy beard who stood next to a fixed silver cannon.

'Yes, of course,' he said and turned to me, doubtless to urge me to get below decks right away.

But before he could speak, Charles Adams appeared on my other side.

'I will make sure your wife comes to no harm,' he offered cheerfully.

Jacquard kissed me lightly on the cheek, simultaneously squeezing my hand so tight it hurt.

I realised after a while that it was not necessary to guard myself against disclosures in the presence of Master Adams. I did not need to speak at all. He was the most voluble of young men, talking of galleons and the cloth trade and his doting mother. His conversation spread to others standing around us. He became the centre of attention, and I could confine myself to smiling and nodding. Every few minutes I looked up at Jacquard, with the captain and the officers. Perhaps because of the large sums of money he had paid, they assumed he would want to share the bridge with them. I hoped Jacquard could see I was maintaining near muteness.

The galleon sailed faster and faster. Everyone commented on the good time we made. It seemed the winds conspired to bear me out of England. I edged away from Master Adams and farther up, closer to the bow of the ship. The wind whipped harder through the flapping sails, blowing my dress this way and that.

The Thames widened as we continued east. Looking straight ahead, I could see the point where it would open to the sea. That point was not so distant – we'd reach it in perhaps an hour. And then I would be gone from England. My head spun as I gripped the wooden railing of the surging galleon. When would I return – and with what terrible knowledge gained? I'd never be the same person as I was today.

'Are you feeling the seasickness, Mistress Rolin?' came the friendly voice of Charles Adams. He had left the others to speak to me.

'If you'll forgive me for saying so, you've lost your colour,' he said. 'You're not worried about pirates, are you? We are well armed, and this captain is most formidable.'

I nodded, and hoped he would return to the others. But he didn't.

'Mistress Rolin, may I share some of my fruit with you? It's nothing but salted meats and bread on board, so I brought it with me. I believe fruit aids the humours.'

Master Adams fished in a small bag he carried and removed a wrapped parcel. In it was a bunch of red cherries, perfectly ripened.

'My mother insisted,' he said, smiling sheepishly.

'Then I definitely could not take any, since they are meant for you,' I said.

But he would not desist. And so I slipped a ripe cherry into my mouth. Its pulpy sweetness delivered a moment of pleasure. When we grew cherries in the priory orchard, they were my favourite treat.

As we stood there, the ship dipped and surged and a fringe of water sprayed us. We jumped back from the railing. Master Adams laughed. As for me, I flicked the water off my hat, but a few drops landed in my mouth – I was startled by its salty taste. The sea mingled with the river here.

'Another cherry?' he pressed me.

I accepted a second. This one was even sweeter. I closed my eyes; the sun warmed my face as I savoured the taste. The sails snapped in the wind.

'Thank you,' I said. 'I've always loved cherries.'

'My mother does too – and my sister. We have them specially grown in an orchard outside London. They can be difficult to nurture, I'm told.'

'Yes,' I said. 'Our trees in Dartford required careful nurturing.'

The instant the word *Dartford* escaped me, I froze.

'Did you live in Dartford before you married?' he asked.

'No, never,' I stammered. 'I ... I visited friends there.'

Such a contradiction only compounded my blunder, but Master Adams seemed to think nothing of it. He put the cherries away and began to speak of the books he wanted to buy in Antwerp. I nodded, barely listening, as I watched Jacquard make his way back to me. I was profoundly grateful he had not heard my slip.

'My wife may need to rest,' he said to Charles Adams.

'Yes,' I said quickly. 'I'm weary.'

Master Adams cocked his head and said, 'Of course, though I thought the cherries refreshed you, mistress.'

'They were delicious,' I said with a weak smile.

Jacquard ushered me to the cabin, which was hot and airless. But I welcomed its confinement after my foolishness on deck. I considered telling Jacquard what I said, but I did not want to alarm him further. I was certain that Charles Adams would forget the remark – he had probably already forgotten it.

I curled up on the borrowed officer's bed. Jacquard did not return to our cabin until after I'd fallen asleep. The sound of the door being unlocked and opened woke me. It was as black as ink in this room – I could not see him. But I could smell the wine on his breath and hear him as he moved about, settling on the floor. I fell back asleep quickly. Something about being on this massive surging ship sent me deep into oblivion.

There was a small glass window in the cabin wall, enough to let the light flood in. The morning sun weighed on my eyes. I rubbed them, turning to wake.

Jacquard stood inches from me, looking down.

I stared back at him. There was no desire in his expression. Quite the opposite – he looked at me with colder eyes than I'd ever seen.

'What's wrong?' I said, my voice raspy.

'Nothing.'

He'd changed his clothes – I was grateful that he'd managed it while I was asleep to avoid embarrassment.

'I'll have food sent down,' he said. 'Stay below decks until I come to fetch you. We have excellent wind and should dock at Antwerp well before nightfall.' He paused. 'Do you understand me, Joanna Stafford?'

'How could I not understand you?' I asked, taken aback.

He left the cabin.

After I'd splashed water in my face from the basin and dressed and broken my fast, I decided that Jacquard's coldness was only to be expected. This was a dangerous mission. He'd had disturbing news moments before we left shore yesterday and hadn't slept much last night. Today we'd set foot in the Low Countries, a prospect that perhaps unnerved him as much as it did me, although we showed it in different ways.

I was sweaty and restless by the time Jacquard came to get me. 'They will fetch our trunk soon from here and bring it up top.'

He led me out into the cramped walkway. The steps leading to the deck were a few feet away. 'We will see Chapuys later tonight. When we get to Antwerp, we will have something to eat and drink first. I know a place.'

'Why not see Chapuys at once?' I asked. 'What could be more important to him than our mission?'

Jacquard did not answer me.

Once I reached the deck, I forgot about Jacquard's curtness, for it was wonderful to feel the wind and sun on my face again. Our ship had crossed the brief stretch of sea while I was belowdecks. Now we sailed east in a wide channel between an island and the coast of the Low Countries. This was the prosperous land of Brussels, Antwerp and Ghent. More people lived along this coast than the English one, there was no question of that. Roofs and steeples, jammed close together, filled the horizon. Our ship eased into a river – the Scheldt. Like the Thames, it was a major waterway and would lead us to the city we sought. The river was crowded with ships. There were galleons as large as ours as well as many, many smaller ones.

'I'd forgotten about this, how it feels as if the whole world is bound for Antwerp,' said Charles Adams as he joined us.

'That's because it is,' answered Jacquard. 'Portuguese spice traders, German printers, Milanese silk merchants, Venetian glass blowers,

Dutch printers, and' – he bowed to his companion – 'English cloth merchants. All base their business *here*. The Hapsburgs are the monarchs of the Netherlands, but truly, the bankers are the princes of Antwerp. They've even created a safe haven for the Jews – the persecutions of Spain are frowned on in Flanders.'

For the rest of our sail up the Scheldt, Jacquard and Charles Adams conversed happily, of books and wine and music. I could tell by their familiarity that they'd spent hours on these subjects already today and perhaps even last night as well. Jacquard had taken a distinct liking to this merchant's son.

I will never forget arriving in the port of Antwerp. The sun was low in the sky behind us, and so it reflected in all the windows of the houses and guildhalls and taverns of the city. A golden light flashed, shuddered, and then sank into dusk as we found a place for anchoring. While waiting for the rowing boats to reach us and take us the rest of the way, Charles Adams shared with me the meaning of the word *Antwerp*.

'It has to do with a legend – a story about a giant,' he said. 'The giant lived on the river Scheldt and demanded a toll, and if a person refused, the giant cut off his hand. To throw a hand weapon in Dutch sounds like *Antwerpen*. And so you have it.'

'Oh,' I said.

Even in the twilight I could see him flush. 'Oh, perhaps that's too gruesome a story for a bride – I hope you're not angry.'

'My wife likes gruesome stories,' Jacquard said, with a strange intensity.

Just then the rowing boats came, and we were on shore. To my surprise, Jacquard insisted that Charles Adams come with us to sup and drink. Charles himself tried to beg off, saying he was weary.

'Come now – you're five years younger than I am, and I'm not tired,' Jacquard teased him. 'Just one tankard of wine?'

Flattered, Master Adams agreed. I was grateful for it; this meant Jacquard would spend his time talking to his new friend and not needling or lecturing me.

Although night beckoned, there was no sign of curfew in Antwerp. The flat streets teemed with people. I heard a little French and Spanish but mostly a strange language I was told was Dutch. Music poured out of the doorways and windows, all flung open to the balmy evening.

Another way Antwerp was different to London was smell. I assumed all large cities smelled the same. But along with the inevitable filth of a huge metropolis, there was the acrid odour of newly printed books as well as a pungent brew of spices: cloves and ginger and peppers and other exotics I'd never even dreamed of.

Were I in the Low Countries for another reason, I might have felt ecstatic about exploring such a city as Antwerp. But we'd entered this part of the world on a mission laced with darkness.

Jacquard led us down a quieter street to a tavern. The establishment was not as well situated as I expected. But he was known there; he called out to one man, nodded to another. They spoke to him for a moment, saying how long it had been since they saw Jacquard. Then both of the men left the main room.

We sat down at a table. Jacquard boasted that the finest wines in the world were found in Antwerp. 'The silver and spices from the Americas keep pouring in, so the lowliest tavern of Antwerp boasts a better selection of French wines than Paris.'

Charles Adams sipped the wine Jacquard ordered.

'Isn't it magnificent?' Jacquard demanded.

Master Adams hesitated, then said, 'The wine is a bit sour, I am sorry to say, Master Rolin.'

'*What?*'

Jacquard flew out of his chair and out a doorway to the back. No more than three minutes later he returned. He beckoned for Charles Adams. 'The owner of this tavern has apologised – and offers us a drink from his best collection in his private chamber. Wine from Madeira. Come.'

Glancing at me, Master Adams said, 'And your wife?'

'She will be fine. We can start the wine here and then return to her. It's from a casket – it has to be poured in the back and tasted immediately.'

The minute Charles Adams left with him to try the wine, I noticed how quiet the tavern was. There was no one else being served. A sad-eyed woman polished glasses in the corner. I could hear music, faintly, from another establishment up the street.

I don't know how I knew it. There was no noise. No strange sights. But I did.

I ran to the same doorway that the men had passed through. The woman polishing glasses looked up as I sped by.

The door did not lead to the room of the owner of the tavern. It led to a very narrow stone passageway. At the other end, a torch was fixed to the wall. Under it Jacquard bent over Charles Adams. He'd just cut his throat.

43

'Do you think I wanted to kill this boy?' Jacquard said to me, his face rigid and slick with sweat. 'I had no choice.'

He had dragged me back into the tavern. The door to the street was shut and locked. One of the men who'd greeted us when we entered clamped a hand over my mouth a second after I screamed; I hadn't heard him come after me. Before I was dragged away, I glimpsed the other one dragging Charles Adams to the far end of the passageway. They were all Jacquard's confederates from past missions.

The old woman put a glass of something in front of Jacquard and he drank it down in one gulp.

'Why?' I wept. 'Why would you do such a terrible thing?'

He pointed at me. 'The blame belongs with *you*. After all my instructions, repeated and reinforced, you tell him you are from Dartford an hour after we board?'

I stared at him, frozen.

'Yes, I saw you two talking and sharing fruit and I made it my business to find out exactly what you'd told him.' Jacquard beckoned for another drink from the old woman.

'But to kill him – you didn't have to do that,' I said brokenly.

Jacquard slammed his fist on the table. 'Gardiner is *hunting* you. It's only a matter of time before he learns you are no longer in Hertfordshire – perhaps that you never were in Hertfordshire. If he knows I left for Antwerp on that ship, he could investigate my supposed wife. He'd be bound to learn which other Englishmen were on the boat and interview them. And you told Adams you were from Dartford. Not Derbyshire – Dartford. How could you do that?'

I sobbed into my hands, convulsed with guilt and grief over the death of this kind young man.

'Stop it,' Jacquard spat. 'I can't bear the sound. Not after what

I've endured the last two days. You must gather yourself. We leave for Chapuys' house now.'

'No,' I said. 'I go no further with this. There have been two deaths already – I cannot bear the burden of these mortal sins committed on my behalf. No penance can cleanse me.'

Jacquard rose to his feet. 'You either walk with me to the house of Ambassador Chapuys or I'll have you trussed up and carried there in the back of a wagon. Choose.'

I also rose. I gripped the back of the chair as I leaned forward and said, 'I will walk, Jacquard. But after that I only proceed if it's of my own free will – do not forget that.'

He said nothing for a moment – I could see him struggling to restrain himself. 'I don't forget it,' he said finally. 'If you wish to veer off, there's nothing and no one that can force you to stay, it is true. Though I would like to see how you return to England without the aid of the ambassador or myself. You have not a single coin and your papers are forged.'

He paused, allowing this to sink in. 'Before you make your decision, talk to Chapuys.'

And so I walked to the house of Eustace Chapuys at the side of Jacquard Rolin, a murderer, a liar, a plotter, a seducer of young girls – and, according to the papers he carried, my husband.

Jacquard spoke to Chapuys first, just the two of them. Then it was my turn for a private audience. I was ushered into the study of the man, an oak-panelled room filled with books and paintings and precious objects.

The ambassador's sharp features softened as he looked upon me.

'You've suffered greatly, Juana,' he said. 'Ah, I am sorry.'

He led me to a table with food and drink laid out.

'I'm not hungry,' I said.

Chapuys urged me to eat. 'I cannot have you fall ill,' he said.

'Because I am of use to you,' I said bitterly. 'You look on me as a farmer regards his prize pig, to be fed and cared for up until the moment of slaughter.'

'Is that what you think of me?' he said quietly.

'I don't know what to think,' I exploded. 'My journey to the seers has been marked by sin and death. I know that you and others look to me to put a stop to evil. But in so doing, I am *creating* evil. I have sworn that I will do all I can to restore England to the Catholic faith. But these murders along the way? The man who spied for Gardiner in Hertfordshire and now Master Adams? God would not have it so – I know in my heart it's not right.'

Chapuys nodded. After a moment, he gestured to his bookcases of leather-bound tomes. 'Do you know this is why I bought a house in Antwerp? My passion for books. I was a friend of Erasmus, a good friend. I spent long evenings debating the principles of humanism with him and others. Antwerp is the centre of the world for books. You could probably smell the ink in the air when you walked the streets.'

I nodded.

'You also love books, I know that about you, Juana. So you and I would agree, in theory, that printing is good. Come to the window with me, please.'

I joined Chapuys at the large gabled windows, opened to the summer night. His house was on a hill and our window on the third floor of his handsome house. We looked over the many buildings of Antwerp, with the Scheldt gleaming beyond.

'Down there, right now, the presses, more than fifty of them, are turning out books to fuel the Protestant movement. So you see how the good shifts into evil? Sweden, Norway, Denmark, Switzerland – they are, for now, lost. Of course, Germany is riddled with heresy. And the infection spreads fast through France and Scotland. England, as we well know, is engulfed. Our religion must not fall, Joanna. A thousand years of wisdom and devotion cannot be annihilated. One man – just one – stands between the civilised world and anarchy. You know this. The Emperor Charles the Fifth.'

His words were persuasive. But I had a question, the same one that preoccupied me since Canterbury: 'If the emperor is so powerful, then why would he need me to do anything?'

Chapuys grimaced.

'Because the alliance with France is fragile. King François is a liar, without any honour whatsoever. The treaty still stands – but we know François secretly bargains with the Turks. They are as great an enemy to the Holy Roman Empire as the Protestants. My master, Charles the Fifth, is forced to do battles with the followers of Luther on the one side and the followers of Muhammad on the other. Can you conceive of the difficulties in this? But, no matter whether he is allied with

France or not, the emperor will press on. Can you not find it within you to help our holy cause, Juana, to learn the prophecy that concerns you?'

I could feel my resolve to pull away, so firm in that ghastly tavern, beginning to weaken.

'If I agree to push on to Ghent,' I said, 'it will only be after you tell me something of the third seer. Gertrude Courtenay, your operative, told me next to nothing of the second seer and I was ill prepared. Nothing is served by keeping me in complete ignorance. I've asked many times – your refusal insults me.'

Chapuys regarded me thoughtfully.

'If you will eat supper, then I will tell you what I can of this man,' he said with a gracious smile.

I agreed to this bargain. I sat and raised the first spoonful of stew, which Chapuys called *vlaamse stoofkarbonaden*, to my lips. The mixture of peppercorn and cloves, tender beef and carrots, all simmered in beer, left me reeling. I devoured the whole bowl. I was sad and frightened and angry – but I was also ravenous.

While I ate, Chapuys talked of the Lady Mary Tudor, of his fears for her safety now that he had been recalled. 'The removal of the concubine did not restore Mary to prominence as we hoped. The king does not trust her. That is why he arrested and killed the nobles who had ever shown her kindness. I fear this new Protestant queen from Germany will treat her very badly.'

I shared the ambassador's fears for the Lady Mary. In this we were united. And so I folded my hands and asked what I most needed to know – the identity of the third seer.

Chapuys said, 'The man who is being brought to Ghent is a prisoner of the emperor. That is why there was no question of his being sent to England. He is under guard in the Low Countries.'

The beef stew churned in my belly. 'I shall hear my prophecy from a criminal?'

'He's not a dangerous man,' Chapuys said. 'He was questioned as part of a heretical proceeding, and his power of prophecy emerged. After repeated interrogation, he disclosed the prophecy about you. He is without question the most gifted seer of our time, Juana. He spoke of a Dominican novice in England – with Spanish blood – who would change the balance of power in Christendom. He has disclosed a series of visions of you that we've tried to respond to, first through Gertrude

Courtenay and then just myself and Jacquard. The third part of the prophecy can be disclosed only in the city of Ghent, the birthplace thirty-nine years ago of the Emperor Charles. I wish it were otherwise. I am truly sorry for what you've endured so far, Juana. The Dominican friar who first questioned him and learned of your part in the future stands guard over the man even now in a completely secure prison.'

I sat in silence for a good long time, taking this in.

'Is the man a Protestant?' I asked. 'You said he has committed religious crimes.'

'No,' he said. 'The third seer was being questioned by the Inquisition because he was suspected of being a *converso*. In the course of the investigation, the man's prophecies were revealed, of the dog that will fly like a hawk and weaken the English bull forever.'

The Inquisition. Of course I knew of it, although I had never been in the presence of an inquisitor. The Dominican Order oversaw the Holy Office of the Inquisition, created it to root out heresy in Spain. One of its chief priorities was to investigate those of Jewish or Muslim faith who falsely claimed to have converted to Christianity.

Now I had finally discovered the truth about the third seer. He was a man accused of reverting to the Jewish faith of his family – a *converso*.

The ambassador said: 'Ghent is a three-day ride from here, and we must move with all speed. You must hear the prophecy before midnight on August fourteenth, that is the latest information I've received from the Dominican who controls our seer. That is four days from now. But Jacquard knows the land well – he will get us there in time.'

'Must Jacquard accompany us?' I whispered.

The ambassador leaned forward. 'I realise you two do not get on well together. But has he ever physically harmed you?'

'No,' I admitted.

'Nor will he. In any case, from now on, I will be with you, Juana.'

I thought for a moment.

'Very well, I will go with you to Ghent. I have come so far – how can I turn back? But no matter what happens, I will never forgive Jacquard for killing Charles Adams.' I bowed my head. 'And I will never forgive myself.'

44

For this last part of the journey, I abandoned my brown hairpiece and no longer put myself forward as Catherine Rolin, the new bride from Derbyshire. Jacquard insisted that I dress as a young man – there would be no woman in the party travelling to Ghent. Although his continued worry after the murder of poor Charles Adams seemed to me ridiculous, I so loathed pretending to be his wife that I tied up my hair under a hat and bound my breasts under a man's doublet without protest.

I said little during the ride south to Ghent. The roads here were wider than most of those stretching across my native land. We rode through villages and past many prosperous-looking farms. I found myself missing the wilder beauty of the English countryside, the impenetrable green forests and the rocky hills.

I wondered what Arthur was doing – was he happy at Stafford Castle? Had I done the right thing? I longed for Edmund more than ever. I missed not only his sensitivity and kindness but his judgement. I feared to contemplate what he would have made of this decision of mine to pursue my destiny. Would he disapprove – or perhaps be angry that I hadn't taken action sooner?

Chapuys and Jacquard rode side by side, talking. I heard the words 'Ghent' and 'the burghers' and 'the guilds' over and over. They were apprehensive about entering the city, but not because of the third seer. It had something to do with the instability of the people of Ghent.

On the evening of the second day of our travel, Jacquard insisted on doing something odd: Chapuys and I would ride ahead with their servants to a town's inn they knew of, but Jacquard planned to linger. Why, no one told me. I nurtured a hope that Jacquard would leave our party for good, and I'd continue to Ghent with the ambassador.

Chapuys and I reached the inn and secured rooms. I had eaten a late meal and was preparing for sleep when a sharp rap sounded at the door. It was one of Chapuys's servants.

The moment I entered the ambassador's room I saw two things that disturbed me: Jacquard had returned, and the ambassador looked more agitated than I'd ever seen before.

'We've been followed from England by a spy,' Chapuys said, rubbing his forehead.

'Oh, *no*,' I said. 'No, no, no.'

'I sensed that I was being watched on the ship,' Jacquard said. 'I did not see any evidence of surveillance in Antwerp. But once we were on the road to Ghent, I felt it again. That is why I held back and then set my trap for him. He appeared on the road shortly after you left.'

'But who is he?' I asked.

'The same spy that Bishop Gardiner sent to observe you in Dartford,' answered Jacquard. 'The thin one with close-set eyes. He was sent here because he had seen you in Dartford and could identify you. He paid the captain a small fortune to hide aboard the ship. Gardiner did indeed suspect that you left the country with me, posing as my wife. He had a feeling about it and pursued his feeling to the end.'

'This mission cannot continue,' I said. 'Bishop Gardiner knows too much – how can I return?'

'It *must* go forward,' Chapuys said with passion. 'We will find a way to reinsert you into England.'

Jacquard said, 'Gardiner's spy did not send any word to England yet on what he'd discovered. He hadn't taken a good enough look at you to determine if you were Joanna Stafford. And he hadn't the time to send a message to England before shadowing us on our journey. I was able to extract that much.'

The word *extract* made me go cold. 'Is the man dead?' I asked.

Jacquard looked at me steadily. There was no need of reply. Now a third death was laid on my conscience.

After a night of tormented sleep, I woke and once again assumed my costume of a man. The heat was already oppressive, and we would need to ride hard to reach Ghent before nightfall. Tonight was the appointed time for me to hear the third prophecy; we could not delay even a single day.

But the problem of the heat was nothing compared to what I learned next.

'I cannot continue,' Ambassador Chapuys told me. 'No one must know of my involvement in this plot, Joanna. Those are the commands of the emperor himself.'

'You promised you would not abandon me,' I said.

Chapuys gripped me by the shoulders and shook. 'Trust in me,' he said. 'Do you trust me?'

I nodded.

'Solutions will be found,' the ambassador said. 'You will return to your homeland. If, after the deed is done, you cannot live safely in England, then arrangements will be made for you to live in Europe. You could be reunited with the Dominican Order – I can easily find a place for you in a priory in the Low Countries or Spain. You will be taken care of, never fear.'

I knew Chapuys was right. It was too late for me to turn back.

Jacquard and I rode as fast as possible, with two men following. It was so hot that my face and body dripped with sweat; with all my strength, I fought against the numbness of the mind such conditions wrought.

It was nearly sundown when Jacquard Rolin and I came to the place where the Scheldt met the river Leie. Where I would hear the third and final prophecy.

The city of Ghent seemed as large as Antwerp. We passed a magnificent grey cathedral on our way into the city. Elegant houses and abbeys and guildhalls marked the curved streets. But there was a markedly different mood here than in Antwerp. That port city exuded an open and dazzling charm. Here I could see suspicion and distrust in the faces of all the people we passed.

'This is a defiant city,' Jacquard said. 'The citizens have refused to pay the taxes to the Emperor Charles, saying they will not bankrupt themselves to his foreign wars. Without money, the empire cannot be controlled. But the burghers whip the city into a frenzy, saying they must be independent.'

I had never in my life heard of a city rising up in revolt against its monarch. And this was the place where the emperor was born? New questions gnawed at me. If the emperor could not rule Flanders, the cradle of the Hapsburgs, how could he master a huge, sprawling empire – and direct an invasion of England?

The street we followed led to a huge city square – I could see it ahead. But I could also hear something. It was the sounds of people shouting and jeering. And not hundreds of them. Thousands.

Jacquard cursed when we reached that square. A dense mob milled and stamped before us, surrounding a platform raised in the middle of the square. We could not ride any longer.

'The Gravensteen is on the other side of the square and down three more streets,' he fumed.

'What is that?'

'The ancient castle of Ghent, where the seer is being held to await you,' Jacquard answered. 'And we have less than four hours to midnight. It won't be easy to force our way to the far side, or to explain why we're leaving this square when everyone in the city of Ghent seems to have come for some specific purpose.'

He gave the two men the charge of all horses and bade them wait until the square calmed, and then join us at our destination. 'Don't move an inch,' he said. 'I will return with information.'

As I waited, I tried to prepare myself for the place called the Gravensteen. But as the moments crawled by, this milling crowd frightened me more and more. It brought back memories of the bloodthirsty mob of Smithfield that cheered the burning at the stake of my beloved cousin Margaret.

I prayed for strength.

Jacquard returned with horrific news. The city had indeed refused to pay the regent of the Low Countries – the emperor's sister, Mary of Hungary – the taxes imposed on them. The city's leaders, the burghers, vowed to burn the document that bound the city of Ghent in loyalty to the Hapsburg. A deacon still loyal to Charles kept the document locked away, refusing to yield it. But the burghers had held their own trial and condemned the recalcitrant deacon. Tonight he would be executed in the square.

Jacquard pointed at the raised platform. I clapped a hand over my mouth. I was *right*. This was a mob thirsty for a public death.

Jacquard pushed me to walk forward, toward the platform itself.

'No – we can't,' I said.

'This will not take long, for the deacon is to be killed at sundown,' he said into my ear. 'Then we will be able to reach the Gravensteen.'

I could see it better now, this raised platform. Torches blazed at its four corners. I could see the deacon's arms flailing, in terror, as they dragged him to the top. His screams mingled with the cheering of the crowd. A man chased after him with axe raised. This was no trained executioner as I'd seen on Tower Hill. It was butchery before an uncontrollable mob.

The axe rose and fell three times. The deacon died.

I did not falter at it; I felt only a helpless rage at the madness and pitilessness of men.

I looked sideways at Jacquard. He was perturbed, yes; but not sickened. To him, this was but an inconvenient delay in his *mission après mort*.

A burgher rose to the top of the steps and waved something small and light of colour. There was a burst of flame. Over the mutilated body of the deacon they burned the calfskin bearing the signature of the Emperor Charles. And so, destroyed the document binding them in fealty to the Holy Roman Empire.

The people of Ghent danced and sang. Jacquard and I tried to push our way through as best we could without raising suspicion. 'Dance,' people shouted at us. I hid my face in Jacquard's shoulder. As much as I loathed him, I could not smile in the faces of killers.

I don't know if we would have been able to get out of that square in time if it were not for the wind.

Jacquard gripped my arm tighter when he felt it. 'What's this?' he said. He looked up at the sky. 'Minutes ago, the sky was full of stars. How can there be a storm?'

I looked up, too, as the winds encircled me. The clouds stretched across the sky, obscuring the stars, as quickly as the sails had filled on the ship gliding to Antwerp.

The people of Ghent began to react to the windstorm, which gained strength with each second.

An old woman said, 'It's the judgment of God!' Her neighbours shushed her. But others seemed to pick up that fear.

I turned to Jacquard and said: '*Now* we can go to the Gravensteen.'

He peered at me in the darkness and said, 'The storm may make it difficult – be ready.'

'I am ready,' I said. '*You* are the one who may not be.'

We staggered on. The last part of the road we travelled, Jacquard swung his arm around me and pulled me tightly to him, trying to shelter me as he pushed forward with the other arm, fending off the brush and gusts of dirt that propelled toward us. To anyone we might appear a loving couple, desperately trying to reach home.

The Gravensteen was a dread place. I'd thought myself well braced for the prison where I would hear the third prophecy. But when standing before it – that high stone turret with its window slits, the grey walls that spread behind – I felt a fresh spasm of terror. The Gravensteen devoured the stars and the moon and the wind and the light men make. It was the darkest place I'd ever seen.

As Jacquard and I reached the castle, there was a rattling of chains and the massive door came down. Two men leaped out and pulled us inside. The first thing they told us was the Dominican friar in charge of the emperor's prisoner died yesterday from a pain in his chest. I was horrified by this loss, but Jacquard shrugged and said, 'I know what must be done.'

Jacquard, wiping the dirt from his face with a dampened cloth, said, 'Do you want to clean yourself first, Joanna, or drink something?'

'Just take me to the seer,' I snapped.

'I've always liked an eager woman. Saves a great deal of time. Let me speak to the man first while you rest.'

Over my protests, Jacquard strode off. I was led to a small room, where I, too, cleaned my face and hands. A servant poured me wine. Food was offered, but I shook my head. There was no mistaking the serious danger of my situation. Now I was at the complete mercy of Jacquard Rolin, held within a fortified castle, surrounded by a city in violent revolt against its sovereign. Food was out of the question.

Jacquard returned and was, to my amazement, smiling.

'All is well, Joanna Stafford,' he said.

Jacquard led me across the stone floor of the central keep, past an empty fireplace large enough for grown men to stand within. On the other side of an archway was a stone staircase. It led up – and it led down.

'What procedure shall be followed?' I asked.

'A simple one,' he said. 'There are no elaborate necromancy circles to prepare this time, or rabid fits to witness on an abbey floor. He requires only a few … instruments. The Dominican wrote down the procedure and relayed it to Chapuys, who told me everything in Antwerp. I will prepare the instruments that the seer uses to learn his prophecy. While I do that, you and this man will talk together.'

'Talk together?' I repeated.

Jacquard said, 'One of the more interesting aspects of this is he's a man sure to be of your liking. I spoke to him and found him agreeable. He's undemanding. Polite. An apothecary.'

I took a step back. 'Jacquard, what have you done?'

'No, no, no,' he laughed. 'I haven't brought you Edmund Sommerville on a platter.' He gestured for the guard to unlock the door.

'Originally he lived in the South of France. Why he ventured into Spain, into the grip of the Inquisition, I could not say.'

The door swung open. Jacquard went first, and then beckoned for me to follow.

It was a small cell, with straw covering the floor. A bench ran against one wall. Candles had been freshly lit so the room was full of light.

A thin man in his thirties with a scraggly brown beard sat on a wooden bench, his hands in his lap. He looked at Jacquard and then, searchingly, at me as he rose to his feet.

Jacquard said, 'Joanna Stafford, I present to you Michel de Nostredame.'

PART SIX

45

'I'm told you are an apothecary?' My voice quavered in the small, dirty cell.

'I am indeed. But please – do sit,' Master Nostredame said in lilting French. He gestured toward the old wooden bench against the back of his cell. I stepped across the straw and sat down.

'I always wanted to heal others,' he nodded, sitting next to me, a respectful distance apart. 'I tried to learn everything I could about the arts of medicine. My family believed in my dreams of a future; they paid for me to attend two universities.'

Master Nostredame was silent for a while, tugging on his scraggly beard.

'I had tremendous success fighting the plague,' he said. 'My remedies saved lives; I was sent for from all around France. I even have a lifelong pension from one city because of my cures. I grew proud – much too proud. When the plague struck the town I lived in with my wife and children, I was sure that no one would die of it. After all, Nostredame was the physician and apothecary who did not lose patients.'

The man's eyes glistened with tears.

'But the plague struck them down – my wife and both our children. I tried to save them; I tried everything. All that had worked before, on others – on strangers – did not work on the people I loved. That was five years ago. After that, I was lost. I didn't care so much what happened to me. I travelled everywhere. I have had a lot of time to think in the past year, and I believe that inside my soul, I wanted to die. I wanted to join my family.'

I swallowed. 'But the Inquisitors did not kill you.'

He shook his head. 'No. At first they questioned me about a comment I'd made, years ago, about a church statue. The remark suggested heresy, they said. And then they fixed on the faith of my grandfather.'

If I was to accept prophecy from Master Nostredame, I wanted to know everything.

'Are you a *converso*?' I asked.

He shook his head and said simply, 'I'm a good Catholic.'

'Then why are they so convinced of your regressing?'

'My grandfather's name was Gassonet. My father changed it to Nostredame, the most Christian name he could conceive of, one year before I was born. My parents made sure I was baptised and raised in the Catholic faith.' He sat up straighter on the bench. His gentle manner shifted; he did not cool toward me or menace. But he withdrew and yet saw beyond me – ages beyond me. A chill raced up and down my spine.

He said, 'I do not follow the practices of Jews, but I tell you, the people of Israel will prevail upon the world, though the date is not yet set.'

It was true – he *was* a seer.

Nostredame then stood up, his head cocked. It was as if he heard something, though I could detect no noises.

He turned to look down on me, his face long with regret. 'Master Rolin approaches and Mistress Stafford, I have something to tell you.' A few seconds later, I heard a first footfall on the stone steps.

He lifted up his hands; his palms were creased with dirt. 'I'm truly sorry for this,' said Michel de Nostredame.

I stood up to face him. 'No,' I said. 'I'm the one who is sorry, for my fate has cost you your freedom and may yet cost you your life.'

The door swung open, and Jacquard and the guard who'd been posted at the door brought in three things: a shallow bowl filled with water, a brass tripod, and a wooden wand.

Nostredame carefully placed the bowl of water on top of the tripod, in front of the bench. The others left, with Jacquard sending me a searching glance as he left. I pretended not to see.

'Stand as far away as you can, and turn away, please,' said Nostredame, very politely.

I did as he requested. As I stood there, inches from the stone wall, my heart beat so rapidly that I could not hear or breathe or see. All was dead silent behind me. I had no idea what would happen – this was nothing like Sister Elizabeth Barton or Orobas.

Suddenly there was a flash of vivid golden light reflecting off the wall, like a flame igniting. I whirled around to see.

But there was no fire in the prison cell. Only Nostredame, sitting in front of the bowl, staring into it. His eyes were open so wide I feared they would roll back in his head. Slowly, very slowly, he dipped his wand in the water.

He nodded, three times, his eyes still in that fearsome stare.

Nostredame opened his mouth.

'The raven rides the rope,' he said, in a strained voice. 'Now the dog will fly like a hawk. Look to the time of the bear to weaken the bull. It is the only time ...'

He fell silent for a moment.

Nostredame lifted the wand high off the bowl of water – and pointed it directly at me.

'Hers is the hand that touches the chalice. The chalice must be of the Council of Ten. Drink he must before the fourth wife comes to his bed. Or the son named William will come. He will come and he is the one. William is the king who will tear the world asunder.'

Nostredame shuddered and fell back. He dropped the wand on the floor. His eyelids fluttered.

The door flew open. Jacquard came in, and he looked at me, enthralled.

'So now we know what to do,' he said. The guard crept in after him, frightened. Jacquard ordered the guard to remove the instruments. He and Jacquard ignored Michel de Nostredame, who slumped over on the bench, spent.

'You listened outside the door?' I said accusingly.

'Of course I did.' He pulled me out of the room by both arms. He looked so happy, I thought he would twirl me around in some sort of insane dance, as joyous as in the square of Ghent.

'Come to my room,' he said, grinning. 'Now we will make our plans.'

Moments later, I sat on a cushioned stool in the large, tapestried room Jacquard had made his own. I was uncomfortable to see a single huge bed on the other side of the room. For the first time, I wondered where I was supposed to sleep in the Gravensteen.

'Drink this,' he insisted, trying to push wine upon me.

'No,' I said firmly. 'Tell me – what do you mean, "Now we know what to do"? I don't know what to do. What is the Council of Ten?'

Jacquard took a deep draught of his wine and then answered. 'Of course not. You wouldn't. The Council of Ten is a secret school of poisoners. Based in Venice. They are the most skilled in the world. The best.'

Poison.

'And the chalice?' I asked, beginning to tremble.

'I have heard that the council has a certain technique that makes use of a chalice, or a cup. There is a compartment in the base of it that releases a substance when wine is added. The wine is harmless. Can come from anywhere. But in the alchemy of the wine mixing with the substance, a poison is created.' He grinned. 'It's a Borgia trick.'

'And the poison ... it kills the man who drinks it?' I said.

Jacquard said, 'No, it puts him in mind for a nice little nap after dinner.'

I stared at him, confused. He burst out laughing. 'Yes, *of course* it kills him. Within the hour.'

He paused, squinting. 'No, that's not necessarily the case. I've heard of one sort of poison the Council of Ten developed that, if the man drinks a small amount, he suffers profound impotence and other foul humours of the spirit. It's only the full amount that is fatal. But I'm sure, Joanna, that you will find a way to make the king drink his wine to the last drop.'

I rose off my stool. 'You expect me to do that? To serve the king wine in a special chalice?'

'With your noble blood and connections, you're the perfect choice,' he said happily. 'I'm certain that Gardiner's spy never wrote a letter to his master. He intended to talk to the other English passengers in Antwerp, but there was one young man in particular named Adams whom he wanted to speak to.'

Jacquard paused to allow that to sink in.

Then he continued: 'So what we do now is return you to England as quickly as possible and re-establish you as Joanna Stafford, and then insert you into the court of King Henry. We need to stay clear of Gardiner, but Chapuys and I have discussed this, and he believes there are ways to work you into the royal presence.'

'I'm not a poisoner,' I said.

He slapped his hip in frustration. 'What do you think we've been working toward all this time? In all honesty – are you so stupid that you didn't perceive that from the beginning this was a conspiracy to create the perfect assassin?'

I put my hands over my ears. 'Say no more,' I pleaded.

Jacquard made a visible effort to control his temper. 'You're very tired,' he said. 'And you're a woman of difficult humours even when well rested. I shall show you to the chamber that's been prepared for you. We'll talk tomorrow.'

Jacquard led me to the room directly above his on the stone staircase. There were fine blankets on the bed, a change of clothing, food and drink on a side table; he'd even placed a book of Scripture by the bed.

I ate nothing. I read nothing. I did not sleep for hours.

Was I indeed a fool not to see that this was the plan from the beginning – for me to kill the king of England? I'd hoped, and perhaps it was grossly unrealistic, that in the end I would commit some act, such as the abortive attempt to rescue the bones of Thomas Becket, that would turn the tide of history. It would be something decisive but not violent. But how wrong I was, how tragically wrong. This, then, was the prophecy that I'd been intertwined with since I was seventeen. To be a murderess.

What had I done to deserve such a destiny? How could I be the one to carry out a sordid and despicable murder, concocted by the darkest of criminals, the sort first bred in the age of the depraved Borgias?

Yet, as the hours crept by, I began to consider the quest from a different aspect. The Tudor king had murdered my uncle the Duke of Buckingham, my cousin Margaret Bulmer, my friends Henry Courtenay and Lord Montague and others of the nobility. He'd shattered the life of Edmund Sommerville, my father, and Mary Tudor. He'd orphaned Arthur Bulmer. There was a parade of piteous martyrs to his savagery, beginning with Sir Thomas More and ending with the Abbot of Glastonbury. The Catholic Church had been violated, the monasteries destroyed. The pope had excommunicated Henry VIII and called for his deposition. And so it was possible I could receive forgiveness – even absolution – for removing the king from this earth.

But I was not a murderess.

I thought of my parents, of the devotion I felt to my friends at the priory. How close I came to the beauty and power of Christ's wisdom and mercy when I served as a novice. Then how could I have been chosen for profound violence? Did I possess the necessary qualities within me of hatred and rage? I was a difficult woman – Jacquard wasn't wrong about that – and I possessed weaknesses. But in the deepest part of my soul, I refused to believe that I was suited for killing.

I remembered Gertrude Courtenay's desperation: 'You are the one who can save us.' Did she think it was murder – at my hand – that would save her and the kingdom of England? Even knowing her deep obedience to the true Faith, I couldn't imagine that to be true.

And finally, I thought of Edmund. I had stopped fighting the prophecy, I had instead turned around and embrace it as he had encouraged. I sought to restore England to faith and bring back the monasteries – to give Edmund his life back. And mine, too, if possible. But now I was certain that Edmund, of all the people on this earth, would not wish me to commit this terrible act.

Jacquard, as promised, came to see me the next morning. He didn't look as if he'd slept either.

'I sent Chapuys's two men to Antwerp, with letters in code explaining the full prophecy,' he said. 'They left before dawn, one hour apart. If one is killed, the other can get through. It is good they left, because now there is a fresh barricade of men in front of the Gravensteen. Somehow word got out. The city knows that there's a man loyal to the emperor in here. They can't get in – but they won't let us out. It's not going to be easy to leave Ghent.'

'It doesn't matter,' I said. 'I have made my decision. I will not proceed with this. I won't poison the king of England.'

Jacquard looked at me for a long moment. 'When I am buried,' he said, 'on the gravestone will be carved, "He was driven to his death by vexation over a woman named Joanna Stafford."'

46

Jacquard did not return for at least a week. Servants brought me food and drink. I even received a change of clothes. But the door was always barred. I was a prisoner, no different to Michel de Nostredame.

When next he came to my room, he wanted to talk politics at first.

'Queen Mary of Hungary, the regent of the Low Countries, has begged for assistance from the emperor in bringing Ghent into submission,' he said. 'Of course, she would like her brother to come personally, but getting here from Spain is very difficult. Autumn is nearly here, making travel slow. The people in this city are confident that nothing will happen to them, that the emperor would never come to Ghent. They grow ever more defiant. There is always a guard on this castle.'

I said nothing. As much as I hated the Gravensteen, I did not want to leave this place if it meant an assassin's mission to England.

'Yet it is imperative that I get you out of here,' Jacquard continued, beginning to pace. 'The marriage contract for Anne of Cleves is on its way to Germany. Her brother the Duke of Cleves is so ambitious, he sends her to the bed of a wife killer. In three or four months she arrives in England and takes her place as fourth queen.'

'Well, Jacquard,' I said, 'that has nothing to do with me.'

That is when he lost his temper. Jacquard cursed me. He threw things against the wall. He ranted about my stupidity and stubbornness. Then he called for the men of the castle and they came running to serve. I was to be moved, he said, to the cell beneath Nostredame's.

'Now you shall consider the choices before you,' he said, once I'd been shoved into a straw-covered, windowless room with a bench, a narrow pallet against the wall, candles and a privy bucket. 'I shall return soon to find you more compliant, I'm sure.'

He was in the doorway, almost out of sight, when I called out, 'Wait, Jacquard. Wait.'

Smiling, he said, 'Ah, that didn't take long.'

I said, 'I merely thought it prudent to remind you that I was once confined in the Tower of London for four months, in a room not much larger than this one. And suffered no permanent damage.'

His eyes darkened as he stared at me, his hand on the door.

'We shall see, Joanna Stafford.'

Just as when I stayed in the chamber far above, food and drink were brought to me in my new cell below. I had candles. I'd been allowed to bring my book, so there was a means to occupy my mind. I spent most of my hours in prayer. When I was kept in the Tower, there had been regular exercise. I missed that keenly now. But in the Tower I was plagued by uncertainty and confusion, with fear for my father's life. Now was different. I no longer felt lost. I had achieved clarity. I was determined to resist the plans of Jacquard.

The days passed; the weeks passed. It was very hard. I often felt weary and disoriented. My bones ached. Tears slid down my cheeks. But still I drove myself forward. I prayed for strength every minute of the day, and God rewarded me. I held steadfast.

I could hear the men yelling to one another outside my door, though I rarely could pick out Jacquard's voice. To my relief, they made mention of Nostredame. He still lived, and I was glad of it. His visionary powers frightened me, but I also sensed a true benevolence in the French apothecary. He had been caught up in something uncontrollable, just as I had.

On those stone steps, there was much complaining about Master Rolin – of his harshness and arrogance. No surprise for me there. But also the men grumbled about the possibility of food running out. It would seem that the city had inflicted a siege upon us. How long, I wondered, before we were starved out of the Gravensteen?

The answer came one day in the form of Jacquard Rolin, holding a flask of wine in one hand and a letter in the other. I knew that I must look very poorly from these many weeks of imprisonment – but he did not look so handsome any more either. His doublet was dishevelled; he was not bothering to trim his whiskers.

After he ambled in, he said, 'Joanna Stafford, I need to celebrate. These men of the castle are not worthy companions in my revels. So I have no choice but to turn to you. But after all, we are married by documents accepted in any court. So I've come to pay a call on my wife.'

He dangled the letter before me.

'This came through a window today – Chapuys found someone skilled enough to infiltrate Ghent with bow and arrow to do that. Imagine. And now I have all sorts of news to share with you.'

'Such as what?' I said.

'Ah, she speaks.' He chuckled. 'Madame Rolin speaks. She is so excited that the ambassador reached out to us. You've always had such admiration for Eustace Chapuys. It moves me.'

I leaned forward on the bench.

'Tell me,' I said.

'The first piece of news is that the Emperor Charles is so angry with the city of Ghent that he very much wants to grant his sister's request and come here – with his imperial army – and punish the rebels personally. He has submitted a formal request to the king of France that he be allowed to travel through that country.'

'Then we will be freed,' I said. 'When?'

'Perhaps as soon as January,' he said. He drank very deep from his flask. 'Ah, but there is a complication. Queen Mary the Regent has granted the English king's request to allow Anne of Cleves to travel from Cleves to England through the Low Countries. She leaves very soon with her grand German entourage – she may already have left. If I had been able to communicate directly with the Regent, I would have pleaded with her not to do that, to instead delay Anne of Cleves. But she didn't know any better.'

I watched Jacquard intently. There did not seem to be any way that I could reach England before Anne of Cleves. I passionately hoped that this poison plot would be abandoned, and I'd be allowed to leave Ghent when the emperor arrived and try to pick up the threads of my former life.

'So now we have the directives of Ambassador Chapuys,' he said, caressing the letter. 'The plan goes forward on two prongs. The first is that you and I, using diversionary tactics, endeavour to escape from this castle as soon as possible and race to London.'

I shook my head. 'I don't agree to that, and I expect you'll have a difficult time getting a "wife" out of the Low Countries who resists you every step of the way.'

Jacquard threw back his head and stared at the ceiling of my cell. 'It was assumed that would be your attitude, and yet there was some small hope inside of me that you'd see reason.'

'What is the second prong of the plan?' I asked.

Jacquard said, 'The chalice was swiftly crafted by the Council of Ten and has already been sent to England. If necessary, someone else will complete the task outlined in the prophecy.'

My mouth dropped open. 'Someone *else*?'

'We have a candidate in position,' he said. 'The person won't know what is in the chalice, just that it is important that it be filled with wine and served to His Majesty. A very obedient person – which brings all of us untold joy, after these many months spent with you.'

I was stunned by this development. 'But the prophecy is very specific that I must be the one to serve the chalice.'

He grimaced. 'Yes, that is a drawback, and why it serves as second position. It would be preferable for you to carry out the prophecy.' He leaned forward. 'Do not think that if you continue to refuse, it will be looked on kindly.'

I stared into the gold-flecked eyes of Jacquard while bidding goodbye to the hope I'd cherished, of pulling together the threads of my life after abandoning the assassination plan.

Jacquard said, 'When the emperor reaches Ghent, he is sure to bring his Inquisitors as well as his high nobles and his officers. The Inquisitors will take custody of Michele de Nostredame – and most certainly burn him – and then they will consider the case of Joanna Stafford.'

I recoiled. 'What crimes have I committed? Or Master Nostredame, for that matter? He is a good Catholic.'

'Oh, come,' he said. 'You have both trafficked in sorcery and the arts of necromancy. That is forbidden by the Inquisition.'

I sprang to my feet. 'It all took place at the *instigation* of the emperor and his representative, Ambassador Chapuys,' I shouted.

'Is that so?' he asked. 'How can you prove it? Do you have anything written?'

'Chapuys did not order you to deliver me to the Inquisition,' I said. 'That's impossible.'

Jacquard held out the letter. 'Do you want to read it? I will have to give you the code to decipher it, but I am happy to do so if that is what is required.'

As I stared at the letter quivering in his hand, it hit me like a blow.

Jacquard did not need to give me codes. Chapuys had betrayed me.

'If you come with me willingly, then you don't have to fear the Inquisition,' Jacquard said urgently. 'You may not believe this, but I don't want you to burn, Joanna Stafford. I have seen people burn.'

'So have I,' I blurted, and a horrible memory appeared of billows of black smoke rising as Margaret died in Smithfield. And now I would join her? Before I could stop it, I began to laugh, but it was a mad laugh, hysterical and twisted.

I sucked in air, hard, desperate to calm myself. Finally, I looked straight at Jacquard. 'Is this the worst that you have?'

'I know you would like me to say yes,' he said. 'But it gets even worse.'

'Worse than burning? I don't see how.'

'Because it's not your own fate in question but that of someone you hold dear,' Jacquard said. 'If you do not agree – and the fires of the Inquisition do not motivate you – then we may need to welcome another guest to Ghent.'

I gripped the bottom of the bench. He was correct – this was worse. Just as Gardiner used fear for my father's life to force me to act for him, now Jacquard would exert similar pressure through threatening someone I loved. But whom?

'You can't mean Arthur,' I babbled. 'Your men could not steal him from Stafford Castle and bring him all the way here.'

'I'm not talking about a child,' Jacquard said.

A cold, sick dread congealed in the pit of my belly. It was so terrible that I could not speak.

'We're not going to be kidnapping people from England,' Jacquard said. 'We have resources and a certain amount of skill – Señor Hantaras is a man most formidable. But no, one of our spies saw a familiar name show up in the list of licences requested for departure from England. The licence was granted and this person, who wanted so much to leave Dartford after unfortunate circumstance, is now travelling through the dominions of the Emperor Charles. I think there is much you would do to prevent harm from coming to him.'

'No,' I moaned. 'No. This can't be. It can't be.'

'Yes, efforts are being made to secure Edmund Sommerville, and bring him to you. Won't it be nice for you to see your friar once more?'

I leaped off the bench and sprang on him, closing my hands around his throat and pressing hard. 'If you hurt Edmund, I will kill you, Jacquard!' I screamed. 'By sacred oath, I swear it.'

Jacquard ripped my fingers from his throat and threw me across the room. I stumbled and fell onto the straw. 'Now that's the side of you I love to see,' he said.

He pulled open the door to my prison cell – and paused.

'You're not going to kill me, Joanna Stafford. You're going to kill Henry the Eighth.'

47

I do not know how much time passed – I believe it was three days – when the voices of the men in the Gravensteen clamoured louder. Then the shouting died away, and I heard nothing. No one came with food or drink for a day. I had not felt well enough to eat the maggot-ridden meat or drink the sour ale brought yesterday, so this was the second day without food or drink. And I was down to my last candle. Perhaps the siege had lifted and everyone had left. I thought it unlikely that Jacquard would leave, too, without one last attempt at pressuring me to comply. But the possibility also existed that the castle had been breached, and Jacquard was taken or killed.

My cell door had a barred opening at top, as did Michel de Nostredame's. It allowed a very faint light to come into the room. I pressed myself against the door, straining up, and cried, 'Hello? Hello? Hello?'

There was no answer.

Though I'd tried to fortify myself for death with continual prayer, this was a ghoulish end to contemplate: to die of thirst and starvation in a dark cell. And I raged against Jacquard for denying me the right of a Catholic to make confession to a priest before death.

Dazed with hunger, I slept on my pallet in the straw – whether it was day or night, I could not know. When I finally woke, I beheld a row of fresh candles on the floor, all of them lit. A platter of food sat next to it: meats and cheeses and breads. There was a jug of ale, too. And other things: a dress, hung over a chair; a basin of fresh water; lye soap.

Fingering the dress's brocade fabric, I knew where it came from. Jacquard. He was alive and this was his latest move in the great game.

Put on the dress, come with me out of the castle and to another place, another kingdom. There we will plot and kill, and kill again.

There'd be one more confrontation between Jacquard Rolin and

Joanna Stafford, I decided. When it was over, there would never be another.

I ate the food. I took off my soiled bodice and kirtle and cleaned myself. Then I put on the dress. It was tawny and crimson, with a square bodice. It was made of fine fabric but not a dress of a lady. And it smelled musty. Where had he acquired it, I wondered.

A key rattled in the lock. It was one of the sullen-faced guards of the castle.

I followed the guard not to the main keep but up the stairs. He was taking me to Jacquard's room.

Master Rolin awaited me with two full goblets of wine on a gleaming silver tray, and smiled when I walked in.

'Oh, you put it on – you put it on,' he exulted. But then he cocked his head.

'It's not laced right,' Jacquard said. 'Turn around.'

His fingers flew up and down my back, expertly relacing the dress. To my embarrassment, the dress now clung to me and dipped low in the bosom.

Jacquard whispered in my ear. 'You are being cooperative. It pleases me immeasurably.'

I remained silent.

Very slowly, he put his hands on the tops of my shoulders and turned me around to face him.

'The last keeper of the castle kept his whore here. She had fine clothes and pretty trinkets and drank wine served on silver' – he pointed at the tray on the table – 'but she was never allowed to leave. Not such a bad existence, though. Wouldn't you agree?'

Still I said nothing.

In a more serious tone, he said, 'The emperor is coming to Ghent. He's already begun moving his army north toward France. He brings twenty-five white Spanish horses as a gift of gratitude to King François for allowing him safe passage. Naturally, the people of Ghent are in full panic; the word reached here two days ago. To save their lives, they are now trying to win favour again with the queen regent, although it's too late for that. They've decided that those few who are loyal to Emperor Charles must no longer be suppressed.' He reached for his glass and raised it to me. 'That would be us. And so there is no impediment to us simply walking out the door of the Gravensteen today. If we move with all speed, we will reach England before Anne of Cleves.'

'Jacquard,' I said, 'I'm not leaving this place in order to kill the king.'

The disappointment flashed in his eyes and then was gone.

'Do you like the dress?' he murmured, reaching out to finger a sleeve. 'It's all I have to offer you that is clean. If you'd agreed to go to Antwerp, I could buy you six new dresses there.' He grinned. 'But I confess, I've always wanted to see you dressed like a whore. And I was right – it suits you.'

I took a step back.

'I shall go back to my cell now.'

He fingered the dagger handle that was slipped into his doublet.

'I think we will be changing your room permanently. You refuse to leave to carry out your mission? Very well. The emperor should arrive, I calculate, in January or perhaps February. It's past the time of year for easy land travel. Why not wait in comfort?'

'I don't seek comfort,' I said.

He laughed. 'I knew you would say that. It's almost as if we *are* married. I know what you're going to say or do before it occurs.'

A realisation struck.

'You don't have Edmund,' I said. 'Or else you would use him to force me to go to England.'

Jacquard spread his hands. 'Even the most diligent of the emperor's men have a difficult time penetrating the Black Forest.'

Although 'the Black Forest' had an ominous sound, I felt a surge of relief. Now the only threat remaining was of the Inquisition. And I was ready to face the judgement of the Dominicans and of Christ, if need be.

Jacquard crooked his finger to beckon me to his side. 'Since we are man and wife, shouldn't we share this room for the two months until the emperor arrives? I let all the men go but one. But we have enough food to last. I have the keys to the castle.' He patted his pocket and I heard a jingle. 'Ah, they could be very cold weeks. Best sleep here by the fire.'

How he had always enjoyed embarrassing me. Even now, it gave him such pleasure to see me discomfited.

'Perhaps,' he said, 'if you're a very good wife, I'll let you escape before Emperor Charles enters the city of Ghent.'

Now I was the one who laughed. 'You would never do that,' I said.

'You think I have no feeling for you – that I hate you?' he asked, puzzled. 'You're wrong. I am extraordinarily frustrated by you, Joanna Stafford. Many times I've felt anger. But at least we have the full prophecy now, and can make use of it with the person in place.' He laughed. 'I have to admit that you are most unusual. Your strength of will, it amazes me. It amazes us all. I'm telling you the truth when I say I don't want you to die.'

'But I would rather die than have you touch me, Jacquard, and I would rather die than serve you any longer,' I cried. 'I can't bear it any longer. You and Chapuys – and your emperor – are all abhorrent to me.'

The bantering tone vanished.

Jacquard said, 'There is no quicker way to raise anger in me than to decry the emperor.'

I retorted, 'The king of England is excommunicated and ordered deposed by the pope. But the Emperor Charles does not engage the English with honour, on the field and at sea. To save himself the trouble and cost of it, he has his minions try to force a woman to commit the foulest of murders instead. I call that cowardly. You don't *deserve* the kingdom of England. It's better ruled by a heretical king.'

Jacquard went very still. 'You call me minion?'

'That's what you are,' I said. 'Nothing but a scheming … lying … murdering … *minion*.'

Jacquard's face darkened. 'You English bitch.'

He pulled out his dagger and, in seconds, the point was at my throat. 'I've taken more from you than any other woman in my entire life.'

With his other hand, he grabbed the front of my dress. 'You'll learn respect today, Joanna Stafford. I tried to do it the other way. I tried very, very hard for a very long time.'

He dragged me, the knife balanced on my throat, to his bed. Jacquard pushed me down and got on top of me, pressing my arm back with his elbow. He shoved my legs apart with his knee. I tried to kick him, but when I did so, the knife pierced my skin. It hurt; tears sprang from my eyes.

With the other hand, Jacquard pulled his leggings down, and that shift gave me a chance. I wriggled away so fast, he did not have a chance to pierce me with his knife. He lunged for me, and caught me, but I struck out at him with all my might, and the knife flew out of his hand and clattered to the floor. We wrestled across the bed. He was strong, yes, but I was pumping with terror and hate and desperation. I fought back, shoving my knee in his groin. He crumpled and cried out in pain.

I leaped off the bed and ran for the door. I heard Jacquard stumble out of the bed, cursing. I knew that if he caught me, he would kill me. There would be no mercy.

The silver tray gleamed in the corner, and I ran for it with only a few seconds to spare. I picked up the heavy tray with both hands, whirled around, raised it, and smashed Jacquard over the head.

He slithered to the floor.

I dropped the tray, my hand shaking. I knelt and touched Jacquard's throat. A vein danced. He was unconscious but alive.

I pulled the keys from his pocket, and a cloth sack of coins spilled out. I took it.

In the doorway I hesitated. Would Jacquard die of his head wound without medical treatment? I had put myself through great suffering because I refused to commit the mortal sin of murder against King Henry VIII. But was it not as great a sin to murder Jacquard Rolin?

I looked at his slumped body for one moment more.

Taking a deep breath, I locked the door to the room, pocketing the key. I made my way down the stone steps.

I did not see the guard anywhere. I slipped through the keep to the stairs I remembered from that August night we arrived at the Gravensteen. Within minutes I found it, and I opened the door to the cell of Michel de Nostredame.

The French apothecary was much calmer than I'd expected.

'I must find a way back to my own country,' I told Nostredame. 'I fear that Antwerp, the city of Ambassador Chapuys, will be a dangerous destination. I've seriously injured Jacquard Rolin, but if he survives and manages to free himself, he will follow me to Antwerp.'

Nostredame smiled. 'France. That is the way for you. I will take you myself to Calais, the English-owned port city. Is not your Dover across the channel?'

I stared at him, unsure. 'Is it possible for us to travel there?'

'It is indeed.'

My excitement dimmed as I remembered what Jacquard said, that I could not possibly return with forged papers and no money.

'I may be in Calais forever,' I said. 'I have taken Jacquard's coins, but I don't know if it's enough money to get me all the way to England. This could be hopeless.'

Nostredame's eyes took on that faraway gleam as he said, 'You're wrong. There is hope indeed.'

48

Michel de Nostredame and I set out for Calais. It was true that the town was less than one hundred miles from Ghent. But it was now November. I was shocked when I emerged from the stone fortress of the Gravensteen to cold, grey skies. I had been confined for nearly three months.

The roads were muddy – close to impassable – all the way to the Gravelines, the French coastal city. When we could, we hired a cart. But when the muck was too deep for horses' hooves, we walked, past farmland and a few villages. At night we stayed in an inn if we could find one, or paid a farmer to lend us a room. We posed as brother and sister, just as I had with Edmund when we ventured forth on our quests. Nostredame did all of the talking; my English-accented French was rarely heard. For the first few days I looked over my shoulder, fearful of Jacquard's following. But there was no sign of him. Either he died behind that locked door or he made his way to Antwerp.

At all of the inns I overheard talk of the Emperor Charles's historic progression through France, accompanied by five thousand armed soldiers, the Duke of Alva and his high nobles, chamberlains, and cooks, and, yes, the Dominican friars of the Inquisition. It was widely agreed on that being a citizen of Ghent was a sorry prospect.

Nostredame never asked why I was determined to get to Calais as quickly as possible. The night we reached Gravelines, we stayed in a large inn with a tavern. The owner agreed to serve us fish soup before retiring. We ate in a lonely corner of the tavern, in exhausted but companionable silence, until I said, 'I must reach the court of Henry the Eighth before it's done.'

Nostredame regarded me over his steaming bowl of soup.

'Then you will seek to prevent it?' he asked. 'How will you accomplish that?'

'I don't know,' I answered. 'Certainly it won't be easy for me to present myself at court. But I feel certain that *this* is what I'm meant to do. I first started feeling it in my cell at the Gravensteen. Jacquard told me of their plans – if I did not agree to hold the chalice, there is a second person will be put into motion, in England. It will be close to the wedding, and in the time, somehow, of a bear.'

Nostredame blew on his soup to cool it. I watched him for reaction to my disclosure but there was none. And then I knew why.

'You knew that this was what would happen,' I said, awed.

'Not precisely,' he said, and blew on his soup again. 'It's difficult to explain.'

'Why was I chosen?' I asked. 'When was the prophecy born? Was it the day I saw Sister Elizabeth Barton?'

Nostredame shook his head. 'The future is never immutable. But there are ... points ... that are set, that are known long ago. I can't tell you how long.'

'What do I have to do with those points?' I asked, baffled.

'Everything,' he said simply.

I looked around to ensure no one could hear, and then I said, 'I know that by preventing the poisoner from carrying out his act, I am clearing the way for the fourth wife to have a son by the king, and that son will be an enemy to the true Faith. That is a terrible burden, but the alternative – to clear the way for the emperor and the king of France to plunge a land into chaos and then carve it into pieces – is not right, either, Nostredame. I've been lost for months, for years, ever since I was forced to leave my priory. But now, I've found my purpose.'

I was overcome by this confession to the third seer; my eyes filled with tears.

The next morning there was a break in the dreary weather. I felt a surge of determination when we walked to the part of the town overlooking the blue-green sea, sparkling in the sun. High waves crashed against the shore. Peering down the beach, I could see a fleet of fishing boats working their catches.

England was across this channel – I would be home at last.

Nostredame, who had spoken at length to the innkeeper, said, 'We have to hire a wagon across the causeway to reach the Pale and then the town of Calais. There is just one way there. It's a risky journey. There is nothing on the causeway. No house, no man, nothing. It's a

long stretch of wild and desolate marshes – and should there be a gale
and we be exposed to it unprotected, we die.'

'Very well,' I said, peering up at the clear sky. 'But it doesn't look
as if a gale will hit later.'

Nostredame gave me a meaningful look.

'Ah,' I said. 'Of course. Yes – let us go at once.'

We secured a wagon, driven by toughened men with many lines
on their faces and few words on their lips. By midday, the sun had
vanished; within the hour the gale came. Nostredame and I huddled
under a canopy that soon collapsed. We clutched each other, shivering
in the icy, vicious wind.

'If I die on the Pale of Calais,' I cried to Nostredame, 'can anyone
else stop the chalice from being given?'

'No,' he said. 'Yours is the only hand.'

The sky grew yet darker, and the gale more fierce.

I was colder than I'd ever been in my life – and in tremendous pain.
Perhaps if I were to sleep, it would be God's blessing.

Nostredame shook me: 'No, stay with me,' he shouted. 'Hear my
voice.'

But a darkness enveloped me, and in the middle of it emerged
Edmund's face. I was seeing him just as he was when he came to the
Howards' manor house in Southwark. His hair was long and his shoes
muddy. I didn't hear Nostredame any longer. I heard only Edmund.

'I've come to take you home, Sister Joanna. I've come to take you home.'

'Edmund,' I moaned. 'Help me.'

I fell into a sort of dream and he smiled at me, a little shyly, his
brown eyes full of quiet wit, not the dull blankness when I saw him
last. We were in Dartford, betrothed, and he had his book of poetry in
his hands, marked with the page he planned to read from next.

Edmund, I cried in my thoughts, *why did you leave me? You said you
would never leave me in the chapel of Blackfriars, don't you remember? But
you did. You left me, and I'm cold and weak.*

There was nothing for a while and then I wasn't moving any more.
Voices sounded all around me, but strange ones:

'She's ice – as cold as death.'

'We must fetch a physician at once, have you coin?'

Nostredame spoke then: 'I'm a healer, I will take care of her.'

*

I opened my eyes – it was dark, but there was no more rain beyond a fine drizzle. There were people in the streets of a city staring at me as I floated by. I looked up, and into Nostredame's face. He was carrying me through Calais.

'Where are we going?' I croaked.

'To the place beyond the Pale,' he said.

I didn't hear more, for the darkness claimed me again.

When I woke up what seemed like moments later, I lay in a bed next to a window. The sky was light grey; I heard seabirds calling to one another.

A pretty dark-haired girl stood up and clapped her hands. 'She's awake,' she cried in French, and ran out of the room.

Moments later, Nostredame appeared. 'How do you feel?' he said, holding my wrists for a moment, then stretching back my eyelids.

'I believe I am all right,' I said. 'Where are we?'

'With friends,' he said.

'How long have I been here?' I asked.

'Three days. You did come close to death on the Pale. Forgive me. I knew there would be a gale, but not such a terrible one.'

I sat up in the bed. I felt a little weak. 'You said when we got to Calais that we would go beyond the Pale – I remember that,' I said. 'What did you mean? How can we be beyond it?'

He said, 'Joanna, this is a house of Jews. I went to the temple first, and asked them for help.'

He waited for me to respond.

'I am grateful to them for their kindness, and wish to tell them so,' I said.

Later that day I came downstairs and met the entire Benoit family: a shopkeeper, his wife, and three daughters. The youngest was Rachel, and she had volunteered the most often to sit by my bed. 'Is she ready to see it?' asked Rachel, very excited.

'What is there to see?' I asked.

'Something that has bearing on your journey to England,' said Nostredame. 'Something good.'

'Then I want to see it,' I said immediately, overriding his protests that I might not be strong enough for the required walk. No one would tell me exactly what I'd see – Rachel wanted it to be a surprise, a happy one, and though I was impatient to receive good news, I agreed to do it her way.

After proving my mettle by eating a large dinner, I set out with Nostredame and Rachel. The Benoit house lay outside the high walls of Calais, in a small settlement set aside for Jews. The guards watching over the gates to the city nodded as we passed, and we walked through the centre of town. Finally I was in Calais, the famous port conquered by Edward III after a lengthy siege and now the sole remaining possession of the English Crown in the kingdom of France.

Rachel pointed at a large church with a soaring tower and said, 'That's the best way.'

I turned to Nostredame, puzzled.

He smiled and said, 'The Church of Notre Dame gives the best view of the harbour from this part of town. Let's see if we can get permission to climb the tower.'

When we reached the door, Rachel pushed me forward with an excited smile. 'I wait outside,' she said. Nostredame and I walked through the entrance to the church.

The priest was agreeable to our request and slowly we climbed the steps to the top of the tower.

'Here's a proper view,' he exclaimed. 'Look!'

I joined him in the window. From this vantage point, we could see beyond the high harbour walls to the churning waters of the channel. There were a great number of ships anchored there. The smaller ones bobbed in the stiff winter breeze of Calais. There must have been twenty. Studying the flag of the largest galleon, I gasped. It was the flag of the House of Tudor.

'Those are English ships,' I cried.

'They are sent by the king of England to convey his new bride to Dover,' Nostredame said. 'Anne of Cleves didn't travel to Antwerp to make the crossing. She's passing through the Low Countries to here, to Calais. The princess will be here very soon.'

49

One week later, Anne of Cleves arrived in Calais amidst an entourage of more than two hundred German lords and ladies, maids, and servants. The gunners on the largest ships fired one hundred and fifty rounds to salute her; close to five hundred soldiers wearing king's livery lined the streets to cheer her. The young princess was lodged in a grand house called the Exchequer while I remained with the Benoits outside the Pale. We were not likely to cross paths.

But the ruinous winter storms of the channel make everyone equal. Anne of Cleves was forced to wait in the port town, day after day, until it was judged safe to sail. I waited, too. The day before the Germans reached Calais I'd booked passage on one of the smaller English escort ships bound for Dover. I paid for it with all the francs left in my possession; I used a new set of forged documents to represent myself. My name was real this time; what was forged was a French councillor's signature on the paper that said I had permission of the government to leave the country.

Nostredame supplied me with the document, advising me not to ask where it came from but to be assured that it would suffice. I thanked him for it, as I thanked him for everything he'd done for me since the Gravensteen.

'No,' he said. 'It is you I shall always be grateful to – you freed me from that prison cell when you did not need to, Mistress Joanna.'

I insisted that Nostredame leave me in Calais, with the Benoit family, who'd taken me in. 'We've been here for weeks. I knew we shall sail for Dover at some point – we have to,' I said. 'You must go and continue with your own life.'

We went on a last walk together, along the shoreline of Calais. We strode past the shacks of herring fishermen just north of the sand dunes. No one else was out there – the winds of December were harsh. But I'd experienced worse.

Gazing out, I was suddenly struck with the realisation that I was leaving the continent where, somewhere, Edmund wandered.

'Have you heard of the Black Forest?' I asked Nostredame.

'It is in a corner of Germany, a vast forest so dark and impenetrable it is called "black".'

Taken aback, I said, 'Why would anyone want to go there?'

'It is also a place of knowledge and legends and myths and mystical powers,' Nostredame said. 'For those courageous enough to conquer their fears, it can be a forest of magic.'

We walked in silence for a while and then I turned to Nostredame. '*Why* was I chosen?' I asked.

'I don't know,' he answered. 'Reasons are the most difficult thing for me to see.'

I tried it another way. 'But do you know why it happened to me this way? Why did I have to learn of the prophecy through two other seers and then you and always bit by bit – and of my own free will?'

Nostredame squinted into the wind. 'There is something in you, an alchemy of human qualities, that will come into play when the moment arrives. That alchemy is not just the human nature you were born with, that God gave you. Each encounter with a seer changed you – brought you closer to the person you must be at the critical moment.'

'But what are those qualities?' I asked, distraught. 'I fear it is my rage and recklessness, Nostredame, and not the more faithful spirit I've tried to build through service to God.'

'Faith is a quality I've struggled with myself, Joanna, and what I can tell you is – I have faith in you,' he said.

And so we bade each other farewell, the third seer and the subject of his fateful prophecy. 'We shall meet again, but it won't be for quite a long time,' he said with a smile, and left for the journey to his home village in the South of France.

That same day that Nostredame departed, I made a trip to the shop in the town of Calais. I needed new silk threads for my needle-work project with the Benoit girls. To keep myself from fretting over-much – and to try to make myself useful in the household – I'd started lessons in embroidery for the three girls.

I stood at the shop, chatting with the clothier whom I'd met before, when I felt someone tugging on my piece of sewing. I turned, surprised, to face a stout, middle-aged woman wearing a wide hat.

She turned to two men. One was young and thin and resembled a scholar; the other was ageing and dressed as a nobleman. The woman spoke a language I didn't know. The young man listened, and then spoke in French to the older. The nobleman nodded and turned to me.

'I am the Earl of Southampton,' he said. 'I am charged with the protection of the Lady Anne of Cleves, the bride of the king of England. Mother Lowe is the head of the maids of the household. She wants to know who you are, because she says she hasn't seen such good needlework since she left Germany.'

Revealing myself was happening much sooner than I desired – but there was no help for it. I could not enter the orbit of the royal family without a name and background. 'I am from England,' I said. 'My name is Joanna Stafford.'

Southampton's eyes lit up. 'Stafford?' he asked. 'Related to the Duke of Buckingham?'

'My uncle, my lord.'

'But why are you here?' he asked. 'The English ladies of the queen's household meet her in Dover, in Canterbury, or in Whitehall. It's all arranged.'

'I'm not one of the queen's ladies,' I said, as steadily as possible. 'I've been travelling in Europe and am now, through a happy coincidence, returning to England at the same time. So I've booked passage on one of the ships escorting Her Majesty.'

Mother Lowe said something in German to the young scholar. He spoke in French to the earl – he said Mother Lowe wanted to know about me at once.

Back and forth it went in such a way, German to French to English.

'Yes, yes – why not?' said the Earl of Southampton. 'There are few families more esteemed than the Staffords.'

He turned to me. 'Mother Lowe says that the Princess Anna will wish to meet an English lady from a noble family who does good needlework. We hope to sail tomorrow. Your belongings will be transferred to the galleon that conveys the queen to England, so that you may attend her.'

My heart pounding, I made a curtsy.

We did not sail the next day. Or the next. Spotters were stationed on the line of water, day and night, to give word when the weather cleared enough for the thirty-mile sail across the channel. On the third,

Saturday 27 December, as dawn broke, they fired their guns. The signal was given.

I raced to the shore and was ferried to the largest ship.

No one spoke to me on board; the princess and all of her German ladies were already below. It was too cold to observe the unfurling of the sails on deck. I assumed myself forgotten, which I was content with, when the Earl of Southampton came to collect me.

What a large crowd was gathered around Anne of Cleves. I couldn't even see her for the ring of German ladies and English gentlemen.

A young man pushed his way forward, looking me up and down, and said, 'I didn't think that there were any Staffords on this journey. Especially not ones this lovely.' He bowed. 'I'm Thomas Seymour.' So this was the brother of the dead queen, the 'wastrel and lout' Mary Howard Fitzroy refused to marry.

Southampton said, impatiently, 'The princess is waiting.'

Mother Lowe and the scholar stood to the left of a young woman, ornately dressed, sitting on a cushioned chair, bent over her needlework. She wore an enormous hat, folded into three corners.

Mother Lowe spoke in German to the young woman, who raised her head. She nodded, and looked over, toward Southampton, and then at me. She appeared to be in her late twenties, with skin not as pale as most Englishwomen's. It was a complexion closer to my own. She had a long nose, a delicately pointed chin, and large hazel eyes with long lashes. Her gaze was steady and dignified, as befitted a queen.

The princess's voice was low as she spoke that same harsh-sounding language to Mother Lowe. Evidently she had no English, either – or French. I wondered how she planned to communicate with her husband.

'Her Majesty would like to see your needlework,' the earl informed me. 'That is her favourite occupation, sewing.'

I watched as the future queen inspected my embroidery. As she turned my work this way and that, a delighted smile lit up her face. I suddenly felt apprehensive to think of her being handed over to Henry VIII. Her brother, the Duke of Cleves, must be not only ambitious but heartless.

Translations passed back and forth, and I was asked to tell the queen about myself.

Southampton said, 'She wants to know if you are married.'

I shook my head no.

The next question was where I lived with my parents.

'You may tell Her Highness that my parents are dead and I live in a house by myself,' I said.

Anne of Cleves looked confused when Mother Lowe informed her of my status, and I was asked how it was possible for a woman of noble birth – or any woman – to live alone.

I sighed. There was no use trying to conceal things.

'Please tell Her Highness that I was a novice in a Catholic priory, one that no longer exists,' I said.

Southampton winced.

'That is the truth,' I said.

He finally told the scholar, who glanced over at me, nervous, and then spoke to Mother Lowe. To my amazement, when Anne of Cleves heard what her mistress of maids said, she beamed another delighted smile.

Southampton said to me, 'Her Majesty's mother is very fond of nuns and counts an abbess as a close friend.'

I stared at him, dumbfounded. The earl leaned closer to me: 'The mother still practises the Roman Catholic faith, while her son, Duke William, is Lutheran.'

There was a flood of German. The princess said that someone like myself, who was of good family, possessing excellent housewife skills – should be married at once. Now that I was no longer a nun, arrangements must commence. If I agreed, she, the queen, would speak to her husband, the king, about a match.

The earl turned a bit red after relaying this. He knew, as did all English officials, of the Act of Six Articles that forbade the ex-religious to marry. He waited, apprehensive, for my response.

'I thank Her Majesty for her great kindness. But I must now turn my attention to my business enterprise. In my town of Dartford, I've nearly finished my first tapestry, and must search for a buyer.'

This led to many excited questions from the queen, which Southampton conveyed to me. The ship rocked and pitched as we sailed toward the coast of England; several of the queen's German maids became seasick. But the princess herself was unimpaired.

Unfortunately, Anne of Cleves returned to the topic of my marriage. Southampton said, 'Her Highness feels most strongly that you should contract a marriage and have a family. She says that children are the greatest joy a woman can experience. God willing, she hopes to bear the king of England sons and daughters. She hopes he will grant her family's humble request to name their eldest son after her brother, William.'

I stood there, on the swaying ship, looking at the sweet and sincere face of Anne of Cleves, and was filled with terror.

'Are you not well, Mistress Stafford?' asked the earl of Southampton.

'No, I fear not,' I murmured.

My apologies were conveyed. Before I could edge away, the earl said, 'Her Highness requests that you accompany her party on the progression to Whitehall, where she will meet the king. Is that convenient?'

I stared at him.

'Mistress Stafford, is it convenient?' he repeated, annoyed.

'Yes, of course.' I dropped a deep curtsy, and left the cabin.

What should I do? I could not bear the thought of my kingdom being devoured by the Emperor Charles and his allies after the king was poisoned. But now I had proof that the prophecy of England's future, should Anne of Cleves bear a son, was true.

A few hours later, when it was nearing sunset, our ship reached the coast of England. We landed at Deal and were taken to Deal Castle by order of the Lord Warden of the Cinque Ports. All of the queen's party was to stay in the castle overnight, including, now, myself. Tomorrow we'd progress to Dover, and then on to Canterbury. I'd heard that the queen was expected to reach London the third or fourth of January.

I joined the trail of attendants walking to the entrance of Deal Castle, lit with blazing torches. A thin crowd lined the path, braving the cold to look us over. There was a small group of dignitaries greeting us – I assumed I would now see the Lord Warden.

But when I reached the front of the line, a lavishly dressed couple awaited: a tall stout man of middle years and a very young woman. I heard someone say 'the Duke and Duchess of Suffolk'. I remembered hearing about them at the Red Rose a year ago. Catherine Brandon was the daughter of Maria de Salinas, who married the closest friend of King Henry.

When it was my time, I curtsied before the couple.

'I am Mistress Joanna Stafford,' I said.

The young duchess, dressed in a long velvet cloak, peered at me more closely. A large dog poked his head forward, too.

'Are you the woman who served with my mother?' Catherine Brandon asked. 'I would like to speak with you later this evening.'

'I am at your service,' I said, and then joined the throng stepping into the castle itself. The queen and Mother Lowe and her ladies had been taken upstairs to the royal apartments, along with the earl of Southampton. The duke and duchess of Suffolk must be with them, too.

The rest of us were ushered into a great hall where food was laid out on long tables. The room roared with conversation. I found a place and nibbled some supper as I struggled to come up with explanations for the Duchess of Suffolk – and those who would doubtless come after her – that would make sense as to why I was in the party of Anne of Cleves.

'Pardon me, Mistress Stafford?'

I looked up into the smiling face of Sir Thomas Seymour.

'I've been asked to fetch you,' he said. 'Beseeched, actually. There's a young lady who says you know her and she most urgently needs to speak to you.'

'Young lady?' I asked, confused. 'No one with the queen's party?'

'I'm not sure,' he said. 'May I take you to her – and then perhaps later, should there be dancing, you'll allow me to partner you?'

'Please just take me to the person who wishes to speak to me,' I said coolly.

A spark lit in Seymour's eyes; this was, unfortunately, a man who enjoyed a challenge.

He steered me down a passageway that led deeper into the castle, which filled me with suspicion. Just when I was about to charge him with mischief, he led me to an alcove where a young woman stood, holding a candle.

It was Nelly, my servant on Saint Paul's Row. She wore a long cloak, but even so, I could see that she was with child. Her eyes were full of pleading.

'Do you know this girl?' Seymour asked.

'Yes,' I said. 'Thank you, Sir Thomas.'

'I shall see you later, I'm sure,' he said meaningfully, and left.

'Nelly, what are you doing here?' I asked. With a sudden chill, I said, 'Señor Hantaras is not with you, is he?'

'No, my mother and I are now in service in a household in Dover,' she said. 'I came to see the new queen arrive at the castle – but then I saw you, Mistress Stafford. And I wanted to talk to you about … Jacquard. He's supposed to be back in England by now.'

If only I had protected her in London, this wouldn't have happened.

'Is Jacquard the father of your child?' I asked.

'Yes,' she whispered. 'And he has been gone from England for so long with no word. I don't want anyone to hear us, please – I think we can use a room down here.' She pulled me down the passageway, and pushed open the door to a small, cluttered room.

'Nelly,' I said. 'I am sorry to have to tell you this. But it's only right you should know. Prepare yourself – Jacquard may never return to England.'

Nelly didn't say anything. The candlelight glowed as an odd expression filled her eyes.

'Yes,' she said. 'I know.'

At that instant, she looked over my left shoulder. A new shadow leaped across the floor. The last thing I saw was Señor Hantaras, holding something in his hand. Something he raised over his head, and then swung directly at me.

There was pain. And then an enveloping darkness.

50

I knew nothing for a very long time. Then I began to swim up from the nothingness. I couldn't see and I couldn't move. Eventually I realised it was because there was a cloth tied around my eyes and ropes tightly binding my hands. But I did not mind it. I enjoyed the sensations coursing through me. I felt serene and calm, floating in this sea of darkness.

A cloth was untied from around my eyes. Blinking, I looked up at a dark-haired woman I had never seen before – she was in her late thirties.

'Drink this,' she said curtly, and gave me a sip of weak ale.

'Thank you,' I said. I drank and looked around. I was tied up in the back of a large wagon, not moving. There were blankets heaped on me to keep me warm. The wagon had a roof and walls, concealing us from whatever was outside. It was as if I were in a travelling box. Daylight peeked in from the cracks of the roof.

'Are you Nelly's mother?' I asked.

'Of course she is,' said a man sitting in the opposite corner. Señor Hantaras shimmied over to where I lay on the floor of the wagon.

'It will save us time and a great deal of pain on your part if you tell me why you arrived at Deal Castle in the party of Anne of Cleves,' he said.

I knew that his words were threatening. I should have felt fear. Instead I said, 'Hello, Señor Hantaras.' And, incredibly, I smiled.

He turned to the woman and said, 'You gave her too much.'

She looked down at her lap. She held in one hand a bottle, it resembled an apothecary's bottle. At the bottom were black beads.

The stones of immortality.

I recognised the beads from Edmund's priory infirmary. He gave them to our dying laundress to ease her suffering. And later he confessed that he ground them to make a tincture for himself. I was being given the same sort of dose that Edmund grew addicted to. The red flower of India, he called it.

Something stirred, frantic, in the corner of my mind. This is serious, I thought. But how could it be serious when I felt so peaceful?

Señor Hantaras shook me. 'Tell me why you were with Anne of Cleves,' he said.

The grip of his hands hurt, and I was glad. It helped to clear my head. 'I am carrying out the prophecy of the third seer,' I said. 'Why else would I be with her?' I tried to peer out the back of the wagon. 'Where are we now? You'd better return me to the royal party at once. I must be with her when she meets the king at Whitehall.'

'Why did you attack Jacquard Rolin?' he countered.

He knew what happened, and he did not say 'kill' but 'attack'. So Jacquard lived.

'I was defending myself,' I said.

Hantaras regarded me for a good long time. Then he shook his head. 'If you were still working with us, you would have gone to Antwerp and reported to Chapuys.'

A laugh bubbled up. I couldn't help it. 'Jacquard told me that Chapuys planned to hand me over to the Inquisition for practising sorcery. And I was supposed to go to him?' I shook my head. 'I went to Calais because it was the only other route to England. I decided to carry out the prophecy myself – I can't trust Chapuys any more.'

Señor Hantaras stared at me, frowning.

I tried to say as seriously as I could, 'I know what to do. I understand the prophecy better than anyone.' But it sounded like giddy boasting.

I tried not to look away from him; I prayed that my bluff would work.

'We shall see,' he said, and turned to Nelly's mother. 'Bind her mouth again – and watch her. Don't give her so much the next time.' He edged his way to the back of the wagon.

'What about the blindfold?' his mistress asked.

'She's already seen us,' he said. 'And it doesn't matter in any case.'

Señor Hantaras eased out. I heard him say to someone else standing outside the wagon, perhaps someone standing guard, 'We can't eliminate her until the deed is done.'

They are planning to kill me. I must defend myself.

The wagon began to move. Horses pulled us forward. Nelly's mother sat in the dim back of the closed carriage, watching me every second. I strained to hear what was said outside. At first it was just a jumble. Nelly's mother gave me no more of the tincture and my powers of perception sharpened. I was rewarded by hearing 'Rochester'. And then 'the queen's retinue'. So we were following the progress of Anne of Cleves into London. She had gone from Deal to Dover to Canterbury, and now the queen was in the city of Rochester. In two or three days' time, we could be in London.

Nelly's mother undid the strip around my mouth again to give me food. She sliced a loaf of brown bread – while trying to look as if I didn't notice, I tracked where she put the knife. She returned it to the bottom of an open box against the side of the wagon.

I ate the bread silently, trying to show as much compliance as possible. I ate every bite. This was my chance. I still felt the effects of the dose, but I might not get another opportunity. Edmund had performed all of his duties while taking small amounts of the tincture. I would have to force myself forward through this lingering peacefulness to an act of darkness.

'I need to use the privy again,' I said.

She lifted me up to a kneeling position and then half pushed, half dragged me to the part of the wagon where the bucket was kept. When we had almost reached it, I collapsed and rolled so that my back was to the side of the wagon, in front of the box. 'Forgive me,' I said. With my hands, I reached until I felt the blade of the knife. I twirled it around so I could grab it by the handle. The sharp edge pierced my skin, but I did not flinch. The tincture was an aide to me; it blunted pain.

'I'll have to bind your mouth again before you use the bucket,' she said, suspicion darkening in her eyes.

I said, 'I understand.'

I had the knife.

She pulled me up and lifted the cloth toward my mouth, and as she did, I tore away and then made a swift circle, the knife in my hand.

I stabbed her in the leg.

She cried out in agony as I scrambled to the very back of the wagon. I turned the knife this way and that, tearing at the ropes around my wrists.

Nelly's mother tried to follow me, but the wound was too painful and she collapsed, writhing and gurgling.

She found her voice: 'Help!' she screamed. 'Help, she's escaping!'

I only had seconds.

I ripped the last bit of rope from my wrists and smashed open the back door of the wagon with my left shoulder, the knife still in my right hand.

A man stood a few feet away from me, his mouth gaping. He was breathless – he must have been running to the wagon, in response to the scream. It took me a few seconds to recognise him – this was the red-haired fellow spy who came to talk to Jacquard right before we left Gravesend.

The red-haired man lunged for me. I jumped out of his grasp – and then counterattacked.

Pivot, drop, and thrust.

The man scrambled to get out of range of my knife. His shock was obvious. That was my initial advantage – his disbelief that a woman would fight in such a way. He did not know what I'd been trained to do by the best – by Jacquard. I started laughing, I could not stop myself.

Pivot, drop, and thrust.

He leaped away again, but a determined glint came into his eyes. He was planning a way to overpower me.

We tangled at the end of a quiet road. Yet suddenly it was not so quiet. As the red-haired man turned to come at me another way, a man at the top of the street called out, 'What's this?'

I heard running feet. At least two men thundered toward us.

The red-haired man turned and sprinted in the other direction. He had slipped through an opening in two houses by the time the two men had reached me. I had already tossed the knife on the ground, behind a mound of rubbish. It would be hard to explain a bloodied knife in my hand.

'What was that about?' one asked me. 'Have you been injured?'

The two of them looked me up and down. After being tied up in a wagon for three days, I must have appeared dishevelled indeed.

'Are we in Rochester?' I asked.

They exchanged glances. 'Of course this is Rochester,' the other one said. 'Do you need a constable? A justice of the peace?'

'Do you know the constable here?' I asked. Perhaps that was prudent – to go to someone for help. Señor Hantaras and the red-haired man would most certainly try to kill me, especially if Hantaras's mistress bled to death in the silent wagon not ten feet from where I stood. Although what explanation could I give to a stranger?

'I know all the constables in this part of Kent,' replied the first man.

'Do you know Geoffrey Scovill, in Dartford?' I asked. 'Can you send for him? Is that in any way possible?'

The two of them looked at each other again, with sadness.

The second man said, 'We know Geoffrey well. He used to be a constable in Rochester. His wife died two weeks ago, in childbirth. The baby was born dead, too. He cannot be troubled with anything at present.'

And with that, the numbing tincture receded and I felt a twist of real grief.

'Mistress, you look so distressed,' said the first man. 'What can we do to help you?'

I swallowed, and then I said, 'Is Anne of Cleves in Rochester?'

They nodded. 'She's at the Bishop's Palace.'

I managed to draw out of them direction to the Bishop's Palace. In minutes I was on my way. I had no cloak and it was bitter cold on these streets. But I welcomed it; the cold helped clear my mind. There was no ice, nothing to prevent me from running. I picked up my skirts and did just that, following the streets as they slanted toward the large building silhouetted against the winter sky – it could only be the Bishop's Palace.

I was forced to slow down a short distance away. There were so many people clogging the streets; perhaps they were drawn here, eager to catch a glimpse of the new queen.

I heard a muted roar, a strange one – and one that made my knees begin to tremble. Just then a young blond man passed me on the left, leading a large dog by a rope.

'Where are you taking that dog?' I cried.

The blond man looked over his shoulder to answer, 'The bear baiting.'

I scrambled after him. To the side of the Bishop's Palace was a circle of boards, a pit for bear baiting.

'Look!' shouted an old woman. 'The new queen likes the bear baiting.'

I squinted to see. Yes, the old woman was right. The third-floor windows of the Bishop's Palace were flung open, and a woman wearing a triangular cap stood at it, peering down. It was Anne of Cleves. I also recognised stout Mother Lowe next to her.

Although it was so cold, a sweat broke out of my forehead.

I darted around the bear-baiting pit to the front of the Bishop's Palace. At least twenty of the king's guard clustered in front of it. How would I best gain entry? Would Mother Lowe or Southampton remember that the queen wanted me in her party?

'It's the king!' shouted one of the guards.

'No,' said another. 'He's in London.'

But there were more voices, raised in recognition. They pointed at a line of horsemen in the distance, bearing down on us.

The king was not waiting for Anne of Cleves to arrive in Whitehall. He wanted to see her now – today – in Rochester.

Look to the bear to weaken the bull. When the raven climbs the rope, the dog must soar like the hawk.

51

I edged toward the entranceway to the Bishop's Palace, desperate to make my way past the guard. But I was noticed at once. One of them pushed me back, but then I spotted Sir Thomas Seymour chatting to another man just inside.

'Sir Thomas!' I shouted. 'Sir Thomas, it's Joanna Stafford.'

Ladies of noble birth did not shout for gentlemen to come to them. Heads turned. One guard poked another in laughter. But I did attract the attention of Seymour. He pulled himself away from his companion to approach me, grinning.

As he drew closer, the smirk changed to a grimace of distaste.

'What's happened to you?' he asked.

'Please, I would be so grateful if you'd tell the Duchess of Suffolk I need to speak to her,' I said, trying my best not to beg.

Seymour turned to look at the party of men who'd almost reached the Bishop's Palace. 'Christ's blood, is that the king?' he exclaimed. He'd lost all interest in me.

At the moment that everyone turned in that direction, I scrambled for the door. I was inside, moving as fast as I could, when I heard a man shout behind me, 'Hold her! Hold her!'

I looked across the long chamber and spotted Catherine Brandon, the daughter of Maria de Salinas, with her husband, the Duke of Suffolk, on one side and her dog on the other. She wore the same sweeping, dark velvet cloak as at Deal Castle.

She hurried over to see me.

'I looked for you everywhere at Deal and could not find you – no one could,' she said, frowning. 'Southampton's been concerned. Where have you been?' She looked me up and down. 'What happened to you?'

'Your Grace,' I said, 'you must help me.'

She took a step back, alarmed. I must have seemed mad to her. Perhaps I *had* gone mad.

'For the sake of your mother,' I said. 'I know you are a follower of Reformer faith, but your mother loved Katherine of Aragon almost her entire life. As did mine. We both have Spanish mothers. For their sake, will you help me?'

Something flickered in her eyes. This was a woman who loved – and missed – her mother.

But then she said coolly, 'You took vows to become a nun, didn't you?' I remembered what I'd heard at the Courtenays' table. She was a passionate believer in religious reform.

'Yes,' I said. 'Our beliefs may differ. But you have to help me get upstairs. I must go to the Princess.'

At that exact moment, the king and his party burst in the door. Dressed not in royal garb but in a gentleman's coat and hat, he strode eagerly across the room, one of his legs slightly dragging, as everyone bowed low. His friend Charles Brandon hurried to his side, and the two talked near the staircase.

Thomas and other gentlemen clustered around the king, laughing at something His Majesty had just said. Charles Brandon returned to his wife. Ignoring me, he said, 'The king is going to do some play-acting. He plans to call upon her without telling her he's the king, and then reveal himself. If all goes well, he may advance the wedding ceremony or at least one aspect of it.' He chuckled and returned to the king's side.

I watched the group of men ascend the stairs. But I could not follow, for the head of the king's guard had found me. 'Your Grace,' he said to Catherine Brandon, 'this woman gained entry without permission. The king is here – we can't have it. She'll have to go.'

Something about the man's tone disturbed the duchess's dog and he growled. 'Hush, Gardiner,' she scolded her animal.

'Did you say "Gardiner"?' I asked. 'You named your dog after him?'

'Yes, I did,' she said with defiance.

There was nothing I could do to prevent it. The lingering effects of the tincture, the fear, the exhaustion, everything. I doubled over, nearly choking with laughter.

'Are you well, Mistress Stafford?' Catherine Brandon asked.

'I am quite well,' I said, straightening. 'I apologise, it's just that I am acquainted with the Bishop of Winchester and that is an excellent name.'

Catherine Brandon blinked in surprise, and then a smile split her young face.

The head of the king's guard repeated his demand that I leave. She turned on him and said, 'This woman is a friend of mine. And the queen has requested that she be part of the royal party. So there is no need for concern.'

'But Your Grace, I—'

'Leave us,' she snapped. 'At once.'

He retreated.

I saw none of the king's party at the top of the landing any longer. He could already be in the presence of Anne of Cleves.

'Give me your cloak,' I said.

'What?'

'Give it to me,' I said. 'I can't see the king like this.'

'The king?' she said.

'I implore you, the cloak,' I said. *'Por favor.'*

Her eyes wide, Catherine Brandon unbuttoned her long cloak and handed it to me. I threw it over my soiled dress and fastened the top buttons, smoothed my hair.

I made my way to the stairs. I didn't dare run up the steps. But, clutching the cloak's top buttons, I moved as swiftly as a lady possibly could.

On the third floor was a long gallery with windows on one side. There were about thirty people clustered in small groups. They were all looking at two people in the middle of the gallery. One was tall and obese – the king. The other was short and female. But she was not Anne of Cleves.

The other woman was Catherine Howard, holding up an object to His Majesty: an elegant silver chalice with a jewelled base.

I darted to the left, toward the windows. Heads turned. I had no choice but to abandon the stately movements of a lady. The king had taken the chalice from Catherine. I had to move fast – as fast as a hawk to its prey.

I raced past the Duke of Suffolk and then Thomas Seymour. I was fifteen feet away ... then ten ...

The king lifted the chalice to his lips and tilted it back to drink. He had just begun to swallow when I called out, 'Your Majesty, stop!'

Everyone in the gallery stared at me, stunned. Catherine Howard gaped in disbelief.

Henry VIII lowered the chalice to look at me. 'Yes?' he said, in his high-pitched voice.

'I'm your cousin Joanna Stafford,' I said. 'I have not been to court in a very long time.'

A puzzled, verging on annoyed, expression came over him. 'What of it?' he asked.

'May I take the chalice now?' I said, with a smile that no doubt carried the glow of the tincture. 'I've had the honour of meeting and attending on Anne of Cleves. I wanted to assure you that she is a noble young woman, and I think you will find her most seemly. You must not delay any longer. There will be plenty of wine to partake of in her company.'

The king held the chalice in his hand as he stared at me.

I could feel the courtiers' eyes on me, hear their shocked whispers. To throw myself in the king's path, to try to take wine from him, was unprecedented.

The seconds crawled by as the king continued to examine me with those narrow, cold blue eyes, sunk deep in his fleshy face.

The king held out the chalice and I seized it with my right hand. As my fingers curled around its smooth rim, a roaring filled my head. It was as if a wind rose, but it was inside only me, and it carried a cacophony of sounds: Sister Elizabeth Barton's cries of pain, the conjuring chant of Orobas, and the wailing words of Nostredame.

My hand trembled, and the chalice began to slip. I seized the other side of the rim with my left hand. I rooted my feet in the floor so I would not collapse. The unearthly sounds slowly faded.

The king noticed nothing, for he had turned away, lumbering toward the door at the far end of the gallery, which led to the apartment containing Anne of Cleves.

A man posted at the door bowed. Just as he reached the doorway, the king faltered. He reached out to touch the side of the door.

Holding the chalice, I began to tremble.

But then the door was opened and he strode through it, followed by five of his attending gentlemen. The door shut behind them. No one in this room could hear what happened.

'Joanna, what are you doing here?' asked Catherine Howard. 'I'm happy to see you, of course, but you're not on the list of ladies of the queen. I am – I'm a maid of honour. I officially began serving her in Canterbury.'

'I'm happy for you, Catherine,' I said. 'May I ask, where did you get this chalice?' I held it up to her – it was most certainly fit for royalty to drink from. Our Lord Jesus Christ drank from a vessel made of silver at the Last Supper – the Council of Ten's choice to fashion this instrument of death in the same precious metal was blasphemous indeed.

Catherine beamed with pleasure. 'It was a gift from Queen Mary of Hungary to the Howard family, Joanna. A very nice Spanish gentleman gave it to my uncle the duke, but said that the queen regent specifically requested that it be used to serve the king of England wine *before* he marries. They said it is a wedding custom of the Low Countries. The Spanish gentleman asked me to be the one to give the king wine! What an honour. Just now, he told me that the king was coming to see my mistress the queen incognito and this was a perfect opportunity, because he'd be thirsty from the ride.' Catherine looked up and down the gallery. 'I don't see him any more. He was here before. Well, it's very exciting – only you kept him from drinking most of it. Look.' She pointed at the red liquid swirling in the chalice I still gripped so tightly.

'Let me take it to be cleaned,' I said. 'I will get it back to you afterward.'

'But Joanna,' she said stubbornly, 'why wouldn't you let the king drink his wine?'

'Let me tell you something, Mistress Catherine Howard, and I won't want you to forget it,' I said. 'You can't trust the Spanish.'

With that, I turned and made my way out of the gallery. Still holding the chalice, I found a place near a window on the second floor, and waited. Nearly twenty minutes later, the king came storming down the stairs. The whole palace was in an uproar.

'He doesn't like her,' I heard over and over again. 'He doesn't like her.'

I was with Catherine Brandon when her husband rushed to her side. 'I've never seen him take such a dislike to a woman – and she's to be his wife,' he murmured. 'It's as if he's sickened by her. His mood is most foul. This is a disaster.'

The king then summoned Brandon, the Seymours, the Earl of

Southampton, and several other nobles and gentlemen to a room on the first floor of the bishop's palace. There was some sort of furious meeting within, and then the king burst out the room, red-faced, and limped to his horse.

I watched him ride away – angry and full of wretched humours, but alive.

I returned Catherine Brandon's cloak to her, and bade farewell to Catherine Howard. She was so agog over the disaster of the king and queen's first meeting that she'd forgotten my strangeness over the chalice.

But one person hadn't forgotten. And after the havoc died down, I sought out Señor Hantaras, who stood outside the Bishop's palace, in the shadow of the bear-baiting pit.

His eyes burned as I walked to him, the chalice extended. Just before I reached him, I finally poured the poisoned wine into the ground. The bear howled on the other side of the fence as I did so.

'Unless you want members of the Howard household to drop into their graves, I suggest you take this,' I said. 'Do you have another one, to substitute and return to the Howards?'

'Of course I do,' he said.

'Is your mistress dead?' I asked.

'The wound was not that deep,' he said, not sounding overly concerned about the injury. 'She will recover.'

I said, 'This was my destiny and I fulfilled it. Michel de Nostredame confirmed it. The king was not to be killed. This poison concocted by the Council of Ten is the sort that, in a small dose, turns a man impotent and full of mad humours. That is what the king consumed. There will be no second son. And some day, when the king is dead and Prince Edward is dead, the Lady Mary will be queen and the true Faith will be restored. That is what we all desired, correct? That is what I was recruited and trained to bring about?'

He said nothing.

'So tell Ambassador Chapuys ... it's over,' I said, and I turned away.

I left the bear pit and the Bishop's Palace, to find Watling Street, the one, I knew, that would finally take me home.

52

Early on, one of the tasks accomplished by the builders of the king's new manor house of Dartford was the moving of graves. It was a delicate matter. Prioresses, nuns, and friars were commonly buried where they lived. But it would not do to demolish a building and raise a new one on top of the coffins of the faithful. It could bring bad luck to the king.

The new cemetery for the religious was on the far side of the road from the priory. So the dead looked upon the long stone wall, and the grove of trees, but were not forced to know of the grand new building. This was where Prioress Elizabeth Croessner, who welcomed me to Dartford, rested, and tapestry mistress Sister Helen and the brilliant Brother Richard, and dozens of others. My father, Sir Richard Stafford, lay there; he had died at the priory, reaching Dartford in his last weeks. I'd wanted my father near me forever.

This cemetery was also where Geoffrey Scovill chose to bury his wife and daughter.

I went there the first day I returned to town. My house was strangely unchanged. I'd thought in Gravesend that I would never be the same person after what awaited me on the island I loved. But I found my surroundings neither comforting nor alien when I came back to the house on the High Street. It had been paid for the entire time I was away. Jacquard Rolin insisted we pay the house's rent six months ahead before we left; he used to say we must have several paths open to us always.

Should I send for Arthur, persuade my cousin Henry to allow me to raise him as I'd promised my father? I wasn't sure that I was a fit person to care for a child any longer. I had persevered in Rochester, I found strength to carry out the deed I was convinced was right and just. But all my terrible mistakes along the way, the lives ruined and lost, made me go cold with shame.

But then, what was to be my future? I took a seat at my loom and stared at the finished tapestry. A powerful green-and-violet bird rose from the brilliant flames of its nest, on the verge of rebirth.

A knock at the door sounded. I almost didn't answer it. I did not feel ready to speak to anyone.

It was Agatha Gwinn, my one-time novice mistress. She'd heard at Holy Trinity Church that someone saw me step inside my house.

'Wherever have you been?' she exclaimed.

'Travelling,' I said.

'Oh, is it to do with Edmund – is he coming home?' she asked. 'We miss him greatly in Dartford.'

'I don't know,' I said, bowing my head.

Agatha told me that Oliver Gwinn, with the aid of Master Hancock, had petitioned and finally received permission to remain married to her, even though she had once been a nun.

'I'm happy for you,' I said.

There was another knock at the door. I was to have no peace.

But this time it was a royal page. He said, 'Her Majesty Queen Anne sends me from London to acquire the tapestry of Mistress Joanna Stafford.'

'She wants my tapestry?' I asked, stunned.

The page nodded. 'She intends to give it as a present to the king. She instructed me through the interpreters to tell you that you can name your price – within reason.'

'What a great honour,' Agatha cried. 'For your very first tapestry to go to the king himself? You will have a sea of commissions after this.'

'Yes,' I said, and dipped my head lower to hide the tears shivering in my eyes. I saw again the sweet, trusting face of Anne of Cleves, on the ship from Calais. So determined to be a good wife and queen.

'It needs finishing,' I said. 'Not all the details are what they should be.'

After I'd made arrangements to send the finished tapestry, I said good-bye to Agatha and walked up the High Street to the main road. It didn't take all that long to reach the cemetery.

The markers for Beatrice Scovill and her child were on the far side, next to a young oak tree. Although the ground was hard and icy, I knelt to say my prayers.

A man's voice said, 'I didn't know you'd returned.'

I looked up at Geoffrey Scovill. His blue eyes were dull and shadowed. A few white hairs sprouted among the brown, and he just thirty years old this year.

'I am sorry, I can't even find the words for how sorry I am,' I said.

'I'm lost, Joanna,' he said. 'I'm so lost.'

I caught my breath. 'I know what it's like to be lost,' I said.

'I don't know how to live with it – the regret,' he said thickly. 'I never gave her the love that she had a right to.'

'You were a good husband, I know that,' I said quickly.

He shuddered. 'No,' he said. 'I was forever thinking of *you*. No one can understand. It was like a fever, these last two years of my life. I tried, but I could never get free of you until now, Joanna. I couldn't see what God gave me, a beautiful and giving woman who cared for me more than any other person ever has, or ever will.'

I wept to hear this.

'I've suffered, too, Geoffrey,' I said, choking.

'I know that.'

Geoffrey had a book in his hand. He nodded, seeing that I noticed.

'It's the Bible of William Tyndale,' he said. 'You won't understand, Joanna, how could you? But it is the only thing that gives me a moment of solace.'

I took a deep breath. 'If it helps you, then I am glad of it.'

I clutched my hands and resumed my prayers. After a moment or so, there was a soft thud. I looked down. Geoffrey had tossed the small bag on the ground next to me, the one that contained the opal he said was called Black Fire.

'God's truth is, I would give anything in the world if I could have Beatrice back for just a few moments.' His voice broke. 'I want to tell her how sorry I am.'

I shut my eyes. I prayed, over and over, for peace for Beatrice, for some measure of serenity for Geoffrey. He didn't say anything more. I heard the sound of his shoes crunching on the ground as he moved around the tombstones, and then all that was left was the wind again, in the trees.

Something stirred on my head and both my arms. My eyes flew open. Snow had begun to fall. My knees and fingers ached from the cold. I struggled to my feet.

I looked over at the spot on the ground where he'd tossed the bag.

It was not there. I searched for a few minutes. Geoffrey must have taken it away with him.

There was no other person here. The shadows of the desiccated trees stretched toward me. All else that remained were the souls of those who had gently passed through Purgatory and now resided with Christ and the Virgin in the Kingdom of Heaven.

The snow had stopped falling when I completed my prayers. It was still and dim in the graveyard, with twilight approaching. I forced myself to walk quickly back to town, so that movement would send warmth back into my flesh.

Night came by the time I reached the High Street. There were only a few people left out. In the darkness, with my hood pulled around my face, I hoped to be unrecognisable.

As I approached my house, I could see a man standing in front of it, holding a large bundle. He stood very still, as if waiting for me. Was he sent by Señor Hantaras? It was so foolish to think I would be safe from those who wished the king dead, whose plot I had subverted.

I was completely alone in the town now, no friend on the High Street to turn to. Geoffrey Scovill, even if I wished to seek him out, lived far from the centre of Dartford.

'Sister Joanna?' came a man's voice. 'Have you returned?'

'Yes?' I took a steadying breath. 'Can I be of service, sir?'

The man took a step toward me, and in the moonlight I could see his features. He was familiar to me – and yet not so.

'I am John,' he said softly.

Without the beard, I had not known him until that moment. And he wore clean clothes. Moreover, he had never addressed me in such a fashion, as if he were any other townsman.

'Are you well, John?' I asked cautiously.

He nodded. 'I am, Sister. Since just after Christmas, I've not heard the voices. I live with my cousin now.' He tightened his grip on his bundle. 'I help gather firewood, and I go to Mass every day.'

'John, you are cured?' I asked, awed. 'Truly?'

'Yes, Sister. They say it is a miracle.' But his voice sounded subdued – sad. He shifted his bundle in his arms and then said, 'Brother Edmund, shall he come back too?'

'I'm afraid I don't know, John.'

'He was my friend,' John said.

'Yes,' I said, trembling. 'Thomas Aquinas once wrote, "There is nothing on this earth to be prized more than true friendship."'

He bowed his head. 'Thank you, Sister. I pray I shall see Brother Edmund again.' He stepped back, and then turned to go. But before he did, he said one thing more: 'There is much to be forgiven.'

The night was savagely cold but I stood before my house and watched John lope away, carrying his firewood, until he'd melted into the dark stillness of the High Street.

53

Bishop Stephen Gardiner led me over the walkway stretching across the moat of the Tower of London. The senior yeoman warder signalled to him as we approached Byward Tower.

'Bishop Gardiner, Sir William Kingston apologises that he cannot greet you, but he's questioning a prisoner at present,' said the man.

'I understand,' said the bishop with a pleasant nod.

All of the guards bowed low to him. Gardiner was more valued than ever. The king had insisted that the Bishop of Winchester preach before him every Friday during Lent, I had heard. When not preaching, Gardiner was busy persecuting those Lutheran followers who crossed the ever-murky boundary between obedience and heresy. Who knew how long the pendulum would swing in his favour? During that time, he'd take full advantage of his ascendance.

Beauchamp was a short distance. I knew the walls of that three-storey-high tower so well, for it was a place that lived in my dreams, nearly three years after my imprisonment.

Finally the bishop broke the silence.

'There is news from Ghent,' said Bishop Gardiner.

Keeping my voice calm, I said, 'Yes, Bishop?'

'The Emperor Charles entered the city on the fourteenth of February with his army. The leaders of the revolt have been arrested – yet I'm told the emperor will be merciful. Less than thirty will be executed.'

I thought of the citizens who screamed for blood in the square of Ghent. Violence begets violence – and more violence.

'This infamous rebellion had to be quashed utterly,' the bishop said, his voice edged with anger. 'If a kingdom's people throw off their monarchy and believe they can govern themselves – this bizarre idea cannot be tolerated. The fine its citizens must pay will cripple the city for generations to come.'

He paused, as if waiting for me to speak.

'That is most interesting,' I said.

'Yes,' the bishop said, whipping around to scrutinise me. 'But then a great many interesting things occur in the Low Countries. Wouldn't you agree?'

I'd often wondered if Gardiner suspected why the spies he sent after me disappeared from the earth. Was he ever able to confirm that I'd left England with Jacquard Rolin, posing as his wife? Gardiner knew the same story I had told everyone, that I travelled abroad in search of Edmund Sommerville but was unable to find him. No one had probed the details of my journey. I had not seen Señor Hantaras again. And Jacquard had not returned to England – as far as I knew.

We reached Beauchamp. Another yeoman warder greeted the bishop and then offered to escort us.

'There is no need, for I know the way,' said Gardiner.

I followed the bishop up the worn stone steps of the central staircase to the second floor. I remembered how they dipped in the middle from so many years of use.

'The king was at Winchester House again last night,' Gardiner said. 'I was honoured to be able to host a feast and party. I haven't seen him so merry in months. Little Catherine Howard danced and danced.'

I stopped short. 'Catherine Howard attended your party?'

'Yes of course,' he said. 'Ah, this is the right passage.'

We walked to the second door from the end. A guard was waiting.

Bishop Gardiner said, 'Sister Joanna, I forgot to tell you something. The king wishes to summon you to court for an audience. He desires to commission a series of tapestries from you. He dislikes everything about his fourth queen, with one exception: the phoenix tapestry she has given him as a wedding present. The one that you wove.'

I stared at him, unable to conceal my dismay.

With a small, satisfied smile, the bishop signalled to the guard to let us in.

Gertrude Courtenay sat in a chair by the fire, a book in her hand. The room contained many comforts. Her friends had contributed all the funds, since the Courtenay money and property had been seized many months ago.

She wore a green dress and dainty slippers but no jewels. That would have been unseemly. Her face was more lined than when I'd last seen her – yet her brown eyes blazed with as much vigour as ever.

'Joanna – you have no idea how I have missed you,' she said. Her sweet, melodic voice had not changed a whit.

'I shall be back within the hour,' said Bishop Gardiner.

'I thank you for this, Bishop,' said Gertrude. 'I will never forget your efforts on my behalf.'

'You know I will continue to do all I can – but you must be patient,' he said, and then gestured for me to join her in the cell. The door closed after me.

'You look well, Joanna,' she said. 'Come embrace me.'

I hugged her frail, fierce body.

I said, 'I hear that you may be released from the Tower.'

She stiffened. 'But not my son,' she whispered. 'He will not leave this place while the king lives.'

Gertrude took a deep breath, forcing herself to be calm. We walked to the fire to sit down together. 'I hear that the Cleves marriage was never consummated,' she murmured.

'No,' I said. 'Everyone knows the king took a strong dislike to her from the very beginning. They say that his councillors are seeking grounds for a divorce. She will not be mother to a son. He won't have a second son by her.'

We stared at each other. Then she touched her finger to her lips – we shouldn't speak any more freely than this. In the Tower, it was always possible that people listened.

'Tell me all the news,' she said lightly. I shared with her what gossip I had. Once I had avoided all news of London, of the world. But now I felt it best to be informed. She passed me some embroidery and we stitched together. We did not talk of loved ones who died – or loved ones who left. It was as if I was spending time with her in her receiving room in the Red Rose.

It seemed like only moments later that the key stirred in the door – it was time for me to go.

Bishop Gardiner loomed in the doorway to Gertrude's cell.

'Must she leave me?' asked Gertrude. She attempted to make the question light, but her voice trembled.

I hugged her again. This time, she clung to me as if I alone had the strength to redeem her.

'Do you regret it?' I whispered in her ear. This was what haunted me. Seeing all that she had lost – her husband's life, her own freedom, her son's future, her homes and fortune – and all that had been done to me, was she sorry she entered into conspiracy?

'*Never*,' she said.

With a last nod, I bade Gertrude Courtenay farewell. And within moments, I was on the green once more. The worst of the winter had passed. Lingering patches of snow looked sullen and beaten. A weak spring sun struggled through the clouds.

The Bell Tower was not far. The place where I met Edmund.

Yes, it was Gardiner who brought us together. Was it the bishop who forced us apart? Now Edmund was far, far away, whether still in the Black Forest of Germany, I had no idea. If only it were possible for me to learn where he was, to, as Geoffrey had put it, speak for just a few moments more.

I had found the courage to ask Gertrude what I'd long burned to know. Now I could not restrain myself from confronting Gardiner.

'Bishop,' I said, 'did you personally write the article that forbids the religious from marrying with me in mind? Did you know that Edmund Sommerville and I pledged to marry?'

He shook his head. 'I told you in Winchester House, Joanna, that His Majesty does not want those who've taken vows in a monastery or priory to ever marry. He is a king of great principle, you know.'

He stopped walking and looked at me. A faint smile stretched across his face. 'Did you really think that religious policy for the entire kingdom was written just to strike out at *you*? Revenge, perhaps, on my part, for your failure to secure the Athelstan crown – or perhaps for more recent flouting of my will?'

I stared without flinching at the Bishop of Winchester, not answering. Finally, he gestured for me to resume walking. Jacquard Rolin, the Duke of Norfolk, even Ambassador Chapuys – they had threatened me, used me, and hounded me, never caring for my happiness or even my life. Yet Stephen Gardiner, Bishop of Winchester, was still the most formidable man I had ever faced.

'You have never been a consideration of such import.' When we reached the narrow walkway that bridged the moat, he continued, 'Not everyone is meant to play a significant part in the affairs of the world, Joanna.'

'I will remember that, Bishop,' I said.

And as the late-winter sun burnished the river Thames, I followed Stephen Gardiner out of the Tower of London.

ACKNOWLEDGEMENTS

I wrote much of *The Chalice* in the Wertheim Study of the New York Public Library, Stephen A. Schwarzman Building. I would have been lost without a place at the table and my own Shelf 92. Thank you, Jay Barksdale, for admitting me to the study. I watched autumn of 2010 turn to winter outside the study's windows and then slowly warm to spring and finally to summer as I worked on my manuscript. When 2011 ended and I completed the first draft, those first snowflakes of the season fell in Bryant Park.

There are some amazing people I turned to while researching the tense and troubled late 1530s of England. I am deeply grateful, once again, to Mike Still, assistant museum manager at Dartford Borough Museum in Kent; historian Hans van Felius, who helped me in particular in my research of the Low Countries; Emily Fildes, curatorial intern at the Tower of London; and, most profoundly, to Sister Mary Catharine Perry, OP, Dominican nuns, of the Monastery of Our Lady of the Rosary. Close to home, the Cloisters Museum and Gardens of the Metropolitan Museum of Art provided me with inspiration. The Cloisters is truly the gem of the city.

I am grateful to my writing teachers, to Russell Rowland, for once again steering me in the right directions in his workshop; to Rosemarie Santini, Max Adams, and Greg Fallis, for the lessons in craft that are never far from my thoughts. These readers of the first draft were my vanguard: Harriet Sharrard, Rachel Andrews, Emilya Naymark, and Elena Fraboschi. Sue Trowbridge is a fantastic web designer.

This book would not have been possible without friends, employers, and colleagues. I thank Ellen Levine, editorial director of Hearst Magazines. Without her generous support, my books would not have been launched so well. I'm also grateful to Gary Marmorstein, Lorraine Glennon, Donna Bulseco, Megan Deem, Isabel Gonzalez-Whitaker, Nikki Ogunnaike, Tish Hamilton, Anthony DeCurtis,

Evelyn Nunlee, Elaine Devlin Beigelman, Brec and Sandy Morgan, David and Illisa Sternlicht, Bret Watson, Sean O'Neill, Bruce Fretts, Michele Koop, Kitty Bell Sibille, Dave Diamond, Doug Solter, David and Nikki Gardner, Olga Cheselka, and Maggie Murphy. A special thanks to Jason Binn's fantastic team at *DuJour* magazine, led by Keith Pollock and Nicole Vecchiarelli.

I must thank the online community that has been so essential from the beginning: the Yahoo Tudor group led by Lara Eakins; English Historical Fiction Authors, led by Debra Brown; On the Tudor Trail, led by Natalie Grueninger; the wonderful comrades in arms at Book Pregnant; and the incomparable bloggers who supported *The Crown* and *The Chalice*. Amy Bruno and MJ Rose, I hope you know how much I appreciate you. I delight in the new friends I discovered through the Historical Novel Society, Mystery Writers of America, and International Thriller Writers. And shout-outs to writer and filmmaker Christie LeBlance, who created the book trailers, and writer and producer Thelma Adams, who believed enough to option my first book.

I was fortunate to work with a very talented and insightful team of editors on *The Chalice*. I am grateful to Heather Lazare, senior editor at Touchstone Books, Simon & Schuster, and Genevieve Pegg, editorial director of Orion Publishing Group. At Orion, I enjoyed working with Eleanor Dryden, Juliet Ewers, Laura Gerrard, Gaby Young and Angela McMahon. I'm also grateful to Jessica Roth, senior publicist at Touchstone; Meredith Vilarello, marketing manager at Touchstone; Cherlynne Li, Touchstone's art director; and Marie Florio, associate director of subsidiary rights at Simon & Schuster.

I thank Heide Lange, my agent at Sanford J. Greenburger Associates, for her ceaseless support of my fiction, and her ace assistants, Rachael Dillon Fried and Stephanie Delman. Kate McLennan at Abner Stein has been my rock throughout; and I'm grateful to Hannigan Salky Getzler.

And of course I could not be a novelist without the encouragement of my family: my husband and children; my mother and sister; and my wonderful cousins, aunts, and uncles; sisters-in-law and nephews and other extended family. I hope you know how much I love you.